THE HOMECOMING

Mary Jane Staples

CORGI BOOKS

THE HOMECOMING
A CORGI BOOK : 0780552160780

First publication in Great Britain

PRINTING HISTORY
Corgi edition published 2001

1 3 5 7 9 10 8 6 4 2

Set in 11/12pt New Baskerville by
Phoenix Typesetting, Ilkley, West Yorkshire.

Corgi Books are published by Transworld Publishers,
61–63 Uxbridge Road, London W5 5SA,
a division of The Random House Group Ltd,
in Australia by Random House Australia (Pty) Ltd,
20 Alfred Street, Milsons Point, Sydney, NSW 2061, Australia,
in New Zealand by Random House New Zealand Ltd,
18 Poland Road, Glenfield, Auckland 10, New Zealand
and in South Africa by Random House (Pty) Ltd,
Endulini, 5a Jubilee Road, Parktown 2193, South Africa.

The Random House Group Limited supports The Forest Stewardship
Council (FSC®), the leading international forest certification organisation.
Our books carrying the FSC label are printed on FSC® certified paper.
FSC is the only forest certification scheme endorsed by the leading
environmental organisations, including Greenpeace. Our
paper procurement policy can be found at
www.randomhouse.co.uk/environment

MIX
Paper from
responsible sources
FSC® C018072

Printed and bound in Great Britain by Clays Ltd, St Ives PLC

To the people of my world.

THE ADAMS FAMILY

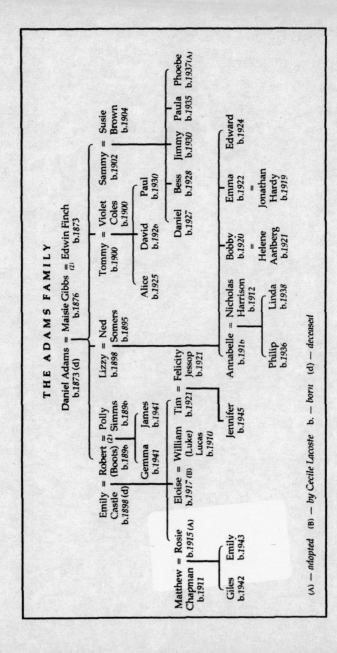

Daniel Adams = Maisie Gibbs = Edwin Finch
b.1873 (d)   b.1876   (2)   b.1873

Emily = Robert (Boots) = Polly Simms
Castle   b.1896   (2)   b.1896
b.1898 (d)

Gemma   James
b.1941   b.1941

Eloise = William (Luke) Lucas
b.1917 (B)   b.1910

Tim = Felicity Jessop
b.1921   b.1921

Jennifer
b.1945

Matthew = Rosie Chapman
b.1911   b.1915 (A)

Giles   Emily
b.1942   b.1943

Lizzy = Ned Somers
b.1898   b.1895

Annabelle = Nicholas Harrison
b.1916   b.1912

Philip   Linda
b.1936   b.1938

Tommy = Violet Coles
b.1900   b.1900

Alice   David   Paul
b.1925   b.1926   b.1930

Daniel   Bess
b.1927   b.1928

Bobby = Helene Aarlberg
b.1920   b.1921

Emma = Jonathan Hardy
b.1922   b.1919

Edward
b.1924

Sammy = Susie Brown
b.1902   b.1904

Jimmy   Paula   Phoebe
b.1930   b.1935   b.1937(A)

(A) — adopted (B) — by Cecile Lacoste b. — born (d) — deceased

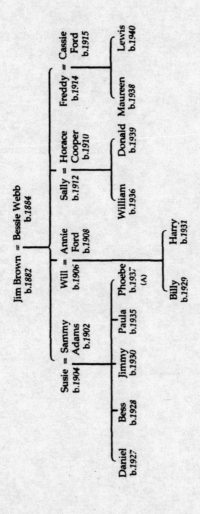

THE BROWN FAMILY

Jim Brown = Bessie Webb
b.1882   b.1884

Susie = Sammy Adams
b.1904   b.1902

Will = Annie Ford
b.1906   b.1908

Sally = Horace Cooper
b.1912   b.1910

Freddy = Cassie Ford
b.1914   b.1915

Daniel   Bess   Jimmy   Paula   Phoebe
b.1927   b.1928   b.1930   b.1935   b.1937
                                            (A)

Billy   Harry
b.1929   b.1931

William   Donald
b.1936   b.1939

Maureen   Lewis
b.1938   b.1940

Prologue

The Russians were in Berlin itself, the Americans and British advancing on the Elbe, west of Berlin.

An SS officer, one Major Erich Kirsten, notorious for speeding up the process of extermination in concentration camps, escaped the closing Russian trap in Berlin and succeeded in reaching Belsen. There he ordered the camp commandant, Kramer, to finish off all surviving inmates before forward units of the advancing British arrived.

Too late.

The British were there in the afternoon, aghast and outraged at what they beheld: mounds of dead inmates and hundreds of dying; scores of totally enfeebled men and women who were merely skin and bone and a great pit in which lay a mass of naked corpses. Typhus and other diseases were rampant, revolting odours spilling from huts filled with the dead and dying. The SS personnel of the camp included women as disgustingly callous as their male counterparts.

Major Kirsten, along with Kramer and every other German there, was placed under arrest by soldiers ferociously inclined to shoot them all on the spot.

Major Kirsten, however, did not seem in the least perturbed by the searing animosity of his captors. Nothing, as far as he was concerned, warranted his arrest. He was a man who dutifully obeyed the orders of his superiors in Berlin.

The next day a British staff officer, Colonel Robert Adams, arrived to investigate the horrors of mass murder. His inspection of the camp and its broken, suffering inmates caused him unimaginable revulsion and anger. How was it possible for men and women to do this to other human beings? He advanced slowly along the line of SS men and women guards, looking into their faces, faces that seemed to shrink in an effort to disappear. He guessed, however, that they were uneasy not about what they had done to the inmates, but what might now be done to them. The women were coarse female louts, most of them bulky and bulging in their uniforms. One woman did meet his direct glance, just for a second or so, a woman whose eyes were reflective not of shame but a kind of sneering defiance. He stopped to look her up and down, his contempt and disgust reducing her to lip-biting discomfort, and then walked on.

With Commandant Kramer already on his way to be tried as a war criminal, Colonel Adams interrogated Major Kirsten, whose demeanour was that of an untroubled man.

'What is your connection with this revolting camp?'

In fluent English, Kirsten replied, 'Who wishes to know?'

'I do.'

'I have given you my name and rank, and as a prisoner of war that is all I am required to give.'

'You are not a prisoner of war, you are a miserable specimen of total inhumanity, a wormlike creature of Himmler's, and if you don't answer my questions, I'll have you delivered to whatever inmates of this camp have strength enough to tear you to pieces.'

'*Herr* Colonel,' said Kirsten, a sharp-featured man in his thirties, 'I'm not prepared to end my days in the stinking hands of Europe's filth, and will tell you that in every aspect of my work for the good of the Third Reich, I have committed no crimes. I have only ever obeyed orders. You have no right, under any military law, to arrest any soldier for obeying orders.'

Deep grey eyes showed the blue of razor-sharp steel. The eyes regarded him, looked him over from head to foot, and stripped him of his untroubled air. Kirsten sensed the increased threat of a lynching at the hands of Jewish inmates, and he visibly twitched.

'I'm listening to an animal calling itself a soldier?' said Colonel Adams. 'According to depositions from several of the camp's guards, you came here to arrange the massacre of all inmates still alive.'

'I was obeying orders from Berlin. Obedience

to our superiors is the first principle of our service to the Third Reich.'

'I wonder,' said Colonel Adams, 'whenever you are out of that uniform, do you walk on two legs or four?'

'I request, *Herr* Colonel, as an officer of the SS, to be spared your insults.'

'I take the view that it's impossible to insult a piece of filthy garbage. But you'll get a trial before you're hanged, and I hope to God you take time to choke to death, along with other animals who, like you, have reduced innocent human beings to not knowing if they are human beings at all.'

Major Kirsten, now a dusky red, obviously considered this denunciation totally unjustified. He again insisted he had only ever obeyed orders.

'Further, *Herr* Colonel, we are arguing about opinions. Your opinion, I suggest, is that these filthy creatures are on our level. My opinion, shared by every true Aryan, is that they are subhumans whose objective is to contaminate the whole world. The whole world should thank us for all we have so far done in reducing their numbers.'

Colonel Adams, tolerant of common failings, regarded this infamous servant of Himmler with a freezing disgust that matched the feelings of the contingent of sickened British soldiers.

At the liberated Dachau concentration camp, American soldiers, appalled and outraged at the sight of a huge mound of naked, skeleton-like corpses, meted out summary justice on the spot. They shot to death more than a hundred SS men.

Here at Belsen, Colonel Adams might have shot Major Kirsten himself. Instead, he forced him to join the men and women guards in the gruesome task of burying the mounds of dead, a punitive exercise that lasted many days. It turned Major Kirsten into a livid, filth-encrusted spectacle of degradation, took the blood from the inhuman faces of the guards and made grey, haggard creatures of them.

Subsequently, they were all despatched to prison under escort, to be tried as war criminals along with Commandant Kramer. Colonel Adams frankly hoped every last one of them would be hanged. He was not advised that during the difficult journey to Nuremberg gaol, two of the SS guards, a man and a woman, escaped. And so did Major Kirsten.

Chapter One

Early October, 1945

The war with Germany and Japan was over, Japan devastated by what atom bombs had done to Hiroshima and Nagasaki. In Britain, the Conservative Party, tainted with the appeasers who had supported Chamberlain and been hostile to Churchill, had lost the July election to the Labour Party. Churchill, the bulldog, was out of office, but as a tired man he was now able to enjoy a well-deserved rest combined with the therapeutic recreation provided by paintbrush and easel.

Demobilization of the men and women of the Services had begun. Vera Lynn, sweetheart of the British Forces, was singing songs of welcome on her radio programme, and making 'The White Cliffs of Dover' more popular than ever. Into the ports of the United Kingdom came the first of the men from the overseas theatres of war, where scarred battlefields were strewn with the remnants of smashed armour and soaked with the blood of the countless dead.

At the same time, the last of the young men to be called up before the war ended were taking the places of veterans returning from recaptured Empire outposts like Singapore and Rangoon. And there were other spots requiring an Army presence, such as Palestine. Daniel, the elder son of Sammy and Susie Adams, called up eight months ago, had been posted there with his company. Daniel had an American fiancée, Patsy Kirk. Patsy had returned to Boston with her father, a radio newsman, after Japan's surrender. She did not intend to stay there indefinitely. She was happily committed to marrying Daniel sometime during 1946.

Evening in Haifa, Palestine, the Middle East country that was currently turbulent with political and racial strife. The Jews were pressing vigorously for part of Palestine to become their national homeland. The Arabs were just as vigorous in their determination to cede nothing of what they had owned for centuries. The Jews referred to the millions of their people who had been murdered in concentration camps. That, they said, was more than enough to justify the establishment of a safe homeland, and Palestine, by reason of history, was the natural choice. Not when it means untold thousands of our people being dispossessed, said the Arabs.

Arabs and Jews were now electing to hate and kill each other, and Britain, the mandatory power, had the unpleasant task of policing the country and trying to keep the opposing factions apart. This, of course, was beginning to make British troops unwelcome to both sides, the Arabs suspecting Britain's Government meant to betray them, the Jews suspecting interminable procrastination along with military measures to suppress them. They were certain nothing could be accomplished in their favour unless they were left to deal with the Arabs themselves, which meant inviting the British to leave and soliciting help from sympathetic Americans. The more militant Jewish factions were quite ready to go to war with the Arabs, and underground help from American Jews was already placing a steady supply of smuggled weapons into their hands, despite British border controls.

The street being patrolled by a quartet of British soldiers was dark. Here and there light issued from a dwelling window or a café. Life murmured in the cafés, but apart from that all was quiet.

'Not a bad night so far,' said Corporal Frank Wallis, in charge of the patrol.

'The fresh air, you mean?' said Lance-Corporal Daniel Adams. The sea breezes that flirted around Haifa's port gave the air a welcome freshness at night. 'Or the situation?'

'Both,' said Wallis.

There was trouble sometimes, trouble that mainly occurred when the sun went down, and it went down fairly quickly in the Middle East. Daniel had no quarrel with the weather, apart from missing the lingering balmy twilight of an English summer. Nor did he have any real quarrel with the Palestinians, Arab or Jewish. He simply wished that now the war in Europe was over and done with, neither faction would start one here.

He walked on beside Corporal Wallis, his closest Army mate, their eyes alert for any kind of suspicious movement. Sometimes, in the dark, hidden hands would go to work, discharging stones. Large stones, not pebbles. Jew or Arab, none of them mucked about with piffling pebbles. Half-bricks were their favourites, their targets either each other or a suffering British patrol. Half-bricks, however, while painfully injurious, weren't fatal. Bullets were, and occasionally a patrol had to dive for cover. That often resulted in the Palestine police making an arrest, securing a conviction and the imprisonment of the convicted, Jew or Arab. That didn't improve the Jewish or Arab relationship with the British.

Corporal Wallis came to a sudden stop.

'Watch out,' he said, and all four soldiers unslung their rifles. With eyes used to the darkness, they glimpsed quick-moving figures turning into the street. Two running men came pelting over the sidewalk, following which the noise of a car engine burst on the ear, and the vehicle, lights blazing, skidded as it turned into the street at a crazy speed. The running men, bent low, kept going. The Army patrol, at a halt in the middle of the street, was caught by the car's lights. Corporal

Wallis thrust his rifle up and forward, holding it crossways as a signal to stop. The car came rushing on. 'Bloody blimey,' hissed Wallis, 'the bugger's going to mow us flat.'

The line of four soldiers tensed to split apart and give way, but if the car driver had thought about mowing them down, he changed his mind. He stood on the brakes and brought the vehicle to a screeching, shuddering stop. At once, out leapt four young Arab men. Carrying bulbous-headed clubs, and indifferent to the soldiers, they took up a foot-chase of the two fleeing men.

Corporal Wallis and Daniel moved fast, rifles outstretched to form a horizontal barrier, the other two men solidly backing them up. The Arabs came to a stop, and Wallis addressed them.

'Now come on,' he said, 'don't make trouble. We've all got mothers, you, us and them. So go home.'

The Arabs, vibrating, said nothing. Eyes dark with dislike and hostility stared at Corporal Wallis and Daniel from under the hoods of body-covering burnouses. The hostility was un-mistakeably menacing, the more so because the prey, still running, were disappearing into the darkness, going towards that part of Haifa predominantly Jewish. An arm whipped upwards, and a club whirled to smash down on Daniel's cross-held rifle. But the menace of silent hostility had kept Daniel alert and expectant, and the club smashed empty air as he took a quick step back.

The next moment all four Arabs were staring at the barrels of pointed rifles.

'Go home,' said Corporal Wallis, 'or we'll run you all in.'

It was a request to be reasonable. All British patrols were briefed to exercise persuasion of a reasonable kind. Armed aggression exacerbated the riotous nature of incidents, and made the British Army's difficult job more so. Daniel knew that in depriving these Arabs of the pleasure of beating two Jews senseless, or even lifeless, the patrol probably now stood on the brink of a dangerous confrontation. Arab and Jewish tempers flared at the drop of a hat. Orders regarding the use of rifles meant one was to fire only if the situation allowed no other alternative, and even then one only fired the first shots over heads.

The silence of the four Arabs created increased tension until they suddenly turned in on each other, exchanged whispers and then returned to their car, an old and battered vehicle that was probably stolen. The car moved off, although not without fists being shaken out of open windows.

Daniel, watching them go, said, 'Hairy!'

'Who's got the wind up?' asked Corporal Wallis.

'Me,' said one of the privates.

'Personally,' remarked Daniel, 'I'd have felt better if they'd said good night to us. No hard feelings and all that.'

'Some hopes,' said the other private.

'Come on,' said Corporal Wallis, 'get your feet moving and let's complete our round.'

They went on their way over a prescribed route to finish their duty patrol, and did so without further incident. Daniel was able to give his mind to thoughts of Patsy, far away in America but still, he was sure, a girl of light and joy.

Chapter Two

The Wareham train was late, exemplifying, perhaps, the tired state of the country after six years of exhausting effort that had drained resources and people alike. However, there was nothing jaded or weary about the slender brunette standing by the car outside this station in rural Dorset. An air of vitality kept winning company with elegance. Sunshine after a morning of rain cast warm light over her, enriching the maroon of her narrow-waisted jacket worn fashionably over a turquoise blue dress of pre-war silk jersey, carefully preserved and restyled. From her wartime wardrobe, which she considered pathetic, she had elected for colour. She could still carry off colour, despite her age. Of all things affecting her person, she disliked her age most. God, she had just turned forty-nine. Fifty was now lying in wait for her. Fifty. How frightful.

From the interior of the open Riley came a voice.

'Mummy, is Daddy lost?' That was Gemma, three months short of four.

'Only if the train is.'

'Well, fancy a train getting lost,' said James, Gemma's twin brother.

At which point, Polly Adams, wife of Colonel Robert Adams, heard its approaching whistle in the near distance. She quickened. Saints and sinners, even at her age her pulse rate was suddenly erratic. She waited. The locomotive, steaming slowly, pulled into the station.

'Mummy,' called Gemma, 'the train's come. Can me and James get out now?'

'Yes, out you come,' said Polly. She would have liked a few seconds alone with Boots, but there was no way she could deny his children fair shares in the welcome. They scrambled from the car with an energetic exercise of arms and legs, Gemma's curling hair now as darkly sienna as her mother's, eyes as brilliantly brown as her Aunt Lizzy's. James was like his father, his hair a deep brown, eyes a fine grey with a hint of blue. By no means identical in their looks, they were nevertheless inseparable playmates. They placed themselves beside their mother, Gemma on her left, James on her right, and sensing their excitement she took the hand of each to restrain them. 'I don't think we'd better jump all over Daddy,' she said, 'he's been travelling since yesterday, all the way from Germany, and may be tired.'

A middle-aged couple emerged from the station, followed by a young woman carrying an umbrella, followed by an old bloke carrying a bicycle wheel, followed by a large woman carrying a lot of weight. Some seconds later, out came an American Army officer carrying his raincoat, to be met by a young lady of Dorset, who hugged him, kissed him and took him away with her. No-one else followed.

Polly bit her lip. Where was Boots?

'Mummy, has Daddy fell asleep on the train?' asked Gemma.

'He might have, if he's tired,' said James.

At which moment, a long-legged British Army officer in a trench coat emerged, a packed valise depending from each hand.

'Mummy, he's here!' exclaimed Gemma.

Polly wondered why she should suffer misty eyes. Ye gods, all these years, and he still touched her most sensitive emotions. There he was, home from the war, Dunkirk far behind him and Germany's horrendous concentration camps his most recent memory. And here she was, not at all sure of her self-control. He was her own age, forty-nine, if two months her senior, but nothing seemed to change him, except perhaps the war's bitter winter in Europe had left its weathering mark. She felt the twins break her handclasps to make their dash to their father. Boots put his valises down, stooped and brought them up into his arms, perching them on the insides of his elbows. Beneath the peak of his khaki cap his eyes resolved for him the individuality of each young face. If his almost blind left eye saw not much more than a blur, his sound right eye, as always, did the work well enough for both. He kissed Gemma, and he kissed James.

'Let's see, who's which?' he asked.

Gemma, determined, it seemed, to make

herself unforgettable by noise alone, yelled, 'Me, Daddy, I'm me!'

'So am I, I'm me too,' said James logically.

'Come to that, so am I,' said Boots.

'And me?' There was another face. The face that always seemed to retain something of the piquant charm of a flapper of the wild Twenties.

'Hello, Polly,' said Boots with warm affection.

'Hello, old thing,' said Polly throatily, and Boots set the twins down, wrapped his arms around his wife and delivered a telling kiss on her lips. Polly's response was emotionally ardent.

Gemma and James looked up at their parents.

'They're kissing,' said Gemma.

'Oh, well,' said James, not old enough to think up a more pertinent comment.

'Delighted to see you looking so good, Polly,' said Boots.

'How good?' asked Polly.

'On a par with springtime?' said Boots, quite sure the moment called for a compliment.

'Oh, you lovely old sport,' said Polly.

'Shall we go home?'

'Happily to our present one,' said Polly, 'and for the rest of our lives to our next, wherever it happens to be.'

That was to be their first priority, the purchase of a home of their own and the end of her time in a rented Dorset cottage.

Boots's younger brother, Sammy, phoned the cottage that evening. Polly answered.

'Hello?'

'That's my high-class, well-educated sister-in-law?' said Sammy.

'I know who you are,' said Polly, 'my brother-in-law. The fast-talking, comical one.'

'It's me, I can confirm that,' said Sammy. 'Did Boots make it, Polly, is he home?'

'He made it, Sammy, he's home.'

'Glad to hear it,' said Sammy, 'it's time we had him back. How is the old feller?'

'I object to old,' said Polly.

'So do I,' said Sammy, 'but some of us are getting on a bit, y'know.'

'Well, fight it, Sammy old sport, as I do,' said Polly. 'But I can tell you Boots is fit, healthy and standing up.'

'Well, that ought to guarantee a lovey-dovey reunion,' said Sammy.

'If you mean what I think you mean,' said Polly, 'you're trespassing.'

'Polly, I'm just happy to say good luck to his health and strength,' said Sammy. 'I'd like to talk to him in a minute, but first in regard to you and him getting back to this part of the world, I've been scouting around on your behalf like you said, for a highly desirable residence not far from your respected Ma and Pa.'

'So you have, Sammy, and I've mentioned it to Boots,' said Polly.

'Well, in my usual modest fashion I can say I do have an eye for highly desirable residences,' said Sammy.

'You've got an eye for a lot more than that, Sammy.'

26

'Like the firm's overheads? Granted,' said Sammy. 'Anyway, I'm able to inform you that this afternoon I clapped my peepers on a very good-looking family house in East Dulwich Grove. You know the Grove, of course, it's on top of Dulwich Village, and so close to your Ma and Pa's mansion you could lob a lump of brick straight through their conservatory.'

'Lumps of brick are out, Sammy, but East Dulwich Grove, yes, that's in,' said Polly. 'Top of the list, old sport, as long as it doesn't cost the shirt off Boots's back.'

'It's up for sale, I can tell you that,' said Sammy, 'and on offer at nineteen hundred and fifty.'

'That's the shirt off Boots's back and mine as well,' said Polly.

'Very handsome family castle, Polly, and you've got to dig a bit deeper in your finances for rubbing elbows with Dulwich Village, highly posh and exclusive,' said Sammy. 'I'll be sending you a photograph. I've had a friendly chat with the owner himself, Mr Humphrey Waterloo-Bridges.'

'Come again, Sammy?'

'Well, it might've been Warden-Bridges, but he had a Victoria plum in his mouth. There's a lot of Victoria plums in and around Dulwich Village.'

'I'm a native of Dulwich Village,' said Polly.

'Well, so you are, Polly,' said Sammy, 'but if I've got it right, didn't you eat your plum while you were driving an ambulance in the other war? I mean, you speechify very flash, but not plummy.'

'Very flash? Sammy, I'll sue you.'

'Don't do that, Polly, let's stay friends, eh?' said

Sammy. 'You talk musical, like Boots talks educated, and Susie's admiring of both of you. Anyway, I've got first refusal for you and Boots on Waterloo-Bridges' house, but you'd have to come and look it over inside a week. I'll put the estate agent's name and address on the back of the photograph. Oh, and by the way,' he added in friendly throwaway fashion, 'tell Boots that Adams Properties will make him a director's loan of the necessary two thousand quid, which he can pay back when he's shaking hands with prosperity.'

'Sammy, you helpful old darling, I think you'd better talk to Boots right now,' said Polly. She called Boots, had a few quick words with him, then handed him the phone.

So Sammy began to chat with Boots, telling him he was tickled pink to know he was back from the war all in one piece and standing up as proud and healthy as a Roman gladsome, according to Polly. Boots said he supposed gladsome meant gladiator, then asked if Sammy was treating him to a select load of old cobblers.

'Not me, Boots, just letting you know I'm glad you're back and very admiring that you finished up a general.'

'Colonel.'

'Not half, and I really am tickled pink—'

'So's Polly,' said Boots. 'She's killing herself at being known as Flash Polly.'

'Well, good old Polly,' said Sammy. 'I feel like she does – rapturous that the war's over.'

'It's not for millions of displaced persons, Sammy, or for surviving concentration camp victims, it's still a bloody kind of hell for them,' said Boots, who still carried images of the hideous nature of Belsen. 'But tell me about this house you've just recommended to Polly.'

Sammy repeated much of what he'd told Polly, and went on to point out it was what she'd had in mind, a place close to her parents, now getting on a bit.

'Further, Boots, this particular house isn't far, either, from our respected Ma, Chinese Lady. It's no secret she's against any of us living in foreign parts, like Clapham or Shoreditch or Dorset.'

'Well, you're right, Sammy,' said Boots, 'Polly and I had already decided we'd look for a house somewhere near her parents. Sir Henry's over seventy now, and it's fair that he and Lady Simms should be able to see more of the twins.'

At which Sammy said if Waterloo-Bridges' place suited him and Polly, but the price hurt them a bit, Adams Properties would let him have a director's loan of two thousand smackers, which he could pay back a lot later. Boots said directors' loans weren't allowed to be indefinitely outstanding.

'Am I acquainted with that piece of unfortunate company law?' mused Sammy. 'Now you mention it, I think I am.'

'However, if I repaid it yearly,' said Boots, 'you could immediately re-issue it until I was able to settle in full.'

'I knew it,' said Sammy.

'Knew what?' said Boots.

'That you could still kick holes in a problem,' said Sammy. 'Like I've mentioned before, when the family invested in your education, it paid us dividends. I don't mind now about all the hard-earned dibs I handed to Chinese Lady out of me savings sock to keep the family going.'

Boots, who had heard all that flannel before, said, 'Loaned her, Sammy, at exorbitant interest rates.'

'It's a long time ago,' said Sammy. 'Anyway, the property company can easily make the loan, Boots. We've banked handsome profits from buying and selling bombed sites for development, and Rosie's getting a happy return for investing that inheritance of hers. Listen, when d'you think you can come back in the business?'

'I'll talk to you when Polly and I travel up to look at Waterloo-Bridge,' said Boots.

'Eh? Oh, see what you mean. It's Humphrey Warden-Bridges, actually. Not my fault I misheard the bloke. As I told Polly, he had a large Victorian plum in his north-and-south. I suppose you'd like to talk to our respected Ma now.'

'I would,' said Boots. 'Much obliged, by the way, for doing some house-hunting, and for the offer of a director's loan.'

'All in the family, Boots, all in the family,' said Sammy. 'Hold on.'

There was silence for a moment, then, 'Boots?'

'That's you, Susie?' said Boots, a smile in his voice.

'Yes, just a quick word before Mum gets here,' said Susie, 'and just to say so happy you're back, we're all longing to see you and Polly and the twins. Ever so much love from everyone.'

'Who's a sweet woman, then?' said Boots.

'Tell me more,' said Susie. 'Oh, here's Mum—'bye, Boots.'

'So long, Susie,' said Boots. 'Hello?'

'So there you are at last,' said his mother, Mrs Maisie Finch, known to her family as Chinese Lady because in her striving Walworth days she'd taken in washing and enjoyed a friendly acqaintance-ship with Mr Wong Fu of the local Chinese laundry.

'Yes, here I am at last, old lady,' said Boots.

'Well, I'm glad you're back safe and sound,' said Chinese Lady, 'but why you ever went off in the first place after all your time in the trenches of that other war, I'll never know. Mind, you always were one to look for what was on the other side of a brick wall, like one of them explorers. Now, you're all right, are you? You haven't come back with any wounds or only half a leg, I hope.'

'No, I've still got everything I started with,' said Boots. 'Nothing's missing. If there is, Polly will let me know, and I'll send you a postcard. How are you, old lady, and how's Edwin?'

'I can't grumble about myself,' said Chinese Lady, sixty-nine, 'and thank goodness Edwin's retired at last. I don't know what the Government was thinking of, letting him work well past his retiring age. Still, the blessed war's over now, and he's doing what he likes, a bit of pottering in the garden and teaching Jimmy to play chess.' Jimmy was Sammy and Susie's younger son. 'Boots, he'd like to see you when you can manage to come up.'

'Polly and I will be up with the twins in a day or so,' said Boots.

'That's nice,' said Chinese Lady. 'I hope you're not still in the Army, are you?'

'I'm on three months paid leave prior to my retirement, old girl,' said Boots.

'It's time you stopped calling me old girl,' said Chinese Lady.

'Will Maisie do?' suggested Boots.

'Maisie? Well, that's very respectful to your own mother, I don't think.'

'It's a tribute, old lady, to the fact that you're still young at heart,' said Boots, 'but don't run up ladders or climb drainpipes. Love from Polly and the twins.'

At the other end of the line, one of Chinese Lady's rare smiles appeared.

In bomb-shattered Nuremberg, the top Nazis, imprisoned, were awaiting trial as war criminals. Twenty-one of them, headed by Goering, Hess and Ribbentrop, were to answer above all other nominated crimes for the extermination of six million Jews.

Goering, who considered himself a soldier first and foremost, challenged the right of the Allies to put him on trial at all. His reputation as a portly figure of beaming goodwill had led his captors to see him as a buffoon, but they found him as quick-eyed as a ferret, with a tongue that could deliver irony and satire far removed from the inanities of a clown. When shown his indictment, he glanced only casually through it before boldly writing down his response.

'The victor will always be the judge, the vanquished the accused.'

There were no sins, no crimes, to answer for as far as he was concerned. Nevertheless, the Allies held a different view. He had time to reflect on his fate, for the trial would not begin until November.

Chapter Three

'No digging,' said Mrs Emma Hardy, younger daughter of Lizzy and Ned Somers.

'I'm just suggesting', said her husband Jonathan, 'that together we could get a kitchen garden going in no time at all.'

Emma, who had spent most of the war working for a farmer down in Somerset, said, 'Jonathan, I've done all the digging I ever want to do, so I'm going to leave garden spade work to you exclusively. I've grown unwanted muscles.'

'Ah, so you have, Emma,' said Jonathan, Sussexborn, 'you're a strong girl, that you are.'

'So I am,' said Emma, 'which means if you bring a spade anywhere near me, I'll flatten your head with it. You do all the digging, Jonathan, and I'll do all the cooking and let my muscles fade away. I don't want to end up looking like a man.'

'Be a terrible shock to me, that would,' said Jonathan.

He had been conscripted into the militia before the outbreak of the war with Germany. Accordingly, he was among the first of demobbed servicemen, and he and Emma lost no time in taking up residence in Ferndene Road, off Denmark Hill. Their house had been acquired by Sammy on behalf of Adams Properties, and Jonathan was buying it by means of monthly instalments that included simple interest. He had accepted the offer of a job with a firm of accountants in the City of London, a well-paid job. Although a wound suffered during the Eighth Army's campaign in the Western Desert had left him with a gammy knee, it gave him no problems, apart from a limp, which he had in common with Emma's dad, whose artificial left leg was a souvenir of the Great War. After hospitalization in the UK, Jonathan had served as a sergeant gunnery instructor at a Royal Artillery training camp in Somerset until the end of the war.

He hadn't lost his Sussex brogue. It surfaced frequently on his fluent tongue. Emma liked him because of his Sussex self, his never-say-die buoyancy, and his vibrant body. Well, one did like a good build in a husband. And as Jonathan had an equal liking for her own kind of body, they got on very well together whenever each body transmitted certain signals to the other.

Well, they were both still young and vital, Emma twenty-three, and Jonathan twenty-six, and both had been brought up to believe in healthy togetherness.

The Army had toughened Jonathan, but hadn't spoiled him. It had made a fine sergeant and a resilient man of him. Emma liked him very much as a husband. But here he was, trying to persuade her to help him dig up half the overgrown garden.

Emma was having none of that lark, not after years of quite heavy farm work.

'I mean it, Jonathan, you're the gardener and I'm the lady of the house,' she said. 'What're your feet doing on my kitchen floor?'

'Nothing much, Emma, just—'

'They're wearing gumboots.'

'Well, so they are, Emma. They've been gardening with me.'

'They're not to garden on my kitchen floor,' said Emma. 'Still, I'll forgive you just this once, then you can go out again and get on with digging the vegetable plot. Wait a bit, what's that smell?' She sniffed at his old open-neck Army shirt.

'Not me, Emma, it's woodsmoke,' said Jonathan. 'I'm burning twigs and the hedge clippings. If the weeds in this garden were overgrown, so were the hedges. But the clippings will make good potash.'

At which point, the sound of a voice reached their ears.

'Hey, put that bloody fire out!'

'Oh, Lord,' said Emma, 'it's Cheerful Charlie again.'

Mr Charles Duckworth and his wife were immediate neighbours. Emma and Jonathan had only moved in ten days ago and in that time had received complaints about the seed spread by their garden weeds, their dirty chimney smoke and the sound of hammering. The latter was to do with the garden shed. Falling to pieces, Jonathan's first outdoor job had been to repair it.

He looked at Emma. Always worth a look, his

Emma was, with her wealth of chestnut hair and large brown eyes.

'I'll talk to the fusspot,' he said, 'or he'll spoil our Saturday afternoon.'

'Yes, do that, lovey,' said Emma, 'do Sussex talking.'

'Hi, you there, Hardy?' bawled the fusspot from the other side of the dividing hedge.

Jonathan emerged from the kitchen and directed himself at the hedge. At the top of the garden, hedge clippings and leaves were burning merrily, smoke spiralling upwards.

'That you, Mr Duckworth?' he called.

'You bet it is,' shouted the unseen neighbour. 'What's the idea, lighting a bloody bonfire? My garden's all over smoke, and it's creeping into the house, and making the wife cough.'

'Well, from where I am, Mr Duckworth,' said Jonathan, 'that old smoke be going straight up. I don't rightly know I ever saw straighter smoke, and I've seen a durned old packet of it in my time. I've seen it going all ways, right, left and round corners, and I've known some crafty stuff creep up the legs of my trousers.'

'Eh?'

'Can you see my bonfire smoke?' asked Jonathan.

'Course I can bloody see it and smell it too,' growled Mr Duckworth, a choleric old buffer of fifty-five. 'Didn't the people round here suffer enough fires and smoke with the air raids?'

'Ah, so they did, Mr Duckworth, like my Ma and Pa in Walworth, but that was the evil smoke of war,' said Jonathan. 'The smell of burning twigs and leaves, well, I like it myself. I were brought up in the country, where the smell of woodsmoke were on a par with the smell of Lifebuoy soap used for washing down a dairy. A good smell, Lifebuoy soap, I reckon, but I be certain sure smoke going straight up can't be making Mrs Duckworth cough. Have you called the doctor?'

'Eh? Eh?'

'Could be a chest cold, poor lady,' said Jonathan. 'Is she bronchial?'

'Now look here—'

'Mrs Wheeler in our village, she were bronchial once, as I remember,' said Jonathan, 'Only once. It carried her off. Mind, she were eighty-nine at the time. Anyway, about my bonfire smoke that's going straight up, you sure it's coming over the hedge, Mr Duckworth?'

'There's smuts, and I don't like the smell, nor does Mrs Duckworth,' bawled the crochety old buffer. 'Put it out, and get your chimneys swept sometime.'

'I'll get a sweep in,' said Jonathan, 'but I don't fairly see my garden bonfire's a worry, and there be stuff I've got to burn up, so I be asking for your kind tolerance as a good neighbour. It's been a fair old ugly war, and I daresay you and Mrs Duckworth be as glad as Emma and me that it's over and everyone can live in peace with each other. Mr Duckworth?'

Mr Duckworth had retreated, growling, and Jonathan went back to the kitchen, where Emma was brewing a pot of tea.

'Well?' she said.

'I talked to him,' said Jonathan, 'but I wouldn't say it did a lot of good.'

'Well, bother him,' said Emma, 'let's have a cup of tea – no, look at you, you've got your gumboots on my kitchen floor again.'

'Little devils, these boots,' said Jonathan.

'Oh, well, it's done now,' said Emma, milking cups. Her head came up. 'What's that?'

Jonathan, going to the open door, saw what it was. The nozzle of a hosepipe was protruding through the hedge at the top of the garden, and a powerful jet of water was falling just short of the bonfire.

'I don't think much of that,' said Jonathan. The nozzle disappeared, and the next moment the jet of water was rising over the hedge and coming down on the bonfire. It hissed and a cloud of smoke billowed.

'Jonathan, stop him,' said Emma.

'So I will,' said Jonathan, and with the resolution of an ex-sergeant who had caused recruits to quiver, out he went.

Emma heard a yell in a little while. She darted to the open door and saw Jonathan taking measures to subdue the enemy. He was using the garden hose, directing the jet high up over the hedge. Mr Duckworth was bawling. He was wet all over.

'I'll have the law on you, Hardy!' he shouted.

'You be drowning, Mr Duckworth?' called Jonathan, turning off the outside tap.

'You wait, just wait!'

'Come round and have a cup of tea,' said Jonathan. 'Bring Mrs Duckworth, and Emma and me'll show you our wedding photographs.'

No answer. Mr Duckworth had retired, wet, fuming and set on showing his umbrage to Mrs Duckworth.

'Oh, dear,' said Emma, when she and Jonathan were sitting at the kitchen table drinking tea, 'I never imagined after nearly six years of war with Germany, we'd have a silly war with neighbours.'

'That's what I tried to point out to him, that it was time to live in peace,' said Jonathan, 'but don't you worry now, Emma, we'll calm them down.'

'Turning the hose on him didn't calm Mr Duckworth,' said Emma.

'Made him a bit damp, though,' said Jonathan.

Emma laughed.

'You're a manly man, Jonathan,' she said.

Three days later, a bloke in a blue suit and a bowler hat called on Emma and Jonathan. He arrived in the evening, not long after they had finished supper. Jonathan answered the door, and there the bloke was, on the doorstep.

'Mr Hardy?'

'That's me.'

'Good evening. I'm Mr Robinson, from your local council.'

Jonathan, fit, muscular and with years of varied Army life behind him, looked the bloke over. He seemed all right, if a bit hollow-chested and distinctly middle-aged.

'What can I do for you, Mr Robinson?'

'Unfortunately,' said the council bloke, 'we've had a complaint from your neighbour, Mr Duckworth.'

'A wet one?' said Jonathan.

'Pardon?'

'Come in,' said Jonathan, and took the visitor into the front room, which Emma called the parlour because her family's cockney history was associated with same, but which many modern young couples would have called the lounge. 'Take a seat,' said Jonathan.

'Thank you,' said Mr Robinson, and sat down, bowler hat in his hand, his hair neatly parted down the middle.

Emma came in.

'Oh, hello,' she said, and Mr Robinson came politely to his feet.

'My wife,' said Jonathan. 'Emma, this is Mr Robinson from the council. He's here to ta' about a complaint.'

'Why?' said Emma, looking very nice in a white shirt-blouse and navy blue skirt. 'I haven't made a complaint. Have you, Jonathan?'

'It's a complaint from a neighbour,' said Jonathan, and the council bloke coughed.

'I'm sure it can be settled without fuss,' he said. 'Um – it appears you're lighting bonfires in your garden, Mr Hardy, and the smoke is affecting your neighbours, Mr and Mrs Duckworth.'

'We've only been here two weeks,' said Jonathan, 'and there's only been one bonfire, last Saturday afternoon. That old smoke went straight up. It might have wandered about if the day had been windy, but it wasn't.'

'Mr Duckworth insisted the smoke affected Mrs Duckworth, and that she had to put up with smuts,' said the council bloke.

'Well, as Mrs Duckworth was indoors,' said Emma, 'is Mr Duckworth accusing the smuts of floating down his chimney and seeking her out?'

'Seeking her out, that's a good one, Emma,' said Jonathan. 'Can you picture that, Mr Robinson, a platoon of smuts charging down the chimney to catch up with Mrs Duckworth?'

'A platoon?' said Mr Robinson, looking startled. That led to an involuntary little chuckle, which in turn led to another cough. 'Er – um – not without stretching my imagination,' he said. 'But it seems your chimney smoke also delivers smuts.'

'Look, I tell you what,' said Jonathan, 'I won't light another bonfire without asking Mr Duckworth if he minds, and I've already arranged for a sweep to clean out our chimneys.'

'That's very agreeable of you, Mr Hardy,' said Mr Robinson. 'I live in Sunray Avenue myself, and thought if I called this evening on behalf of my department, I might find you at home. Well, I'm sure Mr Duckworth will be satisfied with your proposal. Thanks for your co-operation.'

Emma and Jonathan saw him out.

'Not a bad chap,' said Jonathan.

'An improvement on Ducky,' said Emma.

On Saturday afternoon, Mr Duckworth himself called, presenting a portly frame, a mottled complexion and a new complaint. Emma, having opened the door to him, was the unfortunate recipient.

'Now look here, if you don't do something about your bloody dog, I'll do something myself.'

'Excuse me,' said Emma, 'but who are you?'

'I'm Duckworth.'

'Oh, yes, I recognize you now,' said Emma. She and Jonathan had introduced themselves to their neighbours on both sides on the day they moved in. 'But what's happened to your manners?'

'Never mind my manners.'

'But I do mind,' said Emma. 'Hitler didn't have any manners, nor did his rotten SS, and that upset me and a lot of other people.'

'Well, your mangy dog has just upset me and my wife,' said the choleric old trout. 'It's left its filthy mess on our front lawn.'

'Not our dog,' said Emma.

'What's that, then?' Mr Duckworth turned and pointed at a shaggy collie sitting by Emma's front gate and happily thumping its tail.

'It's a dog,' said Emma, 'but it's not ours. We don't have one, or a cat, or a budgie or a parrot.'

'Blasted dog,' said Mr Duckworth, and departed muttering and grumbling, and without apologizing.

Later, when Jonathan came into the kitchen from the garden, gumboots off, Emma told him about Mr Duckworth and the dog.

'Thought it was ours, did he?' said Jonathan. 'I'll bet he was disappointed when you told him it

43

wasn't. We could get one, if you like, Emma, and teach it to bite him.'

'No dog, thank you, Jonathan,' said Emma, looking decoratively domestic in a pretty apron.

'Cup of tea, then?' said Jonathan.

'The kettle's on,' said Emma.

'Well, while we're waiting,' said Jonathan, and pulled her onto his lap.

'Well, I'm blessed, did I invite this?' said Emma. 'Jonathan, if you – Jonathan – oh, help.'

Still, it was a nice change from having Mr Duckworth on the doorstep.

Chapter Four

Walworth, South-East London, the following Monday

Walworth was the cockney heart of the area south of the Thames, and had been sadly knocked about by German assaults from the air, not only by conventional bombing raids but by the V1s and V2s.

Mrs Cassie Brown answered a knock on the door of her house in Wansey Street, one residential thoroughfare that had been spared any grievous damage. On the step stood a bulky woman, renowned for her good neighbourliness and a heart as generous as her buxom bosom.

'Oh, hello, Mrs Hobday, nice to see you,' said Cassie, her ever-present lively look given extra sparkle by an air of happy excitement.

'Mutual, ducky, mutual,' said Mrs Hobday, cardigan worn over her straining blouse. 'I was never more pleased than when you come back from the country for good with yer nice kids and yer dad. Look, I've brought you a small side of back bacon. Well, like you know, me old man still works at Nine Elms depot, and he's still managing to pick up what falls off a goods waggon occasional. I know he's a bit useless, but he's still got more sense than to try and put the stuff back. He come 'ome yesterday with a pack of four small bacon sides. So here's one for you and yer fam'ly.' She handed a brown paper parcel to Cassie.

'Mrs Hobday, it's bacon?' said Cassie. Bacon was still rationed, like too many other foods. 'I don't know how to thank you.'

'Have you got a sharp carver for slicing it, dearie?' asked Mrs Hobday.

'Oh, yes,' said Cassie, 'and I've also got me kettle on for an afternoon pot of tea. The children are at school, so come in and have a cup.'

'A pleasure, I'm sure,' said the good lady, and waddled into the house. Cassie closed the door and they went through to the kitchen, the hub of life for any Walworth family. 'I must say you're looking nice and happy today. Mind,' the good lady went on, as she eased her largeness into a chair and made the kitchen table look small, 'things is a lot more peaceful for all of us now that there's no more bombs, although me old man says he still feels a bit punch-drunk from all them perishing doodlebugs. Have you 'eard from yer husband lately? I can't help remembering what a nice bloke he was that time he come home on leave, just after you'd gone back to the country. He—'

'He's coming home,' said Cassie, managing to get a word in. Her husband, Sergeant Freddy

Brown, had been serving in Burma with the British 14th Army, conquerors of the formidable Japanese land forces. 'I had an airmail letter today, which said by the time I received it, he'd be on a ship. He's been given early demob, with a lot of other men. Mrs Hobday, isn't that great? I don't know I ever received happier news.'

'Oh, I'm that pleased for yer, ducky,' said Mrs Hobday, as Cassie filled the teapot from the steaming kettle. 'We'll enjoy that cup of tea now, eh?'

'In his letter, Freddy asked to be remembered to you,' smiled Cassie. 'He said he'll never forget that supper and breakfast you gave him.'

'Well, what I always say is this, if you got nice neighbours, you treat 'em nice, specially when there's a war on,' said Mrs Hobday. 'If we didn't 'elp each other in a war, we wouldn't get nowhere. Me old man says Hitler only ever 'elped hisself, and look where he got, in a hole in the ground and no coffin and no flowers, and the Russians doing one of their dances on his corpse. Well, that's what me old man said. No, I won't take none of yer sugar ration in me tea, love.'

'Yes, you will,' said Cassie, happy indeed that Freddy was on his way. 'A side of back bacon and a nice neighbour are worth a whole packet of sugar.'

'Well, just a small spoonful, love,' said Mrs Hobday. 'Ain't it a real blessing, no more of them bomb explosions— Oops!' A huge rumbling noise reached Wansey Street. 'Oh, me gawd, I've spoke too soon.'

'No, you haven't,' said Cassie, 'it's only the walls of the ruined school and houses in Sayer Street that workmen are knocking down so that they can start rebuilding.'

'Mrs Davis up the street told me the London County Council's going to build big blocks of flat,' said Mrs Hobday, sipping her tea with the relish of all Londoners addicted to the stimulating brew.

'I wouldn't want to live in a flat without a backyard,' said Cassie. 'Nor would Freddy. I mean, where would you keep your dustbin? And your coal and firewood? And where would you hang your Monday washing? No, they ought to build what suits London people, lots of terraced houses with railings and gates and backyards.'

'Well, yer know, ducky, I said all that to me old man,' observed Mrs Hobday, 'and of course, him being a bit useless, he just scratched his 'ead for a bit. Then after about ten minutes, he come up with one of his bright ideas. He said keep the dustbin under the kitchen sink and 'ang the washing on a lamppost. I said some 'opes, yer daft lemon, and what about the coal, anyway? And he said he'd have to think a bit more about that. It'll take him a week of Fridays. Still, he ain't all useless, and he always wears a nice line in fancy braces and keeps 'is boots polished. I like a man that's got pride in 'is braces and a shine to 'is boots. You don't have to go after a man so much when he's got some good points. I'm pleased yer hubby's on his way home. Well, thanks, dearie, I will 'ave another cup.'

'Oh, you're very welcome, Mrs Hobday,' said

Cassie, whose hospitality could always stretch the contents of a teapot.

Aboard the troopship that was bringing home a number of time-expired conscripts from Burma, Cassie's husband, Sergeant Freddy Brown, was leaning on the rail and thinking about his one and only wife, and if they ought to consider acquiring a house with a garden. A garden would suit Cassie. Best wife a feller could have, and what a lovely bit of all right she was in bed, especially on the occasions when a particular kind of event came to pass, and confirmed for a bloke that the difference between a man and a woman was one of God's first-class ideas. Was there a God, though? He hadn't shown up much in Burma, nor, apparently, in those stinking German concentration camps that the 14th Army men had heard about, and nor in the filthy prisoner-of-war camps that the Japanese guards had turned into hellholes. Still, whatever, the fact was Cassie had sex appeal, not half and thanks very much. And when a bloke was away from a wife like Cassie for a long time, well, you couldn't help thinking about the first thing you'd like to do at a reunion. Give the kids a tanner each and send them out to buy sweets. Wonder what Cassie will look like in the two saffron sarongs I'm taking home to her? Could she use them as nighties?

'Watcher, sarge.' Private Monty Cutts put himself beside Freddy at the ship's rail.

'What's on your mind?' asked Freddy.

'Nothing much, sarge, except you haven't

caught a sea fever, have you? Only you're looking a bit flushed.'

In an office in Baker Street, London, Captain Bobby Somers, RA, and Lieutenant Helene Somers, FANY, were coming to the end of their final meeting with Colonel Buckmaster, head of SOE(French). Colonel Buckmaster had made a name for himself as the intelligent mastermind of all that related to British support for the French Resistance movement, supplying arms and agents to strengthen its effectiveness. It had not been easy, for a certain amount of anti-British feeling had existed among many of the French, brought about, it has to be said, by the bitter fact that France had surrendered to the Germans, while Churchill and his people had used their island fortress to stand and continue the fight.

Colonel Buckmaster had always shown compassion and understanding, and he cherished his memories of the men and women who had lost their lives as agents. His admiration for the two agents in his office now was frank. After several hair-raising but successful missions, they had spent seven months prior to the end of the war training new agents at an establishment in the New Forest. That was all over now.

'It's a particular pleasure to me that you both survived after so much dangerous work. I hope, Helene, and I hope, Bobby, that I'm not saying goodbye to you, only *au revoir*, and that I shall see you at any reunions that I'm sure will take place. France can be proud of you, Helene, and we in this country should salute you, Bobby.'

'Any salutes for Bobby are for me too,' said Helene, still a robust and good-looking woman whose auburn tints in her dark hair reflected her tendency to be mettlesome. 'I'm his wife, *mon Commandant*.'

'Yes, of course.' Colonel Buckmaster smiled. 'I wish you well of your lady wife, Bobby.'

'Wishing me well gives me hope that I'll be able to turn her into my little woman,' said Bobby, a grin coming and going. 'Baking cakes in a pretty apron.'

Helene uttered a little yell.

'Listen to him! The war is over, but he's still making jokes, and every one is still terrible. What have I done? I have married an English clown. I said so at the time, I have said so since, and I say so now. *Mon Commandant*, why are you laughing?'

'Dear young lady,' said Colonel Buckmaster, 'I'm laughing because in marrying a man full of terrible jokes, you must suffer a lifetime of them.'

'That makes you laugh?' said Helene.

'It might make other men weep,' smiled Colonel Buckmaster, 'but yes, it makes me laugh. I think you're both going to enjoy each other. Invite me to the first anniversary of your marriage. Good luck in your new work, Bobby.' He had helped Bobby obtain a position in the French section of the Foreign Office, starting in October. 'Goodbye now.' He shook hands warmly with them, and they both made it very clear that it had been a privilege to know him and to have worked for him.

Outside, in the light of a quite balmy day, Helene slipped her arm through Bobby's. She was still in her FANY uniform and beret, Bobby still in khaki and cap, both having received their discharge papers together with their war gratuities from their respective Services only this morning.

'Bobby, I didn't mean I was sorry to have married you.'

'Sure?' said Bobby.

'Of course I'm sure.'

'Right, give us a kiss, then,' said Bobby.

'Out here, in this street? No, the kisses I give you are only for when we're alone.'

'Fair enough,' said Bobby, 'so let's find some place that'll serve us what's coming to be called an austerity lunch before we go home.' Home at the moment was with Bobby's parents, Lizzy and Ned Somers. 'Over lunch we'll talk about where we might like to live, and what kind of a house we can afford.'

'Oh, yes.' Helene became happy. 'Bobby, wouldn't you like to have children?'

'I'm unanimous about that,' said Bobby, as they strolled arm in arm, 'but not over lunch.'

'Over lunch? Over lunch?'

'Yes,' said Bobby, 'let's wait till we've found a home and have settled down. Don't let's draw attention to ourselves over lunch.'

'Oh, my God, you're still doing it! Having children over lunch? I'm going to scream, I tell you.'

'Don't do that, not here in the street,' said

Bobby. 'Look, the war's over and it's time for laughs, isn't it, my French Fifi?'

'Oh, yes.' Helene tugged his arm. Baker Street traffic flowed by, and for all the post-war conditions that pointed to a long period of austerity, people seemed to be walking with a spring in their step, perhaps because of the sunshine. 'I don't really mind your crazy jokes. I've written to my parents three times since the end of the war, and have said the same thing in each one.'

'What same thing?' asked Bobby.

'That I like being married to my English idiot.'

'Good-oh,' said Bobby. 'Over lunch we'll discuss how to go about making our first baby. That'll be OK, a discussion. I'd like the details. In our family, that kind of thing isn't discussed, so I'm hopelessly ignorant. It's lucky you're French, since I'm sure French families are more forthcoming.'

Helene stifled a scream.

Late October

Autumn was fighting the early onset of winter, its russet-hued mornings crisp with sunshine, its afternoons cold and grey beneath chilly clouds. Fuel and various foods were still rationed, and quality material for clothes was hard to come by. The British people, having soldiered on throughout the war, were having to soldier on in peacetime.

Demobilized men were now flooding back into the UK from the worldwide battlefields, leaving behind them many countries in political upheaval.

Sergeant Freddy Brown arrived home, lean, bushy-haired and laden with optimism for his post-war future with Cassie and the kids. The kids were at school, but Cassie was at home, and she jumped into his arms. Freddy said he was glad to have her there, and was she busy at the moment? Not specially, said Cassie, just ever so happy that he was home for good at last. But she could bake a cake later as a celebration, she said.

Freddy said later sounded all right, so did a homemade cake, but wasn't there something they could do until then? Cassie asked if he had any bright ideas about that. Freddy said he was stuck with just one idea. Cassie, bright-eyed, asked was it the kind of idea she'd like? Freddy said if she'd try on one of the sarongs he'd brought home for her, they could carry on from there and find out.

Well, of course, Cassie in a saffron sarong inspired a carry-on that was a lot more memorable than baking a cake.

The following day, an Army car pulled up outside a cottage near Bere Regis in Dorset. An officer eased himself from the passenger seat, and the driver, a REME corporal, alighted and opened up the boot. He hefted luggage out, and the officer took hold of two large suitcases. He thanked the driver.

'Pleasure, sir, honest. Hope you enjoy your civvy street, I'll be there myself in a month. Goodbye, sir, glad to see the back of that ruddy grim war in Eyetie country.'

'We're still alive, Corporal Davis. We've left a hell of a lot of unlucky ones behind. Goodbye.'

The car moved off, the cottage door opened, and Mrs Rosie Chapman, adopted daughter of Boots, appeared. The officer, Captain Matthew Chapman, REME, turned, a smile of unrestrained delight creasing his weatherbeaten and darkly tanned features.

'Are you Mrs Rosie Chapman?'

'Oh, I be her, sir, and be you Captain Chapman home from the mighty seas?'

'Ah, so I be and so I am.' Dorset-born Matthew Chapman laughed and brought himself and his suitcases along the path to the doorstep, the short walk revealing his permanent limp. 'God bless you, Rosie, for showing yourself. Blow my boots off if you don't beat the shirt of Venus herself.'

Rosie, hair the colour of ripe corn, blue eyes dancing, looks as striking as ever, laughed.

'Matt, Venus doesn't wear a shirt.'

'Ah, the lady turns blue in the winter, does she?' said Matt, and set his cases down, on which cue Rosie put herself into his arms.

'Matt, you dear man, here we are, all yours.' She kissed him, and their children appeared, three-year-old Giles and two-year-old Emily, the latter named after Rosie's late adoptive mother. They looked shyly up at their father. His smile melted their reserve, they sensed affection and the fun of games, and they wound themselves around his legs.

'By God, Rosie,' he said, 'whatever Italy means to the Italians, I know what this old country and you three mean to me. Everything that's worthwhile.'

'I like that, very much,' said Rosie, 'and I hope you'll still think the same when supper's on the table. We're having fatted calf. Actually, one of the chickens, poor thing. But she was past her best time as a layer. There, be you coming in, Captain Chapman, sir?'

Matt, always responsive to Rosie's effervescent nature, picked his children up, one under each arm, and took the last steps of his journey from Italy into his home.

His luggage remained on the doorstep. Who cared? Not Rose, not her husband, not their excited children, and not the chickens.

There was no-one else in the cottage, for Felicity, Rosie's sister-in-law, blind friend and companion, knowing Matthew was on his way home, had departed with her child to stay with her parents in Streatham, and there she was waiting for husband Tim, as Rosie had been waiting for Matthew.

Emma, answering a knock on her front door, found her neighbour on the step. Not the fussy and troublesome Mr Duckworth, who was discovering something to complain about twice a week, but Mrs Duckworth, plump and fluttery.

'Oh, I'm ever so sorry to bother you, Mrs Hardy,' said the nervous lady, 'but Mr Duckworth, my husband, well—' She gulped. 'He wants to know what all the hammering's about, and who's doing it.'

That was like the cantankerous old goat, thought Emma, not only to fuss about a bit of hammering, but to make his wife take a turn at delivering a complaint, when he must know she wasn't that kind of woman. She was so embarrassed about her errand, in fact, that even her pink jumper seemed fluttery.

'Oh, it's only Jonathan, Mrs Duckworth, and he's not really dangerous.'

'Jonathan?'

'My husband,' said Emma. 'He's been putting up some useful shelves in the garden shed, and now he's knocking new nails in its roof. He says the old ones have rusted away, and that we don't want the roof to blow off in the wind, especially as it might land in your garden just when Mr Duckworth's doing some autumn pruning.'

'Oh, I can see you wouldn't want that to happen, it could land ever so heavy,' said Mrs Duckworth. On the old goat himself, with any luck, thought Emma. Mrs Duckworth, gulping again, said, 'Yes, it's got to be fixed, of course, but Mr Duckworth says does it have to be on a Sunday afternoon, which is a time for some peace and quiet. He says. I'm sorry to ask about it, but—'

'That's all right,' smiled Emma, 'I do understand. Come in and have a cup of tea. I've just put the kettle on, as it happens.'

'Oh, how kind.' A smile broke through nervousness, but didn't stay long. It simply came and went. 'Oh, I don't think I will, Mrs Hardy, I'd best get back and put my own kettle on for me and Mr Duckworth.'

'You're very welcome to step in, really,' said Emma, who felt that if Mrs Duckworth could only overcome her timidity and give Mr Duckworth a couple of old-fashioned wallops with her rolling-pin, it might do him a bit of good, as well as reshaping his silly head.

'No, I'd best get back,' said Mrs Duckworth. 'Oh, about the hammering—'

'It's stopped now,' said Emma, 'and Jonathan will be coming in for his cup of tea. I'll tell him to give any more hammering a rest.'

'Oh, so kind, thank you,' said Mrs Duckworth, and hastened away to carry the good news to her choleric old fusspot.

Jonathan received Emma's order to give his work a rest in amiable fashion, except that he did say old Duckworth's head needed more of a hammering than the shed roof, which coincided with Emma's thoughts of what a rolling-pin could do for the bloke.

Chapter Five

Eloise, French-born daughter of Boots and wife of
Colonel Lucas, Commando Officer wounded in
action following the Allied crossing of the Rhine,
had finished her time with the ATS and was living
with her husband in a flat in Chelsea. Luke, whose
worst wound had meant the loss of his right
arm, was nevertheless still in the Army. A regular
with an outstanding active service record, he now
worked at the War Office. Eloise was settling into
a domestic routine, for Luke generally was a nine-
to-five desk soldier, and already adapting himself
to his disability, as well as to the radical change
that had brought him from the violence of war to
the restful calm of being a providing and attentive
husband to Eloise.

It was not precisely humdrum, however. Eloise,
like Helene, did not go in for the humdrum. And
also like Helene, she expected a husband to be
very attentive. Accordingly, she insisted Luke go
shopping with her on Saturdays. Shopping?
Shopping? Yes, why not? You're not serious, said
Luke. Yes, I am, said Eloise, it will be fun, doing it
together. I'm not cut out for shopping, said Luke.

Oh, I will show you how to enjoy it, said Eloise. The devil you will, said Luke. I shan't ask you to carry the shopping basket, said Eloise. You're damn right you won't, said Luke. But you'll come with me, said Eloise, won't you? Not if I can help it, said Luke. But it's something for us to do together, said Eloise, so you must. Not shopping, never, said Luke. I insist, said Eloise.

So every Saturday he went shopping with her.

It was the old story of a determined husband's determination falling to pieces.

Sammy and Susie were still living with Chinese Lady and Mr Finch, along with their children Paula and Phoebe, and, additionally, Bess and Jimmy who, long absent as evacuees in Devon, were back at last. Bess, seventeen, was a good-natured girl studying hard in the hope of following her cousin Alice into Bristol University. Jimmy, in his sixteenth year, was a humorous lad and still being educated.

The large house, with five spacious bedrooms, accommodated the eight residents comfortably, while Sammy and Susie, having commissioned an architect to draw up plans for a new house, interested themselves in his proposals and suggestions, many of which related to ideas of their own.

In mid-November, Polly and Boots moved into their new home, the house close to Dulwich Village. It was, as Sammy had said, a handsome property indeed, but certainly not the last word in residential grandeur, a relief to Boots when he and Polly had first looked it over. He had no wish to live like a squire. He saw it very much as a handsome family house with a conservatory and a delightful garden. House and garden offered the twins acres of space in which to run about. The kitchen, abutting on a utility room with a walk-in pantry, was large but crying out for modern equipment. That priority would be taken care of when manufacturers were able to supply the home market. The most attractive features of the house were the sitting-room facing the garden and the handsome oak-panelled hall. Upstairs, and suitably sandwiched between the twins' bedrooms, was a playroom. Good, spacious enough for three, said Boots to Polly. Three? Yes, James, Gemma and me, said Boots. I need to make up for lost time, especially on the rocking-horse, with the twins riding pillion. Some rocking-horse, said Polly, and there isn't one, anyway. And they've disappeared from toyshops. I know what that means, said Boots, the twins will want donkey rides. And you'll be the donkey, of course, said Polly. So there'll have to be a rocking-horse, said Boots, which means having a word with Sammy's old friend, Eli Greenberg. Which he did, and Mr Greenberg, whose Camberwell yard was the treasure chest of South London, produced one of solid, enduring Victorian vintage from under a mountain of chairs.

'There, Boots, ain't that a proud beauty?'

'Is the tail in good order, Eli?'

'Not vun missing hair, Boots,' said Mr

Greenberg, 'not vun. A brush and comb, that's all it needs, ain't it?'

'What's the damage?' asked Boots.

'For a friend, Boots, say a fiver?'

'A fiver?' said Boots, noting the excellent condition of the desired object. 'You're robbing yourself. It's worth twenty pounds at least.'

'Vell, say a tenner, and I von't take a penny more,' said Mr Greenberg.

'Let me add an extra two quid for delivery on your cart,' said Boots. 'Will that suit you, Eli?'

Mr Greenberg cast a warm glance at the man he regarded as the most distinguished member of the Gentile family that had only ever shown him kindness and friendship. There were the other kind, yes, the ugly-minded louts who had been followers of Britain's Hitler-lover, Oswald Mosley, but the people of the East End had consistently fought them. Boots was typical of a people tolerant of political bumblers, but intolerant of thugs and political extremists. He was a gentleman, if not a born one, then one by nature. He wore, as always, his easy-going air, but Mr Greenberg knew, as many other people did, he was not a man who conceded ground to the devil or any of his acolytes.

'Vill it suit me, Boots, my friend? I should say no? Vhen did business vith the Adams family ever do me a bad turn?' Mr Greenberg had aired this rhetorical question on many occasions, usually for Sammy's benefit, but that still didn't stop him airing it this time, or from taking his handkerchief out of his capacious coat pocket and blowing his nose. 'Ain't I known vhat happy friendship means to a man, and ain't it good to see you back from the var, and such a terrible var, vasn't it?' Mr Greenberg cast another glance at Chinese Lady's eldest son, a sober glance this time. 'Sammy tells me you saw vhat Himmler did at Belsen.'

'D'you want to hear about it?' asked Boots.

'I do, Boots, don't I?' said Mr Greenberg. 'I know much, but vill you have a cup of tea vith me in my office and tell me more?'

Boots gave him an account over a cup of tea, an account that filled in radio news gaps and shocked Mr Greenberg into silence. What could one say about the totally unspeakable? One could find no words that fitted one's horror and complete disbelief. Accordingly, Mr Greenberg could only numbly grieve for the Jews of Belsen.

'I know how you feel,' said Boots.

'And how do I feel, Boots? I vill try to tell you. I feel Himmler vas born of the devil. I feel how fortunate I am to have had a father farseeing enough to bring his family out of Russia to this country many years ago. I feel that God smiled on us, and then turned aside from millions of others. Vhy should God have done that, Boots, vhy should He have blinded His eyes to such suffering?'

'I've no answer,' said Boots, 'except to suggest that in providing us with a world beautiful and life-giving, God then expected us to get on with it, to gratefully behave ourselves, and not to bother Him with the troubles we make for ourselves or others make for us.'

'But such suffering,' said Mr Greenberg again, shaking his head.

'I've still no real answer,' said Boots.

'Some of us so fortunate, Boots, and so many so unfortunate,' said the sad Mr Greenberg.

'I don't understand, Eli, any more than you do,' said Boots, and wondered if Goering and the other Nazi leaders, in their slavish acceptance of Hitler's pathological hatred of the Jews, had considered the extermination of six million of them merely a job well done.

Perhaps, he thought, the German nation as a whole agreed with that, for there had been no great outpouring of remorse from the people, no great outcry for the perpetrators to be brought to justice, only implications and suggestions that they felt uncomfortable about what had come to light. All too many Germans were of the opinion that the Allies were being unfair in putting fat, jolly Goering on trial. And all too many professed themselves ignorant of the purposes of the concentration camps, or even of any ill-treatment of the Jews. Boots would have pointed them to a day and a night in November, 1938, when throughout the Third Reich, Nazi thugs smashed and destroyed Jewish shops and synagogues in every town and city, beat and humiliated thousands of Jewish people and murdered scores, while the German people looked on and did nothing. He had asked himself, if such brutality had taken place in the countries of the Western Allies, would the American and British people have tolerated it? He thought not, and fervently hoped not.

As he drove out of Mr Greenberg's Camberwell yard, Boots dwelt on his conviction that for once a war had been justifiable.

To Polly the house in East Dulwich Grove was the home where she and Boots would spend the rest of their lives, where in their kind of compatible and stimulating companionship they could help each other grow old gracefully. The brittle, restless and demanding Polly had become a woman who asked for nothing more than that which she now had, the husband she had always wanted and the children she thought she never would have. His children. Well, perhaps there was one other thing.

'Darling?' she said some days after they had moved in.

'I suspect that,' said Boots.

'But why should you? You have always been my darling.'

'I still have suspicions.'

'Well, dear old thing, it's true I'm going to ask a favour.'

'I believe you,' said Boots.

'Only a small one.'

'I suspect that too,' said Boots.

'There's no need. I'm only going to ask that when you start working for the firm again, and have agreed with Sammy what you need in the way of a salary to keep your loving Polly and your twins in the style you think they deserve, well, when this has been arranged—'

'My suspicions have taken a turn for the worse,' said Boots.

'Darling, how droll you are, and I love it. Do you think at the right moment we could engage a maid-cook?'

'Good God,' said Boots.

'That's an affirmative?'

'It's a cry for help,' said Boots.

'I could pay her wages out of my own money,' said Polly. She owned a healthy bank balance originating with a bequest from her mother, who had died when Polly was a young girl.

'I don't mean that kind of help,' said Boots. 'Your money is your own.' Polly made a little face. He had always been insistent about that. 'If anything should happen to me—'

'Don't say that, don't ever say it.'

'You'd really like a maid and a cook, Polly?'

'I'm not the world's greatest cook myself, we both know that, and a little help with the housework would be nice, but if you think we couldn't afford—'

'Engage one,' said Boots.

'A maid-cook? Boots, you're saying yes?'

'You may not be a great cook, but you're an asset as a gardener,' said Boots. 'You've grown first-class onions and runner beans in Dorset, and I daresay you will here. Plus, there's your gift to me of the twins. So yes, treat yourself to a maid-cook.'

'Love you, you adorable old sport.' Polly hugged him.

'Let her know I don't like lumpy custard,' said Boots.

Polly, her whimsical husband's most devoted fan, gave laughter an airing.

Their new home provided her with the opportunity to make frequent visits with the twins to her parents' house, to spend time with her ageing father and her very likeable stepmother.

Kate Trimble, who had made a home with her and Boots in Dorset until she joined the WAAF, maintained contact with them by letter and phone while waiting to be demobbed. And Eloise and her husband Luke regularly visited. The twins fascinated Eloise, and their existence, intriguing her, prompted her on one occasion to say to Boots, 'Ah, you are a dangerous man, Papa.'

'To people?' said Boots.

'To the women you have known. You look at them, and voila! – you make mothers of them.'

Susie had once said much the same thing, and Sammy had accordingly requested his eldest brother to keep his eyes off her.

'Eloise, I think that's a serious exaggeration,' said Boots.

'But it's almost true,' said Eloise.

'If so,' said Boots, 'what should I do, live in a cupboard and be a hermit?'

'No, of course not,' said Eloise, 'you are too nice to hide yourself. Women must take their chance.'

Emma had established a neighbourly friendship with timid Mrs Duckworth, regularly inviting her to share a pot of afternoon tea. Mrs Duckworth became happily responsive to that, but never on any occasion said anything about the cantankerous nature of her husband. In fact, she assured Emma he didn't ever really mean to be unkind. It was just that now and again the mood took him to look around for something he could grumble about.

Emma thought it was a bit more than that, for poor Mrs Duckworth often looked a harassed woman. Jonathan's attitude towards the lady's husband made him remark that he'd like to drop in on the awkward old bugger sometimes, and talk unkindly to him. Emma told him he wasn't to interfere, ever.

Meanwhile, her dad was recovering from a debilitating attack of flu. The illness had brought his family and his close relatives rushing to his bedside in concern. Ned had been a steadfast husband to Lizzy, and a good old dad to his sons and daughters without ever giving them a mistaken inch too much. He was fifty now, and had looked as if his artificial leg was helping his sound one to carry him effortlessly into the realms of longevity. His hair, thinning a bit and greying a little, seemed his only failing. But the attack of flu completely downed him.

Lizzy was sure she knew why. Ned was still manager of a wine merchant's business in Great Tower Street, the premises having escaped air raid destruction. Since the end of the war he'd been working long hours with the re-establishment of wine imports from the Continent involving re-organizing the cellars. This after the stresses of the long war, when he'd kept the business going without staff, had, in Lizzy's opinion, taken its toll.

However, not having indulged in a misspent youth or taken to drink, which would have impaired his palate as a wine connoisseur, his constitution helped him to make a recovery, for which Lizzy gave thanks. Everyone else experienced the pleasure of deep relief. Good old Ned had his place in family affections, and that went for his gammy leg as well. His firm, Spanish-owned and well-known for its sherry, informed Lizzy he was to spend time convalescing.

Boots phoned daughter Rosie.

'Rosie?'

'Daddy old love, happy to hear you – oh, how is Uncle Ned?'

'Much better. He's up and about in a modest way.'

'Oh, good show, now I'm even happier,' said Rosie.

'Listen, poppet, he'll need a change of air well away from London, and your Aunt Lizzy could do with a break herself. So as Dorset air is high on the list of purity, and your Uncle Ned will need rather more home comforts than he'd get in a hotel, I'm wondering if you and Matthew could find time and room to—'

'Say no more,' said Rosie. 'I'll phone Aunt Lizzy as soon as I've finished speaking to you. We've four bedrooms and Matt and I are very kindly disposed to our favourite relatives, his and mine.

Truly, we'd love to have Aunt Lizzy and Uncle Ned, and we'll take them out to coastal areas where the sea gives extra tonic to our well-known air. Would you think two weeks?'

'Two weeks should work wonders, Rosie. Bless you, poppet.'

Rosie laughed.

'I said years ago that you'd still be calling me poppet when I was an old lady.'

'Are you an old lady, Rosie?'

'Oh, getting on a little, I suppose. I'm thirty.'

'And that's getting on a little, is it?'

'Well, it's a far cry from the days when I was nine or ten.'

'How are Emily and Giles?'

'Asleep at the moment,' said Rosie, 'after a rollicking day. Matt calls them Rollicker One and Rollicker Two. I don't know what the chickens call them, except that they run for cover every time the rollickers appear.'

'Kids,' said Boots.

'Yes, lovely,' said Rosie.

'How's the rebuilding of Matt's garage coming along?' asked Boots.

'Slowly,' said Rosie. 'Priority for building materials in our South-West is given to the bombed towns, like Southampton, Plymouth and Bristol. Matt's doing freelance farm work. He worries about how little he's earning. But we manage comfortably enough because of all I'm earning from my investment in your property company. Matt would prefer to be the main bread-winner, though. He has all these old-fashioned ideas about the responsibilities of husbands and fathers.'

'Are they old-fashioned, Rosie?'

'Virtuous?' said Rosie.

'Sound,' said Boots.

'I think I'll go along with that,' said Rosie, 'being a little old-fashioned myself. Daddy old dear, I'll phone Aunt Lizzy, I promise. Love to Polly and the twins, and lots of love to you. Isn't peacetime wonderful?'

'It was a long time coming, poppet.'

Chapter Six

Letter from Miss Patsy Kirk of Boston, Massachussetts, to Lance-Corporal Daniel Adams care of BFPO (British Field Post Office).

Darling Daniel,

I'm in happy receipt of your last letter giving me the news that your company will finish its time in Palestine in April or May, and that you'll then be getting home leave. I'll be there waiting for you, because I'm going back to the UK in March, to stay again with your Aunt Vi and Uncle Tommy.

I do miss you, I really do, and your family, and you can bet I'm looking forward to the day when we can be married. Daniel, when do you think that can be arranged? Pa won't need me to keep house for him after February, he's decided to take a second wife, a woman journalist he met in Europe at the end of the war. The date is fixed, and it'll be when they come back from their honeymoon that I'll be booking my sea passage back to the UK. I just can't wait to get there.

I like you telling me in your letters that I've got a great amount of American sex appeal, and in your next letter could you tell me what your idea is of American sex appeal, because I think you mean it's different. How different? Could you explain, as I think I might find it very interesting.

Take care, Daniel. I'm glad you're not having to fight in any war, but we sometimes get news of Palestine that makes me feel it's far from peaceful for you. Think of me lots, as I do of you, and don't forget I love you.

Yours for ever,
Patsy

Daniel received the letter during a period of relative quiet, when street patrols in Haifa were of an untroubled kind. Daniel, as adaptable to the twists and turns of life as his uncles and most of his cousins, had fitted himself into the Army without suffering feelings of being hard done by, and although he was among the younger conscripts of his company, he had done well enough to earn his stripe. His time in khaki would run for two years, which meant he'd be demobbed early in 1947.

On reading Patsy's letter, he felt he must decide whether to marry her when he received home leave in about five or six months, or wait until his discharge. Well, there was Patsy's American sex appeal. That could help any bloke to make a quick decision. So he wrote a reply telling her first of all that American sex appeal was what she had, and the difference was that other girls had their own kind, which wasn't something he knew a great deal about, since he'd always had other things on

73

his mind until he met her. A short while after the meeting, he wrote, he realized he had something else on his mind, something that had a kind of oomph to it. He did a bit of analysing, and realized oomph was another word for her American sex appeal. How did she rate that as an explanation?

As for marrying her, he felt he'd like that sooner than later, and would come across with a suggested date when he knew for certain what day his company would embark for home leave. The blokes would be given that information in the New Year. Meanwhile, he'd take care to keep out of trouble, she could bet on that, as he was set on being a healthy A1 when he finally came into legalized contact with her oomph.

Lizzy and Ned had spent two enjoyable weeks in Dorset with Rosie and Matthew, Lizzy delighting in the children, Giles and Emily, and telling Rosie how happy she was that the little girl had been named after Boots's first wife, the family's god-send during the First World War. Ned found the fortnight both restful and recreational, the latter coming from outings that enabled him to take in lungfuls of pure country air. He also struck up a warm friendship with Matthew, a man very much like Boots in his easy-going ways and tolerant attitudes to life and people. Ned, like Lizzy, wondered if that similarity had been his chief attraction for Rosie, who had always adored her adoptive father.

*   *   *

At this stage, the country was struggling to come to terms with the cost of victory. Industry generally was trying to make do with machinery rapidly becoming out-of-date. The Marshall Plan, America's great and generous contribution towards the recovery of the ruined economies of Continental Europe and the Far East, meant that Germany and Japan, the nations that had plunged the world into war, were seeing the building of new factories equipped with the most modern machinery, while Britain was struggling in the doldrums, a country literally beggared by the prolonged conflict.

There was a critical shortage of houses in London, half a million having been destroyed and thousands of others severely damaged by air raids and flying bombs. The Labour Government under Prime Minister Clement Attlee was planning the creation of a Welfare State to look after the sick, the poor and the unemployed, but was unable to provide instant new housing. The alternative solution for the dispossessed people of Inner London was the erection of huge blocks of flats, a quicker way of providing homes than rebuilding those that had been destroyed. No more slums, said the Labour Party. Well-designed, centrally-heated flats, that was what the working classes should have, and what they're going to have, at affordable rents.

For people outside Inner London, the problems of rebuilding their homes lay with the fact that the building industry was handicapped by a shortage of materials, particularly seasoned and imported timber. Timber, in fact, was as good as rationed. For that matter, rationing still existed in respect of meat and other foods.

Sammy stood on the edge of the site of his bombed house on Denmark Hill. Sammy had connections, and accordingly his new house was going up, the footings in, the outer brick walls three feet high. No, Susie hadn't wanted a house they could move into immediately, she wanted a new house on their old site, and the overgrown garden put back into shape. And for the new house she wanted lattice windows. She liked the look of them inside and out, and didn't care a ha'penny for the fact that self-elected arbiters of taste would call them the product of silly pretentious suburbia.

'Susie, lattice windows require good quality lead.'

'Yes, all right, Sammy.'

'Manufacturers of lattice windows can't get anywhere near enough of the right kind at the moment.'

'You can get it, Sammy.'

'Susie, there's no spare lead on offer even at the best scrap metal yards.'

'But you know people, Sammy.'

'Scrap metal spivs, Susie?'

'Now, Sammy, you know I don't hold with spivs.'

'Well, of course, I'd never invite any such geezers to tea, Susie.'

'Don't even think of it, Sammy. Try Mr

Greenberg, he's always been able to oblige you, and he always knows where to lay his hands on this, that and the other.'

'Susie, you doll. Good old Eli, of course. Come here.'

'Sammy, is that your hand on my person?'

'I can't tell a porkie, Susie, it is, but look at it as a touch of gratitude for pointing me at Eli.'

'Sammy, be your age.'

Sammy called on Mr Greenberg at his Camberwell yard and explained his requirements.

'Lead, Sammy, you vant lead?'

'Believe me, Eli, I don't want a rocking-horse like you dug out for Boots.'

'For his children, Sammy, vhich I vas pleased to find, vasn't I?'

'I'm after good lead, for Susie's lattice windows, like I've just said, but I don't want it lifted off church roofs. Susie wouldn't like that, and I'm nearly as reverent as she is.'

'Sammy, Sammy, vhen did I ever do that kind of business?'

'Sorry, Eli, slip of the tongue.'

'You vant lead that I ain't got?'

'That'll be a sad disappointment to Susie.'

'Vell, Sammy, it so happens—'

'There's a good bloke, Eli, I knew I could rely on you.'

'Between you and me, Sammy, I know there's a pile of bomb-damaged stuff under some closed-in railvay arches in Bermondsey, vhich some people have forgotten about, but it ain't going to be cheap, buying the scrap, stripping the lead and getting it carted.'

'I'll look after the costs of buying the scrap and stripping it, Eli, and the window manufacturers will look after collecting the lead and agreeing the right kind of price that'll cover your costs and mine, and give us both a bit of profit.'

'Vell, Sammy, a small profit, that's fair, ain't it?'

'Fair's fair, and Susie'll be tickled.'

'Ah, Susie, vasn't she alvays more fond of laughing than crying?'

'By the way,' said Sammy, 'I believe you told me you're helping to raise donations for concentration camp survivors. Am I right?'

Mr Greenberg sighed. His white-flecked beard itself took on a sad look, and his eyes clouded with moist grey.

'Ah, Sammy, vas there ever more evil in the minds of the dark vuns than in the mind of Himmler? Boots told me about Belsen, everything, didn't he? Vas there ever more grief for my people, for all the dead and all those that are only half-alive? True, Sammy, I do now have an interest in a relief fund that—'

'Say no more, Eli, old cock, and take this.' Sammy handed a folded cheque to the man he had known since a boy, a man whose word was his bond and whose little foibles had turned him into one of South London's most likeable characters. Unfolding the cheque, the enduring rag-and-bone merchant laid blurred eyes on the amount. The blur vanished beneath a surge of warm pleasure.

'Two hundred and fifty pounds, Sammy, two hundred and fifty?'

'It's a charitable donation from the firm, Eli, with best wishes from me and Boots,' said Sammy. 'I can't recall ever getting a bad deal from any of your people, or from you. That contribution won't go far among the suffering, but if it helps a bit, then good. I'm suffering myself in a way, on account of Himmler cheating the chopper.'

'Sammy, vat can I say?'

'Only that you and me can count our blessings,' said Sammy in serious vein, 'along with the rest of the people that never had jackboots walking over them. If Boots told you exactly what those jackboots did to your people at Belsen, he hasn't told me or anyone else in the family. He lets us get it out of the wireless or from newspapers, probably because all the worst facts might make Susie, Lizzy and Vi sick for a week.' Sammy shook himself and brightened up. 'Anyway, you get that lead available to the manufacturers, old cock, and Susie'll bake you and your family one of her special sultana cakes, if she can get some sultanas.'

'Susie vants sultanas, Sammy? Vell, I do happen to know—'

'Crafty old Joe Honeypot? So do I.'

'Ain't it Joe Honeyvell, Sammy?'

'Same thing,' said Sammy. 'You can leave the sultanas to me. Only don't tell Susie I got 'em from crafty old Joe. He's a spiv, and she knows it. She's got a rolling-pin specially reserved for any spivs that come knocking.'

'That Susie of yours, Sammy.' Mr Greenberg

smiled. 'Vasn't she alvays a caution, and ain't I fond of her?'

'So am I,' said Sammy, 'but she still don't like spivs.'

All that had been some weeks ago. Now the new house was going up, the architect's plans, specifications and sketches having been approved by all concerned, including the local council, while a specially appointed Government authority had promised reimbursement appropriate to the value of the old house. Sammy had put the builders in touch with certain sources that could overcome shortage of materials except the right kind of pure lead. Good old Eli, as promised, had come up trumps with that kind of quality, and it was now in the hands of the window manufacturers, which meant a promise from them of early delivery instead of a six-months wait. That was how it was with orders for manufactured goods in these early post-war days. Yes, you could order, but you'd have to wait for delivery. You could even order a car, but you weren't likely to get it for a couple of years.

All the same, what Susie wanted, Susie was going to have, lattice windows and all. Susie was one by herself. All through the war she had never wavered, never run screaming from those ruddy flying bombs, and never believed less than a hundred per cent in Winston Churchill.

The old boy was taking time off now. The Labour Party, having ousted the Conservatives, was doing its best to sponsor the rebuilding of bomb-ruined houses and factories. All in all, though, things were kind of grey. Still, the business was holding its own, the factory once more turning out ladies' fashion garments for the firm's shops and other outlets. There were always three things people had to have, a roof over their heads, food and clothes.

Sammy had a word with the site foreman, then got back in his car and drove to the firm's offices at Camberwell Green, where he was in time to receive a morning cup of coffee from Rachel Goodman's daughter Leah, a lush young beauty and no error. There was going to be a mixed marriage in the family, for Leah was engaged to Lizzy's younger son, Edward, a pilot in the RAF.

Every time he looked at Leah or her mother, Sammy silently thanked his Maker and the RAF for the fact that Hitler's planned invasion of the UK had been knocked on the head. Looking at Leah now, he thought he detected brightness in her velvety brown eyes.

'Leah,' he said, 'have you got some good news falling about on your tongue?'

Leah had, very much as Cassie had had a little while ago.

'Uncle Sammy – Mr Sammy – isn't it lovely news? I've heard from Edward – he'll be out of the RAF and home from Cyprus before the end of May – that's next summertime—' Leah, delivering herself in excited bits and pieces, paused for breath. 'He wants our wedding to take place sometime in June, and for me to name the day. Mr Sammy, I'm so happy.'

Bless the girl, thought Sammy, bless her for

being like her mum, warm-hearted, generous and as natural with Gentiles as with her own kind. A highly valuable shorthand-typist for the firm, at eighteen she was a richly endowed brunette, and a bit like Elizabeth Taylor, the young up-and-coming film star. Lucky Edward. Not every bloke married an Elizabeth Taylor lookalike.

'Well, that's a welcome piece of news, Leah.' Sammy smiled. 'A church wedding, might I ask?'

'Edward's parents and Mama, and Edward and I, well, we've all talked about it,' said Leah, 'and we think it has to be a civil ceremony, at a registry office.'

'Fair enough,' said Sammy, who was not going to lay down any ideas about that himself. He wasn't always backward in poking his nose in, but he had sense enough to realize this was one time to keep it out. 'You let me know the date sometime, and I'll let Mr Greenberg know. Then he'll arrange to carry you to and from the wedding in his pony and cart. It's an old family custom. Would you like that, Leah?'

'My life, not half I wouldn't,' said Leah in cockney fashion. 'Mr Sammy, I'm going to jump feet first into all your family customs, but no-one will mind if I keep faith with Rabbi Samuels, will they?'

'No-one in this family, Leah,' said Sammy. Chinese Lady would put any defaulter on the rack and wind the ratchets herself. Chinese Lady simply did not allow any kind of family disharmony. An argument or two, or one of the wives standing up for her rights (of which there seemed to be a lot more than a bloke had bargained for), that was accepted, but festering disharmony, no. 'We're all going to like being related to your family, Leah.'

'That makes me happy too, Uncle Sammy.' Leah and her sister Rebecca had always called him that. 'My family knows how lucky we were to be born here. I still can't believe what happened to European Jewish people in those dreadful concentration camps.'

'There's going to be a reckoning,' said Sammy. 'All those perishing Nazis are going to be tried as war criminals.' At Nuremberg, the prosecuting counsel were due to open their case against the indicted war criminals later this month. 'Me, I'd hand 'em over to the suffering survivors. Well, I'll start my day's work now, and call you for dictation in a while.'

'Yes, sir, right you are, sir,' smiled Leah, and left.

Her mother, Rachel, was still with the firm, working as secretary and personal assistant to Sammy, and Boots was back in his old position as general manager, looking after the administration of all three companies, Adams Enterprises Ltd, Adams Fashions Ltd, and Adams Properties Ltd. He was presently engaged in correspondence with the local council concerning the proposal to erect a three-storey block of flats on the site of the old Southwark Brewery, the site having been acquired by the property company from Adams Enterprises. Boots's approach was that of practical sensibility. London was badly in need of new housing of every kind. The council's response was hedged about by rules and regulations. Boots, never inclined to let bureaucracy get the upper hand, called by appointment on the department concerned. His appointment was with a Miss Jardine, deputy planning officer.

She looked up from her desk as he entered her office, her horn-rimmed spectacles perched on the end of her fine nose. She pushed them into place to observe him, grey Homburg hat in his hand, overcoat over his arm, his manner comfortable and much in keeping with his expression of easy self-assurance. She straightened her back in a sudden defensive gesture. He in turn observed the fly in the ointment. In her thirties, she had a smooth cap of shining blue-black hair, an attractively neat face, a firm mouth and, he thought, an obvious determination not to let any man get the better of her. Boots indulged in an inward smile. He had met her kind in the upper echelons of the ATS, most of them with sufficient belief in their own worth to stand up to the thunder and lightning of battle-scarred warhorses.

'Mr Adams?'

'Good morning, Miss Jardine.'

'Please sit down. I can give you a few minutes.'

'Then we'll suit each other,' said Boots, taking a seat, 'I can spare only a few minutes myself.'

'Pardon?' She took another look at him. He smiled. Miss Jardine blinked.

'We're both busy people,' said Boots. 'We're going to talk about problems?'

'I have to say your application—'

'Of course,' said Boots.

'Pardon?'

'Another fund of paperwork for your department,' said Boots, 'so let's do our best to get rid of it. We don't have any problems ourselves. What exactly are yours? I keep getting letters from you quoting extracts from the Town and Country Planning Act.'

'We have to be absolutely sure the relevant part of the Act is strictly observed,' said Miss Jardine, looking into fine grey eyes that seemed to be offering peace and goodwill to all, and herself in particular. We – I—'

'Yes, I sympathize,' said Boots, whose fine grey eyes included one still impaired. 'Be assured, Miss Jardine. Adams Properties specialize in very strict observance of everything that's relevant. You understand our project on completion will provide good living accommodation for some of these unhappy people still homeless? Yes, of course you do.'

'Well, yes, but all such developments should be centrally heated if the application is to receive favourable consideration.' Miss Jardine experienced a moment of triumph for pulling that one out of her hat. 'Council policy is to discourage coal smoke pollution.'

'What could be more commendable?' said Boots, so very agreeable in his manner that Polly would have said his sex appeal was showing.

'Well, I – we – this department—'

'Yes, as you've obviously noticed, our plans

show a central heating system,' said Boots. Miss Jardine sagged a little. 'By the way, I'm delighted to find myself talking to a young lady. Local government departments are usually headed by – um – elderly officers very set in their ways, and very insistent on the crossing of T's and the dotting of I's even if urgency is on the boil. You're a welcome change from what I daresay we both regard as awkward old codgers.'

'Pardon?' Miss Jardine was faltering badly. Boots thought how absurd it all was in comparison with events still fresh in his mind, the final devastating months of the war and the uncovering of the extermination camps. However, the family business had to forge ahead. He needed the income it gave him, and although he had never had any desire to be stinking rich, he was set on keeping Polly in style and providing the twins with the best kind of education possible. 'You were saying?' said Miss Jardine.

'That my company agrees with your policy concerning central heating? All the way, Miss Jardine, and I'm glad you mentioned it.' His smile implied she was the most agreeable woman he had ever met, and Miss Jardine had a helpless feeling that her spectacles were going to steam up. 'May I suggest how we can jump the present hurdle? You write us a letter detailing the relevant part of the Act in plain English, together with local provisions, and we'll send a reply guaranteeing our strict observance of same. How's that?'

'Well, I should need to confer with – with—' Who should she confer with?

'Of course,' said Boots, coming to his feet. 'But I feel I can rely on you, Miss Jardine, to help us get the application passed. I can't thank you enough. A pleasure to have met you, and to have had a thoroughly enjoyable discussion with you. Very refreshing, believe me. My compliments.' He extended his right hand over her desk and smiled down at her. Her glasses steamed up.

She staggered to her feet and allowed him to shake hands with her. His grip was firm without being annoyingly masculine.

'Oh – er – goodbye, Mr – Mr—'

'Goodbye, Miss Jardine.'

She sat down again on his departure, and was still looking at nothing in particular when an assistant entered three minutes later.

'Miss Jardine—'

'Have I just received someone?'

'Yes, Mr Adams of Adams Properties.'

'Have I had coffee this morning?'

'Not yet, Miss Jardine.'

'I'd like it black and strong.'

Chapter Seven

Boots's son Tim, a Commando officer, was released from the Army in late November, at a time when swirling fog was creeping up nightly over the Thames and the Labour Government was busy constructing a Clean Air Act. Tim phoned Felicity, his wife, on his arrival at Euston station. An hour later, he was on the doorstep of his parents' house in Streatham, where she was staying with their infant daughter, blue-eyed Jennifer.

Felicity's parents tactfully arranged for the reunion to take place in the parlour, by the fireside, where a good five minutes of expressive cuddling, kissing and touching went on before anything really coherent was heard. Tim knew all too well that touch and feel were Felicity's way of seeing.

'War over, uniform ready to be chucked, and here we are, you and me, Puss,' he said.

'Oh, good, you're talking,' said Felicity. 'Now I'm certain it's you in person.'

'Believe me, it's not the milkman,' said Tim.

'I know,' said Felicity. 'I'm still as blind as a bat, curse it, but I can smell it's you.'

'Good smell?' said Tim, looking into the dark glasses that held her scarred eyes.

'Familiar,' said Felicity. 'Warm and musky, with a touch of the foggy stuff this time.'

'Yes, there's going to be a lot of it about tonight,' said Tim. 'It's pre-war stuff, so the taxi driver reckoned, and it's rolling up the river from Southend as if it's coming home. How are you, Puss? God, I'm bloody glad to see you.'

'I'm telling myself we're two of the lucky ones,' said Felicity, which was a sentiment presently common to people who had survived the bombing of their cities, to men who had survived land, sea and air battles, and to Jews who had escaped Himmler's dragnet. 'Yes, we are lucky, Tim, even though we're both carrying lousy scars.'

'I don't think you're exactly lucky, but I know I am,' said Tim. Wounded several times, and badly during a raid on German positions in the Western Desert, he had body scars that Felicity had touched and traced to give herself mental maps of them. 'Jesus, Puss, how did some of us escape when so many others were shot to pieces?' He winced. It was going to be a long time before the savagery of fighting fanatical Germans faded from his mind. There was one thing that would never fade, however, the uplifting aspect of comradeship. He had come to know what old soldiers of the last war meant when they spoke of that. Boots his dad had once said it was the only worthwhile thing to have come out of the slaughter of trench warfare.

He winced again, and Felicity found and touched his mouth with her fingers.

'Don't ever feel undeserving of life, Tim,' she said. 'From all you've told me, it usually amounted to one simple thing, didn't it? Some of you ducked and some forgot to.'

'I've known two great fighters,' said Tim. 'Colonel Lucas against Hitler's fanatics and you against your blindness. Yes, he got his head down at the right moments, but you never had a chance in your case. All the same, you and me, Puss, we've come out of it together, we're alive and we've got a future, and I'm going to be grateful for that. I'm remembering now that Boots my dad was always grateful for surviving the trenches of the other war, which was why he never quarrelled with life's perversities.'

'He and Polly came visiting with their twins,' said Felicity. 'I've never had the pleasure of actually seeing your father, but I still find him a lovely bloke.'

'Well, he takes after me,' said Tim blithely. 'Where's our Jennifer?'

Felicity smiled. She was blind, incurably blind, but she had Tim, supportive, sexy and yes, very much alive, and she had Jennifer, a gurgling gift.

'Upstairs in her cot, and probably burping in her sleep,' she said. 'I miss living with Rosie and her two, but must admit my parents have been a great help.'

'Well, listen,' said Tim, 'if your parents could

put the kettle on after I've taken a look at Jennifer, we could have a cup of tea, drink to our future and talk about where we'd like to live.'

'Tim darling,' said Felicity, just a little husky, 'I'd live in a shed with you.'

'Fair enough,' said Tim, 'we'll look for a shed with a cooker and a bathroom.'

'I should have said except there's Jennifer to consider,' countered Felicity.

'No problem,' said Tim, 'we'll fork out for a large, roomy shed with a library and a nursery. Nothing's too good for you and Jennifer.'

'In that case, old soldier, Jennifer and I can be grateful too that we have a future,' said Felicity.

Within a week of Tim's return, he and Felicity and Jennifer were living with Boots and Polly, who had insisted on having them until they found a place of their own. Sammy dropped in one evening on his way home from the office to have a private word with Tim, and Tim received the offer of a job, as well as the further offer of a loan to help him and Felicity buy a suitable house.

'You're a bit reckless, offering me a job, Uncle Sammy,' he said. 'What I know about the working of the firm's business you could put in a teaspoon and still strain your eyeballs trying to find it.'

'Listen, Tim my lad,' said Sammy, 'your late mother, God bless her, did a good job with the firm, so did your cousin Emma, and your dad is back as half its backbone. I'm the other half. Now we all know you didn't get to be a general by a fluke—'

'Captain,' said Tim.

'I had the same argument with your dad,' said Sammy. 'Now, anyone who performed like you did during the war can perform just as well for the business, especially if your name is Adams, which yours has got to be, seeing you're Boots's son. You and Daniel, when he's demobbed, are going to be the managerial department of the property company. That'll take the weight off my shoulders and stop me having to get medical treatment for a bent back. You take time off now, as much as you want, after all your years knocking holes in Hitler's gorillas, and then when you start with the firm, your dad and me will show you how to turn yourself from a demobbed Commando into a business asset.'

'How can I say no to that?' said Tim.

'As for somewhere to live,' said Sammy, 'it so happens I can put you in touch with the Musgroves of Poplar Walk.'

'Who are they?'

'Oh, a couple of people I got to know,' said Sammy. 'Their daughter married a Canadian general—'

'General?' Tim smiled. 'You sure about that, Uncle Sammy?'

'Well, a lieutenant, was it?' said Sammy. 'I never know the difference myself.' He frowned at himself. 'I could get a bit depressed about being ignorant, but I can't find the time. Anyway, you know Poplar Walk.' It was off Denmark Hill, and accordingly found favour with Chinese Lady, the matriarchal octopus. 'The Musgroves are emigrating to Canada to share all the snow with their daughter. If you and Felicity are interested in taking a look at their house, here's their phone number. They're asking seven hundred. It would've been five before the war, but there you are, Tim, house prices are going through the roof. It's the shortage. Sad for young people. But our property company will buy the place for you and arrange repayment on simple interest terms that'll cost you a lot less than a building society mortgage.'

'I think I'm getting sentimentally touched by all this,' said Tim. 'But before I fall overboard, tell me what simple interest will amount to.'

'Well, as a straightforward example,' said Sammy, 'if we can beat the Musgroves down to six hundred and forty, the firm collects seven hundred and twenty from you by way of repayment.'

'Eighty quid interest?' said Tim. 'Uncle Sammy, that's twelve and a half per cent.'

'Twelve and a half per cent on the capital outlay at the end of a repayment period of seven years, say, is fair do's, Tim,' said Sammy. 'If the firm invested that amount at four per cent gilt-edged, it would collect twenty-five quid a year, adding up to a hundred and seventy-five over seven years.'

'Got you,' said Tim, 'you're giving Felicity and me fair do's right enough. Uncle Sammy, I think you've turned into a big-hearted philanthropist.'

'Never heard of it,' said Sammy, 'it sounds like some of your dad's educated talk. The firm's done the same thing for Emma and Jonathan, and it'll offer the same to Edward and Leah. It keeps the money in the family all the way. Anyway, think about it, Tim, eh?'

'There's one thing the war hasn't changed,' said Tim.

'And what's that?' asked Sammy.

'You, old man,' said Tim. 'You're still generating electricity.'

'Hope I don't get short-circuited by my competitors,' said Sammy. 'Some of 'em are spivs who've taken to wearing shirts, ties and City suits.

With the country at peace, Chinese Lady's fretful days were over, and she was able to count her blessings. Most family members were home, including Annabelle's pilot husband Nick. Only Tommy's son David, Sammy's son Daniel, and Lizzy's son Edward were still serving. David was in England with the RAF, Daniel in Palestine with the Army, and Edward in Cyprus with the RAF. If some of the family carried the scars of war, well, better that than being dead, like poor Emily, although she thought that Tim's wife Felicity, in suffering the terrible burden of blindness, could hardly be called lucky.

Ned was fully recovered from his illness, a blessing for him and Lizzy. And although Daniel's young American lady, Patsy Kirk, had gone home to Boston with her father, well, she was going to come back to marry Daniel in time. As for David, there was talk that one day he might turn up with a young lady called Kate Trimble on his arm. She was in the WAAF, and supposed to be getting demobbed soon. Yes, there were blessings, thought Chinese Lady, and it was to her pleasure that Boots and Polly had moved from Dorset to a house in East Dulwich Grove, although she had to accept the possibility that Boots's lovely daughter, Rosie, would remain in Dorset with her husband and children. Everyone missed Rosie and her happy ways with the family. Still, she used the phone regularly to keep in touch with those closest to her.

The war had taken Emily, yes, and millions of soldiers and innocent people on all sides, including an unbelievable number of Jewish men, women and children. Not a vindictive woman, Chinese Lady was nevertheless very much in favour of Hitler's gang of warmongers being tried and hanged as criminals.

That trial had begun. In Nuremberg's Palace of Justice, Goering, Hess, Ribbentrop and seventeen other notorious Nazis filed daily into the dock to listen to prosecutors outlining acts of murder, torture and extermination for which they claimed the defendants had been responsible.

One defendant had escaped the prosecutors. Robert Ley, head of the German Labour Front and responsible for the recruitment of millions of foreign slave workers, had managed to hang himself in his cell, despite being under constant watch. More than one of the other defendants envied him his successful suicide.

Ned Somers told his wife Lizzy that the Nazi monsters who had bestrode conquered countries in their jackboots, boasting of the military might of Hitler's Germany, were obviously hating the fact that the trial would reveal exactly what they had done to the conquered.

Lizzy said it was a pity that the Allies hadn't acted on Mr Churchill's suggestion, to shoot them all five minutes after capturing them. Ned said it was news to him that Churchill had made such a suggestion. Oh, Dad told me all the leaders discussed it, said Lizzy. She was referring to Mr Finch, her stepfather.

'He picked up a whisper that was running round the corridors of Government, I suppose,' said Ned.

'Well, I've always thought his Government job was a bit special,' said Lizzy, whose affection for Mr Finch went back a long way. She had no idea, however, that he had been much more than a mere Civil Servant. Nor did she know anything of his true history or suspect he had secrets. Of all the family, only Boots knew that Mr Finch's birth roots lay in Germany.

'But would Churchill, Roosevelt and Stalin have suggested shooting that whole gang of Nazis out of hand?' murmured Ned.

'Good job if they did,' said Lizzy.

It was Stalin, actually, who had made the suggestion, but Roosevelt and Churchill both turned it down in favour of a trial.

Boots came off the phone after a long conversation with his stepfather. He spoke to Polly.

'How would you like to spend a day in the

Nuremberg courtroom, watching the Nazi dregs and listening to the proceedings?'

Polly, disbelieving, said, 'Before I answer that, old love, I'd like to know if you're serious or slightly off your chump.'

'I'm serious,' said Boots. 'We'd have to leave tomorrow, and take our seats the day after. The invitation's come via Edwin and Intelligence, it's a privileged offer because of my association with the uncovering of Belsen.'

'And to Edwin's association with a Government department?' said Polly, who had long suspected Boots's stepfather had never been a mere civil servant.

'Well, he knew quite a bit about what went on in Whitehall before he retired,' said Boots ambiguously. He had never disclosed Edwin's secrets to any of his family, not even to Emily or Polly. 'He'll be with us if we go. We have three seats, just for the one day. Not even the King of Siam could get a seat in the spectators' gallery – even if he offered to swap his hundred most bewitching concubines for a ticket. Wouldn't you like to see a small piece of history being made?'

'Sit in on the trial of Hitler's leading monsters?' said Polly. Like many people, she had been following the proceedings by reading newspaper accounts and listening to radio broadcasts. It was a trial likely to last for months, which some people thought would be a waste of time. They saw it as an extension of the long war, and wanted the whole thing over and done with, and the

defendants dead and buried for their mass extermination of Jewish people, never mind their other
crimes. Cynics said months of repetitive detail
would end up boring the pants off a cast-iron
virgin. Nevertheless, a great many people would
have agreed with Boots, that the trial represented
history in the making. 'We'll see Goering himself
at bay?' said Polly. 'I wouldn't call that a privilege
exactly, more of an ordeal, but who could say no
to the offer of being there for a whole day? You
want to go, don't you, old scout?'

'Yes, Polly, I'd like to sit in for a day,' said Boots.
'The offer includes flying there tomorrow.'

'What about the twins?' asked Polly.

'I'm sure Tim and Felicity will gladly look after
them,' said Boots. Until negotiations for the
house in Poplar Walk were completed, Tim and
Felicity were still resident. 'We'll only be away two
nights.'

'What shall I wear?' asked Polly, who was what
Sammy called a female woman. Accordingly, she
practised the art of tasteful adornment to please
herself, to please an assembled company and, of
course, to please Boots.

'Bear in mind that the worst of these thugs are
going to be found guilty and hanged,' said Boots.

Polly looked at him. For all his easy-going
nature and his tolerance of idiots and misfits,
Boots did have this streak of steel, and Polly knew
how he felt about Belsen and the people responsible for turning such frightful places into
extermination camps. He would, she thought, be
able to watch Goering being hanged without

a single regret for what the savage rope did to a man's neck. But then, when the time came, perhaps most people of the civilized world would feel as he did.

'My dear man,' she said, 'are you suggesting I wear black?'

'Black's for mourning, of course,' said Boots, 'but it can be very smart and stylish. Like your black costume with the white buttons.'

'Ye gods, you want me to wear that?' said Polly. 'It'll turn me into a ghoul. But I'll do it, old love, I'll be a ghoul for a day.'

'Well, I just don't know,' said Chinese Lady to Mr Finch. 'Going to that trial with Boots and Polly? Edwin, I suppose you all know what you're doing?'

'I think so, Maisie,' said Mr Finch, silver hair by no means diminishing his distinguished looks. He was seventy-two and retired.

'I'm not sure I'd want to be in the same room as Hitler myself,' said Chinese Lady, frowning.

'Hitler's dead, Maisie.'

'A pity he was ever born,' said Chinese Lady tartly, 'but you know what I mean. Those men all represent Hitler.'

'Well put, Maisie, they do indeed,' said Mr Finch, 'and I can't resist the opportunity to find out if their kind of evil shows in their appearance. Have they, in fact, taken on something of the look of Satan himself?'

'I suppose you mean they've all come to look a bit like Hitler,' said Chinese Lady. 'Well, wasn't he the devil himself?'

'It doesn't show in current newspaper photographs,' said Mr Finch, 'but in person and face to face with the judgement of the world? I can't resist going, Maisie.'

'Well, I could resist very easy, Edwin,' said Chinese Lady. 'After a war like we've just had, I don't want to be anywhere near Germany or Germans.'

'Who could quarrel with that?' said German-born Mr Finch, and a little sigh escaped him.

'And if Boots and Polly weren't going with you, I'd ask you to stay at home,' said Chinese Lady. 'You're supposed to be retired.'

'Ah, well,' said Mr Finch, and received a look. 'I am retired, my dear, and I'm counting my excursion to Nuremberg with Boots and Polly as a little holiday.'

'I shouldn't think it'll be like a holiday in Margate,' said Chinese Lady, 'and will you be all right, going up in an aeroplane?' She obviously had doubts herself. Aeroplanes to her were even more dangerously new-fangled than the electric toaster Sammy had come up with a month ago. Only yesterday, the blessed thing had burned the toast and set it on fire.

'I'll be quite all right, Maisie,' said Mr Finch. 'It'll be far less tiring than trains and a Channel crossing.'

'Well, just make sure you take care of yourself,' said Chinese Lady who, to tell the truth, felt Edwin, Boots and Polly would all have something interesting to tell her when they came back. No-one could say that actually seeing Hitler's pack of devils was going to be something ordinary.

It was just a pity that Hitler himself wasn't in the dock. Still, he probably wasn't having a happy time down in hell with Satan.

Chapter Eight

Nuremberg, the medieval city that had become the spiritual home of the Nazis, the centre of their rallies that embraced militarism, triumphalism and idolatry, had been bombed to smithereens by the Allies, and was now a vast graveyard of shattered grey stone, wherein its inhabitants fought to stay alive with as much resolution as they had endured the bombing. However, not every house or building had been wrecked, and by some kind of a miracle, the imposing Palace of Justice had escaped destruction. It was here that the Allies had decided to bring the top Nazis to trial, to indict and, hopefully, to convict them in the heart of what had once been their pagan citadel of light.

Preparations for the opening of a new day's proceedings had begun. Boots, Polly and Mr Finch, after an overnight stay at the Grand Hotel, also a surviving miracle, took their allotted seats in the spectators' gallery, while noting the presence of white-helmeted American guards and the solemn judgemental aura of the courtroom. Dark panelling and heavy green drapes sounded a brooding note, and thick carpeting ensured that every footstep was silent.

People were talking or whispering as the preparations continued, but the atmosphere was subdued. The white-helmeted, white-belted American guards imposed sober behaviour on all who entered. Polly, her coat off and draped over the back of her seat, for the courtroom was warm, looked far from ghoulish in her stylish black costume and white fur hat. Chic was the word. She received a wink from an American guard overseeing ticket-holding VIPs into their seats. That momentarily amused her. A come-on wink from a handsome military policeman of the United States? At her age? And at a time when a whole world of displaced or unhappy women were all asking God to provide them with a home-going GI and an entry into the land of golden prairies, abundant food, resourceful people and matchless freedom?

But the little incident and her mental reaction to it were an irrelevance in such a place as this, with all it meant. Everything drew the eye, the sombre appearance of the court, the filing in of clerks, scribes and defence counsel, the admission of people to the spectators' gallery, and the uneasy gaping emptiness of the dock waiting to receive the accused. Against the wall at the back of the dock were six American guards in stiff standing postures.

Other guards watched the movements of everyone entering the courtroom. Security was as tight as it could be to ensure nothing happened to diminish the standing of the international tribunal or to effect a surreptitious delivery of the means of suicide to any of the accused.

Boots and Mr Finch were both as absorbed as Polly, Boots dwelling on the horrors of Belsen, Mr Finch on the self-destructive characteristics of the nation of his birth. The more he reflected on the appalling inhumanity not only of Hitler and his gang, but of thousands and thousands of men like Himmler's Gestapo and Goering's SS, the more thankful he was for having turned his back on Germany years and years ago. Imperialistic though Britain was, its Empire seemed entirely benevolent compared to that brutally acquired by Hitler and Goering. And there was always his ready-made family, a family that had risen from the cold rags of poverty to the warm coverings of affluence, and had never given him less than trust and affection.

A little sigh escaped Mr Finch.

In filed the prosecuting counsel, French, American, British and Russian. They had spent preceding days recounting crimes of aggression and crimes of horrendous murder, and were far from finished in all that they wished to lay before the court. They took their places with a rustle of documents, some conferring earnestly with each other.

Polly picked out the British prosecutors, bland-looking Sir David Maxwell-Fyfe and dapper Sir Hartley Shawcross. Her pulses energized. She waited for the next development, which surely had to be the entrance of the accused, the men who had helped Hitler unleash terror on the world. That sense of anticipation induced silence throughout the spectators' gallery.

They came, the accused, they arrived and they appeared, not as a body but one by one.

There was a perceptible stir as they began to enter, having been escorted from their prison cells by guards. Boots and Polly both tensed, and Mr Finch drew a little breath, for suddenly, there below in the well of the courtroom, were the moving figures of Goering, Hess and Ribbentrop, Goering leading as the chief defendant. His bloated corpulence had wasted away, and his plain uniform sagged around him. His thin, straight mouth was tightly shut, a look of contempt on his face. He considered the whole thing a spiteful attempt by the victors to humiliate the losers, and he had already stated there was not a shred of legality to the tribunal.

Hess, vacant-faced, hollow-eyed and gaunt, was maintaining the air and incomprehension of a man who did not understand what was going on. He was, in fact, promoting himself as a case for a sanitorium, not a courtroom. Ribbentrop, Hitler's foreign minister, who had given himself the airs of an arrogant German nobleman and a lofty diplomat, looked hopeless, gutless and shapeless.

In came the rest of the accused, the bankers who had financed Hitler's drive towards war, the generals who had signed orders of criminal intent, the men who had been the architects of a slave-driven industry, and the sadists directly behind the formation, purpose and administration of the extermination camps. Shuffling or peering, apprehensive or querulous, each filed uneasily into the dock, save for the loutish Jew-baiter, Streicher, who bruised his way to his seat, where he sat muttering and scowling. God Almighty, thought Boots, what a collection of fallen idols. There isn't one real-looking man among them. Shattering defeat had robbed them of their omnipotence, and arrest and imprisonment had drained them of their arrogance. Goering alone seemed unintimidated, but he was still physically unimpressive, his face pasty.

The two rows of the dock filled with the accused. The court seemed a restless place then, the prisoners shifting about, nervous defence counsel harrying their papers, and prosecuting counsel flipping pages of their documents.

Boots felt Polly's gloved hand touch his. He took hold of her fingers and gently pressed. They looked at each other, and each read the other's mind. Ghastly lot, that was Polly's message. Minus their jackboots, what are they? That was Boots's reflected thought. And yet they had exercised the power of life and death over eighty million German people, and many millions of conquered people.

'Attention!' The word was shouted in English by the marshal of the court. 'All rise! The tribunal will now enter!'

The whole court, including the prisoners, came to their feet, and the judges entered, Russian, American, British and French, two of each, together with the tribunal's president. The American and British justices were wearing plain black robes, those of the French were decorated with white bibs, wrist ruffles and ermine. The Russians, in dark brown uniforms with green trim and gold epaulettes, looked sternly severe.

The judges took their seats, and so did the president, Sir Geoffrey Lawrence of Britain.

Papers were shuffled again, whispered conferences resumed, and several of the defendants attempted to adopt an air of composure. It turned the atmosphere fidgety. But at 10 a.m. precisely, Sir Geoffrey brought the court to order and opened the day's hearing. It began with the accused listening to an indictment concerning the aggressive annexation of Austria. A transcript of Goering's phoned directive was all-revealing in that it required the German Army's entry into Austria to be 'uncompromising'. It was given word for word, and almost every word related to brutality and deceit. Goering, listening, was by no means embarrassed, however. Polly saw him smiling at Ribbentrop and even winking at other prisoners. Much was made by the prosecution of the subsequent fate of Austria, which became a mere vassal state of Hitler's Third Reich and was subjected to the anti-Semitic German laws.

Goering smiled again, and during a brief break, Mr Finch was among others who heard him say quite clearly to his co-defendants, 'Aggression? Our union with Austria? Didn't the Austrians pave the Fuehrer's way from the border to Vienna with flowers? Didn't they show sheer joy?'

Mr Finch, sitting on the other side of Polly, whispered, 'That smiling hero of the Third Reich, Polly, is also a merciless wolf and a cunning fox. But look at him. I'm damned if he doesn't have more defiance in his little finger than the rest of the defendants put together. He doesn't have to square anything with his conscience, for he has no conscience.'

Polly conveyed this to Boots.

'Tell Edwin,' murmured Boots, 'that I'm thankful the gentleman in question has never been a friend of mine.'

'Darling, I'm as grateful about that as you are,' whispered Polly.

Defence counsel were arguing that to classify the takeover of Austria as a criminal act was absurd, since the Austrian people and their Government had demonstrated in favour. Prosecuting counsel pointed out that Chancellor Schuschnigg, Head of the Austrian Government was summarily arrested by Austrian Nazis and despatched to a concentration camp when he showed resistance to German demands. Further, there were documents detailing the arrest and murder of thousands of people opposed to the annexation.

The arguments went on and on until the President of the court called an adjournment for lunch.

Chapter Nine

'Can you swallow a meal, Polly?' asked Boots, accompanying her and Mr Finch out of the court-room.

Polly said that so far her stomach was fairly normal, and Mr Finch said nothing had put him off lunch himself.

'Let's eat, Boots,' he said, 'it may help to give us some needed staying power.'

'To see us through the afternoon?' said Polly.

'I've had a whisper to the effect that the afternoon session is going to be on a different level from this morning's,' said Mr Finch, the vaulted hall of the Palace booming to the sound of many feet and many voices.

'Is that a threat, Edwin?' asked Boots.

'I think I can say it's a promise,' said Mr Finch.

His old colleague in Intelligence had laid on a car for them during their stay, and they drove back to the Grand Hotel. Its façade was tatty and pitted, but the interior offered a pre-war elegance. Outside and in the foyer, German women of Nuremberg loitered, lingered and solicited in the hope of earning a meal in surroundings civilized, plush and, above all, warm. Dressed in the best garments they could muster, make-up covering the paleness of extreme privation, they were all willing to offer their bodies in exchange for a meal, and to look for the chance of becoming the well-fed mistress of an American.

It was the energetic Americans who controlled Nuremberg and the prison that held the accused. American civilians and Army personnel had practically taken over the hotel, and their gregarious nature and generous dispensation of largesse had earned them the worldwide reputation of being the kind of men every woman's starving daughter ought to get to know.

And there they were, the daughters of ravaged Nuremberg, clusters of them, lips strawberry-red, as Mr Finch, Polly and Boots alighted from the car at the hotel entrance. Some were young, others not so young. Hungry eyes took in the distinguished look of Mr Finch and the tall, long-legged masculinity of Boots. The same eyes reflected envy of the woman with them, a woman of elegance, her white fur hat surely the emblem of a mistress richly provided for. A lucky German woman, they assumed, the men American, of course. Whose mistress was she? That of the elderly but distinguished gentleman, or the arresting man with the long legs?

Boots, Polly and Mr Finch sought to find a way into the hotel through these groups of women whose primitive living conditions and empty larders made supplicating creatures of them. It showed in their eyes and their expressions. Some people, perhaps many people, would have told them that they were deservedly reaping the bitter fruits of the vile seeds sown by their beloved Fuehrer.

A voice reached Boots's ears.

'*Mein Herr*?' Then in English, 'Let me join you, please, yes?' The English was good, although the German accent was very noticeable, the plea edged with desperation.

The desperation of the starving? Boots supposed so as he and Polly took note of the owner of the voice. It belonged to one of the creatures of the damned, damned by devastating onslaughts from the air, the violent deaths of friends and neighbours, the loss of their men to the savagery and cruelty of the war with Russia, and the shattering consequences of a defeat unimaginable in headier days. Economic help was yet to reach Nuremberg. The victorious Allies seemed to be saying first eat what you have reaped: the whirlwind. The woman at Boots's elbow wore a fairly presentable coat, and was tall and thin, her high cheekbones sharp, grey eyes dark and huge. Beneath a rakish black beret, her bleached blonde hair was tied at the nape of her neck with a black bow in what Polly construed as an attempt to project girlishness, very appealing to young American soldiers, except for what was obvious. She was near to thirty.

She fought off sisters in distress who tried to displace her from the side of a man whose looks they all liked.

'You need a meal?' said Boots, as Mr Finch opened up a way for them.

'I am starving, truly,' said the woman. 'Starving. *Mein Herr*, take me in with you?'

Boots glanced at Polly.

'As a matter of interest?' murmured Polly.

Yes, would it be interesting to hear what an English-speaking German woman had to say about the war, about Hitler and the Jews, and about Goering and the other defendants?

Boots thought it would, if the food and wine loosened her tongue.

'Very well, come with us,' he said.

'Oh, thank you, thank you,' she said, and much to Polly's amusement, she slipped her hand around Boots's elbow, and entered the hotel foyer arm in arm with him. Mr Finch, intrigued but unsurprised, led the way to the saloon bar adjacent the restaurant. They were all in need of an aperitif.

'Your name?' said Boots.

'Lili.'

Boots thought they all probably called themselves Lili, or even Lili Marlene, in an attempt to glamorize the moment for the men who picked them up. He knew the restaurant was a place of colour and opulence, a warm glittering oasis in the cold grey, rubble-strewn desert of Nuremberg. Such a restaurant probably represented a land of milk and honey to any of the citizens deprived by the war of everything resembling even a basic need.

The bar offered waiter service only. They chose

a table, at which Lili seated herself with a quickness that suggested she was fearful of Boots changing his mind. Her eyes kept darting, looking, glancing. Polly, sitting down, smiled. Like Boots, she was intrigued by the possibility that a good lunch would induce the hungry-eyed woman to tell them what the people of Nuremberg now thought of Hitler, Himmler and the appalling concentration camps.

A waiter arrived. Mr Finch, acting as host, invited Lili to name her preference. She asked if she could have schnapps. Polly asked for a gin and tonic. Boots and Mr Finch opted for neat Scotch without ice. Lili glanced at Polly, noting her white fur hat and the black fur collar of her coat. A flash of bitterness showed in her dark eyes, and her reddened lips tightened.

'How lucky you are,' she said.

'Am I?' said Polly. 'How do you know?'

Polly's well-spoken English seemed to surprise Lili, who looked at Boots and then at Mr Finch.

'You are Americans, *ja*?' she said.

'English,' said Boots.

'English? English?' Lili thought about that. 'Yes, of course, you don't speak as Americans do. There are English here as well as Americans, but many more Americans, many more. I was reading English at university before the war. I am pleased to meet you, and I thank you for having me at your table.' She glanced at Polly. 'You are English also?'

'You're surprised?' said Polly.

'I thought—'

'I understand,' said Polly.

113

The drinks arrived, and Mr Finch signed the chit and added his room number. Lili made short work of her schnapps, and Boots thought her every movement and gesture spoke of an afflicted nervous system.

The saloon was almost full of people now, and above the chatter, he asked, 'Have you always lived in Nuremberg?'

'Always, except when I was at university.'

'It was there you learned to speak good English?'

'I learned good English before.'

'The war brought you home, perhaps?'

'Yes, I volunteered to do work in the hospital.'

'Were you in favour of the war?'

'Ah, not in favour, no, only in favour of winning it and enjoying peace.'

'That's an honest answer.'

'It is true,' said Lili.

'What do the people of Nuremberg say about the war and its consequences?' asked Polly.

'You wish me to answer questions as payment for lunch?' said Lili.

'You can answer or not, as you wish,' said Boots.

'I will tell you no-one thought we would lose. Our Army was the best in the world.' Lili looked at her empty glass. Mr Finch signalled the waiter and ordered another schnapps. 'Of course,' continued Lili, hungry eyes still darting, 'no-one knew the *Fuehrer*—' She checked, as if mention of Hitler's idolized title was a mistake. 'No-one knew Hitler was going to use it to make war on Russia.'

'No-one?' said Mr Finch. 'But it was all there in his bible.'

'Bible?' said Lili.

'*Mein Kampf.*'

Lili looked dismissive.

'Not many of us read it,' she said. 'Perhaps every family had a copy, but not always for reading, just for showing they were good Germans, or pretending they were. We are being blamed for many things the Nazis did, but what could we do when Hitler and the Party were so strong? There were no Nazis in my family, but everyone had to be careful not to show they were against the Party.'

Polly made a face. It was all too common now, the denial by many Germans that they were Nazis or that they approved of the excesses of the SS and the torture chambers of the *Gestapo*. As for the Jews, simply no-one knew about the real purpose of the concentration camps. Or so they said.

'You, perhaps, belonged to an underground German resistance movement?' suggested Boots drily.

'I would have liked to, yes,' said Lili, taking up the second glass of schnapps brought by the waiter, 'but in Nuremberg who could have found one? You must know Nuremberg was Hitler's cathedral, where he was worshipped.' She sipped the fiery schnapps, which was bringing a little colour to her face. 'We were forced into kneeling at his altar.'

'Were you?' queried Mr Finch.

'Ah, it is easy for you to question our actions. At the beginning, Hitler did many good things for Germany.'

'Which helped to foster worship?' said Polly.

'You can understand that he restored our self-respect?' said Lili.

'The rebirth of your self-respect was worth accepting the actions of his Stormtroopers?' said Boots.

'Not all of us liked their behaviour, no.'

'Or what went on in the concentration camps?' said Polly.

'No-one except Himmler knew what was happening in those places. Everyone is shocked—' Lili checked and stiffened. Boots turned his head to follow her gaze. At the door of the saloon stood an officer of the American Provost-Marshal's department, two white-helmeted corporals at his back. His searching eyes encountered Lili's blonde hair, and at once he and his men marched straight towards her. The impact of this sudden military intrusion startled everyone in the place.

Coming to a crisp halt, the officer apologized to Mr Finch and his companions for interrupting, then addressed Lili.

'You are?'

'Lili Moeller,' she said through stiff lips.

'Sure?'

'*Ja.*'

The representative of the occupying power, America, said curtly, 'Show me your papers.'

Boots, Polly and Mr Finch were silent as Lili opened her handbag, took out her identity document and handed it to the officer. He inspected it with care.

'Almost as good as the real thing,' he said, 'but it won't do, lady. We know you to be Hanna Beckendorf, formerly a sergeant in charge of a platoon of women guards at the Auschwitz concentration camp and personally responsible for the murder of a number of women inmates. Stand up.'

He was uncompromising in his attitude, a man who had come to know the barbaric nature of concentration camp personnel.

Lili, white-faced, breathed, 'I protest.'

'You all protest. I guess all of you have gotten degrees in the subject. You're under arrest. Stand up.'

'Help me,' begged Lili of Boots.

Boots, looking at her, thought of the women guards he had seen at Belsen and of the ghastly suffering of the inmates. He remembered the one woman who had held his gaze and shown nothing in the way of remorse. Her expression, in fact, had been a sneer.

'Were you at Auschwitz?' he asked.

'No – yes – but I was good to the Jews—'

'Not one of your kind was good to the Jews of Auschwitz,' said Boots, and Polly saw the steely hint of blue in his eyes. Mr Finch sighed. 'You will have to help yourself,' said Boots.

Lili drew a hissing breath, and venom sprang and spat.

'You English – ha! – you should all be burned alive for what you did to Dresden!'

'Take her away, men,' said the Provost officer, and his two corporals brought the woman up from her chair and marched her out of the saloon. If most patrons were staring, the two German waiters chose to be unaffected. 'My apologies, ma'am, for any embarrassment,' said the officer to Polly, then gave Boots and Mr Finch a nod before marching out.

'My God,' said Polly, when her breath was back, 'you picked up a Nazi she-wolf, Boots.'

'Luck of the draw, would you say?' said Boots.

'I wonder why she chose to hide herself here, in Nuremberg of all places?' said Mr Finch.

'Possibly because she has an SS lover here?' suggested Polly. 'One of the SS men from Auschwitz? There are hundreds of such men awaiting trial, aren't there? Are they allowed visitors?'

'Yes,' said Mr Finch, 'and it's possible you could be right about a lover, Polly. Yes, that might have brought her here with her dyed hair, or perhaps she thought Nuremberg was the last place the authorities would look for her. But what alerted the American Military Police? Is she the victim of an informer?'

'Edwin old dear,' said Polly, 'could you call a woman like that a victim?'

'No, not if she is a woman like that,' said Mr Finch.

'What do you think, Boots?' asked Polly.

'That whoever and whatever she is,' said Boots, 'she missed what I thought she most needed, a good lunch.'

'But perhaps it wasn't chiefly the food,' said Polly, 'perhaps she knew the American military police were after her, and thought that if she could attach herself to us, she'd have been seen as one of us instead of an SS woman on the run.'

'One of us?' said Boots. 'Not with her kind of lipstick.'

'You old cleverclogs,' said Polly.

Boots smiled and touched her arm. She accepted it for what she knew it was, a light caress to tell her he shared all her present reactions and emotions.

'Well, whatever, I fancy she thought she was safer with us than among the women outside,' he said. 'And in any case, she'll get a meal. They'll feed her in prison, whether she deserves it or not.'

'Don't let's miss our own lunch,' said Polly, 'just in case the afternoon session spoils our appetite for dinner.'

Chapter Ten

As Polly feared, the afternoon session proved unbearable to almost everyone present.

One of the American prosecutors referred the tribunal to a motion picture entitled 'Nazi Concentration Camps'. It was compiled from films taken by accredited Allied cameramen during the advance that effected the liberation of a number of such camps. The American prosecutor now offered it as evidence, and the tribunal ordered that it should be admitted and shown.

The courtroom was plunged into darkness, except for the dock. Security demanded that special lighting be used to illuminate the accused. Goering scowled and fidgeted. Hess contrived to look blank and detached. Ribbentrop advertised petulance. Hitler's Army chiefs, Keitel and Jodl, known to have signed orders authorizing the killing of hundreds of innocent hostages, stared into space.

A screen, mounted on a wall, sprang into bright receptivity as the projector light caught it. Polly sat stiffly between Boots and Mr Finch, anticipating with a shudder what she was certain she would see.

Boots, knowing what it would be, took her hand again. Her fingers curled tightly around his. She had witnessed the ghastliness of trench warfare during her years as an ambulance driver from 1914 to 1918, but she suspected the concentration camp horrors were going to test every sensitive nerve.

The pictures hit the screen, pictures of the camps, of the dead, the dying and the tottering skeletal men and women whose liberation might or might not have saved them from terminal collapse. One did not know how they had fared since being freed, but one did know every scene was horrific in what it represented, the deliberate degradation and systematic murder of men, women and children.

There was a ghastly similarity for the audience to endure, in that if any of them thought the revolting horrors of one camp could not possibly be repeated elsewhere, the flickering black and white screen images quickly showed they could. However, there was one scene that stood alone, the appalling piled on the horrific when the film revealed a mountain of naked, bony, dead-white corpses being bulldozed into a gigantic grave. The bodies flopped, tumbled and sprawled, the bulldozer heaping scores on top of hundreds. Elsewhere, American soldiers wearing medical masks in surroundings hideous with the stench of rotting bodies, were shown regarding hundreds of corpses that had been stacked like firewood.

A captured American serviceman who had

been incarcerated in the Mauthausen extermination camp, was able to address the recording camera and describe the fiendish treatment of inmates. They were forced to carry blocks of quarried stone on their backs, and this went on interminably until they collapsed and died. To amuse themselves, guards sometimes dropped an inmate to the bottom of the quarry, laughing as the victim's fall smashed him to death. They called it 'the parachute drop'.

By now, the court was in strained, suffering silence, except for the sounds of a woman trying to stifle sobs of anguish and heartbreak. The accused, stark in the light that never left them, were variously affected. *'Mein Gott, mein Gott,'* breathed one prisoner over and over again. Uneasiness sat on some faces, the pallor of shock on others, particularly those who had planned extermination but never actually witnessed the end results. Hess was muttering aimlessly, Ribbentrop ghastly in colour, Goering unmoved. Polly thought his indifference to these recorded scenes of Nazi brutality and murder an horrendous indictment of his inhumanity, astonishing in a man who in pre-war times had been known internationally for his wit and his gregarious good fellowship. What had been wittier than his expressed opinion of Englishmen?

One Englishman, an idiot, he said. Two Englishmen, a club. Three, an empire.

The film was not yet finished. Boots stiffened as the uncovering of Belsen was shown in all the horror of death, squalor and decimating disease,

British soldiers stark with frozen disbelief. A slow-moving officer came into the picture. Polly, shuddering, suddenly became rigid. Boots stared at the officer.

Himself.

He was joined by an infantry captain, both covering the ground with the slowness of men unable to believe what was before their eyes, the suffering, the dying, and mounds of naked male and female corpses. It was a relief to see himself disappear from the screen as the camera panned.

'Dear God,' breathed Polly, and Mr Finch expelled a long, silent breath. None of them had expected the day's proceedings to take in this filmed record of the worst excesses of concentration camps. Even if they had, they would not have expected to see Boots himself appear amid the sickening desolation of Belsen.

More was to come in the form of films taken by the Germans themselves. One reel covered the kind of infamous liquidation frequently favoured by the SS, a number of them seen driving two hundred hostages into a barn and closing up all exits. Petrol was then used to swamp the outside walls. That done, the SS men set fire to the place, and the fire became a leaping conflagration of flame, consuming barn and hostages. Some did manage to burst free, only to be shot down.

Boots looked at the accused, to note their reactions. Keitel, Hitler's chief of staff, was perspiring, and one of the bankers had a handkerchief to his mouth and nose. Albert Speer, chief architect, looked close to vomiting, Hess fidgeted uselessly with his earphones, and Streicher, Hitler's premier Jew-baiter, belched.

Goering yawned.

Polly, wondering how much more she could endure without being violently sick, remembered how often Hitler and his menagerie of animals had been referred to at home as monsters. Proof that they actually were was before her tortured eyes.

The compiled motion picture ran for two frightful hours, when the court abruptly adjourned, almost in disorder, such was the effect the film had had on everyone from the president downwards. Mr Finch, Polly and Boots, silent, watched as the prisoners were led out under the escort of guards grimacing with disgust and loathing.

Polly said, 'Is that what we came for, Boots, to look at sheer horror and its perpetrators? What do you say, Edwin, do you say that's why we came?'

'We came, I think, to see a day's history recorded,' said Mr Finch, 'but I didn't expect it to be so bitter and revolting.'

'I found Belsen unbelievable at the time,' said Boots, 'I've now seen hell itself, a man-made hell. I suspect what Polly means, Edwin, is that although we've survived the showing, will any of us sleep ever again?'

'Boots,' said Mr Finch, 'it's given my stomach an infamous hiding.'

As they began to move to the exit, Polly said, 'I need only one thing.'

'And what's that?' asked Boots, an arm around her.

'I need to go home,' said Polly.

They had spent one night in the reserved rooms at the Grand Hotel, and were due to fly back to London tomorrow. Mr Finch contacted his old colleague at the hotel, the Intelligence man who had arranged everything, including the plane reservations. He was, however, unable to secure them seats for a return flight this evening, much to Polly's bitter disappointment, and it was not until the next afternoon that she, Boots and Mr Finch took the flight home on their pre-arranged reservations. There were special daily flights to and from Nuremberg these days.

They came off the plane at London Airport with thanks for their deliverance from the corruption and infamy that were on trial in Nuremberg. Once home, Boots and Polly gave Tim and Felicity a full account of their day in the courtroom, reducing them to stunned silence.

In bed later, Polly watched as Boots came in from the bathroom, wearing just his pyjama trousers. To Polly, his body looked firm, streamlined and clean. He was always that, clean of body. He had his faults, what man didn't? But he was so much more of a man than any of those creatures in the dock at Nuremberg. Born of his old-fashioned cockney mother, she wondered, not for the first time, what had given him that which set him apart from his brothers and all other men she had known? It made him his own kind of human being, yet no-one could have untied the knot that bound him to his Victorian mother or any other member of the family.

He was deeply disturbed by the hideous revelations of Nuremberg, she knew that, but as he slipped on his pyjama jacket and saw that she was watching him, his smile surfaced.

'Tell me the worst,' he said.

'About what?'

'My ageing condition?'

'Your ageing condition is a joke.'

'Do I need to ask what's on your mind, then?'

'I was thinking of all that I have, this bed, these clean sheets, this house, the twins and my marriage.'

'Polly?'

'And of those young girls, murdered by the thousand at Auschwitz. Boots, not one of them was given the chance to grow and flower. Not one of them came to know even a little of what you and I have. Not one came to know that outside of Hitler's ghastly Third Reich, there were fine young men to be found, young men like our nephews David, Edward and Daniel, or the young Jewish men who served with our forces. Those girls were murdered and burned to ashes. My God, Boots, millions of people lived a life of hell and died in hell. How much do we owe to the Channel that kept us free from Himmler and his Gestapo?'

'My dear old mother will tell you God made the English Channel, and took a hand in sending us Roosevelt's Americans,' said Boots.

'Come to bed,' said Polly, and he switched off

the light and slipped in beside her. She at once put herself as close to him as she could. They were both in their fiftieth year, but she was able to be grateful to unpredictable Nature that she was not yet dried up, not yet an invalidated woman.

Arms around her, Boots said, 'If the pictures get worse before they're better, Polly, count to ten.'

'And if you ever need to talk about Belsen,' she said, 'you know now you can talk to me. We can lay its ghosts together.'

'Polly, dear girl, we're home, and I've left all the worst ghosts behind in Nuremberg,' said Boots. 'I know yesterday was an ordeal for you—'

'For everyone, except Goering,' said Polly. 'He belongs in a sewer.' She sighed and relaxed. 'I'm going to say we had an unforgettable day that would be best for us if it was forgotten. How does that strike you?'

'It's a classic,' said Boots.

'It would be,' said Polly, 'if it weren't for the fact that we both know we can never forget.'

Mr Finch had assured Chinese Lady he was in fine fettle, and that the court proceedings had been interesting.

'Interesting?' Chinese Lady looked sceptical. 'That wasn't what the wireless news said.'

'Ah,' said Mr Finch, sipping a reviving whisky. He had intended to play down the more frightful aspects of the Nuremberg proceedings. 'Interesting in an unbelievable way,' he said, and gave Chinese Lady, Susie and Sammy an account that reduced them to shocked silence. Recovering,

Chinese Lady said she shouldn't have let him go, that no-one could have sat through all that without having nightmares, especially as it meant being in the same place as those wicked men responsible for such dreadful things. You'd best have an aspirin before you get into bed, Edwin, she said, and you'd best go up now. It was ten o'clock. Mr Finch, looking a little tired, said he would but he'd finish his whisky first.

Susie said imagine having seen that awful lot of murderers in person, and having to watch a film all about the horrible killing of thousands of innocent families. Children, she said painfully, children as well. Sammy said nothing. He looked stunned.

'Sammy?' she said, and he took a deep breath.

'How could it have happened?' he said. 'How the hell could it? We've all heard about it, read about it, but seeing it in front of your eyes, like Boots did at Belsen? We all knew he'd been there, but after listening to what was shown today, Jesus Christ, I've got to ask, how has he managed to stay sane?'

'Boots will never let the evil of men like Goering and Himmler destroy him,' said Mr Finch.

'Well, what you've told us has knocked me senseless,' said Sammy. 'It was a lot more diabolical than anything we heard on the radio.'

He chewed it all over in a helpless kind of way with Susie and Mr Finch until Chinese Lady spoke quietly.

'I think we'd all best go to bed.'

It had occurred to Sammy recently that the ugly

nature of London's ruins made one feel the war was still going on. Perhaps what was coming out of Nuremberg gave Chinese Lady the same feeling.

In America, the farmers of the Mid-West were pursuing their daily lives in the way of people whose inherited affinity with the land was such that most of them had never seen a coast washed by the seas. Most felt they didn't need to. Most worked hard all day, ate a thundering good meal, sat out on the porch and communed with the evening sky and the infinity of the good earth.

Patsy Kirk of Boston was in Kansas with her father, Meredith Kirk. Patsy, imbued with a high level of American effervescence, still had her own very special place in the life of Daniel Adams. Unfortunately, she was several thousand miles away from him in America, and he was equally distant from her in Palestine. They communicated regularly by mail, but while letters could arouse happy sentiments, they weren't as exciting as being within physical touch of each other.

Patsy's father had been born of a Kansas farming couple. Attending high school in Wichita, he was expected, along with his brothers and sisters, to do as his parents and their forbears had done, spend his working life on the land. And his retirement on the front porch. But he broke the mould and went East, and fashioned a different life, in journalism and then as a radio newsman. However, he found time now and again to visit his family, a family certain sure he'd come to no good.

He was staying with them now, in their great rambling farmhouse, and Patsy was there with him.

On the night in Britain when certain members of the Adams family were sleeping off the effects of their visit to Nuremberg, the late afternoon sky in Kansas was an endless vista flushed with pink. Patsy was walking with her Pa along the dirt road leading to the main highway. They were giving themselves a break from too much peace and quiet. Pa Kirk's mother, father and two brothers rarely had a conversation, or encouraged one. A laconic response to an equally laconic comment was sometimes enough to constitute a whole evening's dialogue. They were fine people, sturdy, enduring and God-fearing, but Patsy was jumping out of her skin with restlessness.

'Pa, can you find an excuse for us to go back to Boston tomorrow, instead of the day after?'

'I could, I guess, but should I?' said Pa Kirk, whose sophisticated East Coast look did not exactly harmonize with his family's dungarees. Mind, they did put suits on for Sunday church.

'Pa,' said Patsy, 'if I'm a candidate for a nuthouse by this time tomorrow, you'll be a candidate for bitter sorrow and anguished self-reproach.'

Pa Kirk understood. There was very little here to engage the interest of a Boston girl now in her nineteenth year, especially a girl as cosmopolitan as Patsy. Four years in the UK while that country was at war had put her completely adrift from the insularity of Kansas folks. His own early years in Boston had effected a similar change in himself.

Patsy was a compulsive communicator of her opinions and feelings, a fervent exponent of the spoken word and its infinite variations, a lover of discussion and argument. She was suffering frustration.

'If Hugo phoned to recall me, sure, that would give me an excuse to leave a day early, Patsy.' Hugo Manning was his radio station boss, the big man.

'I'll make the call, Pa,' said Patsy, doing her best to look in keeping with his folks in an outfit of red shirt and blue jeans. 'I'll drive into Wichita and call you from there.'

'Can you sound like Hugo if your grandpa gets to the phone first?' asked Pa Kirk.

'I can sound like Marcia, his gum-chewing secretary. You know, kind of metallic and strangled.'

'OK, Patsy, do it this evening.'

'Pa, you beauty.'

'Hardly,' said Pa Kirk. 'By the way, you're thinking, of course, that there's some mail waiting for you in Boston.'

'What mail?'

'From Daniel Adams.'

'Well, Pa,' said Patsy, 'I'll come clean with you. I do have hopes that Daniel has written, and I also want to renew acquaintance with the rest of the world. Grandma and Grandpa Kirk are great in their way, but they use their radio just to get weather reports and the latest price for corn. Pa, can you imagine Daniel and his family stuck on weather reports when those Nazis who bombed the heart out of London and did a genocide act on the Jews are on trial in Nuremberg?'

'No, I don't think they'll be listening to weather reports,' said Pa Kirk, 'I think they'll be listening to the indictments of every last sonofabitch.'

'Pa, you know I'm definitely going back in a few months, don't you?'

'I know, honey, and I'm now too wise to talk you out of it.'

'Like Daniel would say, good on you, Pa.'

Chapter Eleven

December

When they were dressing one morning, Susie had a word with Sammy. Well, several.

'Sammy?'

'Yes, my love?' said Sammy.

'What?' said Susie.

'You have a question, my dear?' said Sammy.

'Stop talking like that,' said Susie, 'or I'll think you're somebody's insurance man.'

'Susie, my good woman, how could—'

'Sammy Adams, d'you want a bump on your head that wasn't there before?'

'Well, no, Susie, I don't.'

'Then take that silly grin off your face and listen,' said Susie. 'When we move into our new house – when will all the walls be up, by the way?'

'When I've convinced the builder that if he keeps making excuses about a shortage of bricks, I'll send a bloke round to injure his wife,' said Sammy.

'Yes, do what you can to hurry him up,' said

Susie. 'Anyway, when the house is finished and we move in, I'd like some help.'

'Susie, I'm your help,' said Sammy.

'Not with a broom or carpet sweeper, you're not,' said Susie. 'I'm talking about a housemaid.'

'Er?' said Sammy.

'Sammy, there are six of us. You, me, Bess, Jimmy, Paula and Phoebe. There'll be five bedrooms, and carpeting all over. We'll need a housemaid.'

'I grant you, that's not me,' said Sammy. 'Susie, have you been talking to Polly? She's after a maid-cook, isn't she?'

'Yes,' said Susie, 'and I had tea with her yesterday afternoon. She's got a temporary help at the moment. Well, she's still looking for the right kind of permanent daily servant. Polly knows about the right kind, she grew up during the years when her parents had several, including a butler.'

'Am I correct in thinking some of us are getting high-class ideas?' asked Sammy.

'Sammy, we could afford two servants easily,' said Susie, 'but let's start with one.'

'You know what that's called, don't you?' said Sammy. 'Keeping up with the Joneses.'

'Blow the Joneses,' said Susie, 'I'm thinking of the Adamses, our Adamses.'

'Which I like you for,' said Sammy.

'So what d'you think?' asked Susie.

'About a housemaid for you?' Sammy let a grin show, having just realized that employing a housemaid would add to his prestige as a businessman of growing importance. 'Yes, good idea, Susie.'

'You're really in favour?' said Susie.

'Susie love, we've come a long way together since we were kids in Walworth, when I wore darned jerseys and you wore patched knickers.'

'I never did, and how would you have known, anyway?' said Susie.

'Just guesswork, Susie. Yup, we've come on since then, so let's join the gentry along with Boots and Polly, and have a housemaid. Take one on when we move in. Come to that, I ain't sure it wouldn't become me to have a chauffeur.'

'With a chauffeur, Sammy, you need a Rolls-Royce,' said Susie.

'That's another good idea,' said Sammy.

'A chauffeur's not a good idea,' said Susie. 'No, no chauffeur, Sammy.'

'Eh?'

'Or a Rolls-Royce,' said Susie. 'We don't want our friends and neighbours talking about us behind their curtains.' Which made Sammy mutter something about the deficiencies of friends and neighbours. 'What was that, Sammy?' asked Susie, seated at her dressing-table and applying just the right amount of lipstick for a woman of forty-one.

'Oh, only that I've got to talk to the plumber about what's holding up work on the central heating,' said Sammy.

'Eh?' said Mr Toby Talbot, Camberwell plumber and heating engineer, sub-contracted by the builder to do the plumbing work in Sammy's new house.

135

'Come on, Toby,' said Sammy, 'you've got a spare central heating system lying about somewhere, haven't you?'

'I would have,' said Mr Talbot, 'if spare central heating systems did a lot of lying about, like. Only they don't, they come out of fact'ries to order.'

'All right, I know about shortages,' said Sammy, regretting he hadn't thought of finding out in the first place if there was a black market operating in the supply of domestic installations. Mind, if he had, Susie might have got to know, and Susie had the kind of principles that weren't as elastic as his. Spivs and black marketeers made her carry on a bit. 'I'm asking you nicely, Toby, to do a hurry-up job.'

Mr Talbot looked sad about what austerity was doing to the reputations of qualified plumbers.

'As I mentioned first off, central heating systems ain't common, y'know, Mr Adams, not in this country,' he said. 'I don't get too many orders. Mind, the Government's going to get 'em fitted in all the rebuilt schools, which is only right and proper. I remember me own schooldays in the winter, when we all got frozen stiff at our desks, and you could hear our joints crack when we stood up. Crack, crack, just like that. There was poor Lily Marmaduke, as I recall. She stood up once and everything went crack. So, of course, she just flopped, and they had to get her feet and legs in a tub of hot water until the elastic came back to her joints. I tell yer, schools should've had central heating years ago. You might like to know that the blocks of flats being built by the London

County Council will all be centrally heated, so I been told.'

'I'm pleased to hear it,' said Sammy, 'it makes me believe I'm entitled to a system meself.' Central heating was being fitted to the flats being built on the old brewery site, but the heating engineers working on that project belonged to a hefty-sized firm with established connections. Toby was a one-man outfit. 'Well, look at it this way, Toby. I'm having a house built on this site, not a school or a block of council flats. I don't want five hundred radiators, just a dozen or so. That's not much to ask, is it? No, of course it isn't. Glad you agree, and I'm giving you time to install the works before all the walls and ceilings have been plastered. You can get it done while you're still fitting the baths, basins and sinks.'

'Well, I was pleased to have your order, Mr Adams, and I ain't saying I wasn't,' said Mr Talbot, giving his fuzzy moustache a finger-combing, 'but I did say at the time—'

'But me no buts,' said Sammy.

'Eh?' said Mr Talbot.

'Shakespeare,' said Sammy, having a guess.

'What, the undertakers at Camberwell Green?' said Mr Talbot.

'You work it out,' said Sammy. 'I've got to get to the office a bit sharpish, and then make a round of me shops. I'll leave you to sort things out.'

'Mr Adams, there's been a war, y'know, and it means me order for your system is on a waiting list, but I'll do me level best to—'

'I know you will,' said Sammy. 'You're a good

bloke, Toby, and you can work your way round a waiting list. If you need to drop a fiver in someone's pocket, just let me know.'

'That's different,' said Mr Talbot, 'specially if you made it a tenner.'

'Now we're both talking,' said Sammy.

Later that day, when he was making the round of his shops in Kennington, Brixton, Clapham and elsewhere, an unusual depression crept up on him. In the grey wintry cold of December, buildings, shops and houses blown to bits by the bombs of war had left great jagged gaps, some sites providing primitive playgrounds for kids. Others were fronted by ugly hoardings erected by owners waiting for the time when they could go ahead with development. There were similar hoardings to be seen in Walworth, some of which fronted sites acquired by Adams Properties well before the war ended, and subsequently sold to developers who could afford to wait.

But the gaps and hoardings everywhere were all a pain in the eye to anyone who had known the thriving, bustling atmosphere of South London boroughs. Bloody hell, thought Sammy, in a way the ruddy war still is with us, like Chinese Lady feels. Industry was working, but not actually booming, except with manufacturers specializing in exports. The country needed to earn foreign currency, particularly American dollars. Income tax was another pain, a pain in the pocket, and of course it left people with only a small amount to spend outside of necessities. Developers, thought Sammy, wouldn't get going until there was a lot more money circulating than there is at the moment. These bomb-sites could be with us for years, and I don't know what Patsy Kirk, Daniel's young lady, would think if she clapped her go-ahead American peepers on them.

One good thing, though. Girls like Patsy and Leah, and female women like Susie, Polly and Rachel, could light up any kind of winter. Come to think of it, what do I need central heating for when I've got Susie?

He let a grin split his mouth as he drove into Clapham, and his depression lifted.

Mrs Rachel Goodman, widow, received a visitor one evening, a Mr Reuben Cameron, whose surname had emanated from his great-grandfather, an Edinburgh Scot who had married a lady of the Jewish religion and subsequently converted to the faith himself.

Rachel's house in Brixton was an entirely pleasant home for her widowed father, Isaac Moses, her younger daughter Leah, and herself. Her father was presently in Germany, along with a number of other men, all representative of worldwide Jewry, investigating the horrors of concentration camps and trying to solve the enormous problems relating to survivors. And Rachel's elder daughter, Rebecca, was away at university.

Reuben Cameron was, as he explained to Rachel, interesting himself in the post-war needs of Europe's displaced Jews and concentration camp survivors.

'My life,' said Rachel, handsome and well-endowed at forty-three, 'aren't we all doing everything we can for them?'

'Well, of course, Rachel, of course we are,' said Reuben, a fine-looking man of fifty, eyebrows a rich black, eyes a deep indigo blue. He took up causes, mostly for Jewish people in a world not generally well-disposed to them, and he always did so with zeal. 'But there's a call for us to support the Zionist campaign for a homeland in Palestine in practical terms. Including unrestricted immigration for the displaced and suffering Jews of Europe.'

'But the Arabs of Palestine are totally against that,' said Rachel. 'I dearly hope a homeland can be established, but the Arabs have made it clear, haven't they, that they'll fight being dispossessed. Our brethren in Europe were dispossessed by the Nazis, and that is now being judged as a crime leading to genocide. If the Zionists succeed in dispossessing the Arabs, how will they square their consciences?'

'After what was done to the Jews of Europe, Rachel, who among them can afford a conscience?' said Reuben.

'I dislike the fact that we're being caught in the middle,' said Rachel.

'We?' said Reuben, raising his eyebrows.

'Britain,' said Rachel. 'We've a mandate for keeping the peace in Palestine, haven't we? But the Arabs and Jews don't want peace, they want to fight each other, and there you are, we're definitely caught in the middle.'

Reuben sighed.

'I wish the mandate was the responsibility of another country,' he said. 'America, for instance, which is such a power in the world today, and capable of exerting the kind of pressure on the Arabs that Britain can't. However, you and I represent Jewry first and foremost, Rachel. Don't we?'

'Reuben, I've had to tell other people I'm British by birth and Jewish by religion,' said Rachel.

'Yes, we all are,' said Reuben. 'It's difficult, very, but after the terrible events in Europe and the incredible cruelty of those acts of genocide, our first thoughts must be for the survivors. They must be allowed to settle in Palestine, and the Zionist elements of our council insist the British must be forced to leave.'

'But that will mean there'll be nothing to prevent the Arabs and Jews killing each other,' said Rachel. 'It's happening already, you know that.'

'I do know,' said Reuben, 'and we both know, don't we, that the Zionists of Palestine and their supporters are determined to create an independent Jewish homeland there. And in order to bring about the right conditions for establishing that homeland, they insist the British must either leave peacefully or be forced out. It's worrying, Rachel, for those of us who feel reluctant to embarrass the British Government.'

'Reuben,' said Rachel, choosing her words carefully, 'I don't feel I owe the Zionists my support if it means adding to our Government's difficulties. It wasn't the Zionists who invaded Normandy, who fought the war against the Jews' worst enemies for nearly six years.'

'I agree with you, Rachel, word for word,' said Reuben, 'but my patriotism is under strain because of what the British are doing to keep immigrant Jews out of Palestine. They're diverting the ships to places like Cyprus and locking the immigrants into primitive camps, while they unfortunately continue to arouse the animosity of both the Jews and Arabs.'

'I know, and it distresses me,' said Rachel, 'but unrestricted immigration will infuriate the Arabs.'

'Rachel, we must still help our brethren,' said Reuben. 'So to come to the point, could I collect a donation from you?'

'I've certain reservations,' said Rachel, 'but tell me how much you have in mind.'

'Say two and a half thousand pounds,' said Reuben.

'How much?'

'I think we can afford it,' said Reuben gently. 'We can't offer cocoa beans while our American brethren are giving dollars by the bucketful.'

'Very well, Reuben,' said Rachel after a moment's hesitation, 'I'll make the donation to help the cause of the survivors.'

'Thank you, Rachel,' said Reuben. 'I'm sure Isaac, your father, would approve.'

'Yes,' said Rachel.

When Reuben left he had the cheque safely

placed in his wallet. Leah appeared as Rachel closed the front door on the departing visitor.

'Mama, why did Mr Cameron want to speak privately to you?' she asked.

'To satisfy himself we're supportive of the suffering survivors of the concentration camps,' said Rachel.

'And why did he want to do that?' asked Leah.

'To find out if we'd give financial help to the cause,' said Rachel. 'I've donated two and a half thousand pounds.'

'Oh, my life, Mama,' said Leah, 'are you sure it won't be used to help buy guns for the Zionists?'

'Mr Cameron said—' Rachel checked. No, Reuben had not actually specified how it would be spent, he had only said to help the suffering. Did that include the Zionists who were striving to create the homeland?

'Mama, we don't want those guns turned on our soldiers in Palestine, do we?' said Leah. 'Uncle Sammy's son Daniel is one of them.'

Oh, my God, thought Rachel. Sammy's son, yes, he was out there with a unit of the Army.

She phoned Reuben later, and he assured her that her cheque, along with his and certain others, would go into the council's general fund, accompanied by a note specifying these particular donations were to help alleviate survivors who had been robbed of everything by the Germans, except, by a miracle, their lives.

'Which means nothing to do with buying guns?' said Rachel.

'I should not want such donations to be

misused, any more than you, Rachel,' said Reuben.

Rachel hoped she could be sure of that.

That night in Tel Aviv, a hidden marksman opened fire on two off-duty British soldiers as they came out of a café. Both were wounded, one seriously. The marksman, Jew or Arab, melted away in the darkness.

In Nuremberg, the court heard from a survivor of Treblinka extermination camp that to save wasting bullets on mere children, they were thrown alive into a continuously burning pit. Sometimes, SS men would be kind enough to first smash in a child's head, so that with luck it would be dead before landing in the fire.

When details of this came through on the wireless that evening, Chinese Lady sat up stiff and stricken in her fireside armchair.

'Edwin?' she said in a whisper.

Mr Finch was up from his own chair, standing in front of the fire and staring down at the burning coals.

'Children, Maisie, children,' he said. 'Surely, even the devil himself would cry out in protest at this.'

'I can't take it in, Edwin, I can't understand,' said Chinese Lady, and thought of Giles and Emily, Rosie's children. She thought of Gemma and James, Boots's twins, and of Paula and Phoebe, Sammy's young daughters. And she remembered the Blackshirts, and their belief in

Hitler and Nazi Germany. 'Edwin,' she said, 'could it have happened here?'

'No, Maisie,' said Mr Finch unhesitatingly. 'The British people would never accept a dictatorship, not after centuries of democratic governments. Oliver Cromwell's dictatorship lasted only until his death, when the people wanted no more of it. The Germans, unfortunately, have never known democracy, apart from the weak version that existed for a few years after the Great War. When a people allow a man like Hitler to deprive many of them of their rights under the law, to deprive all of them of an electoral vote, and to govern by thuggery, and when that people fall at the feet of such a man and worship him, they have indeed sold their souls to Satan. Nuremberg is demonstrating that day after day. God in heaven, those children of Treblinka.'

'What would you do to those dreadful men, Edwin?'

'With my blood boiling, Maisie, I would hand them all over to the survivors of the camps in the hope that they would be reduced to animal-like creatures and then stoned to death.'

'Lord,' said Chinese Lady in a faint voice. Then, 'Edwin, shall I make a pot of tea?'

'Maisie,' he said, 'you are the most civilized and comforting woman God ever made.'

Chapter Twelve

A Sunday morning, with Christmas not far away, a peacetime Christmas.

Jonathan was in the garden, digging up rose bushes long past their best. It was he who heard the hysterical screams coming first from the kitchen of the house next door, and then from the garden itself. He ran to the dividing hedge, his tinplate kneecap protesting.

'What's wrong, Mrs Duckworth, what's wrong?'

The screams stopped and the lady's voice gasped at him from the other side of the hedge.

'Oh, help me – help me – it's my husband – he's fallen down the stairs!'

Jonathan hared round at a limping run, entering his neighbour's garden by the path at the side of the house. Mrs Duckworth was standing outside her kitchen door, emitting moans and strange little cries, her face pale, eyes staring, body shivering.

'Mrs Duckworth—'

'Oh, go in, go and look – he's not moving – just lying there – oh, do something for him—'

Jonathan dashed into the kitchen and through

to the hall. At the foot of the stairs, Mr Duckworth, clad in a shirt, pullover and trousers, was lying on his back on the polished parquet flooring. His eyes were wide open, fixed and glazed, his hair wet. With blood. His skull was oozing. Jonathan had a horrible feeling that Mrs Duckworth had suddenly been widowed.

'Oh, Christ,' he breathed, and went down on one knee beside the man, whose face was a pallid grey. The open eyes gave not the slightest flicker as Jonathan gently shook his shoulder. 'Mr Duckworth?'

There was not the smallest response. Jonathan had seen dead men, all too many of them, in the Western Desert during the Eighth Army's battles with Rommel's Afrika Korps. Here was another one, he thought, but he placed a hand on Mr Duckworth's pullover to search in hope for a heartbeat, however faint.

Nothing. Like the glazed eyes, the heart offered not the slightest flicker of life.

'Is – is he dead?'

Jonathan looked up. Mrs Duckworth was there, white-faced and shaking, one hand up to her throat.

'I'm afraid he is, but do you have a hand mirror?'

'What?'

'A hand mirror.'

'Yes – yes – just a minute.'

Mrs Duckworth moved on weak legs, going into the kitchen. Jonathan touched the man's face. It was clammy. The head suddenly lolled to one

147

side. Christ, thought Jonathan, I'm looking at a man with a cracked skull and a broken neck. He glanced at the stairs. They were carpeted, but the hall floor was one of hard parquet blocks.

Mrs Duckworth reappeared, still shivering, a small mirror from her handbag in her hand. Her mouth was visibly trembling as she passed the mirror to Jonathan. He placed it close to Mr Duckworth's mouth. The result was completely negative, the mirror did not blur in any way.

'Mrs Duckworth, do you have a phone?'

'Yes – yes. Mr Hardy, is my husband—?'

'I'm sorry, Mrs Duckworth, but I think he's dead.'

Mrs Duckworth moaned. Jonathan made her lie on the settee in the living room, then used the phone to dial 999 and call for an ambulance.

While waiting, he found brandy in a cabinet, poured a little for Mrs Duckworth, gave the glass to her and told her to sip it. Then he used the phone again to speak to Emma. Emma, aghast, came round at once.

In the hall, she and Jonathan looked down at the inert Mr Duckworth.

'Oh, my God, Jonathan, how frightful. The poor man. Where's Mrs Duckworth?'

'In there.' Jonathan pointed. 'Sit with her. I'll wait here for the ambulance.'

Emma did what she could for the shocked and shaken lady, who was finding it an ordeal to even sip the brandy, for the glass shook like a reed in the wind each time she lifted it to her lips.

*   *   *

The ambulance crew, quick and efficient, took only a few seconds to decide emergency hospital treatment could do nothing for Mr Duckworth. The man was stone dead. Accordingly, they contacted the deceased's doctor, and the police.

The doctor, about to leave for church with his wife, hastened to the Duckworths' house instead. After an examination of the unfortunate man, he confirmed for Mrs Duckworth the tragic news that the fall had killed her husband. Mrs Duckworth collapsed. Dr Peters gave her a sedative, and Emma and Jonathan assured him they would stay with the lady until a relative was able to get there. Dr Peters said he would phone her sister in Norwood.

A sergeant and a constable arrived from the Herne Hill police station, conferred with the doctor, and then asked Mrs Duckworth if she was up to giving them the full details of the accident.

'I – I – yes, it's best now, I don't want to think about doing it later,' she said, sitting up on her settee, with Emma and Jonathan on either side of her, giving her the comfort of their presence.

It was about ten-past-ten, she said, and her husband, after fixing a new shelf in the larder, had just that minute gone upstairs to change into a suit. They were going to visit her sister in Norwood, to have Sunday dinner with her. She herself was getting ready to make some coffee for them to have before they left. She heard her husband call her, and she went out into the hall. He was at the top of the stairs, wanting to know where his clean Sunday shirt was. She told him it was in the top drawer of the tallboy, like always. Then he said he'd come down and have his coffee first. He started down, then tripped and fell, and she couldn't do anything to save him. He just fell all the way down, ever so fast, head over heels, and it was his head that hit the floor first, with an awful crash. She screamed, bent over him, and she couldn't help screaming again because he didn't move when she touched him, he just lay there like he was dead, and there was blood wetting his hair.

She ran out into the garden screaming, and Mr Hardy heard her and came round. And Mr Hardy told her he was afraid her husband was dead.

'Well, I'm sorry, Mrs Duckworth, very sorry,' said the police sergeant. 'It's a shocker.'

'There's more domestic accidents that kill people or cripple them real serious than flu victims,' said the constable soberly. 'Falling off ladders, that's one of the regular incidents, and falling downstairs, that's another. Dreadful for you, Mrs Duckworth.'

'And to have seen him fall,' said Emma, arm around the newly widowed lady, whose hysteria and shaking tremors had been eased by the sedative. 'How awful for you.'

Bloody awful, thought Jonathan.

'Have you got all the notes, Durkins?' asked the sergeant.

'If we could just make sure?' said the constable, and Mrs Duckworth, asked if she could possibly confirm everything, took a deep breath, quivered, and gave all the details again. The sergeant thanked her and said he'd arrange for the body to be taken to the mortuary, and that the funeral could take place after the inquest.

'Oh, dear,' sighed Mrs Duckworth.

'There has to be an inquest,' said Dr Peters gently. He had made a second examination of the body, a thorough one.

Mrs Duckworth, eyes misty, nodded numbly.

'My poor Charlie,' she said.

'The burial can be arranged after the inquest,' said Dr Peters.

'He wasn't much over fifty, doctor,' said Mrs Duckworth.

'I know,' said Dr Peters.

Mrs Duckworth coughed up a sob, and little tears fell. Emma's arm tightened around her.

The body had been taken away. Dr Peters and the police had gone, but Emma and Jonathan were still there, letting Mrs Duckworth talk wanderingly about the times that had been happy ones for herself and Charlie. Emma made some hot, strong tea, and they were all drinking it when Mrs Duckworth's unmarried sister, Sylvia, turned up. A teacher, she was an immediate and caring comfort to Mrs Duckworth, and Emma and Jonathan were able to leave, after assuring their stricken neighbour that if she needed any help, to remember they were only next door.

At home, Emma said, 'How ghastly, Jonathan, seeing him kill himself in front of her eyes.'

'I'm going to think about the future, not the present,' said Jonathan, 'and I hope Maudie Duckworth will do the same.'

'What d'you mean?' asked Emma.

'Well, in a year or so from now, maybe,' said Jonathan, 'she could be feeling a lot happier not having him there complaining about us and everything else. And time heals, Emma, that it does.'

'You're not supposed to speak ill of the dead,' said Emma. 'Still,' she said thoughtfully, 'you could be right.'

'Hope so,' said Jonathan.

'Sunday dinner's going to be late,' said Emma.

'Under the circs, I don't think that's going to upset me,' said Jonathan. 'I'll peel the spuds for you, if you like, Emma.'

'I'll take you up on that,' said Emma. 'D'you want to wear one of my aprons?'

'I don't be too keen on that,' said Jonathan.

'Why not?'

'It might get to be too much of a habit for a chap,' said Jonathan.

That was a little piece of light relief, but they were quiet as they went about preparing their Sunday dinner.

The inquest took place on the day before Christmas Eve. Jonathan and Emma attended. They listened to Dr Peters giving his medical evidence, which was a confirmation that the deceased had sustained a fatally severe skull fracture as well as a broken neck consequent on his fall.

Mrs Duckworth, tearful and upset, gave details to a sympathetic coroner, and Jonathan described all that he had done following Mrs Duckworth's appeal for help. The police sergeant gave details of his arrival and inspection of the body, and the constable quoted from his notes.

The coroner summed up and pronounced his verdict.

Death by accident.

Which wasn't a great comfort to the suffering widow.

Jonathan and Emma spent Christmas Day with his parents, Jemima and Job Hardy, and his sisters, in their house in Lorrimore Square, Kennington. Sussex-born Jemima and Job had had a worrying and wearying war, with many a bomb incident taking toll of their faith in the general goodness of human nature, of Job's endurance as an ARP warden, and Jemima's resilience. But they were back now to their habitual belief that country jokes and full-throated laughter provided the best fillip to life and health. They made Christmas Day hilarious for their family and their daughter-in-law, Emma.

Chapter Thirteen

Before Christmas, and when one could have said
Susie's back was turned, Sammy made contact
with a useful bloke he happened to know. A spiv.
A thin, bony geezer, he had a perpetually in-
gratiating grin that managed to look wider than
his face, plus the black market connections that
enabled him to deliver four large plump turkeys
to Sammy at his office, although at a considerable
plucking of Sammy's pocket. When Sammy
brought them home, Susie, of course, wanted to
know how he'd achieved a miracle in these days of
austerity. Sammy said a business friend who knew
a turkey farmer had done him proud.

'A business friend?' said Susie, deep blue eyes
dark with suspicion.

'Well, Susie, if you look at the size of these here
birds,' said Sammy, 'you couldn't say he's not a
friend. Believe me, I was overcome.' He didn't
mention it was the price that overcame him.

Susie drew a curtain over her suspicions. Well,
it was Christmas, the time of showing goodwill to
one and all, including a husband looking as
innocent as a baby duckling. Further, in his

family-mindedness, he was giving one of the birds to Boots and Polly, one to Ned and Lizzy, and one to Tommy and Vi.

Rosie and Matthew, and their children, came up from Dorset to stay with Boots and Polly. They brought a carefully packed box of eggs with them, eggs from their own chickens. Rosie now had four dozen hens, and information to the effect that she and Matthew had bought six acres of land to the rear of their cottage, which land they intended to turn into a chicken farm. Matthew would make that his daily work until his garage was rebuilt. Everyone was in need of eggs, or of chickens for roasting, while all over the country people with gardens were thinking of keeping their own layers. Chicken farmers sold such layers as a profitable part of their business.

Bobby and Helene went to visit Helene's parents in France. Daniel was still in Palestine, his cousins Edward and David both in Cyprus with the RAF, David having recently been posted there. Chinese Lady and Mr Finch, and most other members of their extensive family were invited by Polly and Boots to a traditional cold supper on Christmas evening, for which Ned supplied the wine.

Sammy said he'd like to make a speech.

'What about?' asked Ned.

'Profit and loss accounts, probably,' said Tim.

'He'd better not,' said Susie.

Felicity, blindly feeling her way into the atmosphere, said, 'I've never heard a speech about profit and loss accounts. Have I missed something fascinating?'

'Not much,' said Lizzy.

'Pay attention,' said Sammy, on his feet and looking imposing in his best suit. 'Ladies and gents, and others—'

'Others?' said Rosie. 'What others?'

'Yes, I should like to know too,' said Eloise.

'Most of us?' suggested Polly.

'I feel like one of most of us,' said Matthew.

'Sammy means the kids,' said Tommy.

'Who's looking at me?' asked Jimmy.

'And me,' said Paul.

'Keep 'em in order, Boots,' said Sammy.

'Your problem, Sammy,' said Boots.

'If I might be permitted to say a few words?' said Sammy.

'Edwin,' said Chinese Lady, 'I hope that young son of mine's not going to be common in front of the children.'

'Ah, well,' said Mr Finch philosophically.

'It's like this,' said Sammy, 'we're all gathered together and it's our first peaceful Christmas since Hitler's Huns started chucking hot lead at us. I consider it me privilege to congratulate all of you for coming out of it alive and flourishing. Well, to start with, look at my dear old Ma—'

'I knew it,' said Chinese Lady.

'Good on you, Granny,' said Bess.

'A prime example,' said Sammy, 'of family – um –'

'Fortitude?' said Boots.

'That's it,' said Sammy, 'forty-something. And you've all got it.'

'I've got forty-something?' said Felicity.

'I don't have twenty-something yet,' said Bess.

'I've passed the qualifying date,' said Ned.

'I'm further pleased to inform everybody,' said Sammy, 'that the family business also stood up to the perishing bombs with that self-same forty – what was it, Boots?'

'Fortitude,' said Boots.

'That's it,' said Sammy, 'and I wish I'd been educated meself. Anyway, ladies and gents—'

'And others,' said Annabelle, present with husband Nick and their two children.'

'I daresay', said Sammy, 'a lot of us have been thinking what the family business owes our factory girls, our machinists and seamstresses—'

'I'm ashamed to confess, Sammy old sport,' said Polly, 'that I've actually been thinking of our cook's suggestion that Boots and I ought to keep chickens and have our own supply of eggs, like Rosie and Matthew.'

'Oh, crikey, Aunt Polly,' said Paula, 'could me and Phoebe come and see them?'

'Chickens, what a thought,' said Annabelle's husband Nick.

'I like the idea for you and me, Vi,' said Tommy.

'So do I,' said Vi. 'Our own chickens and fresh eggs, Tommy. We've plenty of room.'

'Ned, could we keep chickens?' asked Lizzy.

'I'll buy a book on the best kind of birds,' said Ned.

'You don't need a book,' said Nick, 'you can study form at the Windmill Theatre.'

'I've heard about the Windmill Theatre,' said Chinese Lady, 'and I don't like the sound of it.'

'It's a kind of gentlemen's club, Maisie,' said Mr Finch.

'Granny, they're all undressed,' said Bess.

'The gentlemen?' said Chinese Lady in shock.

'No, the stage ladies,' said Ned.

'Well, I don't want anyone in this family going there,' said Chinese Lady. 'What sort of ladies are they?'

'Oh, birds of a few feathers, old girl,' said Boots.

'Here, excuse me,' said Sammy, 'but I ain't finished speechifying yet.'

'Carry on, lovey,' said Susie, 'and we'll talk later about keeping our own chickens.'

'It's not going to be me,' said Sammy.

'We'll talk later,' said Susie.

'It's going to be me,' said Sammy. 'Listen, would all of you mind drinking a bit of Christmas cheer as a compliment to our factory girls? I told 'em we'd drink their health. We can couple that with the factory profits.'

That aroused a lot of old-fashioned ribaldry, but the fact was that all Chinese Lady's direct descendants who had come of age held shares in Adams Enterprises, the parent company, the total shareholding having been increased to ten thousand during the war. As well as the direct descendants, Susie, Vi and Ned each had a holding, and Boots, inheriting Emily's, had transferred it to Polly. Accordingly, the Christmas toast to Gertie Roper and her girls was drunk in wine or port or lemonade. Paula and Phoebe spluttered in their lemonade, since it was all a giggle to them. Sammy then proposed a toast to Grandma and Grandpa, which was given with a great deal of ringing affection and respect, and which flustered Chinese Lady somewhat.

After all that, Bess said, 'Daddy, it's still Christmas.'

'Not half,' said Sammy, 'which means you want to know if it's time for some good old-fashioned Christmas games, which it is.'

'Oh, lor',' said Vi.

'Organized by Boots,' said Sammy.

Apart from Chinese Lady, the married ladies uttered despairing cries, and fainted. Well, as good as.

Susie, coming to, said weakly, 'Including "Forfeits"?'

'We'll begin with "Forfeits", Susie, to celebrate the arrival of peace,' said Boots.

The married ladies fainted again, almost.

'What's all the fuss, Aunt Polly?' asked Bess.

'Well, Bess, my young sport,' said Polly, 'perhaps you can't remember the kind of fiendish forfeits your Uncle Boots used to dream up for ladies, but I've a frightful feeling he hasn't lost touch with his devilish inspiration, so before we begin, do as we do – tie your skirts down!'

Which meant that a Christmas party for the family had returned to the pre-war realms fashioned by what Chinese Lady called sociable hooliganism. If she meant social anarchy, her own description turned out to be nearer the mark.

*   *   *

On Boxing Day morning, Bess spoke to Sammy.

'Daddy, you know I've got this office job in Croydon?'

'Like it, don't you?' said Sammy.

'It's all right, but not world-beating,' said Bess.

'Not world-beating?' That was a new one to Sammy, and he appreciated it. He also appreciated Bess, as good-natured and equable as her maternal grandma, Susie's mum. 'Not much of a future prospect, is that it? Well, Plum Pudding—'

'Excuse me, Dad,' said Bess, 'but that's out of order.'

'Slip of the tongue,' said Sammy. Plum Pudding, that had been his pet name for her all through her years of puppy fat. Bess, turned seventeen, now saw herself as a young lady. Blimey, thought Sammy, I think all our young ones are getting to be middle class. Still, it's not against the law, not yet, and not unless Harry Pollit gets to be Prime Minister. Harry Pollit was a leading Communist, and very admiring of Stalin. 'Begging your pardon, Bess. Anyway, what's on your mind?'

'I've been talking to Jimmy,' said Bess, 'and we wondered if you could buy a bit of land so's we could start a chicken farm, like cousin Rosie and Matthew.'

'Eh?' said Sammy.

'Well, don't you see,' said Bess, 'there's still food shortages, and everyone wants a lot more things like eggs, and chickens for roasting. I'm sure Rosie and Matthew will get to shake hands with prosperity as quickly as anything.'

Sammy liked the sound of prosperity. He'd liked it since the age of about nine. By the time he was fourteen, he had it targeted as his future best friend. It had a lot in common with profit, much respected by serious business blokes. Well, profit was the father of prosperity.

'Bess, me pet, you reckon that when Jimmy's left school, and later when you've left university, the two of you would like to have a go at being chicken farmers?'

'Dad,' said Bess. 'I can honestly say I'd like that better than sitting at a typewriter.'

Sammy, who was never going to discourage ambition in any of his children, said, 'Did you have somewhere in mind, like Brockwell Park? It covers some useful acres.'

'Dad, you couldn't buy Brockwell Park, you silly,' said Bess.

'I could make an offer,' said Sammy, 'but I think you're right, there'd be too much paperwork, and I don't suppose chickens would fancy Clapham Common. Too many trams and buses. They'd lay cracked eggs. So where, then?'

'Surrey opens out south of Croydon,' said Bess.

'I think you're thinking positive,' said Sammy, giving her a smile and a pat. 'Well, I tell you what, pet, you and Jimmy get some chicken farming books out of the local library, and study them, and I'll look around for a bit of land. And it might help if you left your office job and got yourself a few months work with an experienced chicken farmer.'

'Dad, you're a real sport,' said Bess, 'and like Mum says, you're not just another man in trousers.'

'I'm touched that your mum thinks that highly of me,' said Sammy.

Chicken farming. Eggs. Chickens for the oven. Food, like clothes and a roof over your head, was a must. Let's see, Adams Food Enterprises, how does that sound? Promising, Sammy, promising.

On the evening after Boxing Day, when the country was slightly bleary-eyed from celebrating its first peacetime Christmas since 1938, Jonathan answered the ringing phone.

'Hello?'

'Oh, is that you, Jonathan?'

'It's me, and is that you, Mrs Duckworth?'

'I'd be ever so glad if you and Emma could come round and have a little Christmas drink with me. I got back from my sister's an hour ago. Well, she insisted on me spending Christmas with her, me not wanting to spend it here, and I've got a nice bottle of port. I'd be happy to have you come round for a glass.'

'Hold on,' said Jonathan. He called Emma. Out she came. 'Emma, Mrs Duckworth would like us to go round and have a glass of Christmas port with her.'

'She's all alone?' said Emma.

'She wasn't for Christmas, she spent it with her sister.'

'Yes, we knew that, but she's all alone now?'

'With her bottle of port,' said Jonathan.

'Tell her we'd like to enjoy a glass with her,' said Emma.

'I think we'll get a glass each,' said Jonathan.

'All right, funny-cuts, just tell her.'

Jonathan told the lady.

'Oh, I'll be ever so pleased to see you,' said Mrs Duckworth, 'ever so.'

'Be there in ten minutes,' said Jonathan. Putting the phone down, he said, 'I think she's already had a glass. Or two. She sounds a bit tiddly.'

'The poor dear's drowning her sorrows,' said Emma. 'She's got to face up to the funeral tomorrow.'

'Well, it's going to be cold, cold ground six feet under for poor old Charlie,' said Jonathan.

'Don't say anything like that to Maudie, Jonathan, you hear?' said Emma.

'That I do,' said Jonathan. 'Your voice be like the bells of St Mary's down by Cuckmere, Emma, clear and ringing.'

'You be a fair old saucebox at times, Jonathan. Well, come on, let's go and have a glass of port with Maudie Duckworth.'

Mrs Duckworth had a glass of port in her hand when she opened the door to them. It was only half-full.

'Oh, there you are,' she said. 'Come in, it's ever so nice to see you. Oh, I've just been having a taste of the port.' She giggled, and she swayed a bit as she led them into her living room. The fire was alight, and there were glasses on a table, together with not one bottle of port, but two. The contents of one bottle were well down. 'Sit yourselves, there's dears. Oh, you do the pouring for me, Jonathan, I don't feel my hand's too steady just now.'

'Maudie,' said Jonathan, 'have you had yours or do you want some more?'

Mrs Duckworth seated herself in a kind of grateful fashion, as if her legs were troubled by failing knees.

'Oh, you can just top me up a little,' she said. Jonathan, picking up the open bottle, gave her a modest top-up. 'Oh, a little more, Jonathan,' she said, and giggled again. 'Port does me good, but I had to make sure Charlie didn't see. Well, a woman needs a nice glass of port at times, don't you think—' She burped. 'Oh, excuse me. Don't you think, Emma?'

'Christmas is a good time for port,' smiled Emma. Jonathan was right. Maudie Duckworth was a bit tiddly. She was drowning her sorrows.

Jonathan poured for Emma and himself, and they sat down to drink their neighbour's health. Their neighbour's health seemed rosy. She drank her port in happy gulps. Then a frown appeared.

'It's the funeral tomorrow,' she said.

'You'll have to face up to it,' said Jonathan.

'Oh, I will,' said Maudie. Her frown went, and a tipsy smile took its place. 'I don't want to be unChristian, but I'll be pleased when he's gone to his rest. I mean—' She took another mouthful of port. 'I mean, if he grumbles about going sooner than he expected, I won't be able to hear him.'

'Was he always a grumbler?' asked Jonathan.

'Well, no, not till the war started – oops –' Maudie did another little burp. 'It's that cauliflower cheese my sister did us for lunch. What was I saying?'

'That your husband didn't start grumbling until the war started,' said Emma, sipping port.

'That's right. Well, he didn't like the war.'

'No-one did,' said Emma.

'Oh, Charlie didn't like it because he was admiring of Hitler and didn't think very much of the Jewish people,' said Maudie, slurring her words a little. She looked happily at her port and treated herself to a swallow that finished it off. 'Well, actually—' Another burp. 'Actually, he didn't like them at all, and complained there were too many of them everywhere. When I said it was only their religion that made them different, he told me I was—' Maudie frowned.

'Told you what?' asked Jonathan.

'That I was a stupid old cow, which upset me.' Maudie inspected her empty glass. 'Mind, he was a good husband till the war started, and then nothing was ever right for him. Jonathan, could you pour me a little bit more port?'

Jonathan obliged, half-filling her glass. What did it matter if she went to bed tipsy? She needed something to send her to sleep, seeing she had to attend the burial tomorrow.

'Happy New Year, Maudie,' he said.

'Oh, it could be a nice happy one for me,' she said, and drank to her prospects. 'Well, there's his firm's pension, which they'll pay to me, and my widow's pension, and I'm still not too old to get a job, like a school dinner cook.'

'Did Mr Duckworth spend the war complaining about the Jews?' asked Emma, thinking of what Himmler and his SS had done to them.

'Oh, he complained about everything, especially about it was a crime to be at war with Germany, which was fighting the Communists on everyone's be—' Maudie, having trouble with her tongue, stumbled over it. She took a helpful swallow of port. She giggled. 'Behalf,' she said. 'Mind, he worked for the Ministry of Food in one of their places in the Midlands, where we lived very comfortably in a hostel, so we never had to worry about air raids, like they did down here. But he still went on about the war and Jews being troublesome, and other things.' She sighed. 'Like what a silly old bitch I was.'

'Well, he's dead now,' said Emma, 'and I shouldn't say so, but he seems to have been no kind of a husband.'

'Oh, he's dead all right,' said Maudie, smiling happily. 'Going on at me last Sunday morning about me being useless, and saying I was always putting his clean shirts where he couldn't find them. So I went upstairs, took his best shirt out of its drawer, and showed it to him. I said it had been where his best shirts always were, in the top drawer of the tallboy. Well, I couldn't hardly believe the way he actually smiled and told me not to fuss. Smiling, would you believe. As if he was forgiving me.'

'Then you went downstairs?' said Emma.

'Beg pardon?' Maudie burped. 'Oh, yes. Well, he's gone now, poor Charlie.'

'And let's hope he's not finding anything to grumble about,' said Jonathan.

Maudie drank yet more port, and giggled.

'Oh, yes, let's hope he's resting in peace,' she said. 'Well, he did give me that smile before it happened.'

'Something to remember,' said Jonathan. 'Maudie?'

Maudie's glass had dropped from her hand, spilling port on her dress. Her head slumped.

'Well, look at the poor dear,' said Emma. Maudie was asleep, breathing little bubbles. Jonathan grinned.

'I think she's drowned her sorrows,' he said. 'Shall we get her up to her bed?'

'We can't leave her as she is,' said Emma.

'No, let's get her upstairs,' said Jonathan. 'Then we'll go home.'

'Yes, I think she'll be all right on her bed,' said Emma.

Jonathan carried the lady up, placed her on her bed, and Emma covered her with the eiderdown. Maudie burbled a little and slept happily on.

'Well, she's all right at the moment,' said Jonathan, 'but come morning and she might find herself with a port hangover.'

'Let's hope she doesn't have to take it with her to the funeral,' said Emma.

'We'll keep a neighbourly eye on her for the

next week or so,' said Jonathan, and he and Emma left after putting the port away and washing the glasses.

The following morning, when Jonathan was on his way to work, Emma phoned her neighbour. Maudie answered the phone quite brightly, and assured Emma she felt fine.

'Mind, I'm that embarrassed about falling asleep like I did,' she said. 'It must have been the port. And I'm ever so embarrassed that you and Jonathan must have had to carry me upstairs.'

'Well, it was no bother, and we thought we ought to get you up to your bed,' said Emma.

'Oh, I'm that grateful at you and Jonathan being so kind and understanding. I did wake up in the middle of the night, when I put myself properly to bed. I had a bit of a headache then, but it's gone now, and I'll get to the funeral all right, with my sister.'

'Well, that's fine,' said Emma.

Meanwhile, Jonathan on his way to the City hoped the funeral wouldn't be too upsetting for Mrs Duckworth. She'd obviously gone through the war as the butt of her husband's general dissatisfaction. Imagine that complaining old haddock being an admirer of Hitler. Well, there'd been others, like Mosley and his Blackshirts, but those thugs had sunk without trace, thank goodness, and Duckworth would be six feet under sometime during today. He and Emma must keep a neighbourly eye on the widow, poor old girl.

Chapter Fourteen

February, 1946

In a well-appointed house on Sterling Street, East Braintree, a suburb of Boston, Massachussetts, eighteen-year-old Patsy Kirk, the dark-haired and vivacious all-American girl engaged to Daniel Adams, was giving a final pat to her father's silver-grey tie and a final look at the carnation in the buttonhole of his immaculate light grey jacket.

'There, you'll do just fine, Pa,' she said. She was well up to the mark herself in a pillbox hat and a skirted suit of jewel-bright colour. 'You're not nervous, are you?'

'No, of course not, this is my second strike,' said Meredith Kirk, a personable man who looked in his prime, even if he wasn't far short of fifty. 'What's the time? Where's my hat? Who's driving us?'

'Pa, you are nervous,' said Patsy. 'There's half an hour yet, and Uncle Brad's driving both of us. Pa, he's your best man.'

'Sure, so he is,' said Pa Kirk. It was his wedding day, his second one, his first wife having died in a car crash many years ago. He'd met Francesca Fantoni, an American woman journalist and divorcée, in Paris just after the end of the war in Europe. Today, he was marrying her, and Patsy hoped her good old Pa wasn't going to find the Italianate lady too talkative. She was a fine-looking woman of forty, but gee whiz, did she like to hog a conversation. All the same, she was obviously nuts about Pa, so she just might allow him a share of their dialogues and bake cookies for him on Sundays.

'Now, we understand each other, Pa?' said Patsy. 'When you get back here from your trip to San Francisco with your bride, I go back to England, OK? I've got my passage booked.'

'Patsy, I promised I wouldn't try to talk you out of it, but I still don't feel too good about you making the voyage alone,' said Pa Kirk, fiddling with his tie.

'I'm a big girl now,' said Patsy, 'and I want to be there when Daniel gets home leave.'

'But surely that won't be till April or May,' said Pa Kirk.

'Oh, April or May, either will rush up on me,' said Patsy.

'You'll catch the winter fogs,' said Pa Kirk.

'I've caught them before, and besides, I think – well, I just think that when Daniel knows how long he'll be home, he might suggest we spend his leave getting married.'

'You think that?' said Pa Kirk.

'There's been that kind of suggestion in his letters,' said Patsy, who had been back home with her Pa since September, after four years in war-time England. 'Pa, I don't want to wait for ever.'

Pa Kirk issued a little sigh. There it was, the near certainty that his lovable daughter was going to make her home in the UK, a country worn out by the war, and therefore not the greatest place in the world for a young couple as vital and energetic in their outlook as Patsy and her English guy, Daniel Adams.

'I wish I could be as confident about your prospects as you are yourself,' he said.

'Pa, you want me to be happy, don't you?' said Patsy.

'I don't doubt you'll be happy in the beginning,' said Pa Kirk. 'In the beginning of most marriages, all clouds are rosy, but they can revert to their natural grey when problems are the kind you can't simply dump in the trash can.'

'What problems, Pa?' asked Patsy.

'I'm thinking mainly about the UK's depressed economy,' said Pa Kirk. 'And the fact that Daniel still has over a year to serve in his Army. If you marry him this summer, you'll have long months without him. And will you have a home?'

'Sure I will, Pa, you know that,' said Patsy. 'With his Aunt Vi and Uncle Tommy. They mailed me, didn't they, to say they'd love to have me back with them? Pa, if I don't get to marry Daniel, I'll wither on the vine.'

Pa Kirk coughed.

'Patsy—'

'I will, Pa, I just will.'

'OK, honey, point taken, even if it was slightly

171

over the top,' said Pa Kirk. 'Was it a quote from a Pearl Buck novel?'

'No, from me, Pa.'

'Well,' said Pa Kirk, 'I'll only ask you to let me make you an allowance of a hundred dollars a month. Say at least until Daniel comes out of the Army.'

'Pa, you're a great guy,' said Patsy. 'I'm not going to say no, I'm going to accept it and appreciate it.'

'I think I hear a car,' said Pa Kirk.

Patsy went to the window, and sure enough there was her Uncle Bradley, Pa's cousin, getting out of his polished black Buick.

'He's early,' she said.

'Great,' said her Pa, 'it'll give us time for a highball.'

'You've already had one,' said Patsy, making for the front door.

'So has Brad, probably,' said Pa Kirk, 'but a second will set us both up for my appointment at the Civic Hall.'

My stars, thought Patsy, as she opened the front door to admit her Pa's best man, will Daniel need a highball when he has this kind of appointment with me?

The ceremony over, the reception was taking place in the banqueting hall of one of Boston's premier hotels, and the new Mrs Meredith Kirk, tall and willowy in dove grey and brimmed blue hat, was making the rounds with her bridegroom. Patsy was with a group of young people. The hall was a swirl of colour, every lady stylishly outfitted, champagne glasses sparkling with light, the buffet gigantic with laden food stands, and Patsy couldn't help thinking everything represented an economy that was high and booming, while two thousand miles across the Atlantic the UK was struggling with the problems of being a country that could not yet provide its people with a full quota of daily calories. The war had been won, but the victory had cost the people dear.

Patsy wasn't too thrilled to find that many of her friends weren't madly interested in the wartime contribution of the British. They rarely mentioned Britain when speaking of how Germany and Japan had been well and truly licked. Having been in England from 1941 until the end of the war, Patsy knew what the UK had gone through, and was a bit sensitive about it. While one couldn't dispute the fact that without the immense resources of America, Britain could never have mounted a successful invasion of France, on the other hand, if Britain had not provided a springboard for the invasion, America could not have stormed the Normandy beaches herself. And that springboard had been resolutely defended for years by Churchill and his people.

It was sad that the British were reduced to a kind of shabbiness, but her friends there, Daniel's family and his many relatives, never had she known them depressed or defeatist. Daniel's quaint old-fashioned granny, always so upright and resilient. His father, Sammy, a man of boundless optimism. His mother, Susie, full of charm and affection, and quick with laughter. His young sisters, Paula and Phoebe, so endearing. His uncles, his aunts, his cousins, all vital and alive. Patsy wanted to get back, to share with them their hopes for a brighter future, and to wait for Daniel to come home on leave.

'Patsy, you dreaming?' A young man, Marvin Baxter, was at her elbow.

'Yes, I guess I was,' said Patsy, making herself heard above the clatter and chatter.

'D'you mind if I ask you if it's true you're going back to the UK?'

'No, I don't mind,' said Patsy.

'Well, are you?'

'Going back? Yes.'

'Hey, that's crazy,' said Marvin.

'Why?'

'There's nothing over there that can't be improved on over here.'

'You mean we've got more of everything?' said Patsy, a little glitter in her eyes.

'We sure have.'

'Then let's be grateful, let's not crow about it,' said Patsy.

'Patsy, I'd like a date,' said Marvin.

'Ask Cecily,' said Patsy.

'Hell, Patsy, everyone dates Cecily.'

'Corblimey O'Reilly, ain't she a lucky gel?' said Patsy.

'Huh?' said Marvin.

'That's cockney for have a banana,' said Patsy. 'Well, kind of. It means "so what?"'

'I can't get the hang of Limey talk,' said

Marvin. 'Patsy, what's over there for you in the UK?'

'People,' said Patsy, 'and four years of living with them in wartime.'

'I can understand how you feel,' said Marvin. 'You went through tough times with them, something we escaped here. The air raids and so on.'

'And the food shortages,' said Patsy.

'The war ended just as I was due to enlist,' said Marvin. 'I never got as close to it as you did.'

'It's OK, Marvin,' said Patsy, thinking of the night when she and Daniel were caught out in the open with bombers roaring overhead. Marvin was a nice guy, but he hadn't been anywhere, hadn't done anything except enter his father's construction business. Still, he'd develop character in time and give off a few vibes. Now how was it Daniel always communicated a hatful of vibes? Oh, some guys did, and some didn't, whether they'd done anything or been anywhere.

'Patsy,' said Marvin, 'I've heard there's an English guy you're thinking of marrying.'

Crowding guests were high on champagne and the convivial infectiousness of the occasion. It was her Pa's wedding reception, but Patsy simply couldn't stop thinking of battered London and of people like Daniel's indomitable old granny.

'See that?' She held up a hand. 'See the ring? It's my engagement ring.'

'From your English guy? I'm out in the cold?' said Marvin.

'You're not out in the cold,' said Patsy. 'You're a friend, your parents grew up with my mother.'

There had been another family friend. Mike Brady. But Mike had lost his life during the German offensive in the Ardennes.

A gong sounded.

'Buffet's open,' said Marvin. 'Come on, let's see what the spread's like, and I'll try to swallow a few mouthfuls, along with my disappointment. All the same, good luck, Patsy.'

People swarmed to the buffet. Enormous quantities had not been provided at the expense of quality. Broiled New England lobsters crowned the repast. Pa Kirk, handsome in his wedding togs, arrived beside Patsy.

'You OK, honey?'

'Sure I am,' said Patsy. 'Where's my stepma?'

'Talking to a reporter who's covering this world-shaking event for the *Globe*,' smiled Pa Kirk. He was well-known to the Boston media. 'How are you, Marvin?'

'Rocky,' said Marvin. 'I guess I had hopes, meeting up with Patsy today, but I've just been struck out by an English pitcher.' He laughed. 'I didn't know they could pitch.'

'There's a guy called Daniel who can throw a curve or two,' said Pa Kirk.

Close by, several guests were running a discussion into an argument, and Patsy stiffened as she clearly heard a man make a statement that touched her nerve.

'The Brits should get the hell out of Palestine, and out of India. They're finished, and so's their two-bit Empire.'

'That's a little hard on them, Simon,' said a woman.

'Well, I'm siding with the kosher guys, and looking forward to seeing them run the Brits out of Palestine. They owe us, the Brits, and Truman should tell 'em so.'

Patsy went hot. Daniel was in Palestine. British troops were policing it because the Jews and Arabs there were at each other's throats. She took a few steps forward. The man in question, swarthy and handsome, glanced at her. She flamed into words.

'That's not fair! The British owe us, I know that, but we owe them something too, and the Jews of Palestine owe them their lives! Yes, for keeping the Germans and the Gestapo out of Palestine in the desert war! How dare you shoot your mouth off like that about our wartime Allies!'

People, shocked, were staring. Patsy put her plate of food on the buffet table and left. Her father went after and caught her.

'Patsy—'

'Oh, I'm sorry, Pa. This is your big day. But that guy's contempt for the British, I just had to speak my own piece and make sure he heard.'

'Simon Oakes forgot where he was, Patsy,' said Pa Kirk. 'Basically, he's OK, and not usually anti-British. Just now, he's very supportive of the cause of the Palestine Jews. It's a cause that has world-wide support because of what happened to the Jews in Germany's concentration camps. I'd appreciate it if you'd apologize.'

Patsy drew a breath.

'I can't do that, Pa.'

People at the buffet were still looking at her. Pa Kirk sighed.

'Do it for me, Patsy.'

Patsy swallowed.

'Pa—'

'I know you will, won't you?'

'All right, Pa,' she said, and went back with him. She made her apology to Mr Oakes, who expressed contrition at having upset her. He assured her he admired her for standing up to him, and that he had no general animosity towards the British.

All this in front of gawping guests, and, of course, it spoiled the day for Patsy, although Pa's bride softened her hurt feelings by taking her aside and telling her that if she had heard Simon Oakes sound off like that herself, she would have told him to save his opinions for other bigots. She could only think he'd let his feelings for the poor, tortured Jews get the better of his manners.

'But I'm glad you apologized, Patsy. That took courage and dignity. I know what your friends in Britain would have called you. A lady. If you're a lady in the eyes of the British, you're tops. I met some of their officers in Paris a while after the war, including a most delightful major, and might have become a lady of England myself if I hadn't already met your father, and if I hadn't known I'm always going to be a little short on dignity. I guess most American women of my kind root for honest and outspoken behaviour, and kick dignity through a hoop. I've done my share of that, Patsy.

You're an exception, and your Pa and I like you for it.'

'Thanks for understanding,' said Patsy.

She longed for contact with Daniel, for circumstances that would allow her to simply pick up her phone and call him.

Chapter Fifteen

The streets of Haifa this evening were dark, apart from light coming from shops and cafés, the majority of which were run by the Jewish population.

Two British soldiers, rifles slung, were patrolling a street. Lance-Corporal Daniel Adams was in company with Corporal Frank Wallis. There seemed very few people about. The quietness wasn't exactly reassuring, and deep shadows looked like giant skulking bats. But neither man was of a nervous disposition. They'd been in Haifa for nearly four months, and there had been incidents, but nothing really alarming or desperate, and their company had just been informed it was due to be relieved at the end of April.

'What d'you fancy, Dan?' asked Corporal Wallis.

'Two more stripes and a sergeant's pay,' said Daniel, lean, lanky and good-humoured. He had his father's blue eyes, and the same kind of whimsical approach to life and people as his Uncle Boots. He also had a lovable girl waiting for him. His American girl. Patsy.

'You've only had a year in uniform – count yourself lucky to have a single stripe,' said Frank Wallis. 'Anyway, I wasn't asking about your ambitions. I meant d'you fancy a swallow?'

'What, for our late supper?' said Daniel. 'No, I don't fancy a swallow or a lark or a blackbird. Just a Palestine leg of lamb with roast potatoes, which I know I won't get.'

'I'm talking about a drink, you daft bugger,' said Wallis.

'Palestine beer?' said Daniel. 'It's baby's water.'

'There's no old ale or Guinness,' said Wallis.

'We're on duty, anyway,' said Daniel.

'Look at that,' said Wallis.

A tracked Bren carrier, as black as the sky, came trundling slowly down the street, a sergeant of the dark-uniformed Palestine police seated beside the driver, and two other men in the back. The policemen and the Bren itself were out to keep the peace or to go into action if trouble flared up.

'Hello, Jacko,' called Wallis, 'who's afraid of the big bad wolf?'

'I bloody am,' said the sergeant, a Northerner, 'don't tha know its bloody teeth bite?'

The carrier rumbled on.

The two NCOs continued their patrol. Both were reliable soldiers, with their fair share of commonsense. Wallis stopped outside a café.

'Solly's,' he said.

'So?' said Daniel.

'Fancy an orange juice?'

'Well, that's allowed,' said Daniel, 'but whose shout is it?'

'Yours.'

'You said that with your eyes crossed and without moving your lips,' said Daniel.

Wallis grinned.

'A real card, you are, Dan.' He looked up and down the street. All quiet. The only time they'd run into trouble had been the occasion some weeks ago, when four Arabs, using a battered old Ford to chase a couple of running Jews, had stopped in a street, piled out to take up the pursuit on foot, and, carrying clubs, run straight into the path of Daniel and Wallis, backed up by two other soldiers. Daniel and Wallis thrust out their rifles horizontally to form a barrier. The confrontation, sudden, was a silent and menacing one until Corporal Wallis told them in simple terms to go home. The Arabs had stood their ground for a few moments, then returned to their heap of a car. The Jews, meanwhile, had vanished. Now, on a night when nothing was happening, Corporal Wallis said, 'In you go, then, Dan. I'll hold your rifle.'

'Listen to you,' said Daniel, 'two stripes to my one are supposed to mean you're more useful to the Army than I am, so why are you telling me to let go of my rifle while we're on patrol?'

'All right, stick to orders, then,' said Wallis. 'Still, it's quiet enough for picking up a couple of orange juices.'

Daniel pushed aside the beaded door curtain and stepped into the café, run by Solomon Gaust, a chubby and cheerful long-time immigrant from Poland. Some Jewish café owners received British soldiers in silent or surly fashion. Most, however, were friendly, like Solly.

There were four customers, all dark, bearded young men in black skull caps. They were drinking coffee, and hardly looked up as Daniel entered, merely flicking their eyes.

'Evening, Solly,' said Daniel.

Behind his counter, gleaming with chromium, Solly smiled.

'Ah, it's you, Daniel my friend. You want?'

'Two orange juices,' said Daniel. Palestine cafés all served very popular orange juice extracted on the spot from the fruit.

Solly put four red-gold Jaffa oranges into the extractor, one after the other, and the sweet juice gushed from the chrome faucet into a glass, filling it. He repeated the process, and pushed the glasses across the counter. Daniel, rifle slung over his left shoulder, took one glass up in his right hand and carried it out to Corporal Wallis. He went back for the other. Solly nodded at his rifle.

'Your best friend, eh, Daniel?' he said, implying that a soldier never treated it carelessly.

'Useful, Solly,' said Daniel, 'but I like people better.' He paid for the juices with Palestine money, and included a generous tip. A bloke from Britain needed friends in Palestine.

'You're a good man, Daniel,' said Solly with some emphasis. The four orthodox Jews took no notice. Daniel carried his glass out and rejoined Wallis, and they downed the pure, refreshing liquid. Wallis took the glasses back.

'Do I look like a dog's dinner?' he asked when he came out.

'Not every day,' said Daniel.

'I think that quartette of the faithful think I'm what the dog left for the monkey,' said Wallis. 'I wonder, by the way, are there still no oranges back home? Bloody shame if there aren't.'

'Plenty in California,' said Daniel.

'You call that useful information?' said Wallis, as they resumed their patrol, eyes peeled from force of habit.

'Fairly useful, if you didn't know,' said Daniel.

'Well, you'd know, wouldn't you,' said Wallis. 'You've got an American bird. How the hell did you manage that?'

'Oh, click-click at first sight,' said Daniel, and thought of Patsy, vivacious, engaging, talkative and kissable. He sometimes felt that on that day of victory celebrations outside Buckingham Palace, his ears had deceived him when she said yes to his marriage proposal. Patsy. What a joy of a girl. She was coming back to the UK in a couple of weeks, and he'd see her soon after his company finished its spell of duty here at the end of April. Home leave was on the calendar then.

A dark-clad woman, approaching, came to a stop. She peered, turned and hurried away on agitated feet.

That alerted the NCOs. They swung round. Too late. Four men, running soundlessly on plimsoled feet, smashed into them. Daniel and Wallis staggered and fell, and their assailants, scarves over heads and around chins and noses, fell with them.

The ground came up to thud into the backs of the soldiers. Their helmets flew off. A furious fighting struggle took place on the ground, and no-one emerged from shop, café or house to find out who was shouting or to see what was going on.

Both soldiers clung to their rifles by the straps the moment they realized the weapons were what the men were after. Punches rained down on them, hands wrenched at their rifles. A fist struck Wallis's mouth, drawing blood from his lips. Daniel quickly turned his head aside to avoid a similar blow from another man. The fist struck his jaw, and stars jumped about. A knee jammed itself into his stomach, hands wrenched at his left arm and then at his rifle again. He hung on. Beside him, Corporal Wallis kicked, heaved and tried to shout again. A hand clapped itself hard over his bleeding mouth. Wallis did his best to sink his teeth into a fleshy palm.

A knife appeared in front of Daniel's eyes. He saw the dull glint of the blade, and his jugular experienced a sensation of horrible vulnerability.

'Rifle! Rifle! Give it!' The words were hissed in thick, guttural English, and the knife pricked at his ribs, not his neck. Every rifle or other weapon filched or plundered from the British containing force gave a tremendous boost to the morale of the faction involved. Fighting, resisting, hanging on, Daniel stiffened his limbs as a rumbling noise reached his ears. He had an instant realization of what it meant. He let go of his rifle strap to immediately find the trigger. A fist struck his temple, and the knee dug tortuously into his stomach. He squeezed the trigger. On patrol, there was always a bullet up the spout. The crack of the rifle whiplashed the air and the bullet struck the wall of a house opposite. The engine of the rumbling, returning Bren carrier burst into noisy life, and the vehicle raced up the street.

The four assailants issued spit and imprecations, leapt to their feet and hared away. From the Bren carrier, coming up fast, came a shout.

'Tha's all right, lads?'

'Get after 'em!' called Daniel, and the Bren carrier raced on in punitive chase.

Someone opened a window, put a head out and took a look. The head withdrew after a few seconds and the window closed again, as if the sight of grounded British soldiers didn't rate a great deal of interest. Daniel, bruised jaw aching, sat up. So did Corporal Wallis, but gingerly.

'Wish I'd never bloody joined,' he said, wiping blood from his split lips. 'Uncle of mine told me I'd enjoy the Army, told me people like soldiers. Never said anything about those who don't. Bloody maniacs, that lot. I heard my own teeth rattle.'

'I think I've got a hole in my stomach you could plant a seed potato in,' said Daniel, climbing to his feet and retrieving his helmet, and Wallis's. Up came Wallis to test his legs.

'Is that one broken?' he asked, pointing.

'Try walking, then you'll know,' said Daniel, bruised back and stomach both sore. 'I want to look in on Solly's, to find out if those four rabbis are still there.'

'Yes, could have been them, so we've got to check,' said Wallis, damaged lips causing him to mumble a bit.

They straightened their aching backs, slung their rifles and returned to Solly's café. They entered through the beaded curtain, and Daniel was sure Wallis was as surprised as he was to find the four orthodox Jews still there. The orthodox elements were supportive of all means to an end. But again these young men hardly bothered to look, again they merely flicked their eyes. Solly stared at the soldiers' bruised faces. He shook his head and muttered like a man who knew what had happened and wasn't in favour of it.

'You want?' he said.

'Nothing, just checking things, Solly,' said Daniel. 'Good night.'

'See you tomorrow, eh?' asked Solly.

'Sometime,' said Wallis. He and Daniel left. They completed their patrol and then returned to the barracks, where they reported the incident to the duty officer, Captain Turner.

'Well, it looks as if you both got a hiding,' said Captain Turner, 'what's more, it looks as if they got away, the slippery buggers.'

'Unless the Palestine police caught up with them,' said Wallis.

'Can't charge 'em, because you can't identify 'em,' said Captain Turner. 'Still.' He grinned. 'If the Bren carrier did catch 'em, perhaps they're getting a hiding themselves. Is that your face I'm looking at, Lance-Corporal Adams?'

'Tell me the worst, sir,' said Daniel.

'Your left jaw's gone missing. There's a blue lump in its place. Report to the MO, both of you. I don't want you spitting blood all week, Corporal Wallis, or you carrying that lump around for a fortnight, Corporal Adams. It's a bad advertisement. Get it seen to.'

Daniel had a restless night, despite treatment. Whichever way he turned, his lumpy jaw got in the way. He thought of Patsy and her ready tongue, and it occurred to him that he much preferred a lively argument with his American girl to tangling with Haifa hotheads.

Two days later, with the swelling subsiding, he felt so much better that he went to the British Army Post Office and filled in a cable form.

Pa Kirk and his bride were honeymooning in San Francisco. Patsy was looking after the house in between taking trips to Boston to buy presents for Daniel, his family and close relatives. Her feelings of excitement climbed high as sailing day became closer. Daniel wasn't going to be at home when she arrived, but his parents would, and his brother and sisters and his granny and grandpa. And his Aunt Vi and Uncle Tom would be in their own home, where they were going to put her up again. So in her close contact with Daniel's family and relatives she'd feel she was in a closer contact with him than here in Boston.

A cable company man arrived on an afternoon that was bitter, with flurries of snowflakes swirling in the wind. He delivered a cable, and Patsy invited him in out of the cold while she read it.

PATSY. LOVE FROM ME. ARRIVING ON LEAVE FOR 14 DAYS MAY 3. IF NOT BUSY COULD YOU MARRY ME MAY 6. MORE LOVE. DANIEL.

Patsy's feet danced.

'Good news, miss?' asked the delivery man, his nose, blue from the cold, welcoming the warmth of the house.

'Good news?' said Patsy. She waved the cable about in a fit of delight. 'Not half.'

'Eh?'

'Oh, it means yes with knobs on,' said Patsy.

'Come again, miss?'

'It's London cockney,' said Patsy.

'You got me there, miss.'

'Thanks a million, anyway, for bringing the cable,' said Patsy. 'Would you like a dollar tip or a cup of steaming hot coffee with a doughnut?'

'Well, little lady—'

'I don't think so,' said Patsy. She was entitled to question that, being five feet seven and a half inches, while the delivery man, despite being a hunk, was only a shortie at about five feet six.

'Well, miss,' he said, 'if it's all the same to you, and my butt being frozen, I'd like hot coffee, a doughnut, and the dollar thrown in.'

He received all that and a warm seat as well. And when he left his butt was thawed out and he had a prepaid reply cable that needed to be wired.

DANIEL, YES MAY 6. YES. NOT HALF. SO HAPPY. LOVE YOU. PATSY.

*   *   *

Since Mr Duckworth's funeral in early January, Emma and Jonathan had been keeping a promised eye on Mrs Duckworth who, on invitation, popped in to have a cup of afternoon tea with Emma twice a week, and to chat to her in quite happy fashion. Of course, she missed Charlie, she said, even his grumbling ways, and he had, after all, been a good husband until the war started. Still, he was gone now and she had to get on with life. Emma gave her sympathy and two cups of stimulating tea on each occasion.

Chapter Sixteen

The ship, due to dock on the morning of Sunday, March 19, steamed past the Isle of Wight on its way to Southampton Water right on time. The day was crisply cold but clear. Patsy, at the rails with hundreds of other passengers, saw the vivid green of the Isle of Wight and, a little later, the coastal variations of Hampshire in the bright light of the sharp winter sun.

And she wondered if the sun was shining on Denmark Hill, and on Daniel in Palestine, where the Jews and Arabs were still in fixed militant disagreement with each other, and with the British peace-keeping troops.

The ship, berthed, was disembarking passengers. Patsy had an enormous amount of luggage. Well, she'd had to allow for permanent residence in the UK. Stewards carried it down the gangway to the quayside, and there she managed to secure the quick services of a porter and trolley, although not necessarily because she had a cabin trunk and two suitcases. More probably because in a dark red

Cossack-style coat and a black fur hat, she looked, to the sprightly young porter, a real bit of all right and no error. The outfit was her Pa's parting gift to her, and he'd also paid for the wedding gown that was in her trunk. He'd be over for the wedding, of course, with Francesca.

'The purpose of your visit, Miss Kirk?' enquired the immigration officer.

'Well, my goodness,' said Patsy, 'you can see from my visa that I'm the intended of my English fiancé, Daniel Adams of London.'

'The intended?'

'Sure,' said Patsy, 'his intended wedded wife. I'm going to be Mrs Daniel Adams.'

'Ah, I see,' said the officer, studying the visa.

'Right now he's in the Army,' said Patsy. 'He's a captain or a corporal, or something. Later on, I guess, he'll be a somebody. Well, he's kind of loaded.'

'Loaded?'

'With career potential.'

'Miss Kirk, enjoy your time with us, and good luck on your wedding day.'

'Well, that's sweet of you,' said Patsy. 'Oh, if I sound a bit lightheaded, it's because I am. Goodbye.'

'Goodbye, Miss Kirk.'

She passed through Customs without any complications, the porter wheeling the laden trolley. Daniel's parents were meeting her and driving her to London. She followed the porter out into the sharp sunshine. From lines of people waiting to meet certain passengers, Sammy and

Susie Adams stepped forward. Susie waved, Sammy called.

'Patsy!'

Patsy saw them, Susie in cosy hat and coat, Sammy in a thick winter pepper-and-salt jacket, dark grey trousers and a dashing peaked cap. She ran forward, and Susie opened her arms to Daniel's intended, the young lady he called his American girl guy.

Polly might once have said that the embrace was a warning of a collective family embrace to come, from which there was no escape, alas. Yes, once she might, during the months when she was waiting to marry Boots and feeling she would end up married to the whole of the possessive Adams family. But after nearly five years at the top of the wives' pecking order, she was an Adams to the core herself.

At the moment, neither she nor Boots had met Patsy.

Sammy was motoring steadily towards Farnham on the A31. Traffic was light, particularly as it was Sunday and car owners hoarded their precious petrol allowance for journeys more important than a spin in the country.

Patsy's cabin trunk, too big to fit into the boot, was on the back seat, Patsy sitting beside it.

'Mrs Adams – Mr Adams – I really am glad to be back.' She had already said that several times. 'And isn't it great, all this sunshine? We've had some bitter weather at home.'

'It'll be cold later, Patsy, when the sun goes

down,' said Susie from the front passenger seat. She was as much delighted as Sammy was tickled that this engaging and outgoing American girl was going to marry Daniel. Sammy had said there were girls and girls, but Patsy was one on her own. He'd also said he was very admiring of Daniel's talents. Susie asked what talents? Sammy said any bloke who had got a promise from a girl like Patsy to walk up the aisle with him had to have talents. Oh, I'm sure, said Susie, except a bride walks up the aisle to the altar with her father, then down the aisle with her bridegroom. Well, up or down, Daniel's still got the kind of talents Patsy likes, said Sammy, and it's up to us, Susie, to give the two of them a worthwhile wedding present. Susie asked what a worthwhile wedding present was. A set of saucepans? No, a house, said Sammy. Sammy, a house? They've got to start with a roof over their heads, said Sammy, and Daniel's got no real money, or a job yet. I know what you're after, said Susie, a house not far from ours, which makes you the clannish son of your mother, but you're still a love, Sammy. We'll talk to them, said Sammy.

From the driving seat, he said, 'Hope you've brought plenty of winter woollies, Patsy.'

'Winter woollies?' said Patsy, conscious of the peace and quiet of the green countryside. 'What does that mean, Mrs Adams?'

'He's thinking about the red flannel worn by the Victorians,' said Susie. 'Grandma's sons have all got a touch of her Victorianism, even Boots.'

'Oh, I've heard a lot about Daniel's Uncle Boots, but I've never met him,' said Patsy.

'Oh, we all adore Boots,' said Susie.

'Count me out,' said Sammy, 'I just respect him.'

Patsy laughed.

'When Daniel and I have gotten our own home,' she said, 'I'm going to talk him into having central heating.'

'Er?' said Sammy.

'Then I shan't need thick winter undies,' said Patsy.

'Blow me,' said Sammy, and thought about the system that was being installed in his new house, which noble home was going up at a criminally slow pace. Still, it wouldn't be long now before it was finished. Chinese Lady would complain about new-fangled contraptions, but Susie was in favour. No more ashpans to empty, no more coal to lug in. He caught her glance and her little smile, as if she knew what he was thinking. And she probably did.

'How is everyone doing now that the war's been over all these months?' asked Patsy. 'Is your business doing great, Mr Adams?'

'It's all forms and permits and regulations,' said Sammy. 'Well, raw materials are still in short supply, and unless you've got one or two useful – um – connections, you go on a waiting list, which I don't believe in. Otherwise, our new house, which Susie and me hoped would be finished last month, wouldn't even be started. I tell you, Patsy, we need a minister of fireworks.'

'Fireworks, Mr Adams?' said Patsy.

'To wake up industry on the dot every Monday

morning,' said Sammy. There ought to be someone in the Government capable of tying a firework
to every manufacturer's shirt tail, he thought.
Boots could do it, and in such a way the bosses and
unions wouldn't even know about until the fireworks went off. Wait a minute, not bloody likely,
not at the expense of him leaving the family business. Boots talked turkey to clients, customers and
buyers, and they all felt they'd been honoured.
There was some female, a Miss Jardine, a local
council officer, who phoned him regularly in
connection with the block of flats currently going
up on the old brewery site. Sammy had a feeling
she just liked to have him delivering his educated
voice into her ear.

'I sure would like to see how your new house is
coming along, Mr Adams,' said Patsy.

'Susie and me'll take you there,' said Sammy,
'and I'll also take you round our garments factory
one day, and let you see our valuable and experienced machinists at work. We've got the best
teams of girls in London. Mind, some of them are
coming up for sixty, but – hello, someone's having
bad luck.'

Ahead, a car was parked on the verge. Its
bonnet was up, and a man had his head under it.
A second man, looking up from the open boot,
stepped into the road and put his hand up, hopefully inviting Sammy to stop. Sammy pulled up
and wound his window down.

'Glad to see you,' said the man, stocky and keen-
eyed. He was wearing a suit and soft cap.

'What's up?' asked Sammy.

'Fouled-up sparking plugs, that's my guess.'
The man, leaning, saw Susie and Patsy. He smiled.
'Afternoon, missus, afternoon, miss. Got a plug
spanner?' he asked Sammy.

'In the tool kit,' said Sammy, and got out.
Nearly six feet, and with a good body, he drew a
smile from the stocky man.

'Thanks, mate,' said Stocky. He turned and
called to his companion. 'Stop trying, Claud, this
gent's got a proper plug spanner.'

'That's a relief,' said Claud.

Sammy opened up his boot, unfolded the
pouch containing tools, took out the plug
spanner and went to the assistance of the second
man, who was also wearing a cap and suit. He was
taller and leaner than his friend, who stayed at
Sammy's car, talking to Susie and Patsy.

'Right,' said Sammy, 'let's have a go.'

'Wish you would,' said the second man, 'I'm no
mechanic myself, I've been trying to release the
plugs with an ordinary spanner.'

Sammy wasn't going to waste time talking. He
wanted to get Patsy home. He slipped his spanner
over the first plug and quickly released it. Taking
it out, he saw that it was oiled up.

'You'll have to clean and dry that,' he said,
handing it to the man, who didn't seem too
interested in it. 'Look, it'll happen again, so get
the car to a garage.' He slipped the spanner
over the second plug, at which moment there was
a scream from Susie.

'Sammy, Sammy!'

He reacted lightning fast, jerking up and aside

as the conventional spanner, aimed to strike the back of his cap and render him unconscious, smashed past his shoulder and down onto the tops of two of the sparking plugs, unintentionally shattering them.

Sammy made his own strike then, using the plug spanner to hit the man hard over his capped head. He collapsed like a folding sack. Sammy, livid, went after the stocky man. This prize specimen, open-mouthed at the quick downing of his confederate, backed away. Sammy charged. The man turned and ran.

Getting back into his car, Sammy said, 'You girls all right?'

'I'm still rigid,' said Susie.

'My stars, Mr Adams,' breathed Patsy, 'I never did see anyone act as quickly as you. That guy's still out, and the other one's still hoofing it. What were they after?'

'Our car, that's my guess,' said Sammy. 'Theirs had oiled-up plugs. But why the hell were they that desperate? Wait a tick, hold on.' He got out again, opened up the boot of the inactive car and found a suitcase. He sprang the locks, and the gleam and glitter of jewellery hit his eyes. He took a look at the grounded man, stirring, then transferred the case to his own car, and for the next ten minutes or so, while he motored into Farnham, Susie and Patsy had an excited discussion with him about burglary most unexpected and burglars most foul.

'Mr Adams, that's the first time I've ever witnessed heroics,' said Patsy. 'Daniel would have been proud of you, he sure would.'

'I'm still shuddering at what that spanner could have done to your head, Sammy, if it hadn't missed,' said Susie.

'Don't remind me,' said Sammy, 'I might faint.'

He stopped at Farnham police station, handed the jewellery to the duty sergeant, gave him exact details of the incident, and the number of the car. The sergeant, despatching a couple of constables to investigate, said it so happened that a burglary had taken place at a country house near Alton that morning, while the family were at church, that the car had been stolen from an Alton garage while in for service, and might he ask what had been done for the man Mr Adams had – er – incapacitated?

'By me? Nothing,' said Sammy. 'I don't give first aid to thieving geezers with ideas of knocking off my own car and laying me out for me funeral. He was rolling about in a bit of agony when I left, and if he's got a headache that'll last a month, bloody hard luck. The other bloke called him Claud. You've sent men after him, haven't you? Good. He's more yours than mine. He can't use the car until he gets new sparking plugs. Here's my card. Got to go now, my motor's full up with valuable cargo.'

'Valuable cargo, Mr Adams?' said the sergeant.

'All right, you tell me what's more valuable than my wife and me intended American daughter-in-law, and I still won't believe you,' said Sammy, and was able to get away a few minutes later. There were no more problems, and they arrived at the house on Red Post Hill just after five-thirty, where

Chinese Lady, Mr Finch, and Sammy and Susie's son Jimmy and three daughters were waiting for them, as well as Tommy and Vi.

Patsy was swept up into the bosom of the family. And then Chinese Lady put the kettle on.

Later that evening, Polly and Boots called. They had promised they would, in order to meet Daniel's American fiancée. Eloise, visiting for the weekend, was keeping an eye on the twins, for Tim and Felicity were now living in the house in Poplar Walk, together with a children's nurse to help Felicity cope with little Jennifer.

Patsy found herself getting to know a couple not at all like Daniel's other aunts and uncles, or his parents. Aunt Polly was just about the most stylish and amusing of ladies, with her own kind of English accent. Daniel's dad had warned Patsy she might find it a bit posh and upper class, but she thought it kind of cultured. As for the uncle, known to all the family as Boots, oh, gee whiz, such a fascinating man, with fine dark grey eyes, the left one, strangely, a little darker than the right. Daniel had said that these two relatives were the oldest of the middle-aged aunts and uncles, but Patsy just couldn't see them in that category. They just didn't have the fading aura of middle age, and she fell easily into enjoyable conversation with them. Knowing from Daniel that Boots had been a staff officer during the war, she asked him how important that was. Boots said that as staff officers were appointed to run about for generals, their importance played second fiddle to their stamina. Patsy said to tell her more. Boots said there wasn't any more, that was it. Patsy laughed and said he was so laid back he was hardly true.

Polly, taken with Patsy's transatlantic buoyancy and her empathy with the clannish Adamses, said, 'What do you think of this family you're going to marry into, my young sport?'

'Oh, that it embraces the many and varied,' said Patsy.

'Is that comforting or frightening?' asked Boots.

'Mr Adams, you don't really mean your family could be frightening, do you?' smiled Patsy.

'Ask me another,' said Boots.

'He meant do you find it frightening that there are so many of us,' said Polly.

'Not yet,' said Patsy. 'I guess time will tell, but I don't see myself running for cover. My problem is that I lose track of some of you.'

'It's the many and varied factor,' said Boots.

'Not half,' said Patsy, which made Polly laugh. 'And then there's Daniel's granny, isn't she cute? Oh, a dear as well. And his grandpa, well, isn't he a perfect English gentleman?'

'He'll be delighted to know you think so,' said Boots quite truthfully.

'You were in England for four years before you went back to America at the end of the war, weren't you?' said Polly.

'I sure was,' said Patsy, 'and I'm never going to forget those years, or the people and the air raids and Mr Churchill.'

'Will that help to compensate you for being so

far from your American home when you're married to Daniel?' asked Polly.

'Daniel will compensate me,' said Patsy, 'he's just about the nicest guy ever. I love my country and always will, it's the greatest, but it's Daniel I'm going to marry. Mrs Adams – Mr Adams – my stars, around here everyone's either Mrs Adams or Mr Adams – I'm so happy to be meeting you.'

'You'll sort us all out in time, Patsy, without getting bitten,' said Boots. 'If you should be, report it to Daniel's grandma and she'll have the culprit executed.'

'At the Tower of London?' said Patsy.

'No, in the garden shed, with the door shut,' said Boots. 'Daniel's grandma regards such matters as exclusive to the family.'

Patsy laughed.

'I'll tell Daniel that,' she said.

'It won't surprise him,' said Polly.

She and Boots were still present when Patsy left in company with Vi and Tommy, to begin a new stay with them. Just prior to leaving, she showed why her large trunk was so full. Half the contents comprised canned foods of every kind, including exotic New England prawns. She was just a little unsure of herself about her gesture, hoping the family wouldn't feel she was kind of taking pity on them because they were still rationed in respect of some foods. There was no embarrassment on the part of the recipients. They accepted the welcome gifts with frank pleasure, and put aside the share for Lizzy and Ned. Tommy and Vi's share was left in the trunk.

Kisses were planted on Patsy, and Polly's little smile was an indication of her conviction that Daniel's young lady was manifestly within the family embrace, and that once she was married to Daniel, ranks would close around her and, under the matriarchal eyes of Chinese Lady, never let her go.

On the other hand, thought Polly, there was the fact that Vi, Susie and she herself had never beaten at the bars, and Helene, Bobby's wife of several months, wasn't even conscious she was in the trap.

Well, the family didn't use barbed wire, just an invisible bond of death-defying loyalty. Indeed, some would have said the watchful spectre of Emily was always present in the ranks.

There was a spectre present at Nuremberg, that of the waiting hangman. It loomed large when the prisoners, taking their daily exercise in the yard, received news that a Japanese general had been executed by the Allies in Tokyo for war crimes. Hans Frank, one of the accused, passed this news to Goering to see how the Fat One reacted. 'You should worry, I should worry?' said Goering. 'Listen, make sure you die with dignity, as I will. You can then be certain that eventually we'll not only be honoured as heroes by our people, they'll also erect a martyrs' monument to all of us.'

It was no wonder that Goering, in his defiance, was a favourite with the guards, and even commanded the admiration of some.

Chapter Seventeen

It had taken Polly months to secure the services of a suitable maid-cook. To begin with, the Labour Government had let it be known that working-class people weren't there to act as menials to toffs and the families of bank managers. No, not any more. Everyone was as good as everyone else, and it was never a socialist principle to encourage or condone a country's poorer female brethren to become domestic servants at wages that made slave labour of them. Further, the war had shown women how capable they were of competing with men for jobs in industry. A girl could expect to do a lot better for herself than be at the beck and call of a toff's wife or some puffed-up middle-class nob.

'Boots,' said Polly at one stage, 'I think they mean us.'

'I suppose they do,' said Boots. 'Well, you're upper class, and I'm a puffed-up so-and-so from a Walworth backyard.'

'Yes, and isn't it a scream, old sport, that a lady toff like me and a puffed-up so-and-so like you go together like caviare and vodka?'

'Caviare and vodka?' said Boots. 'Is that a fact? It's news to me, but I'll take your word for it.'

'Well, whatever,' said Polly, 'shall we cover our heads in shame and hide in a corner?'

'The first time I do anything any politician says I should, or thinks I should,' said Boots, 'you can knock my head off. They mean well, some of them, but when they mistake opinions for wisdom, they turn into interfering busybodies. Carry on looking, Polly.'

'Boots, you're a lovely old darling,' said Polly.

'If you're sure about that, that makes two of us,' said Boots. 'Ignoring the old in your case, of course.'

'Dear man, I spend every day ignoring it,' said Polly.

She resumed her search for a maid-cook and finally, with the help of an agency, secured a bright star, a young woman of twenty-one from Peckham. Flossie Cuthbert. Flossie hated factory work, loved kids, could do wonders with the meat ration, produce the fluffiest kind of omelettes from American dried egg powder, and serve smooth, creamy custard sauce without the tiniest trace of lumps. Nor did she mind giving Polly a hand with the housework or with the twins. She used a bus service to travel to and from the house, arrived promptly at eight, and prepared and served breakfast of cereal and toast within fifteen minutes. Eggs and bacon were still hard to come by. Flossie helped with the children and the housework until twelve, when she did the lunch, and then had an hour's break. She always had dinner ready to be served by Polly at six-fifteen, when she herself then departed to her Peckham home. She had Wednesday afternoons and Sundays off, but she still did near to sixty hours a week. For that, Polly paid her three pounds plus her bus fares, which she thought smashing and a lot more than she could earn in the Peckham sausage factory. Also, it has to be said that by the end of her first week, she adored the twins and had a blushing crush on Boots.

Boots went about with this smile lurking. He seemed to think the whole thing amusing. Perhaps it was to a man who could not relate the present employment of a servant to his standing as a poorly paid clerk during his striving years in cockney Walworth. His Army years, when he had a batman to take care of chores, he put in parenthesis, which was where they belonged. They were a digression, an interval, and nothing to do with his civilian life, past and present.

Chinese Lady had hardly been able to believe her ears. A servant, she said, you and Polly have got a servant waiting on you, Boots? I never heard the like, not in this family I didn't, and I'm not sure I like it. None of us, she said, were brought up to be waited on by servants. I hope, she said, that it doesn't make you a bit above yourself, and too good for the rest of us. All them years as an officer, that worried me a bit, she said, seeing your dad was happy enough being a corporal, but I just don't know that having a servant won't make you upper class. It's different with Polly, she said, she was born that way and couldn't help it, but you're your father's son.

Be of good cheer, old lady, said Boots, I can't see myself as upper class, but if it does happen, I'll ask my doctor if he knows of a cure in three easy lessons. That's not a proper answer, said Chinese Lady, that's one of your airy-fairy ones. Well, old lady, said Boots, we all ought to keep smiling, even if we are running the risk of becoming upper class. Oh, go on with you, said Chinese Lady, and made it her business to call on Polly one afternoon, simply because she happened to be passing, she said.

That enabled her to meet Flossie, to look her over and to decide that at least Polly and Boots had taken on a very respectable young woman. Chinese Lady had been in service herself during her teens, and knew how to sum up respectability in domestic staff. All the same, she still wasn't sure if having a servant wasn't going to make Boots and Polly a bit above themselves. Mr Finch said no, not at all, Maisie, Polly's a woman of the people, and has been since her first days in Flanders as an ambulance driver, and Boots is a natural gentleman, and they'll never be – um – above themselves. Well, if you're sure, said Chinese Lady. Quite sure, said Mr Finch, and Chinese Lady put her reservations aside. She always accepted arbitration from Edwin.

The following evening, at supper with Tommy and Patsy and fifteen-year-old Paul, Vi said, 'My word, what d'you think Sammy and Susie are going to do, Tommy?'

'Paint their new house pink?' said Tommy, the family stalwart insofar as his muscular frame and inbuilt honesty counted.

'A pink house, Dad?' said Paul, curly-haired and, like most of the younger members of the family, able to hold his own with most of the grown-ups. He was attending West Square School in South-East London, along with his cousin Jimmy. It was where some of his relatives had received their education. 'Pink? Crikey, their neighbours'll chuck bricks at it.' He thought. 'And I might chuck a few myself.'

'I think most pink houses are made of sugar,' said Patsy, 'and that the owners have to spend night and day looking out for people who sneak up and bite lumps off them for eating. Of course, you have to have a sweet tooth.'

'And a good dentist,' said Paul.

'Now see what you've done talking about a pink house, Tommy,' said Vi, 'you've got Patsy and Paul in fits. No, I was going to tell you that when the house is finished, and Susie and Sammy move in, Susie's going to have a maid for the housework, like Boots and Polly.'

'A maid like Boots and Polly,' said Tommy. 'Half man, half woman?'

'No, you silly,' said Vi, 'I mean a house servant like the girl working for Boots and Polly. Susie told me when I was on the phone to her this afternoon.'

'Mum, she told you she was going to have a

maid?' said Paul. 'Things will get dodgy for the family. No-one's supposed to have maids these days.'

'Why not?' asked Patsy. 'It's a free country, and a free country is what you all fought to keep.'

'Well, you see, Patsy,' said Paul, 'it's socialism, and under socialism the principle of master and servant is frowned on, which it should be.'

Blow me, thought Tommy, Paul's starting to talk like Alice. Daughter Alice, presently at university, had been talking like a professor for years.

'Help,' said Patsy, 'you're not a socialist, are you, Paul?'

'Yes, of course I am,' said Paul. 'Everyone is. Well, everyone is who believes we're all equal.'

'Now look here, me lad,' said Tommy, 'we're only equal when we're newborn babies. After that, we start getting unequal on account of what we make of ourselves.'

'But, Dad—'

'Eat your rice pudding,' said Tommy.

'It's not rice pudding, it's jam roly-poly,' said Paul.

'Isn't that a cute name for a dessert?' said Patsy. She was used to English food, to the fact that it lacked the meaty body of American food, and that there were no hamburgers. Nor were there ever muffins at breakfast time. But sweet puddings were very eatable as dessert. 'It's lovely, Aunt Vi.'

'Oh, I'm glad you like it, Patsy love,' said Vi, and Patsy smiled. Daniel's Aunt Vi was just the nicest woman, soft-eyed, soft-hearted and uncontentious. She was kind to everyone, even the garbage man, who always growled if the trash can was a bit heavy, which it always was. Aunt Vi set a very nice table, and here they all were, in the well-furnished dining room, the open fire radiating warmth. No-one mentioned the little draughts that whisked around one's feet and ankles. Generally, however, Patsy was delighted to be back among the people she knew so well, and liked so much. She called often on Daniel's parents and grandparents, while counting the days of his arrival home from Palestine in May.

'I'm not sure what me conscience would do to me if mum had a servant,' said Paul.

'Oh, I think I can manage without one, lovey,' said Vi.

'I've got a feeling someone's waving the Red Flag,' said Tommy.

'Of course, I could make allowances for deserving cases, Dad,' said Paul, who could be magnanimous, even if he couldn't yet spell it, 'and I'd consider Mum very deserving of a domestic help, y'know, as long as she treated her as an equal.'

'How about a butler?' said Tommy.

'Oh, my stars, an English butler, Uncle Tommy?' said Patsy.

'Too true, Patsy,' said Tommy. 'English butlers are more equal than anybody, and if we had one he'd even be more equal than Paul. Got that, young feller-me-lad?'

Paul grinned.

'You win, Dad,' he said.

'Tommy, I don't want any butler,' said Vi.

'Well, good for you, Vi,' said Tommy. 'Now we can all be ourselves, which means we're all different, which your grandma, Paul, will tell you is what God ordered.'

'I know, Dad, we all know,' said Paul. 'It's no secret, Patsy, that God had a word with Grandma years ago.'

Patsy laughed. Vi smiled. Tommy grinned. Paul asked for seconds of jam roly-poly.

Sammy and Susie's younger son, Jimmy, was well into his sixteenth year, and contemporary with cousin Paul. He had his own attitude towards his mum's future employment of a housemaid, a daily. The family was due to move into their new house in a week or so. His mum had in mind a pleasant hard-working young woman. Jimmy suggested he'd prefer a sixteen-year-old blonde, since he was approaching the time when his interests might include girls. Right now, he said, he was busy studying science at school and books on chicken farming at home, but he was beginning to feel there could be something else in the offing, like a sixteen-year-old blonde. Sammy said stick to science for the time being, and think about inventing an aeroplane. Jimmy pointed out they'd already been invented, years ago. Sammy said he meant one that ran on clockwork, that a family could keep in its garage and use to fly off to the shops or the office. Jimmy said he didn't think that was a serious suggestion. Susie said well, whatever, she was set on a young woman of forty as a daily.

Jimmy said there weren't many young women of forty about, that he'd never met any himself. Then take a look at your mum, Jimmy, said Sammy, she's a prime example. Jimmy said he was naturally proud about that, but his mum was an exception and so was Aunt Polly. Still, he supposed he could wait, he said. Susie asked wait for what? For my social interests to develop, said Jimmy. Mind you, he added thoughtfully, if such development took too long, he might find himself the same age as young women of forty.

Chinese Lady, on the occasions when Susie's prospective employment of a housemaid was mentioned, said she still didn't know what her family was coming to, what with Boots and Polly already having a servant, and Susie and Sammy thinking about one. She wasn't sure, she said, that everyone wouldn't get above themselves, which if they did would probably mean Lizzy and Ned, and Tommy and Vi, wanting servants too. Jimmy told her it would probably be a natural consequence of everyone getting a bit opulent.

That didn't go down well with his grandma, for she thought the word had improper associations.

In Nuremberg, the trial was proceeding in laborious fashion, hundreds of witnesses and thousands of documents being involved. Some of the accused were restless and uneasy, some surly and muttering, some offended at being there at all, and a few openly penitent. Hess continued to practise vacancy, and Goering remained contemptuous. Early wartime victories may have turned him into a puffed-up braggart and an unscrupulous looter of treasures – drugs and extravagant living may have bloated him – but he did have a brain, an intellect and a shameless boast that the Nazis under Hitler had made Germany a formidable power. He had no intention of apologizing for mistakes. That was how he now spoke of the extermination of Jews. As a mistake, about which, incidentally, he claimed to know nothing. He was quite ready to face up to the prosecutors. American, British, French and Russian, let them all come and he was certain he'd see them all off.

'Mr Adams?'

'Speaking,' said Boots.

'This is Miss Jardine here.'

Ah, the estimable Miss Jardine, frequently in touch with him in connection with development of the old brewery site.

'Good morning, Miss Jardine, are you well?'

'Well? Oh, yes. Thank you.' Her voice was a little throaty.

'Do we have a problem?' asked Boots.

'Pardon? Oh, no problem, no. I believe development of your site is proceeding very satisfactorily.'

'We're very satisfied ourselves,' said Boots. He couldn't fault Sammy's choice of architects and builders. Once his live-wire brother launched himself into a new venture, he made it his business to get to grips with all it entailed. 'And through advertisements placed in the local paper, we already having a waiting list of potential buyers.' It was Tim who had suggested advertising the development, and it had paid off. 'What's on you mind at the moment, Miss Jardine?'

At the other end of the line Miss Jardine's ear tingled to the sound of his mellow baritone. With an effort, she gathered her senses.

'Mr Adams, the council has acquired a large site adjacent to Sayer Street for the purpose of a housing development.'

Sayer Street had been partially destroyed in the Blitz. Its school and many of its houses had been demolished. The damage had extended beyond it.

'Well, there's no better cause,' said Boots, 'but how does it concern Adams Properties?'

'Perhaps if the council leased it to you, Mr Adams?' Miss Jardine now sounded a little breathless. 'Main drainage and electricity will be laid on, and there's a suggestion because of our many housing commitments, that we should offer development in this case to a private company, providing such development is begun within a reasonable time.'

'I know that site,' said Boots, 'but our development intentions are confined solely to the brewery site.' He doubted if the council would seriously consider private development of any of their own sites. In any case, Sammy had long been primarily interested in buying and selling.

'I – we – are thinking in terms of prefabricated units,' said Miss Jardine. 'There's room on the site for a hundred.'

'Prefabs, yes, I've heard of those,' said Boots. Factories that had been building planes were now turning out 'kits' that could be assembled into dwelling units, which were called prefabs and guaranteed to last a good seven years, by which time the Labour Government hoped to have solved the housing shortages. 'Aren't they known as rabbit hutches?'

'Oh, you'd be surprised at the number of families willing to accept them on a temporary basis,' said Miss Jardine, and the throaty note edged back into her voice. 'If – if your company is interested, perhaps – well, perhaps you'd like to come and see me for a detailed discussion.'

'What a happy thought,' said Boots.

'Pardon?'

'Very happy,' said Boots.

'Oh. Thank you.' Miss Jardine's voice seemed to quiver at the prospect of a person-to-person chat in her office.

'I'll talk to my brother and let you know, shall I?' said Boots.

'Oh, please do,' said the infatuated lady.

Boots said goodbye, and then spoke to Sammy and Rachel. Sammy listened with a grin, Rachel with a smile.

'Yes, very amusing,' said Boots.

'Oh, you realize what it's all about, Boots?' said Rachel, who knew, as Sammy did, that Boots had received frequent phone calls from Miss Jardine.

'Sammy's going to tell me,' said Boots, 'unless I tell him first.'

'Well, I ask you, old soldier,' said Sammy,

215

'prefabs rented out at something like a regulated fifteen bob a week? And a hundred of 'em? We pay for them and their installation, collect seventy-five quid a year in total rent, and pay the rates and the cost of maintenance? Not much we don't.'

'These prefab developments are subsidized by funds from the Government,' said Boots. 'I doubt if Miss Jardine had the council's authority to invite the interest of a private developer in this one.'

'Next question, Rachel, is why she invited Boots's interest,' said Sammy, trying to look as if he didn't know.

'Might the answer, Sammy, be more intriguing than the question?' murmured Rachel. 'My life, is Boots a gleam in the lady's eye?'

'Bless me soul, Rachel, that's a shocker,' said Sammy.

'Boots, you're not leading her on, are you?' said Rachel.

Boots, looking amused, said, 'I've seen her just the once.'

'Once is once too much,' said Sammy. 'It's a sign you've still got fatal charm. Talk about knocking 'em dizzy in the Old Kent Road. At your age, you know what Chinese Lady would call it, don't you? Sinful!'

Boots's smile was broad.

'Cut the corn, Sammy,' he said, 'or we'll all die laughing. A good way to go, I know, but I'm not ready for it yet.'

Subsequently he dictated a letter to Leah, who typed it. It was sent off in the post to Miss Jardine, advising her in the most tactful way that Adams Properties, regretfully, were not in a position to take up the offer she had made on behalf of the council.

The lady sighed when she received it.

Chapter Eighteen

Mrs Duckworth was keeping up appearances as a woman bravely adjusting to widowhood, and proving a cheerful but slightly dotty neighbour. Jonathan and Emma saw a lot of her, and she'd burble away about getting a cat or a talking parrot, something to keep her company, although she wasn't too sure about a parrot, since it might be a complaining one which, she said, wouldn't be the kind of company she wanted. Try a budgie, suggested Emma, and Maudie said but the cat might eat it. Jonathan pointed out she hadn't yet got a cat. Maudie giggled and said she was getting soppy in her middle age.

Jonathan helped her with her garden until she suddenly informed him she'd got a part-time gardener, which she could afford and which she ought to have, as she didn't want to take advantage of Jonathan's good nature. Which was a relief to Emma, for Jonathan's good nature might have turned him into Maudie Duckworth's part-time gardener himself. Unpaid.

* * *

Susie and Sammy, with their children, Bess, Jimmy, Paula and Phoebe, were at last installed in their new home on Denmark Hill. Old Walworth acquaintances would have said that Sammy Adams, once an East Street barrow boy, was now lording it in the manner of a Buckingham Palace toff. And those people of Brandon Street able to remember Susie's penurious years in Peabody's Buildings, would have said she was now queening it as a toff's missus.

Certainly, the new house, with its lattice windows, its mellow-toned brickwork and its handsome oak door, presented an attractive frontage approached by a new gravel drive. Susie, in taking on the responsibility of choosing the furniture and all other furnishings, had created a warm, bright and tasteful interior. But lording it, queening it? Sammy would have said well, I grant Susie is my personal queen, but if she ever caught me lording it, she'd make arrangements to dump me on the doorstep with the empty milk bottles. Lord it? Me? I don't even get to wear the marriage trousers more than once a year. Further, Chinese Lady wouldn't allow it. She made sure that even Boots, with his education, never got to lord it over poor old Emily. Mind, he lords it over me, Tommy and Lizzy, but that's different. He's the oldest. All this Sammy would have said, and more, to anyone suggesting he and Susie had turned posh. Sammy didn't believe in a few words, not when thousands were available and every one free.

All in all, he and Susie were delighted with their

new abode, its general spaciousness, its gas-fired central heating that did away with all the work of preparing coal fires, and its large airy kitchen, equipped in as modern a way as the builder and Sammy had been able to devise. It has to be said that one or two of Sammy's black market contacts had helped. There was one slight disagreement, in that Susie said the best room was the lounge, and Sammy said you mean the parlour. No, parlours belong to the old terraced houses of Walworth, said Susie. Susie, it's a parlour we've got, said Sammy. Lounge, said Susie. Sammy said he couldn't invite old friends into a lounge, not without blushing. I've got to put my foot down about this, he said. Well, mind where you put it, said Susie, I don't want to drop a saucepan on it.

Chinese Lady, visiting with Mr Finch, couldn't help being impressed.

'Well, my goodness,' she said, 'I don't know I ever thought any of my family would get to live in handsome houses. There's Tommy and Vi in theirs, and Boots and Polly in East Dulwich Grove. And now you and Sammy in this, Susie, and new too. You sure you can afford it?'

'Oh, it's all paid for,' said Susie, whose parents, Jim and Bessie Brown, had said Hampton Court couldn't look more expensive. 'The business did well for us during the war.'

'Sammy, I hope there wasn't any war profiteering,' said Chinese Lady.

'Now, Ma, you know Susie was always against that,' said Sammy, who'd been against it himself, except in moderation.

'Well, I'm relieved you don't owe anything to the builder,' said Chinese Lady, a little note of pride creeping in. No-one could say her sons had been a disgrace to her. They'd all been good husbands, caring fathers and proper providers, and worked hard in the family business. Mind, Sammy still needed to be watched a bit on account of liking money more than he ought.

'Granny, it's ever so nice here,' said Paula.

'It's nearly as nice as living with you and Grandpa,' said Phoebe, which tactful remark, coming from a nine-year-old, not only pleased Chinese Lady, but brought a smile of affection from Susie, who often wondered when questions would have to be answered about her adopted daughter's natural parents.

'It's a delightful house, Sammy,' said Mr Finch, looking around the well-furnished living room.

Chinese Lady, looking around herself, took on a puzzled air.

'Susie, where's the fireplace?'

'Mum, we don't need any, not with central heating,' said Susie.

'There's no fireplaces?' said Chinese Lady. 'I thought there was something missing. Susie, you don't even have a mantelpiece for ornaments and a clock?'

'There's the wall clock, Ma,' said Sammy.

'It's up there, Grandma,' said Bess. 'Look.'

Chinese Lady lifted her eyes to the wall clock.

'I don't know I could always be looking up at the wall to see the time,' she said. 'I won't say it don't look attractive, but no clock on any mantelpiece, well, I suppose you'll all get used to it.'

'We're working on it, Ma old girl,' said Sammy.

'I don't want any disrespect, Sammy, not in front of your children,' said Chinese Lady.

'Grandma,' said Jimmy, 'we all respect you unreservedly.'

'Crikey, can't he talk, Phoebe?' said Paula. 'Even more than Daniel.'

'Mummy says he'll be like a gramophone when he's older,' said Phoebe. 'I like listening to Uncle Boots best, don't you?'

'Yes, but most of the time we have to listen to Jimmy,' said Bess.

'Fortune favours some sisters,' said Jimmy.

'Come and see the lounge, Mum,' said Susie.

'Lounge?' said Chinese Lady.

'Susie meant parlour,' said Sammy.

Bess, Jimmy, Paula and Phoebe followed in the wake of the adults. They were devoted to Grandma's funny sayings, even if they knew she didn't think them funny herself.

'I can't get over no fireplaces and no coal fires, Edwin,' said Chinese Lady, looking around the parlour/lounge.

'There are advantages with central heating, Maisie,' said Mr Finch, taking in the plush velvet upholstery of Parker Knoll armchairs and settees.

'I've heard Daniel's young lady talk about central heating,' said Chinese Lady.

'It's common in America,' said Mr Finch.

'Well, I hope it won't get common here,' said Chinese Lady, who had her own ideas about what common meant, which included too much of anything or what she called 'language'. 'Specially if it's dangerous, like most new-fangled contraptions. Sammy, you sure it won't electrocute any of you if it goes wrong?'

Sammy grinned. There she was, in her seventieth year, as upright as ever, back straight, bosom firm, and still suspicious of anything that hadn't been built or manufactured in Queen Victoria's time. Her hair, its dark brown colour inherited by so many members of the family, showed only the merest trace of grey, and her only lines were little crow's-feet at the corners of her almond eyes.

'Rest easy, Ma, it won't electrocute anybody,' he said.

'You sure?'

'Believe me,' said Sammy, 'I made a particular point of asking. I didn't want anything in the house that might make me and Susie go up in smoke.'

'And I don't want to come home from school and find just two little piles of ashes,' said Jimmy. 'Of course, I'd know whose was which. Mum's would be a nice tidy heap and Dad's would be next to his old socks, guarding them.'

'Old socks?' said Mr Finch, a twinkle in his eyes as he remembered his years as Chinese Lady's lodger.

'Yes, Dad still keeps pennies and tanners in his old socks, just as he used to when he was young,' said Jimmy. 'We've all heard about it.'

Sammy grinned. Mr Finch smiled.

'Is that boy talking serious?' asked Chinese Lady.

'No, he's just talking,' said Paula.

'Like Daniel does,' said Bess.

'How is Daniel?' asked Mr Finch, whose distinguished-looking figure complemented Chinese Lady's upright carriage. 'And how is Patsy?'

'Daniel's fine, according to his letters,' said Susie, 'but the sooner he's home and out of Palestine, the better I'll like it. Still, we've no worries about Patsy. She's very happy staying with Tommy and Vi.'

'I must say she's a very pleasing girl,' said Chinese Lady.

'She could stay with us now, Mum,' said Bess.

'I don't think your Aunt Vi and Uncle Tommy would like that,' said Susie.

'And with Daniel coming home,' said Chinese Lady, 'it wouldn't be proper for the bride to be living in the same house as the groom, not with the wedding so close.'

'Why wouldn't it be proper?' Phoebe whispered the question into Paula's ear.

'I don't exactly know,' whispered Paula, 'but I expect we'll find out when we're older.'

The tour of the house continued, and it confirmed Chinese Lady's first impression that it was handsome indeed, even if it was common with central heating.

With Patsy still counting the days to the arrival home of Daniel, the United Kingdom under the leadership of Prime Minister Clement Attlee continued its effort to climb out of the doldrums. The wheels of industry were grinding encouragingly, although mainly in favour of export orders. What many people wanted, in order to give a bit of a dash to their post-war lives, was a car. Manufacturers, however, were providing only a trickle to the home market. Boots, Tommy, Sammy and their brother-in-law Ned Somers all had their names down on the order lists of local dealers for new models to replace their worn rattlers of pre-war vintage. Sammy, playing the field, had his name registered with six dealers, for even he, with his many connections, had been unable to find a black market source able to supply him with anything except second-hand models. Indeed, even his old friend Mr Greenberg had been unable to point him at one. Acquisition of a new car was on a par with one's chances of getting hold of the moon, although there were whispers in small back rooms that one day an American daredevil, with the help of captured German rocket scientists, would land on it and bring it home with him. Outside of small back rooms, any mention of scientists made most people feel uneasy. The effects of the atom bombs dropped on Japan were still scary in the mind.

As things were, Sammy declared to Boots that the country was going to the dogs. Boots said they'd know when they were there, the dogs would be at their shirt tails. Sammy said he'd keep his tucked in and tied down. Not a good idea, Sammy, said Boots, far better to let them have your shirt tail than the seat of your pants.

Countrywide, hospitals were preparing to come under Government control, for the Labour Party was determined to provide the nation with a free and comprehensive health service within a couple of years. And the privately-owned coal industry was due to be nationalized, when it would take steps to produce smokeless fuel. Fog, smog and fug born of millions of smoking chimneys had to be aborted, and would be when the proposed Clean Air Act was passed to give the Government power to take a swipe at pollution. Also in the pipeline was legislation that would give workers and their unions the right to secure fair treatment from employers. All this, of course, made Sammy say to Rachel Goodman that Utopia was on its way, that when it landed on her doorstep he'd like her to phone him so that he could go round and have a look at it. Well, Sammy, said Rachel, if the Labour Party can give us half a Utopia, it'll brighten up my doorstep quite a bit. Meanwhile, she kept wondering what donations to the fund for extermination camp survivors were actually being used for, since news items concerning Palestine suggested militant Jewish groups were steadily accumulating arms. Harassment of British troops was increasing, sometimes involving an exchange of fire.

Chinese Lady wasn't sure about the Labour Party which, in her opinion, was full of people who had suspicious connections with Russian Bolsheviks, all of whom she saw as furtive, black-whiskered men with smoking bombs in their hands. That picture, created in her mind by political assassinations before, during and after the Great War, was indelible.

Mr Finch assured her that Britain's Labour Party was entirely democratic and would obey all the rules of Parliament. Chinese Lady said rules could all be blown up in one go by a bomb. She was, as she never hesitated to make clear, a 'Conservatyve'. Well, that Party stood for respectability, which she'd always stood for herself on the grounds that unrespectable people were an aggravating nuisance to everybody. No-one had been more unrespectable or more aggravating than Hitler.

However, all in all, the country was making its effort in this first year of peace, and Sammy and Boots, supported by Tommy in his efficient management of the garments factory, and by Rachel in her own attachment to the firm, were carving out a promising post-war future for Adams Enterprises and its associate companies. Tim was now established with the company, and studying property law. Sammy was approving of his nephew's dedication, especially since Tim's suggestion to advertise the old brewery site development in the *South London Press* had attracted the attention of couples interested in and able to acquire the roomy flats when work was completed. Profitable, that advertisement had been, and you couldn't ask more of a new addition to the firm.

Meanwhile, Tim and Felicity, established in their house in Poplar Walk, were happy with their agency nursemaid as a helpful companion to Felicity and a caring figure in respect of infant Jennifer.

*　　*　　*

Susie interviewed an applicant for the job of a daily help. She had had cards placed in local shop windows. The applicant, Mabel Scott, was a buxom young woman of twenty-six who projected an air of cheerful hustle and bustle, and who soon took over the interview.

'What wages you paying, missus?'

'I thought three pounds a week,' said Susie, knowing that was what Polly paid Flossie. 'I'm looking for—'

'Three pounds? Well, I dunno. Still, what hours you expectin' of me?'

'I thought—'

'I can do from nine till four daily, like, and nine till twelve Saturdays. No Sundays, is that all right, missus?'

'I'd like someone with experience who—'

'Missus, I'm experienced like no-one else. I been doing housework since I was six on account of me invalid mum, and I been a daily from the age of sixteen. I got exemption during the war on account of looking after me mum. Me last job was six years with a nice fam'ly in Herne Hill that moved to Tooting Bec just recent. I've got me references somewhere at home.'

'Yes, I'm sure, but would you do the Monday wash of—'

'Monday wash, missus?'

'Of items I don't send to the laundry?'

'How many in yer fam'ly?'

'Six of us, which might—'

'Six? Well, I don't mind doing unlaundered stuff for six, nor hanging it out. If you'd said ten, well, I'd have had to think a bit, but six, I could manage that. And you'd give me a morning and afternoon break for a cup of tea, like?'

'Yes, of course.'

'Well, I think I could take the job.'

'That's nice of you,' said Susie, who hadn't been given much of a chance to make up her own mind. Still, if the woman was a bit brash, she sounded experienced and competent, and looked it. There'd been two previous applicants, both of them middle-aged cockney women from Camberwell, one of whom said she didn't do things like floor-scrubbing or washing, while the other said she only did afternoon work. Susie wasn't impressed with either. Mabel Scott was different, saying she didn't mind what kind of work she was asked to do as long as her daily time was nine till four. She also said that whenever Susie went out shopping or visiting, she'd guard the house as if it was her own.

'I'm loyal to any employer, missus, and that's gospel.'

Susie took her on at three pounds a week plus lunches. Sammy was pleased to hear it, and said he'd advertise for a bloke to bring the old garden back in order, something Susie was keen to see. She'd like the work done quickly, she said, so that she could look forward to summer roses.

'Orchids, if you want, Susie.'

'Orchids need a greenhouse, Sammy.'

'You want a greenhouse, Susie?'

'Not this year, Sammy.'

'I know a bloke—'

'I don't want a spiv greenhouse, Sammy, this year or next.'

'Now I ask you, Susie, like I have before, do I ever use that kind of geezer?'

'Yes, Sammy, nearly every time I turn my back.'

'Sometimes, Susie, you make me feel I'm a bit misunderstood.'

'Oh, poor old love. Never mind, you're still popular with me and your family, and we wouldn't dream of changing you for anyone else.'

'Well, I'm touched, Susie.'

'You're welcome, Sammy.'

Letter from Patsy to Daniel in Palestine.

Darling Daniel,

Here I am, still living with your Aunt Vi and Uncle Tommy as a non-paying guest. They simply won't take a cent from me, and I love them for making me feel like one of the family already, so I do all I can to help Aunt Vi with her house chores.

Your parents' new house is lovely, you'll like it lots, and yesterday your Pa called to take me, he said, to the family factory, as he'd promised. I asked him if he really meant that, as I didn't think you and everyone else in the family could have been factory-made. He looked kind of blank for a moment, then laughed and said no, you'd all come into the world the same way as other people, and that anyone factory-made would have been sent back by your grandma as a reject.

I enjoyed my visit. Your Pa and Uncle Tommy showed me just how everything gets put together from the time the designs are given the OK. I was so pleased to see how bright and airy the factory itself was, with lots of window space on both floors, as I've heard some factories could make Alcatraz look like the New York Plaza. Your Pa and Uncle Tommy took me round each floor to show me what conditions were like for their workforce. I think they wanted me to know I'm not marrying into a family with a bad record as employers. I spoke to a lot of the women, and no-one had any complaints, they all had nice things to say about the Adams family, and that your Pa, your Uncle Tommy and your Uncle Boots were proper gents. Yes, I'm sure that was it, proper gents, which I know now is a kind of cockney English that translates into American English as real nice guys. Your Pa said all the factory workers were genuine London cockneys from the East End.

I asked what genuine London cockneys were, and your Uncle Tommy said the kind born within sound of the bells of Bow Church in the East End, and your Pa said that although he and his brothers and sister were Walworth cockneys, they weren't considered genuine because in all their years in Walworth they'd never once heard Bow Bells. I had to do some thinking about that, but I still can't work it out. I mean, cockneys are cockneys, and they're all real, like cowboys in Texas or wherever are real, aren't they?

Your Pa told me when he was driving me back to South London that while the factory and the firm's shops are doing well, fashion won't really take off until Europe and the UK are in better shape than now, that the whole of the fashion world is waiting for Paris to stop licking its war wounds and start doing what it does best. He said he can wait, that the fashion *firm's built on a foundation of frost-proof concrete. Your Pa is great on descriptive spiel.*

I'm longing to see you, Daniel, I really am. I've read old-fashioned novels in which lonely heroines go into a decline and only escape expiring when the hero suddenly appears at the deathbed. I'm never going to risk retiring to a bed. You might not turn up in time. I'm going to be a modern heroine and stay on my feet. After all, May is getting nearer every day.

In your last letter, you said there were signs that things were going to hot up out there in Palestine, and that's what the radio news here keeps implying. Daniel, there's shooting going on there now, so please don't get in the way of it. Remember that everything is fixed for our wedding, that I've met the vicar and promised him neither of us will be late for the ceremony. Pa will be over with the lady who's now my stepmother, so make sure you're here too. Meanwhile, I want to say your parents are great, that your Aunt Polly and Uncle Boots would wow the Vanderbilts, and that your brother Jimmy and cousin Paul are almost as cute as you are. There we are, then.

Sackfuls of love from your Patsy.

When the letter reached Daniel, he was just out of hospital. After a concert in Tel Aviv, given by an ENSA company still entertaining overseas troops, a British Army truck carrying a dozen men back to Haifa had been ambushed. Daniel was one of the five wounded men, and was pretty sore about it in more ways than one. He'd suffered a painful shoulder wound, in fact, and a feeling that the shooting up of the truck was a signal from a hot-headed Jewish element that the British had got to pay for not having done an elimination job on Himmler and his concentration camps early in the war.

'No, nothing as far-fetched as that,' said Captain Turner, having listened to this opinion from Lance-Corporal Adams during a visit to the hospital. 'It was simply a message to tell us to push off. We're standing in their way. Without us, they'd take what they want from the Palestine Arabs by force.'

'I'm willing to push off, and that's a fact,' said Daniel. 'I've got a date to keep. At my local church. I don't want it mucked up. Sir.'

'I know, we all know,' said Captain Turner, and addressed the five patients and their bandages. 'Major Jarrett sends his compliments, wants you to know he's sorry the buggers shot you up, and that there's not long to go before the company's relieved by another.' London had come to realize that the policing of Palestine had to be the responsibility of a unit stiff with tried and tested regulars. 'Then we'll all be on our way home to our mothers.'

'We're definitely getting posted home, sir?' said a man who'd had a bullet removed from his ribcage.

'Right,' said Captain Turner, 'and before some of us get our heads blown off, I hope. Our job here is getting to be a lot more uncomfortable, and that ambush could have cost us a few bodies instead of a few wounds.'

'Well, sir,' said Daniel, 'I've got to admit I'm

relieved I'm not just any old body. I wouldn't have anything to look forward to except a military funeral.'

'You're killing me, Corporal Adams,' said Captain Turner.

Out of hospital, Daniel composed a reply to Patsy. He hadn't told her about the ambush and his wound. Patsy had an excitable streak as well as her own share of American get-up-and-go, and he hadn't wanted her to feel she had to come out here and be his Florence Nightingale. His mates would have had hysterics. Now he simply said he didn't feel that either the Arabs or Jews regarded him and his company as their best pals.

He confirmed he'd be home for the wedding, and that he was looking forward to it on the grounds that the marriage certificate entitled him to start up a very close relationship with her. He hoped she'd be in favour, and if so, perhaps she could keep looking for a suitable house, in which they could kind of conduct that relationship privately. They would probably have to rent one until such time as they could afford a mortgage.

Chapter Nineteen

Sammy and Susie called on Vi and Tommy one evening, had a chat with them and then spoke to Patsy by herself.

'It's like this,' said Sammy.

'You mentioned on the phone last night that you've found a house you like,' said Susie.

'Which you feel Daniel might also like,' said Sammy.

'In Kestrel Avenue,' said Susie.

'Very choice, Kestrel Avenue,' said Sammy.

'With a very nice walk to the shops,' said Susie.

'Excuse me, Mrs Adams,' said Patsy, 'but why are you and Mr Adams taking turns?'

'Oh, if I don't get in with my little bits, I don't get in at all,' said Susie.

Sammy grinned.

'Say something else to make me laugh,' he said. 'Patsy, about this house now.' He and Susie had been going out and about with Patsy, searching for something she favoured, but without alighting on anything she thought suitable. Patsy, out with Vi yesterday, had seen a sale board outside a property in Kestrel Avenue. The owner's wife, at home, had happily shown Vi and Patsy round. 'You're really taken with it?' said Sammy.

'Oh, it's a real attractive house,' said Patsy. 'Mr Burton, the owner, is an engineer, so of course his turn of mind took him into thinking of central heating. So he had a system installed, isn't that great? But when I phoned the real estate manager this afternoon, he warned me Mr Burton wasn't thinking of renting out. And when I rang Mr Burton himself an hour ago, he confirmed that.'

'Patsy, how much is he asking for the freehold?' enquired Susie.

'The real estate manager told me six hundred and fifty pounds,' said Patsy.

'Well, look now,' said Sammy, and coughed.

'It's like this,' said Susie.

'We've been thinking about a decent wedding present for you and Daniel,' said Sammy.

'Daniel's our eldest,' said Susie.

'And you being his intended, well, Susie didn't think a set of saucepans was anything special,' said Sammy.

Patsy laughed.

'Mr Adams, you're taking turns again with Mrs Adams,' she said.

Sammy came to the point then. He and Susie, he said, would regard it very kindly if Patsy and Daniel would accept the house as a wedding present.

Patsy gaped.

'We feel that as you're so far from home, and have to make a new life for yourself here with

Daniel,' said Susie, 'we ought to make your wedding present a little bit special.'

'Oh, my stars,' breathed Patsy, 'a little bit special? But it's more special than anything else could be.' It was the kind of gift very prosperous American parents would make to ensure that a son or daughter, when marrying, was given the kind of start befitting the family status. 'Mr Adams – Mrs Adams – oh, thank you.' She hugged Susie, and she hugged Sammy. Susie smiled and Sammy coughed.

'Oh, you're welcome, Patsy,' he said. 'Just leave everything to me, I'll talk to the agents on behalf of you and Daniel.'

'Mr Adams, you and Mrs Adams are so good to me,' said Patsy fervently, and wrote to Daniel that same evening about the ultimate in wedding gifts from his parents.

Boots received a phone call at home.

'Hello?'

'Hello, my dear.' A deeply disguised voice, husky and vibrating, reached his ear.

'Who's that?'

'An admirer.'

'I think you've got the wrong number,' said Boots.

'I'm sure I haven't, I'm sure you're Mr Robert Adams.'

'And you are?'

'I told you, an admirer, and I want to tell you something.'

'Such as?' said Boots.

'I would like to undress you.'

'Not a brilliant idea,' said Boots.

'I would like to see your body.'

'I'd like to know who you are,' said Boots.

'I have a good body myself.'

'Send me a photograph,' said Boots.

'I don't have one, not of that kind. Are you a good lover? What do you do when you make love to a woman?'

'Read the instructions,' said Boots. 'Will it offend you if I hang up now?'

'Don't do that—'

But the line went dead on the caller.

Boots, rejoining Polly by their fireside, said, 'Do we have any odd women friends?'

'Odd?' said Polly. She and Boots, with the twins, had the house to themselves, apart from the hours when Flossie was present. 'Odd, you said?'

Boots recounted the phone conversation with a woman who obviously needed a psychiatrist. Polly blinked.

'No suggestions?' said Boots.

'Right now, old sport, I'm asking myself if I laugh with you or cry for her,' said Polly. 'I can't point you to one of our friends. How about an asylum inmate who picked our telephone number at random?'

'If that's what comes of being picked at random, count me out,' said Boots.

Polly laughed.

'Boots, she actually asked you how you make love to a woman?'

'She actually did,' said Boots, 'and if she phones again and comes up with the same question, I'll pass her over to you for the answer.'

'Well, old darling, I'm a mine of information about that,' said Polly, 'but it's something I keep happily to myself. All kinds of conventions, principles and points of honour took a frightful bashing during the war, but some things are still sacred.'

The phone rang.

'You?' suggested Boots.

'In case it's her again?' said Polly. 'Yes, I'll take her on.' She went to answer the call. 'Hello?'

A pleasant voice responded.

'Oh, hello, Polly my dear.' It was Dorothy, Polly's very agreeable stepmother.

'Welcome,' said Polly.

'I'm on the phone,' said Lady Simms, 'not your doorstep.'

'Your call is still welcome,' said Polly.

'How kind,' said Lady Simms. 'Polly, your father and I would like to know if you and Boots are free to join us for lunch on Sunday.'

'Delighted,' said Polly.

'Bring the twins, of course.'

'Of course,' said Polly, 'and Boots will do his best to see they don't ruin your potted geraniums.'

'I'll take charge of Boots,' said Lady Simms, 'and your father will do his best with the twins.'

'Where will that leave me?' asked Polly.

'In the conservatory, guarding the geraniums, in case the twins outmanoeuvre your father.'

'While you monopolize Boots?' said Polly. 'It's

against all the rules, you know, one's step-mother being a rival for the affections of one's husband.'

'Oh, at sixty, Polly my dear, I can assure you I'll return him untouched to you. There, then, your father and I will look forward to seeing you all at about twelve-thirty on Sunday. Goodbye now, love to Boots.'

'Till Sunday, then, Stepmama,' said Polly.

Boots was pleased to be told the call had been from Lady Simms and not a woman odd in the head.

In Nuremberg the defendants were being made to answer for their crimes as witnesses told what they knew about cruelty, barbarity, murder, extermination, and the razing of Russian villages, together with the massacre of inhabitants. Such witnesses were men and women who had escaped murder, genocide or massacre, and were able to tell the court the extent of the practice of cold-blooded barbarity and calculated inhumanity.

It was too much for one defendant, Hans Frank who, as Governor-General of occupied Poland, had been responsible for authorizing the extermination of a colossal number of Jews. He declared himself damned for his sins. Goering attacked him for his admission of guilt, and for saying that Hitler must have known of the atrocities, for that meant Goering himself would have known too, something he had always denied. He was livid, especially as Frank constantly referred to him as 'the fat one'.

The trial was rolling on, slowly but relentlessly, giving the world details of the sheer savagery of the Nazi regime and the thousands of Germans who became its inhuman tools. Prosecuting counsel for the four Allied countries, America, Britain, France and Russia, all produced witnesses and damning documents, and all took their turn to cross-examine individual defendants.

However, Goering was still a figure of defiance in his contempt for the tribunal and his insistence that while the war had been fought in a total way, the Nazis were no more guilty of excesses than the Allies.

Many of the American guards not only admired Goering, they developed a liking for the Fat One. He could be very amusing. Being amusing made up a lot for being an accessory to extermination.

In late March, he finally took the stand, and did so with confidence. Given the right kind of questions and openings by his defence counsel, he delivered answers and statements that turned into a clever evaluation of how good Hitler and the Nazis had been for Germany, and how the advent of war had come about through the necessity of removing the threats posed by its enemies. He testified to the effect that nothing he had done or ordered could be construed as criminal, that he had only ever acted as a soldier of honour should, and as such he could state he knew nothing of the extermination camps. Such knowledge was exclusive to Himmler. As for the indictment that Germany's conduct of the war broke all the rules and conventions, he quoted the words of one of his country's greatest opponents, Winston Churchill:

'"In the struggle for life and death, there is, in the end, no legality."'

During the lunch adjournment, Sir David Maxwell-Fyfe, British counsel, signalled Whitehall to find out if Churchill had indeed said this, and the Foreign Office replied that the words actually used were, 'There could be no justice if, in a mortal struggle, the aggressor tramples down every sentiment of humanity, and if those who resist remain entangled in the tatters of violated legal convention.'

Goering's brief version had been brilliant.

When cross-examination by the prosecuting counsel began, it was the beginning of a prolonged courtroom duel between Robert Jackson, a master lawyer of America, and the man still thought of by most Germans as a jolly good fellow. Goering, as he had promised himself and his codefendants, was on his toes from the outset. His answers, his sallies, his ripostes and his counter-suggestions came from a mind cleared of drugs by prison routine, a mind sharp and full of well-remembered facts. He could not be shaken from his insistence that he knew nothing of the acts of extermination, although he frankly admitted he did not regard Jews as a good influence on a nation. Robert Jackson derived very little satisfaction from the duel, and found himself bogged down and outwitted at times. At the end, Goering was adjudged a smart old fatso by American reporters present.

Sir David Maxwell-Fyfe began to put the case from the British point of view. Goering actually smiled at him, such was his conviction that he could make them all flounder. Sir David, however, had no intention of going into everything relating to the weighty indictment, as his American counterpart had. He made an issue of two counts only. The first concerned the murder of the fifty RAF fliers, recaptured after escaping from a prisoner of war camp. He suggested to Goering that it was impossible for him and his *Luftwaffe* deputy, Field Marshal Milch, not to have known about it, since the order emanated from Hitler's headquarters, where they were in regular attendance. Goering said neither of them knew, and he said so with the air of a man of integrity.

Sir David shot the next point at him, accusing him, along with Milch, of trying to shift the responsibility for such an unheard-of crime onto the shoulders of their junior officers.

That shook Goering, for it was an attack on his honour as an officer of pre-eminent rank. He shouted that the accusation was untrue. Sir David at once told him he had done nothing to prevent brave men being executed, that in fact he co-operated in a series of abominable murders, totally against the rules of any war, and totally against the principles of honour. Goering himself now began to flounder, and to bluster, as he was harassed and bombarded, and given no time to turn his answers into mocking or witty speeches. Sir David, staying with the incident, kept on at him, and suggested that if the defendant really was unaware of the murders, then perhaps he had been on leave at the time. Goering, seizing on that, shouted yes, it was a fact, he actually had been on leave and away from headquarters during the relevant period.

It was Sir David's turn to smile. Goering had fallen into the prepared trap. Well, yes, said Sir David, it was quite true, the defendant had been on leave until 29 March 1944. Goering perked up. But, said Sir David, most of the executions of the fifty fliers took place in April, not March.

Goering fell from his pedestal, and he took a further hiding when Sir David, taking up the second count, referred to his repeated insistence that he and Hitler himself knew nothing of the extermination of the Jews. Nothing at all, said Goering. Really? Sir David at once destroyed the case for Hitler by quoting his recorded words to the wartime leader of Hungary.

'"The Jews have been treated as germs with which a healthy body has been infected."'

What, asked Sir David, could that mean other than extermination? The shaken defendant fumbled for an answer, but was given no time to voice it, for Sir David quickly attacked his own professed ignorance by referring him to an official area report sent to him in 1942.

'"There are only a few Jews left alive. Tens of thousands have been disposed of."'

On that quote, Sir David sat down, his comparatively brief cross-examination finished, and Goering knew that on these two counts alone he had failed himself, and that the hangman would be waiting for him. While he was not afraid of death, he was appalled at the thought of being hanged.

Mr Finch phoned Boots.

'Did you catch the news report of today's hearing, Boots?'

'I did, yes,' said Boots.

'What did you think?'

'That Goering got trapped and is going to hang.'

'How do you feel about that?' asked Mr Finch.

'Happy,' said Boots.

'You share that sentiment with your mother and me,' said Mr Finch.

Chinese Lady's satisfaction was coupled with a heartfelt wish that once they'd all been hanged, the wireless would at last stop going on about that man Hitler and his heathen Nazis. It was time it cheered people up a bit.

'I've been thinking,' said Jonathan.

'Click, click,' said Emma. They were relaxing in front of the fire and listening to radio music. Music could be relaxing or uplifting. Emma's favourite programme was a daytime one, 'House-wives Choice', for it frequently featured her favourite crooner, Bing Crosby.

'I've been thinking,' repeated Jonathan, who still had fond memories of the pre-war programmes featuring big bands, especially Harry Roy and his most popular number, 'Tiger Rag'. 'Deeply.'

'Deeply?' said Emma.

'Let's see, how old are we?'

'I know how old I am, twenty-three,' said Emma, looking just the job in a snug mushroom-coloured sweater and pencil-slim skirt of chocolate brown. 'Are you having trouble working out your own age?'

'I think I'm twenty-six,' said Jonathan. 'Blow me, Emma, between us we add up to nearly fifty.'

'Fifty?' said Emma. 'Give me some good news.'

'Good memories, Emma, I've got a treasure chest of those,' said Jonathan.

'Good memories of what?'

'Of our time down in Zummerzet,' said Jonathan. 'You in the hay on Sundays in August, and me out of camp and with time to spare to roll with you while old Hitler saw doom coming closer and closer.'

'And me still finding bits of hay in my hair days after,' said Emma. She smiled. 'Saucy memories, they are, Jonathan, and don't I know it.'

'And safety first because we decided to wait until old Hitler was a back number and the war was over before we started a family,' said Jonathan. 'So there you are, I've been thinking, should we start one now, and before we add up to sixty?'

'Would it make you happy, Jonathan?'

'Make me durned proud of you, Emma, that it would,' said Jonathan.

'Well, aren't you a love, Jonathan?' said Emma. While in Somerset, they had discussed having children, but decided in the end to wait until the war was over. 'Yes, it's time we made a start, isn't it?'

246

Jonathan essayed a movement that made her issue a little yell. 'No, not right now, you sexy ha'porth.'

'There's music playing,' said Jonathan.

'Sounds thrilling,' said Emma, 'but forget using the fireside carpet. There's a bed upstairs waiting for us at half-past ten.'

'We'll be older by half-past ten,' said Jonathan.

Emma laughed.

'Not all that much,' she said. 'Let's say tonight's the night. Any more comments?'

'Well, tonight won't be too soon, I reckon,' said Jonathan. 'Years run away, Emma, and you can be directly sure I might not have as much spring by the time we add up to sixty.'

Emma shrieked.

Chapter Twenty

By mid-April, lambs of the fields were gambolling
and springtime's wild cherry blossom was colour-
ing suburban avenues. Young people went to
dance halls, packed the cinemas and bought
gramophone records of their favourite crooners.
Bing Crosby was still at the top, but lurking in
his shadow was a skinny newcomer called Frank
Sinatra. It was said he could make schoolgirls
swoon *en masse*. Lock up your daughters, that was
the advice given to American parents.

Not everyone found that peacetime gave them
peace of mind. People who had suffered frightful
experiences during air raids or from close en-
counters with the flying bombs, were troubled
by sleepless nights or by scarifying dreams that
brought them violently awake. And servicemen
who had known hideous moments on a battlefield
or at sea or in the night air or in other fields of
conflict, they too suffered bad nights.

People of cities like London, Coventry,
Plymouth and Liverpool could dream of their
homes being blown up around them and of themselves hurtling into everlasting blackness. Freddy

Brown could wake up sick and sweating from a sleep that took him back into the jungles of Burma. Tim suffered constant reminders at night of Commando raids, particularly reminders of the blood and thunder nature of the Schledt assault. Bobby and Helene had their unwelcome dreams. For Helene, hers was always of red-eyed Gestapo men chasing them down a black tunnel becoming progressively smaller. Bobby was wracked by similar images. And even Boots, who rarely allowed ugly imaginings to disturb the even tenor of his mind for long, had nightmarish dreams about Belsen.

Cassie Brown awoke one night and knew immediately that Freddy was not beside her. She sat up and switched on the bedside light. Freddy, silent and still, was standing at the window, the curtains drawn back, looking out at the darkness of the night.

'Freddy?' she whispered.

He turned.

'Sorry if I woke you, Cassie,' he said.

'Don't be sorry, Freddy, I know about Burma, don't I?' said Cassie.

'I hope it's not going to hang about for always,' said Freddy. He came to sit on the edge of the bed and to look at her, her dark hair softly spilling. His Cassie, his young street mate of years ago, and his compensation for what war with the Japs had done to his beliefs and to his peace of mind. 'I've got to tell you something I know you know already, Cassie, that the jungles and swamps of Burma were their own kind of hell, and so were the Japs. If you trapped a pocket of them, they wouldn't surrender, you had to kill 'em all, right down to the last man, and it cost us, every time. What I mean, Cassie, is that I never knew the world could be that ugly, but I did know you were here back home, and the kids, and your good old dad, and my Ma and Pa, and that kept one corner of the world like something to dream about. I want you to know, Cassie, that other dreams, bad ones, don't really matter, not while you're here sitting up in bed in your white night-shirt.'

Cassie, eyes misty and a catch in her voice, said, 'Nightdress, Freddy.'

'Which is a bit off-shoulder and not much like a suit of armour,' said Freddy, and climbed back into bed with her.

'Freddy—'

'Let's go mad,' said Freddy.

'Put the light out,' said Cassie.

'Don't worry about it,' said Freddy.

'If we're going to go mad,' said Cassie, 'put it out.'

Out went the light.

On her first Monday as Susie's daily, Mabel Scott proved as good as her word, first helping to sort out what washing was required to be collected by the laundry van. Nothing like an automatic washing machine was available from manufacturers at this time, but the central heating provided gallons of hot water for a manual wash. Further, Mabel sang at her work, and if she was mostly out of tune, Susie wasn't inclined to be critical.

Subsequently, Mabel went through the house hoovering the carpets, tidying up and helping Susie to make the beds. She said what a nice house it was, and that it was going to be a pleasure working in it. Employer and daily parted on very friendly terms at four o'clock.

The following days were also mutually satisfying, Susie happy to have her workload so lightened, and at having found a daily on a par with Polly's Flossie. Chinese Lady, of course, happened to drop in while passing. If she'd had doubts about whether or not it was right and proper for anyone in the family to have a servant, Mr Finch had gradually convinced her it was actually a sign of remarkable achievement. From the depths of poverty, he had said, your sons have climbed ever upwards to the point where two of them were now able to provide welcome domestic help for their wives. Very remarkable, Maisie, he said. Well, if you think so, she said.

She ran her eye over Mabel Scott, who responded in the breeziest fashion to the introduction, and Chinese Lady was able to report to Mr Finch that Susie's domestic help seemed fairly respectable, if a bit loud. Mr Finch presumed not as loud as a brass band? Goodness me, no, of course not, said Chinese Lady. Then I daresay Susie will be able to adjust, said Mr Finch, never known to lack a reassuring or soothing voice.

With the twins seated at the kitchen table and Flossie supervising their mid-morning intake of warm milk and a biscuit, Polly answered a phone call.

'Hello?' No answer. 'Hello?' Further silence for a few seconds before the caller spoke in a gruff, husky voice.

'Are you Mrs Adams?'

'Yes,' said Polly, alerting.

'Mrs Robert Adams?'

'Yes. Who are you?'

'Someone with a message for you.'

'What message?' asked Polly.

'Drop dead.'

So this is the lady lunatic, thought Polly.

'Are you sure you mean that?' she asked.

'Yes. Drop dead.'

'What a silly and unfortunate woman you are,' said Polly.

The caller rang off.

When Boots arrived home, Polly let him know that Mad Martha had been on the phone again.

'She's going to make this a habit?' said Boots.

'I suspect just that,' said Polly.

'Was she unpleasant?'

'Only to the point of telling me to drop dead,' said Polly.

'That's unpleasant, full stop,' said Boots.

'You can say that again, and with feeling,' said Polly. 'I have to ask, have you lately met some sex-starved female who's taken a fancy to you?'

'How does one recognize a sex-starved female without getting into bed with her?' asked Boots.

'The species brush up against you,' said Polly.

'I can't recollect that happening to me, lately or at any time,' said Boots.

'Could it possibly be one of our friends or acquaintances?' asked Polly.

'Acquaintances?' said Boots, and thought then of Miss Jardine and the unnecessary phone calls she had made to him regarding the development of the old brewery site. She had capped that by offering him a discussion in her office about a site earmarked for prefab dwellings. 'Let me tell you about a woman council officer, Polly.'

He gave her all the relevant details.

'You old charmer,' she said at the end, 'that's it, of course. You appeared before her and she crashed at first sight of you.'

'Is that a sensible remark?' asked Boots.

'Top of the list of sound guesses,' said Polly. 'Look here, while I'm fighting off wrinkles during the next ten years, are you going to send dotty females dottier?'

'I've no idea why that should happen,' said Boots.

'You did it to me when we first met,' said Polly.

'I'll agree that when we first met, you were at your wildest and woolliest,' said Boots.

'Those were my suffering days, old sport, the mad, sad days that were a leftover of the Great War,' said Polly. 'Tell me, are you going to do something about Miss Jardine? We both feel, don't we, that it could be her?'

'First let's see if she phones again,' said Boots,

'if she does I'll call her bluff by naming her.'

'Yes, see if that knocks a hole in her head,' said Polly.

Meanwhile, Patsy was on a high. Daniel should be sailing for home soon.

In Haifa, his company was on evening parade, waiting to hear the names of men detailed for patrol duties. Sergeant Clements of C Platoon, laden with the responsibility of having to report absentees, stepped forward, saluted Captain Turner and informed him that Corporal Wallis and Lance-Corporal Adams were not on parade.

'What?' said Captain Turner.

'Have to report, sir, that since going off-duty for the afternoon, they haven't been seen.'

'Did they go into town?'

'Yes, so I was told, sir, about fourteen-hundred hours.'

Captain Turner silently swore. Neither Corporal Wallis nor Lance-Corporal Adams could be called irresponsible. He turned to Sergeant-Major Drummond.

'Sergeant-Major, have the camp searched by C Platoon, while I detail this evening's patrols.'

'Right, sir.'

No sign of the missing NCOs was found. Captain Turner then interviewed all the men of C Platoon. What they had to say confirmed that Wallis and Adams had gone into town early that afternoon, and that no-one had seen them since.

'Well, bugger it,' said Captain Turner, 'didn't that worry any of you?'

'We just wondered why they missed tea, sir,' said one man.

'You just wondered, did you?' said Captain Turner. 'A great help, I don't think.'

'Well, if there'd been any report of an incident—'

'That would have made you do more than wonder?'

'Well, yes, sir.'

'Bloody brilliant,' said Captain Turner, and shot away to report to Major Jarrett. Subsequently, he charged out of the camp in a jeep, taking with him the Sergeant-Major and two men. At the same time, all the detailed patrols were ordered to contribute to the search.

It lasted for hours, but produced no results. No information was forthcoming from any inhabitant, shopkeeper or café owner. Out of hundreds of people, not one, apparently, had seen anything of the two NCOs. Captain Turner had to consider the possibility that if either Arabs or Jews were responsible for their disappearance, neither faction would rush forward to inform on the other, since both hated the British more than they hated each other. Some leading Arabs, including the Mufti of Jerusalem, had frankly favoured a German victory in the war of the Western Desert, although what blessings Himmler would have bestowed on them was a mystery. Blast them all, thought Captain Turner.

'Sergeant-Major,' he said, 'if we're up against a

wall of silence as thick as this, we've got real trouble. It could have been an assassination job, we could be looking for dumped bodies. Corpses.'

'I've got a hell of a headache,' said the Sergeant-Major, 'don't make it worse, sir.' He knew, as well as anyone serving in Palestine, that attacks on British troops in Jerusalem and Tel Aviv had resulted in more than one death, although these had been at night.

The house-to-house search was called off at midnight, with the British Army's headquarters in Jerusalem having been notified of the two missing NCOs from the Haifa camp.

Meanwhile, in a small unlit room with a tiny window, barred by a thick steel rod, Corporal Wallis and Daniel sat on a dilapidated sofa, wrists bound behind their backs, ankles lashed, and gags tight between their teeth. The door was locked, the air stuffy, communication impossible, rage at a peak.

Close to midnight, a key turned, the door opened and in walked a man, face hidden by a balaclava. He carried a jug of water. A second man, similarly faceless, followed, a revolver in his hand. It was fitted with a silencer. The first man placed the jug on a table and released Corporal Wallis's gag. The second man thrust the revolver against Wallis's temple. It constituted a threat to shoot him if he shouted. Wallis, sensibly, used the moment to gulp in air unimpeded by a gag. The jug of water was lifted to his lips and tilted. He drank thirstily and noisily.

The gag was again applied, and tightly tied at

the back of his neck, when Daniel was then given his turn to breathe freely and to take in welcome draughts of water. He said nothing. He suspected he would get no answer other than a hard smack on his mouth from the back of a hand. The two faceless men spoke not a word. They satisfied themselves that the gags were securely back in place, and that the two NCOs remained tightly bound.

They disappeared, locking the door behind them, and leaving Daniel with the feeling they were men with a purpose that could embrace something very nasty.

We're going to be here, like this, all night? Corporal Wallis asked himself the same question. The answer obviously being in the affirmative, he swore into his gag.

I'm bloody dreaming, thought Daniel, and it's a nightmare. If I start believing it's real, I'll have to live with it all night. I'll be gibbering by morning.

He and Wallis had been jumped immediately on entering a café, jumped by masked men, smashed to the floor, smothered and chloroformed all in a matter of seconds. When they came to, they were in this room, bound and gagged. They had not been spoken to, and nor had they had company. None of their assailants had sat guarding them, watching them or letting them know the reason for making prisoners of them. The small room was very much a prison, their bonds and gags emphasizing the restrictive nature of their captivity.

Daniel had a sickening feeling that he and

Frank Wallis were not going to like the outcome. He thought of his home, of his family, and of Patsy.

The small dark room became darker.

Hours into the sleepless night, Corporal Willis twitched, his elbow nudged Daniel, and he turned sideways. Daniel made a similar movement and felt Wallis's fingers fumbling at the cord lashing his wrists. It was an effort drummed up by hours of tortured frustration. Daniel squeezed his wrists tightly together, hoping to loosen the cord a little. Wallis's fingers searched blindly for the knots. The knots were hard and immovable. Wallis gurgled blasphemy into his gag.

I know how you feel, thought Daniel, and I probably feel worse.

The effort was of a hopeless kind. Wallis gave up. They both tried to sleep, for both felt worn out, but their situation kept them too mentally disturbed. However, they managed to snatch moments of fitful slumber, and did so by Daniel easing himself off the sofa and lying on the floor, while Wallis managed to stretch out on the sofa.

The night passed with torturing slowness.

It was a little after dawn when the two masked men reappeared, once again bringing a jug of water, the other pointing the revolver as a threat. The NCOs were given water, and then each in turn was taken to the adjacent lavatory, released from his bonds and given time to relieve himself in the presence of the man with the gun, who stood silent at the open door.

Daniel risked a few quiet words.

'What's this all about?'

'Six million innocent Jewish people asked that question, and the answer for all of them was death.' The man's voice was a sibilant whisper.

'Are we to blame?'

'Yes, you as much as all the others who did nothing.'

'That's—'

'Shut up.' The snout of the silencer jabbed into Daniel's ribs. 'Shut up.'

Daniel and Wallis were given a piece of dry bread, some sardines and water for their breakfast, consumed with their hands free, but both men watching their every move. Well, thought Daniel, they don't intend to starve us, they're keeping us alive, but for what? Wallis thought that given a lucky turn of fate, he'd ask for ten minutes alone with each of these men.

After they'd eaten, he and Daniel were bound and gagged again, and the men left. Daniel existed for a little while on the flavour of the sardines.

Captain Turner and a large search party issued from the camp immediately after an early breakfast. British Army headquarters had given furious orders for the missing NCOs to be found.

In London, the afternoon edition of the *Evening News* contained a paragraph to the effect that two British soldiers were missing in Palestine. It was hoped they were merely guilty of being absent without leave.

259

* * *

Polly, talking about the protracted trial of the Nazi war criminals, said, 'It seems to me, Boots old thing, that the whole gang might have to face the hangman, and if any of them like the look of him, I'll eat your hat.'

'Why not your own?' asked Boots.

'Any of your hats is just a hat, old scout,' said Polly, 'any one of mine is a millinery accomplishment dear to my heart.'

'Spoken like a true woman,' said Boots.

The phone rang. Boots and Polly exchanged looks.

'Yes, I'll go,' said Boots.

'Best of luck, old soldier,' said Polly.

Boots, picking up the hall phone, said 'Hello, yes?'

'Ah.' It was the voice disguised to hoarse gruffness. 'There you are. Do you know how much I would like to go to bed with you?'

'No, I frankly don't know,' said Boots, 'and nor do I know if you'd find me a disappointment.'

'Never. It would be rapture just to have your body close to mine.'

'What gives you these wild fantasies?' asked Boots.

'You. I want to undress you and look at your body and your manhood.'

Boots treated himself to a smile.

'Did something traumatic happen to you during the war?' he asked. 'It happened to many people under the stress of the air raids. Bombshock, I believe, a cousin to shellshock.'

'Nothing happened to me until I met you, and I want to meet you again.'

'Miss Jardine—'

'What?' The gruffness of the voice wavered a little.

'Miss Jardine, yes, I think it's you,' said Boots.

'Who's Miss Jardine? If she's a lover of yours, I'll find her and kill her. I'll watch your house, I'll follow you.'

'I've a feeling, Miss Jardine, that you need a doctor, a specialist—'

'Miss Jardine is a cow, and I don't need a doctor, I need you.'

'I see,' said Boots. 'Where can we meet?'

'You would like that?'

'I'm tempted, naturally,' said Boots.

'Would you like to spank me?'

'That's a temptation of a different kind,' said Boots.

'How exciting. Well, you lovely man, I'll tell you where we can meet when I next phone you.' And the caller rang off.

Boots reported to Polly, and Polly, receiving the gist of the conversation, didn't know whether to laugh or sound alarm bells.

'Boots, she's quite mad.'

'Not quite sane, I agree,' said Boots.

'She actually said she'd like to look at your body, at what makes a man of you?'

'Fact,' said Boots.

'Oh, ye gods,' said Polly.

'I should have told her I'm not a pretty sight,' said Boots.

'Don't be modest, darling, I've never faulted you,' said Polly. 'Did you say she didn't like being called Miss Jardine?'

'It sent her dotty,' said Boots. 'I wonder, have I made a wrong guess?'

'But who else could it be, for heaven's sake?' said Polly.

'Yes, who?' said Boots. 'I'll stick with my suspicions, and when she rings again, I'll have another go at her.'

'When?' said Polly. 'Yes, it's when, of course, not if. How'd you like having an anonymous admirer wild to see how much of a man you are?'

'How much does she expect?' said Boots.

'All of you,' said Polly. 'How do you feel about giving her a spanking?'

'I frankly feel she's in serious need of one,' said Boots.

Chapter Twenty-One

All leave for British troops stationed in Haifa was cancelled, and a daily search was taking place. Two Security men arrived from British Army headquarters in Jerusalem, and conducted an interrogation of the men under Major Jarrett's command in an attempt to jog memories and extract some kind of clue. It was Captain Turner, however, who elicited useful information from a man in C Platoon.

'Don't any of you know anything of where Wallis and Adams might have gone? Out of habit, say?' He'd asked that question on several previous occasions.

'Only that they always went into town together, sir,' said one man.

'There's one thing I've just thought of, sir,' said another man. 'They'd have gone into some café or other. We all do when we're in town. You get real coffee and pukka cream pastries.'

That was the useful information. It put Captain Turner and the Security officers on an organized visit to every café in Haifa. Such places had already been visited during the earlier search, but this time interrogation of proprietors was to be a lot more thorough.

Meanwhile, Wallis and Daniel were lapsing into stubble-chinned paleness, gurgling shouts into their gags at the regular onset of cramp in their legs and wrists. They secured, by bitter complaints one morning, the substitution later that day of handcuffs in place of the biting cords.

British Army headquarters received a phone call from a woman, who refused to identify herself. The call was to the effect that unless three certain men were released from prison within the next five days, the two British NCOs, presently hostages, would be executed. She named the three convicted men. They were all young Jewish men, imprisoned for armed attacks on British troops. She rang off.

The hunt for Wallis and Daniel became desperate. Every café proprietor had been punishingly interrogated. Every one swore he had not served the NCOs that day, or seen anything of them. Perhaps they all feared that any one of them who turned informer would receive a punitive visit from a representative of the rising Jewish underground movement.

Patsy began to worry about Daniel, and so did Rachel Goodman, for the troubles in Palestine were an increasing threat to the safety of the British troops policing this Arab state. She was torn between her deep affection for her country and her sympathy for the aims of the Palestine Jews.

Patsy, who had been expecting a letter from Daniel confirming the day of his arrival in the UK, had not heard from him. Further, the media were reporting that two British soldiers were being held hostage against the release of three Jewish prisoners, and that if such release was not effected, the soldiers would be executed. The Ministry of Defence, out of consideration for the feelings of the men's relatives, refused to name them.

A man in C Platoon spoke to Captain Turner.

'I know you've got nothing out of any of the café owners, sir, but I've got a feeling I once heard that Corporal Wallis and Lance-Corporal Adams nearly always patronized Solly's. I've just remembered about hearing, I can't remember from who.'

Captain Turner, along with the Sergeant-Major, the C Platoon man, and the two Security officers, descended on Solly's. A previous visit had been made, during the general swoop on all cafés, but as in every other case, nothing had been gained, the proprietor adamant that he had no recollection of having seen the two NCOs on the day in question. This time the Security officers first cleared the café of customers and then confronted the proprietor, amiable and homely-looking. He again insisted he had seen nothing of the missing soldiers. Bombarded with demands for a different answer, he stuck stoutly to his negative and complained about being harassed.

The C Platoon man asked the Sergeant-Major to step outside with him.

'Well, Private Jenkins?' growled the Sergeant-Major.

'That bloke's not Solly. I've been in this café a couple of times, and this bloke's like Solly, but he's not him, I'm sure.'

That led to the proprietor being interrogated without any niceties. It only aroused resentment, and a declaration that Solomon Gaust was taking a week's holiday in Tel Aviv, staying with his sister and brother-in-law. He himself, Joseph Hanyah, was a close friend and standing in for Solly. If it was necessary to confirm this, he'd give them the address in Tel Aviv, which, on demand, he did.

At which point, Private Jenkins received a bang in the back from the café door as someone pushed it open.

'Café's shut,' he said, turning. Then, 'Eh?' Then, 'Jesus, you're him, you're Solly.'

The portly, round-faced café owner stepped in, and blinked at the amount of khaki confronting him.

'Excuse me?' he said.

'This is Solly, sir,' said Private Jenkins to Captain Turner.

'Mr Solomon Gaust?' said Captain Turner.

'Yes, myself I am,' said Solly.

'Tell me, who is this?' asked Captain Turner, nodding at the man who called himself Joseph Hanyah.

'My friend. Joseph Hanyah.'

'What's he doing here, in your café?' demanded one of the security men.

'He has been taking my place for a week, yes, hasn't he?' said Solly. 'I have been a week at Tel Aviv, with my wife.'

266

'Staying where?'

'With the sister of my wife, wasn't I?'

'The address.'

Solly gave it. It matched that given by Joseph Hanyah.

'I have heard things,' said Solly. 'What has been happening here?'

'Two of our company's NCOs have gone missing,' said Sergeant-Major Drummond.

'Here? Here in my café?' Solly looked devastated.

'Somewhere in Haifa,' said Captain Turner, 'and we've reason to believe they're the men being held hostage.'

Solly sighed, sank into a chair, and sighed again.

'Yes, that is what I heard, isn't it?' he said. 'Is it permitted to tell me if they are men I know?'

The Security men looked at Private Jenkins. One nodded.

'Corporal Wallis and Lance-Corporal Adams,' said Private Jenkins.

Solly, looking a picture of misery, chewed on a knuckle.

'I am sorry, they are good men,' he said.

'They've got to be found,' said Captain Turner, 'and we need information.'

'Some of us', said Joseph Hanyah, 'have no serious quarrel with the British, and we receive them in our cafés as welcome customers. You must believe this. As for information, I can give you none at the moment, but if I pick up anything, I will come to your camp and let you know.'

'They are good men,' said Solly again. 'I myself will try to find out where they are, yes.'

'And how will you do that?' asked a Security officer.

'It is a hope,' said Solly.

'A hope of what?'

'Of someone saying to me what they would not to you,' said Solly, who seemed to be perspiring with unhappiness.

'Oh, yes? Bloody piffle.' The Security officer was scathing. 'If you know anyone able to say anything at all about this incident, then who the hell is he?'

'No, no, I did not mean that,' said Solly. 'I meant it was only a hope.'

'Mr Gaust, do you think we're idiots?'

'I protest,' said Solly.

The visit was another waste of time. Subsequently, the Security men contacted headquarters at Jerusalem. Nothing, however, was known about the man called Joseph Hanyah as far as anti-British activities were concerned, and Solomon Gaust certainly had a clean bill of health. In the meantime, headquarters had widened the search, taking in Jerusalem and Tel Aviv among other places.

At home that day, Vi was returning from a visit to her elderly mum and dad, known to the family as Aunt Victoria and Uncle Tom. On a tram taking her down Coldharbour Lane to Camberwell Green, she spotted a woman walking up to the front door of a house, a fine, well-built woman. Vi recognized her as Susie's daily, Mabel Scott, who had obviously just finished her day's work and reached her home. Susie had said she lived with her invalid mother. Well, she was a godsend to Susie, cheerful, bustling and efficient, even if she was loud and hearty, and sang out of tune. Vi smiled. My goodness, she thought, Polly and Boots with a daily, and now Susie and Sammy. Still, Polly was used to servants, and Susie and Sammy, with four children at home, had been sensible, really, in employing one. Vi didn't feel in need herself. She took her domestic chores in her stride, and she and Tommy still had the services of old George as their part-time gardener. Life did have its blessings, and peace after the long war was a blessing all on its own. It wouldn't be long now before her elder son David would be home at last from the RAF, and with him, perhaps, would come his fiancée, Kate Trimble, from the WAAF. There were three young people of the family looking into the future, David engaged to Kate, Sammy and Susie's Daniel fixed to marry his American girl Patsy when he returned from Palestine, and Lizzy and Ned's Edward wanting to marry Leah Goodman when he was demobbed from the RAF. Yes, peacetime was offering its blessings, even if the war had tired the country out and the Government didn't have much money in the bank. Still, the family firm was far from broke. Tommy and Sammy had done such a good job keeping it going all through the war, and now that Boots was back with them, it meant the firm had a really solid backbone, and what Sammy called a collection of Adams brain-boxes.

Vi, the most undemanding of the Adams' wives, hummed a little song to herself as the tram carried her to Camberwell Green.

One more traumatic night for Daniel and Wallis. It was close to two in the morning, and the two NCOs were feeling the debilitating effects of their incarceration. They might have let hunger become their main concern, for they were given food and water only first thing each morning and very late each evening. Such food was always meagre, and very much so in comparison with the large doses of silent hostility and contempt that came their way from the faceless duo. It confirmed the obvious, that the Arabs and Jews had a bitter dislike of British soldiers and a fierce resentment of their presence as an occupying power. But foremost in their thoughts was the suspicion that they were being kept alive, no more than that, and only until the moment when they were programmed for execution. That suspicion would not go away.

With the silence of the place almost a stifling presence, they were trying, not for the first time, to slip their handcuffs. Their wrists were raw from previous attempts. Now, for all their efforts, the bloody cuffs simply wouldn't pass over the broad structure of their hands. They had to give up.

Wherever they were, whatever this place was, house or flat, it wasn't empty. Each day they had been conscious of murmurous activity below, activity that ceased sometime after darkness fell. It did not begin again until an hour or so after they had been given breakfast. That, they thought, was a sign of residents up and about. The little window was too high for them to see through it, to give them some kind of clue as to where they were. Were they in Haifa, or elsewhere?

Questions, problems and the ugly suspicions were a constant disturbance in their minds, and the inability to communicate because of the gags was a sickening frustration. And they had lost count of the passing days.

Tiredness induced them to attempt sleep. It was as fitful as always.

Patsy, still hoping to hear from Daniel, looked for a letter when she came down in the morning. There were letters, yes, one for her from her Pa, and two for Aunt Vi and Uncle Tommy, but there was nothing from Daniel. Over breakfast, she spoke of her worries.

'Oh, he'll be here, Patsy,' said Vi. 'I mean, he told you he would, didn't he?'

'That was months ago,' said Patsy.

'Soldiers keep their word, don't they?' said Alice, home from Bristol University for the Easter vacation. Now twenty-one, she was, as ever, the trimmest of young ladies in a typical well-fitting and unfussy blue dress. Although much given to the satisfying nature of education and learning, she nevertheless had to cope with feelings that sometimes actually took her mind off her studies, feelings for a soldier Scot, one Fergus MacAllister, a corporal presently stationed with the occupying British forces in Germany. Here at home, the family's resident guest, Patsy Kirk from America, had her own feelings. For cousin Daniel. 'Keeping their word is a matter of honour for soldiers, isn't it, Patsy?'

'Watch it, sis,' said Paul, 'it's a matter of honour for everyone. Mind you, I suppose soldiers come up against circumstances that can make it awkward to keep a promise.'

'Well, I guess there are awkward circumstances in Palestine,' said Patsy. 'I mean, tomorrow is the last day of April, and Daniel is timed to be home on the third of May.'

'Perhaps he's on the ship now, Patsy love,' said Vi.

'But he mentioned he'd write to confirm his sailing date,' said Patsy.

Tommy knew what was bothering her, and the family too. It was this present crisis in Palestine, where two abducted British soldiers were under threat of being killed unless some convicted Jewish militants were released. Patsy, of course, was being plagued by a worry that one of the soldiers might be Daniel.

'Tell you what, Patsy,' he said, 'phone my brother Boots after breakfast. He's not just an old soldier and a demobbed colonel, he's always had ways and means of finding things out. That's it, phone him at the office.'

'Mr Adams, it's Patsy here.'

'To what do I owe the pleasure?' asked Boots.

'Oh, I'm sorry to disturb you at your office,' said Patsy.

'You're very welcome,' said Boots.

Patsy explained she was worried about Daniel, and what was happening in Palestine, and was there any way of finding out if he was affected? Uncle Tommy had told her to phone and ask. Boots took a few seconds to think, and then said he'd do what he could and let her know.

'Oh, thanks so much, Mr Adams, only the wedding is fixed to take place on Saturday week, and I haven't heard a word from Daniel. Well, he said he would let me know his sailing date.'

'Leave it with me, Patsy,' said Boots.

He phoned his stepfather, Edwin Finch, retired from British Intelligence, but still with contacts.

'I'll do what I can, Boots,' said Mr Finch. 'You're asking, I suppose, if I can persuade old friends in the department to let me have the names of the two abducted soldiers.'

'I'm asking just that, as a favour,' said Boots.

'Boots, a favour for you is a pleasure to me, you know that, and I'll get back to you later,' said Mr Finch.

He did so after thirty minutes, and was reluctantly compelled to advise Boots that Daniel *was* one of the two soldiers in question, and that the British authorities in Palestine were still engaged in an exhaustive search, while determined not to give in to this kind of blackmail. All leave for Army personnel had been stopped.

'Christ Almighty,' said Boots, 'Daniel's out there with his life in the balance?'

'With the utmost regret, Boots, I have to say yes.'

'I can't tell Patsy that,' said Boots, 'or Sammy and Susie.'

'We've only a margin of four days,' said Mr Finch.

'Which means we've a hell of a problem, Edwin, the kind I wish had landed elsewhere,' said Boots.

'You'll have to stall, Boots, and trust to luck,' said Mr Finch.

'Luck?' said Boots. 'That's everybody's fallback in a crisis they're helpless to resolve themselves. And luck isn't a reliable lady. Yes, I'll have to stall.'

He rang Patsy and told her that through his contacts at the War Office, he'd received information to the effect that the names of the abducted soldiers were known only to British Army headquarters in Palestine, that leave had been stopped for all personnel, and so had transmission of mail.

Impulsively, Patsy said, 'Uncle Boots, what do I do now?'

Boots, feeling unusually helpless, said, 'Let's wait a couple of days, Patsy, and see what kind of news comes out of Palestine over the weekend. I'll speak to my brother Sammy, and suggest he and Susie do the same thing. Wait a couple of days, although I think you are going to have to let the vicar know the wedding might have to be postponed.'

'Uncle Boots, that's heartbreaking,' said Patsy.

'I know, dear girl,' said Boots, and hoped that heartbreak would be limited to a temporary postponement of the ceremony. He spoke to Sammy, guardedly, and Sammy said one or two blasphemous things about events in Palestine. He also said he supposed he and Susie would have been informed if Daniel was one of the hostages. 'Yes, perhaps,' said Boots, 'although the official line covers an Army blackout on names.'

'Susie and me, as Daniel's parents, would object considerable to being blacked out,' said Sammy. 'Anyway, I'm personally not going to believe Daniel's one of the blokes up to his neck in hot soup, and Susie's not going to do any believing, either.'

'Sammy, we'll all have to wait and hope,' said Boots.

'Wait and hope?' said Sammy. 'Susie and me, and Patsy, blimey O'Reilly, we're going to like that, you think? Not bloody much, Boots.'

'Nor me,' said Boots; 'but it's all we've got at the moment. In respect of the wedding you'll have to see the vicar and warn him there might be a postponement.'

'Can't you tell me something to make me laugh?' asked Sammy.

'I'm out of jokes for the time being,' said Boots.

Chapter Twenty-Two

The twins were in bed after a day of wearing themselves out, something that Polly encouraged as a natural way of ensuring that once bathed and tucked up by their father, the precious little demons fell into instant sleep.

Flossie had departed, the evening meal was over, and Boots and Polly were engaged in a sober discussion about the situation in Palestine, particularly concerning what it could mean for Daniel and his fellow NCO.

'Are we sure, Boots, that if the Army can't locate them and free them, it would still refuse to release the convicted men?' asked Polly.

'I'm damn sure myself,' said Boots, 'and I'm also sure its decision would have the backing of the Prime Minister. Mr Attlee could no more afford to give in to that kind of blackmail than the Army.'

'My God, Daniel and the other soldier would be sacrificed?' said Polly.

'That's more than likely.' Boots looked as if concern and worry were draining him, and that distressed Polly, for she had never known him other than equal to a crisis. But this was not just a domestic or business crisis, it was far more, a top-level crisis affecting the Army and the Government, with possibly shattering consequences for the family. 'Polly, how the hell can we tell Sammy and Susie?'

'My God, that there might be a funeral instead of a wedding?' breathed Polly. 'That's frightful. Darling, no, we can't tell them, not yet, not while there's still hope. Let's keep the worry to ourselves for the time being.'

The phone rang. They looked at each other.

'You or me, Polly?' said Boots.

'You take it,' said Polly, 'and if it's Mad Martha, cut her dead, and I mean dead.'

Boots answered the call.

'Yes? Hello?'

'There you are, you lovely sexy man.' The gruff, husky voice travelled unwanted into his ear, irritating him in his present mood. 'I have dreams about you.'

'Miss Jardine—'

'Miss Jardine is a cow.'

'Well, whoever you are, get off this bloody line,' said Boots, and put the phone down. He waited. Within a minute, it rang again. He picked it up.

'Don't hang up on me,' said the gruff-voiced woman.

'See a doctor,' said Boots, and again put the receiver down. Then he took it off its cradle and let it lie dead for the time being. He returned to Polly.

They did not enjoy the best of evenings.

*　　*　　*

'Sammy, we really ought to have heard from Daniel by now, one way or the other,' said Susie over breakfast the next morning. Again there had been nothing in the post, and she was sure Patsy would have phoned if she had heard.

'Well, Susie love,' said Sammy. 'I don't think we will hear just yet. Well, not until this Palestine hokey-pokey's been cleared up.'

'I think you mean hocus-pocus, Dad,' said Jimmy.

'I mean hokey-pokey, which is the right wordage for what evil geezers go in for,' said Sammy. 'I've had me share of same from dubious business competitors that weren't brought up right, but I've been fortunate not to have had any from the kind of Dirty Dicks that are operating in Palestine. I'm asking meself when's Daniel going to get home, and I don't know the answer, which is giving us all a headache and Patsy too.'

'Yes, bother it, Dad,' said Bess, looking unhappy, 'it's a rotten time for us, and for Patsy. I suppose those two hostages couldn't be from Daniel's company, could they?'

'Oh, there's hundreds of our soldiers out there in Palestine,' said Jimmy, going in for a reassuring note, 'not just Daniel's lot.'

'I'll have to talk to the vicar tomorrow,' said Sammy. Tomorrow was Sunday. 'I've got to let him know the wedding might have to be postponed.'

'Oh, Lord, that will really mess things up,' said

Susie. 'The ceremony, the caterers, the guests – we'll have to let everyone know in good time.'

'Still, not yet,' said Sammy.

'No, not yet, Mum,' said Bess.

'Mum, what about Phoebe and me being bridesmaids and Bess,' said Paula.

'I know, lovey,' said Susie, 'let's all keep our fingers crossed.'

'Mummy, I've got mine crossed already,' said Phoebe.

'Atta girl,' said Jimmy.

A little after midnight, Sunday

The silent, hostile men had been and gone. Daniel and Wallis had been given water and the usual meagre amount of food. In addition, Wallis received a blow that staggered him when he asked was it Easter or Christmas or what. It was an attempt to let his captors know he wasn't yet completely downhearted, but was losing count of days. The consequent blow, he thought, was probably a reminder that he and Daniel both wore the hated British Army uniform. Palestine in 1946 was increasingly a hotbed of hatred, and Wallis wondered what he and Daniel had done to deserve being pinpointed.

Now the door opened again. That was a departure from the usual routine. Someone entered, dark and bulky.

'Not a word, please, no, not a word.'

It was a whisper, but enough to cause recognition.

Solly? Solly?

The café proprietor moved on cautious feet, like a man suspecting the darkness to be the enemy of noise. Coming close, he released the prisoners' gags and whispered again.

'Not safe, no, to believe we will not be caught, so be most quiet. Quiet, yes. Me, myself, will speak only. I am going to your camp, to tell your officers you are here, above my café. That is where the Zionists caught you, isn't it, after forcing me to go to Tel Aviv for a week. They knew, yes, that you come in most days for orange juice. But here, my friends, here is water.'

He brought a glass of cold water to each of their mouths in turn, and they drank as deeply as they could.

'Solly, you're a great bloke,' said Daniel, 'and if—'

'Be quiet, please. I am going to gag you again, yes. I must leave you as I found you, for who knows if they will come back to check on you before your soldiers get here?'

The faceless duo hadn't made any intermediate calls so far. A visit early each morning and late at night, that had been their routine, and Daniel now understood why. The café was busy from about breakfast time until ten in the evening, and comings and goings by two men who always disappeared upstairs to this room might, under the circumstances, have attracted unwanted attention from the wrong kind of customer. The clever buggers, thought Daniel, locking us up here above the café itself, almost certainly the last place to enter the minds of searchers.

'Stay now, stay, please, and wait,' whispered Solly, much as if he thought they were able to take on mobility once his back was turned. He replaced their gags.

The two NCOs understood. Solly had put himself at great risk in coming back to his café from his home. Eyes were everywhere in the towns and cities of Palestine. He had to take the further risk of making his way to the camp. At the same time, he had chosen to arrange for the Army to release them, and not to get them out of the place himself. A bit of wise thinking, thought Daniel. Any kind of straightforward release would have pointed an immediate finger at the proprietor, and the Zionists gave short shrift to those who worked against them and not for them.

Solly, suddenly, was gone, closing the door very quietly behind him, and turning the key just as quietly.

This, thought Daniel, is going to be a long wait, even if only for an hour, and if I wet my pants at the crucial moment, it won't surprise me. No, hang on to your manly grit, you prawn, you don't want to have to tell Patsy you let yourself down like some incontinent old bloke of ninety.

What's happening to me now?

Sod it, I'm sweating all over.

Wallis was wondering if Solly would make it to the camp, or if friends of the faceless duo would spot him, pick him up and take him out of the ranks of the living.

*　　*　　*

Major Jarrett, Captain Turner and the Sergeant-Major were out of their beds, conducting a rapid question-and-answer session with the man who had appeared out of the darkness to attract the attention of the night sentry and the guard commander. Quick and brief though the questions were, Solly expostulated at time being lost.

'But you have just said you don't expect the men to turn up until morning,' pointed out Major Jarrett, ruddy-faced and barrel-chested.

'Sir, I have also said one can never know, and isn't it so?' breathed Solly.

'All the same, Mr Gaust, it doesn't always do for the bull to rush the gate.' But Major Jarrett gave the Sergeant-Major a nod, and off went the company's senior warrant officer to arouse a score of soldiers. 'Explain your position, Mr Gaust,' said the company commander.

Solly, fretting and issuing not a little perspiration, said he had been approached over a week ago by men he did not know, but who knew him and informed him he was to absent himself, to go with his wife to her sister's at Tel Aviv and to stay there until he was recalled in a week or so. He was upset by this, but he knew he must comply or end up crippled.

'What else did they know about you and your café?'

They knew, of course, said Solly, that two British Army NCOs visited his café almost every day.

'Did they tell you so?'

Solly said no, he guessed that as something obvious. Such men, he said in effect, always knew how to obtain information, and always had friends on street corners or behind curtains who could give them information about the regular or routine movements of British soldiers.

'But if your café had been full of customers at the time—?'

Solly said the Zionists would have restricted customers to those they could trust. Others would have been turned away, a reasonable excuse given.

'Your so-called friend Hanyah. Is he a friend or one of them?'

Solly asked to be excused answering questions about Hanyah, saying it would do him no good to give information that might easily be traced back to his mouth.

'Good sir, I am against having my throat cut. I must look like a true Zionist, not an informer, so when you have released your soldiers, you must come to my home and arrest me, see? Yes? Then you will allow me to prove my innocence of any plot, won't you? Yes?'

'I'm sure that will happen, Mr Gaust, but you'll be held for several days to make your arrest look genuine.'

It was precisely an hour and a quarter after Solly had left the NCOs when a dozen British soldiers, led by Major Jarrett, Captain Turner and the Sergeant-Major, descended once more on the café. This time, however, the exercise took place in pitch darkness, and in silence. Further, entrance was effected at the rear of the premises, and by forcing a window. It was a tactical move, designed to leave the café's front door untouched and accordingly to arouse no suspicion in whoever arrived first in the morning. Armed men stood watch as Captain Turner, the Sergeant-Major and two corporals climbed in through the open window, and made their way upstairs.

A jemmy was used to force open the door of the little room above the café, and nothing could have been more welcome to Daniel and Wallis than the entry of four solid-bodied figures in khaki battledress. That went hand in hand with the physical bliss of being released from their gags and the cords lashing their legs.

'We'll get those handcuffs off back in camp,' said Captain Turner in low key. 'Can you both walk? We ducked using transport for the sake of silence. We want no-one to suspect we've raided the place, or they'll alert the buggers responsible for keeping you here. We want that pretty pair to land in our arms when they arrive in the morning, along with the man who's standing in for Solly. So can you walk?'

'You bet, sir,' said Wallis.

'Happy Christmas,' said Daniel.

'Don't get funny,' growled the Sergeant-Major. 'If I had my way, you'd both be charged for being careless enough to get jumped.'

Blow that for a lark, thought Daniel.

Subsequently, a sergeant and escort called on Solly's home and arrested him, much to the loud and angry protests of his wife, who said such an arrest in the middle of the night was how

284

Himmler's Gestapo behaved. Solly's reaction, for the benefit of his wife, was to join her in her protests, and he was still voicing indignation when he was taken away.

Some time after sunrise, when people were out and about, three men approached the café. One was Joseph Hanyah. Using a key, they entered. While Hanyah began to prepare the café for opening time, the other two men slipped behind the counter and mounted the stairs. Out from the room above and up from the kitchen below poured armed British soldiers to overwhelm them in a rush. It was a bruising, not a friendly welcome, and they crashed.

Other soldiers arrested Joseph Hanyah.

British Army headquarters received the news with a huge gust of relief.

Later, a signal arrived for Major Jarrett.

'Get 'em washed, shaved, fed and tarted up, and fly them home tomorrow. Take care of Mother.'

The reference to Mother meant keep mum, which meant don't inform the press or radio. Headquarters would handle all publicity, as well as signalling London.

That meant Daniel and Wallis could avoid harassment by excited journalists and enjoy a quiet leave. It could also mean Daniel would be home in time for his wedding.

Chapter Twenty-Three

Wednesday, May 3

The time was nine-thirty in the morning. Tommy was at work, Paul at school, Alice on a bus to Trafalgar Square, where she was to meet university friends at the National Gallery. Vi was getting ready to go out, and Patsy, always willing to help with the chores, was hoovering the living-room carpet.

The phone rang in the hall, and Patsy answered it.

'Hello?'

'Hello yourself. Am I smack on target? Is that you, Patsy?'

'Daniel!'

'How's your American sex appeal?'

'Oh, my stars, Daniel, where are you?'

'Good question,' said Daniel. He and Wallis, along with some Army VIPs, had arrived in England at midnight in an RAF converted bomber. The flight had been in two stages, from Palestine to Malta, picking up two more VIPs, and from Malta to an RAF station in Kent, where

Daniel and Wallis had stayed the night. 'Let's see now, where am I, you asked?'

'Stop driving me mad and tell me,' begged Patsy.

'I'm at Manston, near Ramsgate, in Kent,' said Daniel, 'and I'm—'

'Daniel! You're home, you're actually home?'

'Nearly, and for three weeks when I get there,' said Daniel. 'I'm catching a train to Charing Cross in a while, and I'll be arriving there just before twelve. Then I'll catch a bus home.'

'Oh, gee whiz, I'm going to catch me a bus myself and meet you at the station,' said Patsy. 'I simply can't just sit and wait here, I'd be all jumps and twitches.'

'Well, if I'm going to get sight of you when I come off the train,' said Daniel, 'it'll make my day. Wear a Sunday frock, eh?'

'Daniel, oh, I'm so happy.'

'Me too,' said Daniel who, with Wallis, had quickly recovered from his ordeal.

'Daniel, the radio newscasts yesterday said the crisis in Palestine was over, that the hostages had been freed.'

'I give you my word, that was a relief to me and all our blokes in Palestine,' said Daniel.

'Did you know the men, the hostages?' asked Patsy.

'As a matter of fact, yes,' said Daniel, 'and I'll tell you more sometime. Meanwhile—'

'Daniel, isn't it great we can have our wedding now?'

'Great? Not half,' said Daniel. 'Love you, don't

I? Listen, will you let my parents know I'm home? I thought of ringing them first, but you came out on top.'

'Daniel, your mother is going with your Aunt Vi and your Aunt Lizzy to your firm's shop at Brixton to pick up their finished wedding outfits,' said flushed Patsy. 'Won't they just love to know you're home and that the wedding isn't going to be postponed? And I'm going to love meeting you at Charing Cross station.'

'That's my girl,' said Daniel. 'Don't forget your Sunday frock.'

Patsy laughed.

'Get you,' she said.

She delivered the good news to the family, first Aunt Vi, then by phone to Daniel's mother, his Aunt Lizzy, Uncle Boots and Grandma Finch. Susie was full of delight, Lizzy expressed relief and gratitude, and Boots from his office said it was the most welcome item of the week, and that he'd let Sammy know. Grandma Finch said thank the Lord, and that someone had got to stop a young man like Daniel being sent overseas again or she'd write to the Government.

Later, Patsy took a Number 68 bus from Denmark Hill to the north side of Waterloo Bridge. She chose the upper deck because one could always see more from there, and in her mood of giddy bliss she wanted to scan the whole world.

The bus passed the family firm's offices at Camberwell Green, the name, 'Adams Enterprises

Ltd', handsomely evident in gold-coloured paint on each of the windows. She peered to see if she could spot either Boots or Sammy, but the sun was dazzling the windows. The morning was lovely, a gracious gesture on the part of an element known to be perverse enough in this hemisphere to drown the British people even on high summer days like August Bank Holiday Monday.

From Camberwell Road the bus entered Walworth Road, passing streets that had suffered bomb damage and shops that had known Daniel's granny as a customer years ago. From a stop opposite East Street, Patsy saw a crowded market, and she knew, from all she had heard of the family's history, that here Daniel's dad and uncles had, as boys, sought bargains for their hard-up mother, Granny Finch. Herself, she had never known want, her late mother, a lawyer, earning as much as, if not more than, her Pa.

Patsy thought the scene the atmospheric one of a lively, bustling people. Cockneys. Daniel had always said if you met a cockney who wasn't lively, he or she had a run-down perspective probably due to mixing with too many foreigners. What foreigners? Oh, people from places like Hampstead, Potters Bar and Wimbledon, said Daniel. Daniel was a kook, a happy guy.

On went the bus to the junction called the Elephant and Castle, shattered and despoiled by air raids. Patsy sighed at the great ugly gaps visible all round. But she was too blissful to let depression intervene, and when the bus was travelling over Waterloo Bridge, she enjoyed her view of the

Thames sparkling with reflected sunlight. Ol' Man River, that was London's Thames, a flowing highway for Celtic and Roman traders nineteen hundred years ago. Patsy's four years at an English boarding school had put her in touch with Britain's ancient history.

She alighted at the Strand and walked to Charing Cross railway station, her heart as lively as her step. Shops in the Strand had made a great recovery, their window displays colourful and attractive, even if their wares were probably not as diverse as pre-war. When she reached the station, the effects of air raids were still visible. There were scars. But beneath its dome, the concourse was a scene of movement, with passengers either arriving or departing, either hurrying or taking their time, and all with the air of people who knew the war was over.

She began her wait for the train carrying Daniel to her. She paced about, walked about, bought a magazine and an American newspaper from Smith's bookstall, went to and from the platform at which the train was due, and generally fidgeted. She was early by thirty minutes, and the train was late by ten minutes.

It slowly steamed in, coach doors opening, some passengers eager to be first out to avoid a crush at the barrier. The massive engine came to a halt, steam hissing, and from the train descended a confusing mass of people. But way down, Patsy caught sight of the emergence of a khaki-clad soldier carrying a laden valise.

Was that Daniel? Oh, gee whiz, yes, back there,

strolling on his lanky legs. Then he began to look, and amid the crowd of arriving passengers, they saw each other. Daniel waved. Patsy jumped on dancing feet, gloved hand gesturing.

Out he came, through the open barrier, and making straight for her. There she was, a high-spirited, all-American girl when he'd last seen her, and now, well, talk about a high-class young lady and a fair old treat to his eyes. But not in a Sunday frock, no. Patsy, in fact, was wearing the stylish outfit she'd sported on her Pa's wedding day, complete with the pillbox hat.

Up he came, Patsy actually a little short of breath at this, her first sight of him for a year. Always with some of his father's vitality about him, he now had the additional appeal of what his time in the Army and in Palestine had made of him, a firmly structured, sun-tanned and fine-looking young man, even if there were faint dusty rims around his eyes. Sleepless nights because of the crisis in Palestine, she thought, with two of his fellow soldiers held hostage for all of a week.

'Are you my Patsy?' he asked with a smile.

'Daniel?'

'You are my Patsy.'

'Daniel – oh, I'm so happy to see you.'

'Give us a kiss, then,' said Lance-Corporal Adams, putting his laden valise down.

She jumped into his arms, good as, and with people streaming on all sides, she kissed him and he kissed her. Someone whistled, but Patsy and Daniel probably wouldn't have heard a factory hooter at this particular moment.

'Daniel, isn't this great?'

'So are you,' said Daniel. 'I do believe you're getting to be an American beauty. Have you had any American cowboys following you about in Boston?'

'I can't tell a lie,' said Patsy. 'I've had a posse of them chasing me, and all on horseback.'

Daniel laughed, and Patsy thought his tan made him look real sexy. She tingled. Daniel, regarding her warmly, expressed himself earnestly.

'Love you for being here, Patsy,' he said.

'Daniel, that makes me really happy,' said Patsy.

They looked at each other again, took each other in more intently, and perhaps their deep feelings, so mutual, told them they would hold fast and firm together in sunshine or in rain, calm or storm. Whatever, they shared a moment of silent emotion before Daniel spoke again.

'I think I'm just about on time,' he said.

Patsy, drawing breath, said, 'Oh, right on time. We all had worries, because of what was happening in Palestine, and I'm still giddy that you're actually here.'

'If that's a giddy look you're wearing,' said Daniel, 'it's a winner. Patsy, shall we go home?'

'To your parents' new house?'

'I've heard about that.'

'It's lovely, and with central heating.'

'I've heard about that too.'

'And did you get my letter about our own house, the one your parents are buying for us?'

'It arrived just before I left,' said Daniel. It had actually arrived on the day he and Wallis were jumped and laid out. 'Good old Mum and Dad, what a Christmas present.'

'Not Christmas, you goof,' said Patsy, 'wedding.'

'Come on, let's get moving,' said Daniel, 'and you can tell me more about it on our way.'

Much to Patsy's delight, he decided they should take a taxi, if he could persuade the cabbie to go all the way to Denmark Hill. The cabbie in question said he'd be pleasured to oblige one of His Majesty's generals and his lady wife. Daniel said they weren't married yet, and did that make a difference?

'I'll forgive yer,' said the cabbie, 'so hop in. Denmark Hill, you said, where the nobs hang out?'

'It's where my parents hang out, but my dad hasn't been knighted yet,' said Daniel, happily prepared to fork out for the fare. It meant a ride home in comfort and style.

Off went the taxi to travel south through London, the early May sunshine softening the sharper edges of stone buildings.

With the partition between them and the cabbie being closed, Patsy described to Daniel the house she'd mentioned in her last letter to him, and how of all things great, it had central heating. She didn't know how they were ever going to thank his parents enough for gifting it to them. Daniel said they'd find a way some day.

Patsy asked if London's ruined buildings would ever be restored. Not to what some of them were, I hope, said Daniel. The bombs that had blown up slum properties had given councils the chance to see that something a lot better was built.

'But what about all the lovely old churches?' asked Patsy.

'Well, Patsy love, people only pray in churches, they don't live in them,' said Daniel, 'so new houses and flats should go up first. But who wants to talk about that today or tomorrow? We've got other things on our minds, haven't we?'

'Oh, I guess I'm so up in the air that my mind's dizzy,' said Patsy, and looked out over the shimmering Thames as the taxi carried them over Waterloo Bridge. 'Daniel, I guess that old sun has come out just for you and me.'

'It ought to come out daily for you,' said Daniel. 'Listen, you've thought a lot about marrying me and what it's going to mean for you, haven't you? Like the fact you'll be two thousand miles away from your home?'

'Daniel, this is my home now, and I've adjusted to that already,' said Patsy. 'Oh, my stars, you're not trying to tell me you're having second thoughts, are you?'

'I've had second, third and fourth thoughts,' said Daniel, 'and they all lead me to you for my little woman.'

'Your *what*?'

'That's it in this country,' said Daniel, 'you marry the girl you're barmy about, carry her over the doorstep of your abode, show her the kitchen and cooker, and make her your little woman.'

'Ha-ha,' said Patsy.

'Good for a laugh?' said Daniel.

'I think you got all that from your funny old granny,' said Patsy. 'Little woman? You'll be lucky.'

'Fair enough,' said Daniel, 'let's have a modern marriage, shall we?'

'How do you see a modern marriage?' asked Patsy.

'You taking care of the kitchen and the pot plants,' said Daniel, 'and me going out to work to earn our bread.'

'That's a modern marriage?' said Patsy.

'Well, we'll both be beginners, of course,' said Daniel, 'but we can work at it as we go along.'

'Oh, I'm going to settle for old-fashioned happy days,' said Patsy.

'That's it,' said Daniel, 'and I'll treat you to some pretty aprons. By the way, if there's any arguments, who's going to have the last word?'

'Me,' said Patsy. 'Wife's privilege.'

'That's definitely old-fashioned,' said Daniel.

'Some ancient customs should remain,' said Patsy. 'Your mother says so. She's a real sweetie.'

'Well, I'll give it to you, as a real sweetie Mum's always had the last word over Dad,' said Daniel. 'It's caused him a lot of heartburn, I can tell you. Still, you're a great girl, Patsy, and I daresay we could arrange it so that I don't get any heartburn myself.'

Patsy laughed.

Chapter Twenty-Four

Meanwhile, Susie had arrived home in company with Vi and Lizzy, each carrying a long fancy white box in which reposed a finished wedding outfit, ordered from and made up by Adams Fashions Ltd, favourably priced and at a family discount.

Only a few seconds after entering the house, Susie was aghast. The place had been burgled. All silver of any value had gone. Some of it, like a pair of candlesticks, a cruet with cut-glass containers, and a Georgian teapot with milk jug and sugar bowl, had been lovingly acquired by her and Sammy since losing everything when their old house and its contents had been completely destroyed by a German bomb. To add to her distress, the table in the lounge, on which any number of attractively packaged wedding presents had rested, had been swept clean. Oh, the rotten thieves, thought Susie, they've robbed Patsy and Daniel too.

Tragically, she said, 'Now I know I hate burglars.'

Vi and Lizzy were as upset as she was, but Lizzy was able to put her mind to something they had all temporarily overlooked.

'Susie,' she said, 'where's your daily?'

'What? Oh, of course, I'm not thinking, am I?' said Susie. 'Yes, where is she?' From the lounge, she went into the hall. 'Mabel? Mabel?' The call sailed around the house, and its echoes floated back to the hall. But there was no response from Mabel.

'Oh, lor',' said Vi, 'could the burglars have tied her up somewhere?'

'I'm not thinking like that,' said Lizzy, who had her own kind of suspicions.

The three of them made a quick search of the whole house, but there was no sign of the bustling, breezy daily.

Susie was hit hard then by what was obvious.

'I know something else now,' she said. 'I know I hate Mabel Scott if she's responsible. She'll have spent her time here finding out exactly where we kept the valuables most worth thieving. Yes, and knowing about the wedding, she's waited until a heap of presents were there for the taking. Oh, Lord, Patsy and Daniel could be here any moment, and they're going to walk straight into this rotten burglary, which is the last thing I'd want for Daniel after all that upset in Palestine. I feel sick.'

Precisely at that moment, a taxi pulled up outside the house. Vi saw it from the lounge window.

'Oh, my goodness, Susie, here they are,' she said.

The greetings had been glad enough, but Patsy and Daniel had to be told of the distressing nature of a bold and downright crafty act of theft. Daniel, once he'd been given the facts, remembered he was the only person present wearing trousers. That, according to the Victorian rules his paternal grandma attached to the family, put him in charge.

'Let's all stop talking at once, Mum,' he said. 'Where does Mabel Scott live? We need to inform the police or to get round there ourselves before she does a bunk with our goods and her own chattels.'

'Oh, it's in Camberwell Grove,' said Susie, 'it's on a slip of paper she gave me, in the bureau.'

Daniel opened up the roll-top of the bureau, and fished about in a pigeon-hole. He found the slip and noted the address: 6, Camberwell Grove.

'Wait a bit!' said Vi, 'I saw her from a bus a few days ago, I saw her going into a house about half-past four, when she had probably just finished her day's work with you, Susie. The house wasn't in Camberwell Grove, it was in Coldharbour Lane.'

Daniel asked his mum if the woman had supplied references. Susie said she had talked about having them, but had left them at her home, where she lived with her invalid mother. Susie said she took her on at face value. Patsy said that all through centuries of civilization there were cases where face value hadn't been worth a nickel, but victims kept being spoofed.

'Aunt Vi, could you pinpoint the house in Coldharbour Lane?' asked Daniel.

'Oh, yes, I could take the police straight there,' said Vi, placidity disturbed for once.

'It's my guess this Camberwell Grove address is a blind,' said Daniel. 'I'm going to phone Dad, to get him to come here in his car and drive some of us to Coldharbour Lane to find out if we can get the stuff back ourselves. If not, then we'll inform the police.'

'Go call your Pa, Daniel,' said Patsy, feeling for his upset mother.

Sammy, however, was out of his office. So Daniel spoke to Boots, who wasted no time asking questions.

'I'll come myself, Daniel,' he said, 'I'll be leaving inside a minute. Sorry your homecoming coincided with this kind of mess. While I'm on my way, find out from your mother if her daily knew beforehand that there would be no-one at home all morning.'

Boots, a star turn in a crisis, arrived in quick time and received information to the effect that Susie had told her daily yesterday that there'd be no-one at home for most of this morning.

'I think she needed to know in advance,' he said. 'Well, consider what she's helped herself to, all your good silver, Susie, and all the wedding presents that were on the table. She couldn't have put all that loot into a shopping bag or even two.

I'm guessing there might be an accomplice, and that this isn't their first easy haul. So let's motor to Coldharbour Lane, let's go for the house Vi will point out. You'll come, of course, Vi, and you'll join us, Daniel?'

'He sure will, Uncle Boots, and so will I,' said Patsy. 'I've got my own interest in those wedding presents.'

'Boots, shouldn't you go to the police first?' asked Lizzy.

'Mabel Scott will expect us to,' said Boots, 'and she's probably thinking right now that the police are swarming all over this house. I think we're going to be given enough time to catch her out before she disappears with her treasure chest, if that's her plan. On the other hand, she may believe she's quite safe in Coldharbour Lane, and will take her time to plant herself in new pastures. She'll be expecting us, or the police, to be buzzing around in Camberwell Grove. Well, we'll give it a buzz first, before we try the house in Coldharbour Lane, and before we bring the police in.'

'Off you go, then,' said Lizzy. 'I'll stay with Susie. Oh, if that woman does have an accomplice, give him a smack in the eye to learn him some manners. Anyone who steals wedding presents has never been learned any manners at all.'

Boots, Daniel, Vi and Patsy descended on Camberwell Grove at speed, and took only a few minutes to discover that the lady who opened the door of number six didn't know any Mabel

Scott, had never met her and didn't feel she needed to.

They lost no time in heading for Coldharbour Lane, and when Boots brought his car to a stop outside the house indicated by Vi, it was only a yard or so from a pre-war, hundred-pound shabby old black Ford.

'Boots, is that hers, d'you think?' asked Vi.

'Or her accomplice's?' said Boots. 'Stay there, Vi.' He alighted. So did Daniel and Patsy. 'I think Daniel and I can manage, Patsy.'

'Oh, I guess so,' said Patsy, 'but where Daniel goes in search of our wedding presents, I go too. I'm as much a part of the posse as he is.'

'No comment,' smiled Boots, and Patsy thought how controlled he was. A classic phrase intruded. Cool, calm and collected. Come to that, Daniel didn't seem edgy or unsure, either. He and his uncle had an awkward job to do, but both looked as if they could handle it without fuss. The door of the house was solidly shut, its iron knocker challenging. But Boots was disregarding it; he was eyeing the Ford, musing over the old banger. 'Take a look, Daniel,' he said.

'I think I'm with you,' said Daniel. 'Let's see if the boot's locked.' It wasn't, and he opened it up. 'Well, well,' he said.

There were two large cardboard boxes, each full of purloined silver and unpacked wedding presents.

Traffic flowed by, people walked by, and the house door remained shut. Boots stooped and looked through the window at the back seat. Two other large boxes came to his sound eye. They too looked full, but the contents were covered by crammed newspaper. Rest of the wedding presents, he thought. The whole lot had been taken.

'All that, I suppose, is what could be called a haul,' he murmured. Patsy, quick with nervous excitement, was sure someone would come out of the house any moment, and could hardly keep her feet still on the pavement, but Daniel and his uncle were calmly taking their time over everything.

'Uncle Boots,' said Daniel, 'I think whoever owns this car is ready for the off, and I think Mabel Scott and her Bill Sykes are ready as well. Shall we knock 'em up and have a little chat with them?'

'Is that necessary?' said Boots. 'You're right about them being ready to scarper, Daniel old lad. The key's there, in the ignition. I call that an invitation. You take my car, and I'll drive the Ford.'

'That's a great idea for getting the goods back home,' said Daniel. 'Shall we get going before the gang comes out?'

'Oh, gee whiz, are we going to hightail it for the ranch, and leave the rustlers empty-handed?' asked Patsy, exultant.

'Pronto,' said Boots, much to her delight.

A minute later both cars were moving off, at which point the door of the house opened and a man and woman appeared. Seeing the Ford on the move, they yelled and charged. The woman stopped on the pavement to indulge in a screaming fit. The man kept charging. Too late. The cars were away, the old Ford rattling, its exhaust fuming. Mabel Scott's screaming fit died its eventual death, but she was still shaking with the fury she felt at the Ford and its loot being nicked by a bunch of lousy crooks. She hadn't emerged from the house in time to recognize any of the people in the cars.

'Sod me,' grated her confederate through grinding teeth, 'done to a turn by some bleedin' flash buggers – call the police.'

'Call the police? You daft?' bawled Mabel, and clouted the idiot.

''Ere, listen, if you hadn't spent all that time undoing the bloody presents, we'd 'ave been away by now,' complained the idiot.

That earned him another clout, this time for being saucy.

In Boots's old Riley, Vi gasped, 'Oh, lor', I'm losing my breath just sitting here. I never did know anything like this before.'

'Hang on, Aunt Vi,' said Patsy, 'it's giddy-up and back to the old homestead with the family silver.'

'Right, stay in the saddle, Aunt Vi,' said Daniel, 'you're part of the posse too.'

'I just hope I live,' said Vi.

The two cars went at a gallop. In a manner of speaking.

The stolen items had all been restored. The ancient Ford car was now back in Coldharbour Lane, driven there by Daniel and left some fifty yards away from the house in which Mabel Scott and her thieving partner were coming to serious blows over whose fault it was that their loot had been nicked, and the Ford as well.

'Who left the bloody key in the bleedin' car, eh?' shouted Mabel. Bash.

'Who wanted a bleedin' cup of tea before we left, eh?' bawled her accomplice. Bash, bash.

Mabel, big, busty and booming, gave as good as she got. Better, in fact. She knocked the bloke out. Mind, she used a lump of wood.

Boots had followed Daniel to Coldharbour Lane, picked him up and driven him back home, then returned to the offices.

Susie, Vi, Lizzy, Patsy and Daniel treated themselves to some hot coffee and a belated lunch of sandwiches, while discussing events and the audacious method Boots had used in bringing the stolen goods back home.

Patsy said he would have made a great sheriff for Dodge City. Vi asked where Dodge City was. Out in the wild, wild West, said Patsy.

'I'm not sure Polly would fancy that,' said Lizzy.

'The cowgirls might fancy Uncle Boots,' said Daniel. 'And I might fancy being deputy sheriff.'

'You're staying here, my lad,' said Susie, 'you've got an appointment to keep with Patsy, and we're all going to get dressed up for the occasion. So is Patsy. Just wait till you see her in her wedding gown.'

'Daniel, tell us about what actually happened in Palestine,' said Lizzy.

'Oh, nothing as exciting as what's just happened here,' said Daniel, saving his story for when the family was assembled in strength.

A hand reached under the kitchen table and squeezed his thigh. He glanced at the perpetrator.

Patsy's wink suggested there were other excitements to come.

Maudie Duckworth was with Emma that afternoon, and somewhat overstaying her welcome. She was going on about the Nazi war criminals, about their trial going on and on, and how she hoped they'd all be found guilty, especially that man Goering.

'He should be,' said Emma, 'he and Hitler were guilty of the worst kind of crimes.'

'I don't know what my husband would be thinking,' said Maudie, 'except he did tell me once that Hitler did some good things for Germany.'

'Oh, yes, he admired Hitler, didn't he?' said Emma, thinking that Mr Duckworth had been a potential Nazi himself.

'What?' Maudie blinked. 'Oh, no, not Charlie.'

'I thought you did say so once,' said Emma.

'Did I?' Maudie blinked again. 'No, it wouldn't have done, would it, for anyone in this country to have admired Hitler.'

'Especially our Jewish people,' said Emma.

'Yes, didn't the Germans treat their own Jews something cruel?' said Maudie, and left it at that by talking about her gardener. 'Mr Robinson's a real help in the garden considering he's a retired gent. Well, retired from being a Camberwell dustman, and it's nice having a man around sometimes now my Charlie's gone.'

Well, we're not getting any more complaints, thought Emma, but I wonder if her Charlie is bawling some into the ear of his Maker?

'By the way, Maudie, we shan't be at home on Saturday,' she said, 'we're attending a family wedding.'

'Oh, that's nice,' said Maudie. 'Perhaps I'll pop in on Sunday to hear all about it.'

Emma sighed. Keeping an eye on her widowed neighbour had its moments of sufferance.

Daniel, having managed to find time for himself, travelled to Brixton to conduct a purchase before the few days to the wedding ran away from him. He came out of a jeweller's shop at five o'clock, his purchase completed. He had bought Patsy the kind of wedding present he thought she deserved, a 24-carat gold bracelet of linked rectangles, which had cost him the large sum of thirty guineas, but worth every penny. He hadn't been a profligate spender of his Army pay in Haifa, he'd put most of it aside for this particular purpose. A particular purpose was very particular when it was aimed at Patsy, a credit to the high-powered land of her birth and to her good old Pa as well.

The bracelet, snug in its wrapped velvet box, rested safely in his jacket pocket as he boarded a tram that would take him to Denmark Hill via Coldharbour Lane. On the platform, a wartime clippie, still employed, eyed him with all the interest of a woman well-equipped to enjoy a bit of lovey-dovey with six feet of young manhood, even if she was over thirty herself.

'Watcher, handsome,' she said.

'Watcher, gorgeous,' said Daniel, with the tram moving off.

'Pleasure, I'm sure. What can I do for yer?'

'Just for now,' said Daniel, fishing for pennies, 'give us a ride to Denmark Hill.'

'Tuppence,' said Daisy.

'Used to be a penny,' said Daniel.

'There's been a war.'

'Is it over?'

'Course it's over,' she said, clipping his ticket. 'Where you been?'

'In bed,' said Daniel, and the clippie gave him a playful push.

'Gertcha,' she said. Then, 'Who with?'

'Just my teddy bear,' said Daniel, and moved inside, thinking how unpredictable the course of life could be, alternating between the bloody unpleasant and a larky chit-chat, with a robbery turning into a comedy as an interval, and all within the space of a few days. He was still a little lightheaded about coming out alive with Wallis from that dark room.

He sat down and when the tram entered Coldharbour Lane he kept an eye open for the old Ford car he'd left there. It had still been there on his way to Brixton, and he'd supposed the pretty pair were spending their time swearing and cursing over the loss of their loot and their car as well. It was still in position, fifty yards down from their house, but the scene had changed. The car doors were open, its boot was open, and the man and the woman who had come charging out when he and Uncle Boots were driving away, were beside the Ford. They had obviously only just found it, and were at loggerheads because it was empty of the loot. The woman – Mabel Scott, he presumed – was a buxom wench, and giving the man what for, belabouring him with a handbag.

Daniel's grin was as wide as a barn door as the tram ran by.

Uncle Boots! What a character! He'd settled the whole thing in the simplest kind of way. No fuss, no arguments, no bawling, no punch-ups, just a decision made in a second and on the spot.

Further, no police. Not necessary now, he'd said, when the stuff was all back home, and in any case, Daniel, your grandma wouldn't approve.

It wasn't difficult to understand why he'd made colonel during the war, or how it was that Aunt Polly had turned down all proposals from landed gentry in order to make a claim on him if ever fate favoured her. Well, it had favoured her eventually, at the expense of Aunt Emily's life, blown away by a fiendish German bomb. Still, Fatty Goering had been responsible for that, not Aunt Polly. And a bloke couldn't help liking her, or admiring Uncle Boots. Grandma's eldest son was well above the ordinary.

Come to that, her other sons, Pa Sammy and Uncle Tommy, weren't exactly commonplace.

All three had something of Grandma's qualities. And what about their father, Corporal Daniel Adams of the Royal West Kents? Like all his grandchildren, Daniel had never known him: a soldier who, according to Grandma, carried educating books in his kitbag. Well, he must have been quite a bloke, and he must have passed on something priceless to his sons. I've inherited his name, thought Daniel, and although I'm proud of that, I hope it's not all.

'I'm grieved, Susie, grieved,' said Sammy when he arrived home in the evening.

'If you're grieved, Sammy, I'm sick,' said Susie, still shaken by Mabel Scott's deceiving ways. The relief of getting everything back hadn't fully compensated for feeling she'd been made to look stupidly gullible. Never again would she take anyone at face value.

'When I got back to the office and had to listen to what Boots had to tell me about this thieving lark, it nearly ruined me peace of mind,' said Sammy. 'Well, I mean, seeing Mabel had a male geezer helping her, they could've made off with our best bits of furniture, and the piano as well.'

'And our central-heated radiators?' said Susie a bit huffily.

'Well, you know what I mean,' said Sammy. 'I've met one or two dubious females in my time, but Mabel Scott, I tell you, Susie, what she did behind our backs is a blow to me human faith.'

'It's a blow to my pride,' said Susie.

'Still, let's be grateful,' said Sammy.

'I am,' said Susie, 'to Boots and Daniel.'

'Got to hand it to Boots,' said Sammy, 'he's still

in good working order, and it looks like our Daniel has something up top as well. I'm pleased about that. What a performance, pinching the stuff back from right under the noses of Mabel and her Dick Turpin. Not bad, that.'

'Not bad at all, Sammy,' said Susie, and he looked at her. She was still visibly upset.

'Susie?'

'I feel cheated, Sammy.'

Sammy put his arms around her.

'It happens, Susie. There's people out there that look all right and sound all right, but are born wrong 'uns. We all get taken in, so don't blame yourself about Mabel. If you thought she was right for the job, well, so did I, didn't I?' Sammy applied a comforting cuddle. 'We live and learn, Susie. And you've got one consolation.'

'And what's that?' asked Susie.

'You won't have to listen to your daily singing out of tune any more. Next time you interview one, find out what her singing's like before you take her on.'

'I'll do that,' said Susie with a weak smile.

'Anyway, we're going to enjoy the wedding,' said Sammy. 'Daniel's as good as saved London Bridge from falling down by getting home in time. By the way, where is he? I'd like to get a look at him and give him me congratulations for helping Boots do Mabel Shifty-Fingers and Bill Sykes in the eye.'

'He rushed off to Brixton to buy his own kind of wedding present for Patsy,' said Susie, 'and he's probably with her right now at Tommy and Vi's.'

Daniel was. As for Patsy, she had received his personal wedding gift and was riding high over the moon, quite sure such a lovely bracelet was a sign that her favourite English guy considered her special. Really special.

Chapter Twenty-Five

Earlier that afternoon, at West Square School in South-East London, where Boots and other members of the Adams family had been pupils, the class of fifteen-year-old boys had accepted the invitation of their history teacher to state what they considered the main consequence of the Industrial Revolution.

Some said it made Britain the leading industrial power of the world, others that it produced the world's greatest inventors, and others that it gave jobs to people who had faced permanent unemployment.

'Aren't you all overlooking the huge drift of families from the land into cities, and what this did to agriculture and village life?' suggested the teacher, Mr Beckett.

'Well, sir,' said Paul Adams, younger son of Tommy and Vi, 'I'm not personally overlooking it.'

'We await your conclusions,' said Mr Beckett.

Paul's cousin Jimmy, sitting behind him, let a grin slip in. That kind of invitation to Paul could bring forth a speech.

'My conclusion,' said Paul, 'is that the main consequence of the Industrial Revolution was a shocking exploitation of the masses. All the rich bosses got richer, and all the poor workers got poorer. The men and women all worked twelve hours a day in factories for horrible low wages, and their children who were used to running about in country fields with sheep and lambs, and getting free lamb chops for supper, going down the mines and hardly getting any kind of wage at all. I seriously ask, if we couldn't have done without the Industrial Revolution unless, of course, we'd had a Labour Party to look after the workers. That's what the masses needed, in my opinion, a Labour Party, like we've got now.'

Interjections.

'Give him a soapbox.'

'Give him a dictionary, he's swallowed his other one.'

'Give him a cheer.'

'Adams,' said Mr Beckett, 'policies relevant to the subject, yes, allowable. Politics, no. In other words, you can't use this classroom to advance the cause of the Labour Party. Or the Liberal Party. Or the Conservative.'

'Well, sir,' said Paul, 'I was going to say another result of the Industrial Revolution was that it showed our rulers supported a policy of inequality. I mean, they helped the bosses to get rich and to keep the workers down. Not very fair, eh, sir?'

'If it's true, no it's not fair,' said Mr Beckett. 'Let's go into the facts and form our opinions.'

* * *

Jimmy and Paul left together at the end of the day's lessons, and they began their walk along St George's Road to the Elephant and Castle, where a bus would take them to Denmark Hill.

'Listen, Paul,' said Jimmy, 'are you a socialist?'

'You bet,' said Paul.

'I suppose you realize that your dad and my dad are capitalists,' said Jimmy. 'And so's Uncle Boots.'

'That could pain me a bit,' said Paul, 'and it would do if they oppressed their factory workers. Fortunately, for me peace of mind, they treat 'em fair, and although Aunt Polly's upper class, she acts as if everyone's equal, which I admire. I might ask her, when I'm eighteen, if she'd like to join the Labour Party with me.'

'I'd like to be there when you do ask,' said Jimmy with a mile-wide grin.

'Mind you, there's girls as well as politics,' said Paul, 'and I've somehow got to divide my time equally between my social life and my political interests.'

'At your age, you'll get mixed up,' said Jimmy. 'I'd wait till I was older if I were you. I wonder, by the way, if Daniel's going to get home for his wedding now that things have been cleared up in Palestine.'

'Hope so,' said Paul.

'So do I,' said Jimmy, 'or the whole family will collapse in ruins, starting from Grandma downwards.'

When they arrived at their respective homes, they were greeted by the news that Daniel was indeed back from Palestine, and that Saturday's wedding would go ahead. Grandma Finch had been informed and was giving thanks. Further, there was much to listen to in respect of how Mabel Scott had turned out to be a crafty female crook.

Later that evening, at a family gathering, Daniel described exactly what had happened in Palestine, and how he and Corporal Wallis had managed to survive their week-long incarceration at the hands of people who seemed to hate the British as much as they hated Himmler and the Nazis.

Susie and Sammy were shocked, more so because they were aware of the publicized threat to kill their son and his comrade. Chinese Lady said it was outrageous, that she could never take kindly to that sort of thing, never mind what the reasons were, and that it was all Hitler's fault. Hitler, she said, had brought the worst out in everybody, not just his own people. His wickedness, she said, had been like a disease that had spread everywhere outside of Germany. Look what other people had done to each other in the war. We've got to give thanks, she said, that the English Channel stopped it reaching Dover, then London and yes, even Scotland. If it hadn't, she said, we might all have the disease by now. Mr Finch might have smiled, so might Boots, but neither did. Both thought, in fact, that there was more than a grain of truth in Chinese Lady's suggestion that the evil of Hitler and his Nazis had been contagious. Evidence was all in favour.

Patsy, after an outburst of anger at what she, too, saw as outrageous, then embarrassed Daniel by treating him like a hero. Daniel didn't think there'd been much heroic about being gagged and tied up for a week, but Patsy thought his endurance proved her point, so after a while Daniel did the wise thing and accepted her homage. Homage from his bride, he thought, might make a good start to their marriage and establish his status as the senior partner.

Fat chance, said Patsy, when he let the thought slip out. Her admiration for the way he had survived his ordeal didn't mean he could turn her into his little woman, she said.

Worth a try, though, said Daniel.

Thursday morning

There was a letter for Boots and he read it over breakfast.

> *My Dear One,*
> *I long to be with you and to do things with you and to you, especially to you, like tying you down to my bed and—*

Boots blinked. Everything else in the letter could be dubbed pornographic, and not at all suitable for a breakfast table at which he and Polly sat with their innocent twins. There was no address or name. The outpourings of a disturbed mind were signed, *Your Willing Partner in Passion.*

'What's up?' asked Polly.

'Read that,' said Boots, folding the letter and pushing it under her plate. 'But not now. Later.'

'Can Mummy read it to me?' asked Gemma.

'And me?' said James.

'I think she'll opt for reading you one of your fairy stories,' said Boots.

'Oh, is it a grown-ups' letter?' asked Gemma.

'It's not as good as a letter from the Sugar Plum Fairy to the Gingerbread Man,' said Boots. 'Not unless the Sugar Plum Fairy has had a calamitous breakdown,' he murmured to Polly.

'I see,' said Polly, and wrinkled her nose.

'Daddy, what you saying to Mummy?' asked James.

'Yes, you're not supposed to do whispering,' said Gemma.

'Black mark to me,' said Boots. 'I'll put a penny in the whispers box.'

'We don't have one,' said Gemma. 'Do we, Mummy?'

'We'll start one,' said Polly, 'for whispers and hullabaloos.'

'Oh, lor',' said Gemma, all too aware that she and James were regularly blackmarked for hullabaloos.

In came Flossie, pretty to look at in her neat blue dress and white front, and popular in her happy personality and willing spirit. Like Boots, she had a lurking smile that always seemed about to surface. She was carrying a teapot and coffee pot, and she set them down on their respective table stands.

'Coffee for you, madam,' she said to Polly. 'Tea for you and the two little graces, sir,' she said to Boots.

'Count yourself a treasure, Floss,' said Boots, and the maid-cook flowered into a happy smile.

'Oh, you're ever so welcome, sir,' she said, and Polly, noting the smile and very aware of the girl's infatuation, had a sudden frightful thought. Ye gods, was Flossie the Mad Martha?

No, she couldn't be, nor any healthy-minded young woman of twenty-one.

Polly dismissed the suspicion as totally absurd.

After breakfast, she read the letter. It made her unsure as to whether the imaginative description of certain sex acts was totally disgusting or totally hysterical. Her sense of humour inclined her to opt for hysterical, although disgust wasn't far behind.

With Boots home from the office in the evening, Polly referred to the letter.

'I know, of course, that you're every woman's dream of what they'd like to find on their doorstep,' she said, 'but this one has gone right over the top. Boots old sport, she's after you with her imagination rampant.'

'And what happens if she catches me?' asked Boots.

'Something frightful, unless you're wearing a suit of armour,' said Polly, 'but I don't think that's her game, catching you. Isn't her game the sexual vibrations she gets from pouring her erotic self into your ear, or putting it all down in a letter? Now look here, old clever clogs, having done something brilliant to frustrate yesterday's pair of crooks, do something inspired about Mad Martha.'

'There are letters from the council in our office files,' said Boots. 'I've brought one home. It's signed by Miss Jardine. Let's see if her signature matches the handwriting of the lady with the rampant imagination.'

The comparison was made. There were no distinct similarities, none at all.

'Exit Miss Jardine?' said Polly.

'It looks like it,' said Boots, 'especially as the lady of the phone spits on hearing me call her Miss Jardine.'

'I'm going to do some spitting myself if we don't get her off your back,' said Polly. 'There's the psychological consequence to consider. Her dark brown voice and erotic fantasies could take you over. That's not on, old love.'

'Well, frankly,' said Boots, 'I don't fancy becoming the first man to suffer a fate worse than death. I'll fight that all the way.'

'I'll fight it with you,' said Polly.

'United we stand,' said Boots. 'Where are our pickles?'

'Running rings round Flossie in the kitchen,' said Polly.

'I'll give her a break and take them up for their bath,' said Boots.

'Well, let me warn you, any hullabaloo will

cost the three of you a penny each,' said Polly.

'Cheap at that price,' said Boots. 'By the way, I think it's time I taught them how to play garden cricket.'

'With Patsy about to become an American relative,' said Polly, 'we might have to look baseball in the face.'

'I think you dress up for that,' said Boots.

'In what?' asked Polly.

'Um – knickerbockers?' said Boots.

'Count me out,' said Polly.

Kate Trimble, now a corporal in the WAAF and waiting for her demob papers, was on a week's leave. The orphaned daughter of cockney parents who had perished during the air blitz on London in 1940, she had become very attached to the Adams family, mainly due to the time she had spent with Polly and Boots in Dorset. She was staying with Chinese Lady and Mr Finch for the first part of her leave, providing them, at Boots's suggestion, with welcome company now that Sammy and his family were no longer there. Kate, always amenable, was quite happy about that. She had come to know Chinese Lady and Mr Finch, and to like them. Her leave had been arranged to take in the wedding of Daniel and Patsy, and to enjoy a reunion with Tommy and Vi's elder son David, who was arriving at the weekend from his RAF station. She and David were engaged, and planning to marry when they were both demobbed.

Chinese Lady and Mr Finch were delighted

to have Kate, and on this warm May evening they were in the garden with her, taking a little stroll.

Mr Finch, still active in his use of a hoe or the lawn mower, declared that a garden never failed to provide pleasure.

'Actually,' said Kate, 'I used to think gardens were sort of middle class and boring.'

'Did you?' said Mr Finch. 'I've always thought them a particularly pleasant feature of English outdoor culture.'

'Oh, where I lived with me mum and dad in Camberwell before the war, we had a back yard,' said Kate. 'Dad didn't think much of culture, he said it was a kind of plot to undermine the working classes and take the stuffing out of them. He reckoned a back yard was a lot more healthy than culture. We kept rabbits in ours, and I used to feed them lettuce. It was only when I went to live in Devon that I got to like gardens. David thought gardening was joyful.'

'Joyful?' said Chinese Lady.

'Yes, he loved it, and was always whistling while he worked,' said Kate. 'I kept thinking what's he doing with rakes and hoes and things when he could be talking to me? Mind, when we did get talking it was for hours at a time, and great fun. Of course, he was very fond of Devon even then, when he was only sixteen, and later on he chose to work on the local farm before he joined up.'

'True, we saw very little of him all through the war,' said Mr Finch. 'He rarely came home.'

'It would of been nice to see more of him than we did,' said Chinese Lady, who considered that any family member too long absent by choice was out of order.

'Well, he as good as adopted the family he was living with,' said Kate, at twenty-one much less naive than she had been at sixteen. 'He made them his second family, and it won't surprise me, when we're married, if he'll want us to go back to that village and try to buy a farm.'

Chinese Lady didn't look too keen about that. She thought it enough to bear that Rosie and her family seemed permanently settled in Dorset.

'Well,' she said, 'I don't know if Tommy and Vi would like that—'

She was interrupted by the noisy advent of a dog, a frisky Labrador owning what the breed was famous for, an eager desire to make friends. It came out of nowhere to bark at their heels, to skirt them and bark around their knees, each bark an invitation to join it in some kind of game.

'I think you're in the wrong playground, Dandy,' smiled Mr Finch.

'If it's after a bone, it's not having any of mine,' said Kate, putting her legs out of range.

'Edwin, it's the Fletchers' dog again,' said Chinese Lady. Mr and Mrs Fletcher, a couple in their early forties, lived next door. Mr Fletcher was staid and respectable, Mrs Fletcher a little girlish, and their dog an investigator of other people's gardens. 'It'll be living here soon,' said Chinese Lady.

'Oh, it's your friendly neighbourhood dog, is

it?' said Kate. Dandy barked, seemingly in the affirmative.

'I can say it hasn't bitten any of us yet,' said Mr Finch, getting between the eager dog and his vegetable patch. One's vegetables were definitely off-limits to cats and dogs.

A singing voice was heard.

'Dand-ee! Dand-ee! Where are you, you naughty boy?' A figure appeared in the wake of the voice. Mrs Fletcher, fulsome body lightly clad in a pink silk dress, came clumping in search of her dog. 'Oh, there you are,' she trilled, 'you're leading Mummy another dance.' She clumped around Kate, who stared at what was making her heavy-footed. She was wearing old brown boots. A man's boots, unlaced and floppy. She wagged a finger at the dog, which sat back on its hindlegs and thumped its tail. 'Come along now – oh, ever so sorry he's disturbing you, Mr Finch – come along, Dandy, let Mummy take you back home and she'll find you a nice bone.'

The dog, recognizing a promise, bolted away, Mrs Fletcher lolloping after it.

'What a funny woman,' said Kate, 'wearing a man's boots and taking more notice of the dog than of people. Well, I mean, Mrs Finch, she managed to say something to Mr Finch, but you and me could've been somewhere far away on a bus.'

'Oh, she's got her funny ways, but she's a nice neighbour really,' said Chinese Lady. 'She and Mr Fletcher have lived next door for years, and she comes in to have a pot of tea with us sometimes and to talk about my family, not having any children of her own.'

'She arrives wearing boots?' said Kate.

'Oh, they're only what she wears for gardening,' said Chinese Lady, 'except we've heard Mr Fletcher complaining to her that they're his, not hers.'

'I think she's fed her own gardening boots to her dog,' said Mr Finch. 'It'll eat anything, and I suspect it fancies my trousers.'

Kate laughed. Mr Finch smiled. Chinese Lady's firm mouth twitched. Somewhere in the Fletchers' garden, the dog was heard growling happily over a bone. Then Mrs Fletcher's musical trill came floating over the dividing hedge.

'Oh, Mrs Finch, I forgot to say I hope you all enjoy a lovely family wedding on Saturday.'

'That's kind of you, I'm sure,' called Chinese Lady.

'Did I see a girl with you?'

'Yes, it's Kate, a family friend that's engaged to my grandson David.'

'Goodness, an engagement and a wedding, well, I never. Still, I always say everyone should have a wedding some time in their lives – now, Dandy, that bone's for eating, not burying, you silly. Well, goodbye for the present, Mrs Finch.' The voice floated away.

'The lady has problems,' murmured Mr Finch sympathetically.

'Yes, she's not been her best self since a flying bomb dropped not far from a bus she was on,' said Chinese Lady. 'It did damage to the bus, and she was injured along with other passengers.'

'Oh, that accounts for it, then,' said Kate.

'Those flying bombs ought never to have been allowed,' said Chinese Lady. 'Mr Fletcher says it was the shock as much as anything that changed her. But she's still a nice neighbour.'

The defendants in Nuremberg had known far better days than these, each of them compelled to take the stand in turn and to endure hours, or even days, of cross-examination by the prosecuting counsel. None could escape the demoralizing rigours of having to face up to the appointed representatives of America, Britain, France and Russia. The major figures, Goering, Hess, Ribbentrop, Keitel and Frank, had been dealt with over many weeks, and the rest of the accused had witnessed them being mercilessly stripped of their veneer of innocence. Even the redoubtable Goering had taken a beating. One by one the lesser figures were now being reduced to sweat and nervous exhaustion, and enduring perpetual visions of the hangman. If everything was taking a considerable amount of time to unfold, the tribunal proceeded on the principle that no examination by either the defence or the prosecution should be cut short unless clearly irrelevant. The wheels of justice, in grinding slowly, had to convince posterity that the trial had been fair and impartial.

Goering was still popular with a number of the American guards, particularly a Texan, Lieutenant Jack Wheelis, who shared Goering's love of guns and hunting. The ex-*Luftwaffe* chief had given Wheelis his watch as a souvenir, while declaring, not for the first time, that if found guilty he should, as a soldier, be given a soldier's death by shooting, and not visited with the shame of being hanged like a common criminal.

'Ah feel for you, buddy, Ah sho' do,' said Lieutenant Wheelis.

The trial was becoming just a sideline to some people, such as those struggling with critical post-war problems or others with exceptional events on their minds, like Patsy and Daniel. Their wedding day was happily close, and little else occupied their interest. Patsy's father and step-mother had arrived from America, together with an aunt and uncle and two cousins. All were staying at the Waldorf Hotel, in London's Aldwych, and were enjoying some sightseeing prior to Saturday's wedding.

The family was gathering for the big occasion. Bobby and Helene, Emma and Jonathan, Annabelle and Nick, were having a pre-wedding get-together with Lizzy and Ned this evening. Rosie and Matthew would be on their way tomorrow, with their children, and Tommy and Vi's elder son David would be homeward-bound from his RAF station. Eloise was coming from Bloomsbury to spend the weekend with Boots and Polly, Alice had arranged to catch a train home from Bristol, and Tim was assuring Felicity he'd keep her in touch with everything by giving her a running commentary. Felicity said all she needed was a safeguard against tripping up and falling flat on her face. Old Aunt Victoria was telling even older Uncle Tom to embrocate his lumbago so that he could do his sitting, standing and kneeling in the church without seizing up.

Chapter Twenty-Six

Friday morning, eleven o'clock

At the office, Sammy and Boots were studying the audit completed by the firm's accountants for the financial year 1945–46. It covered the parent company, Adams Enterprises, and its associate companies, Adams Fashions and Adams Properties.

'Boots, have you noted what the combined bank balance of all three companies amounts to?' asked Sammy.

'It's not exactly hurting my eyes, Sammy,' said Boots.

'Well, it wouldn't, would it, considering it's a hundred and twenty-eight thousand quid, and no large outstanding owings to allow for except Rosie's investment of twenty-five thousand,' said Sammy. 'Five highly profitable years of Army and Air Force contracts, plus what we've made on buying and selling bomb-sites, that's enough to make us all sing, and to look forward to some juicy dividends. But keep it dark from Chinese Lady, or she'll want to interview you about war profiteering.'

'I'm able to pass on that one, Sammy,' said Boots.

'Well, of course, you think you can, on account of all your time in the Army and not in the office,' said Sammy. 'But now you're back, you'll get interviewed all right if our old lady finds out just how much we've got in the bank. She'll talk about handing most of the oof to war widows and orphans.'

'Sammy, neither you nor I, neither Lizzy nor Tommy, can ever hope to repay Chinese Lady for all she did for us during every year of our time in Walworth,' said Boots. 'We owe her such a debt that none of us should ever be guilty of any act of ingratitude. Deceiving her would be such an act.'

'Blind O'Reilly,' said Sammy, 'your lingo's nearly upper class. It's all that consorting with generals that went to Eton and Harrow. You're not using all those educated words to suggest we let Chinese Lady know we're in clover, are you?'

'I suggest,' said Boots, 'that in respect of all that oof, very useful for a rainy day, we allow Chinese Lady to dwell in blissful ignorance.'

'Dwell in blissful ignorance?' said Sammy. 'Boots, I'm admiring of that, but it's me you're talking to and what you mean, of course, is don't tell her. Well, that's what I mean myself, don't I?'

'You're right, Sammy, she won't believe there hasn't been some war profiteering,' said Boots.

'And what's more,' said Sammy, 'she'll want to go to the bank, count every pound and put half of it in a sack for these war widows and orphans. Or the Salvation Army. Boots, we don't let that kind of money sit in a bank waiting for anyone to count it, it's got to be used for investment.'

'Expansion?' said Boots.

'You got it,' said Sammy. 'We can't stand still, y'know.'

'Weren't you once interested in acquiring sites in the East End for housing development?' asked Boots.

'That's a dead duck,' said Sammy. 'The local East End councils are sticking compulsory purchase orders on all such sites, for building council flats. But there's other ideas, like buying some suitable land and holding it till Bess and Jimmy can start a chicken farm. They're keen and I'm all for giving 'em help and encouragement. Further, me old soldier, there's David and Kate, and the fact that David's sold on some kind of farming. We don't have to let him try his luck down in Devon, not when Surrey's on our doorstep.'

'Are you thinking of one more company, Adams Poultry Farms?' asked Boots.

'I like that,' said Sammy. 'Glad you mentioned it. We'll motor our way into Surrey some time, and see if there's some acres going spare. Any idea of what the cost for ten acres of Surrey might be? Twice over? One lot for Bess and Jimmy, one for David and Kate?'

'Ask me another,' said Boots. 'But your electric lamp's glowing, Sammy.'

'It's to do with what I mentioned, that we can't stand still,' said Sammy. 'Further and also, we've got our other young people to think about. They're all growing up and we'd like to give 'em a chance to enter the business if we expand, wouldn't we?'

Boots smiled. There was no stopping Sammy, even if the only members of the family who knew anything about chickens were Rosie and Matthew.

'By the way,' he said, 'hasn't Rosie asked for repayment of her investment yet?'

'Not yet,' said Sammy, 'but she might now that she and Matt are starting to grow their own chickens.'

'Grow them, Sammy?'

'From eggs,' said Sammy. 'Rosie can have her capital back as soon as she does ask. With that much, she and Matt could buy half of Dorset. Or a large lump of Surrey. Meanwhile, she's getting a handsome return. I'll talk to her over the weekend. They'll all be here for the wedding.'

'Except for Edward, everyone will be visible,' said Boots.

'What a right old reunion, eh?' said Sammy.

'Granted,' smiled Boots, and Sammy gave him a keen look. There he was, after high-ranking years in the Army, a desk bloke now, in one of his dark grey business suits. Some men would have found the change a bit difficult. Some returned soldiers were back driving buses after getting to be sergeant-majors in charge of a lot more than a Number 68. They had to feel it was a bit of a comedown. Boots had taken the change from colonel to business bloke in his stride, like he did everything else. Well, he'd always been family-minded, and reunion with Polly and his kids had been his first peacetime wish, while his coming reunion with Rosie would make his weekend as happy as a Hampstead Heath Bank Holiday.

'Bit of a relief, y'know, Boots, Daniel getting clear of that dangerous set of geezers in Palestine. Rachel didn't like what was going on, and she'd have had a large amount of heartburn if she'd known Daniel was one of the hostages.'

'Not the best time for the Jewish people of this country,' said Boots. 'They're suddenly up against the fact that Britain and the Palestine Zionists are at war. The Zionists expect their support, and will probably get it. Well, what member of the Jewish race anywhere in the world could deny support after the hideous suffering of the concentration camp victims? The whole world will support the creation of an independent Jewish State. Leaving out the Arab nations. They'll fight that. This old country, Sammy, has got itself stuck in the middle, and if anyone's suffering a large amount of heartburn, it's Prime Minister Attlee.'

'I don't go much on politics or politicians,' said Sammy.

'Most politicians, of course,' said Boots, 'are people inexperienced in the nitty-gritty of work and survival. Those like Roosevelt and Churchill only happen once every hundred years. The rest, Sammy, couldn't run a flower shop.'

'So?' said Sammy.

'Open a flower shop,' said Boots, moving to the door.

Sammy grinned.

'Anytime any of your jokes are serious, Boots, let me know,' he said.

Boots, turning at the door, said, 'Let's relax, Sammy, and enjoy tomorrow's wedding.'

'Susie won't relax until she's seen the happy couple float off on honeymoon,' said Sammy.

'Well, Daniel's your first,' smiled Boots. He turned again and his impaired left eye let him down. His left temple came into sharp, stunning contact with the edge of the open door. He staggered and fell. With Sammy looking helplessly on, he hit the floor heavily, and lay there.

'Christ,' said Sammy. He came from his chair in a rush, and went down on one knee beside his brother who, despite his almost blind left eye, had never been the kind of man to walk into doors. 'Boots?'

Boots was on his back and unconscious. Bloody hell, thought Sammy, he's knocked himself out. In came Rachel.

'Sammy, I heard a crash – oh, my God, what's happened to Boots?' she gasped.

'Cracked his head against the edge of the door,' said Sammy. 'It floored him. He crashed all right. Holy Joe, Rachel, look at that.'

An ugly bruise was already forming at Boots's temple, close to his left ear. His breathing was heavy.

'Sammy, oh, my life,' said Rachel, distressed, 'he's badly concussed, isn't he? Don't you think so?'

'And what the hell do we do about it?' asked Sammy.

'I think give him a minute or two,' said Rachel, 'and if he's still unconscious, we'll have to phone his doctor. Wait, I'll fetch a glass of water.'

She hurried out. Sammy remained where he was, down on one knee beside Boots, worry creasing his forehead. Tim was in the City, attending a course on property law. Rachel returned with the water, and together she and Sammy lifted Boots to a sitting position. Rachel then put the glass to his lips. Boots sighed, murmured and opened his eyes. He blinked.

'Who the devil hit me?' he asked weakly.

'The door,' said Sammy.

'Boots, take a little water,' said Rachel, and he sipped from the glass.

'Is my head in place?' he asked.

'It's all there,' said Sammy, 'but Rachel thinks you've got concussion. So do I. Take it easy, don't try getting up yet.'

Boots blinked again.

'Concussion?' he said, face pale and voice slightly slurring. 'I can do without that.'

'Boots, we must phone your doctor,' said Rachel.

'I'll do that,' said Sammy.

'No, give me a few minutes,' said Boots, and drank more water.

Sammy and Rachel watched him. He relaxed and slowly recovered some of his colour. He made a movement, and they helped him to his feet.

'Boots, I really think we should still get hold of your doctor,' said Rachel.

'No, an aspirin and a rest in my office chair are all I need,' said Boots, voice stronger. He touched his bruised temple. He winced. 'I'm an idiot,' he said.

'It happens to all of us, old soldier,' said Sammy, and he and Rachel saw his brother to his office. Boots sat down, and Rachel, exploring her handbag, found a little bottle of aspirins. Boots took a couple, and sank them with water. He drew in a few breaths, and shook his head, as if clearing it.

'There's no problem, apart from a slight headache,' he said.

Sammy and Rachel exchanged glances, and during the next hour they took turns to look in on him every ten minutes. He seemed fine, and he said he was. Certainly, he was lucid and normal enough to have given dictation to Leah. But at the end of the hour, Sammy, looking in again, found him seated at his desk and restlessly turning papers over and over, like a man uncertain about what he was doing.

'Boots?'

'What's going on, what's going on?' said Boots, pushing the papers irritably aside and drumming on his blotting pad. 'Get out of here.'

'Listen, mate—'

'Who the hell are you?' Boots, turning his head, showed a flushed face and dilated eyes.

Christ, he's sick, thought Sammy, and rushed to Rachel's office.

'Rachel, he's relapsing. He's a serious case of concussion, that's a fact, I'm ruddy sure. Keep an eye on him, would you, while I phone his doctor?'

'Sammy, yes, of course,' said Rachel. 'I only hope his doctor is at his morning surgery, and available.'

Sammy was lucky. Dr Piper had just finished his

morning consultations and was about to begin his round of visiting sick patients at their homes. He listened attentively as Sammy carefully explained what had happened, and what Boots's present condition was.

'He's turned restless after seeming to be all right, Mr Adams? And irritable?'

'And he's flushed, as if he's got a fever,' said Sammy.

'I'll be there as soon as I can,' said Dr Piper. 'Meanwhile, do your best to keep him inactive.'

'I'll do that,' said Sammy.

That proved to be easier said than done. Boots was not only restless, he was now strangely excitable, giving vent to all kinds of verbal irrelevancies as Rachel and Sammy tried to soothe him, calm him and keep him in his chair. His responses to their concerned questions were meaningless, his bruise was uglier and very discoloured, and his manner utterly foreign.

Sammy and Rachel were both very worried people by the time Dr Piper, a thoroughgoing and experienced general practitioner, arrived. He wasted no time, he began an immediate examination of Boots in the presence of Rachel and Sammy. Boots, increasingly restless and excitable, gave no coherent answers to any of the doctor's questions, but suddenly changed from restlessness to become quiet and drowsy. At which, Dr Piper made a second searching examination of the patient's eyes, then asked Sammy for immediate use of the phone.

'It's there,' said Sammy, 'but can I ask—'

'I think we need to get him into Maudsley Hospital, to a neurosurgical specialist,' said Dr Piper, and picked up Boots's phone. He dialled.

Rachel stared in alarm at Sammy. Maudsley Hospital was close to King's College Hospital, on the opposite side of Denmark Hill, and it specialized in the treatment of nervous disorders. For God's sake, thought Sammy, what has actually happened to Boots? His brother, still in his office chair, was slumped and actually seemed asleep.

Dr Piper succeeded in contacting Maudsley's neurosurgical unit, and in speaking to a Mr Saunders, a consultant surgeon. Sammy and Rachel listened as he gave all the details of the initial accident and the symptoms. He spoke finally of the present soporific state of the patient. Mr Saunders, voicing concern, ventured the opinion that the impact had brought about a condition known as middle meningeal haemorrhage.

'Good God,' said Dr Piper, who knew that that meant there was a clot of blood building up, and probably causing dangerous pressure on the brain.

'Dr Piper,' said Mr Saunders, 'those symptoms are the classic ones when a middle meningeal haemorrhage condition exists. This man needs treatment as quickly as possible. I'll arrange at once for an ambulance to collect Mr Adams, and have the X-ray machine set up.'

'Thank you,' said Dr Piper, and gave the office address. 'I'll wait here with Mr Adams.'

He put the phone down and looked at Boots, now a man who seemed totally exhausted.

'Doctor,' said Rachel, 'is Mr Adams in crisis?'

'Almost certainly there's a fracture of the temporal bone,' said Dr Piper.

'A fractured skull?' said Sammy.

'And probably pressure on the brain,' said Dr Piper. 'An X-ray will tell. An ambulance is coming, and there's a promise of an immediate examination and any necessary treatment. Mr Adams, I think you'd better let his wife know.'

'Jesus, it's that kind of crisis?' said Sammy, shocked.

'It could be. He does need to be hospitalized quickly, and to be treated quickly, but at the moment he's here, and time's going to run away while we're waiting for the ambulance.'

'Sammy?' Rachel was pale.

Sammy rushed back to his own office and phoned Polly. Polly listened incredulously to what he had to say.

'Sammy, no!'

'Don't I wish I could say it's only what Rachel and I first thought, concussion?' said Sammy. 'But it's a fact that Dr Piper's talking about a fractured skull and pressure on the brain.'

'Oh, my God,' breathed Polly, 'that means there could be haemorrhaging, and that means – Sammy, I know that a victim needs almost immediate treatment for that.'

'Polly, don't let's—'

'Sammy, hang up. I need to ring for a taxi, I need to be at Maudsley Hospital, I need to know exactly what's happening.'

'I'll meet you there, Polly.'

*   *   *

Polly, leaving the twins in Flossie's care, endured a nail-biting taxi journey to the hospital. The effect of Sammy's phone call had made her feel she was living a ghastly dream. It couldn't be real, it had to be a nightmare, Boots suffering a fractured skull and possible pressure on the brain due to haemorrhaging. It was horribly fatal unless an operation was performed in time. She knew enough about that kind of accident or wound to give herself frantic worry. To lose any of her nearest and dearest would cause her great grief. To lose Boots would wreck her. Did she deserve that after all those years of frustrated longing? Was she going to be robbed when she had known only a few years as his wife? Was Emily looking on, was she waiting for Boots to rejoin her? Polly had always been conscious of her inability to push the ghost of Emily aside. There were times when she felt she was an intrusion, usually when overhearing Emily's name mentioned by someone in the family. So many of them seemed to make it their business not to forget the woman said to have been a godsend to Boots during his years of blindness.

Polly struggled with unhappy thoughts and intense worry as the taxi motored down Denmark Hill towards Maudsley Hospital. She was out of it with a flurry of agile limbs as soon as it pulled up outside the entrance. She paid the cabbie, telling him to keep the change as a tip.

Sammy, waiting for her, came out to meet her.

'Glad to see you, Polly—'

'Is it a time to be glad?' Polly was pent up. 'No, wait, does that mean you've some good news? That the crisis is over?'

'Look, Polly,' said Sammy gently, 'there's no news yet, except I was told Boots was given emergency attention as soon as he arrived in the ambulance. He was rushed to the X-ray unit. That's all we know.'

'We?' said Polly, using will-power to hang on to the best part of her self-control.

'Yes, my dear old Ma's here, so's my stepdad,' said Sammy. Polly made a little face. Sammy, understanding, said, 'Well, I had to let Ma know, and I picked her and Pa up on my way from the office. She insisted.'

'Sammy—'

'It's all right, I know you wouldn't want the whole family here and crowding you,' he said. 'Only Ma and Pa have been told so far. Come through.'

He took Polly into the hospital, and there in the hall near reception were Chinese Lady and Mr Finch, talking to a nurse. They turned at the approach of Polly and Sammy.

'Polly my dear,' said Mr Finch, 'the X-ray has been done and Boots is now in the theatre.'

'I'm so sorry, Polly love,' said Chinese Lady, expression taut with concern, but voice gentle. 'It's cruel, and I'm sure I've never known Boots to have such a grievous accident before, not in his whole life, but I'm told he couldn't be in a better hospital, not for his complaint.'

Complaint. Polly couldn't help a painful little

340

grimace. Only Boots's old-fashioned mother could have called compression of the brain a complaint. With an effort, Polly found a few words and delivered them in a dry, husky voice.

'Thank you for coming, Maisie, and you too, Edwin,' she said, and for once she was sure her years were determined to catch up with her, to show her for what she was, middle-aged and, at this moment, probably haggard with it.

They felt for her, Chinese Lady, Mr Finch and Sammy.

'He's in good hands here, that's a fact,' said Sammy, and glanced at his stepfather who, as a man of the world, was bound to be able to offer reassuring confirmation.

Mr Finch, nodding, said, 'Indeed he is, Polly.'

Polly drew a breath and spoke to the nurse.

'Do you know anything more than that the X-ray's been taken?'

'I know that it showed a skull fracture, that Mr Adams is in the theatre and that Mr Saunders, our leading surgeon, is in charge of the operation,' said the nurse.

'So I shan't be able to see him until the operation is over?' said Polly, dragging the words up from her dry throat. 'No, of course not. Forgive such a silly question.'

'It's natural, Mrs Adams, not silly,' said the nurse.

'Polly, we can only wait,' said Sammy.

'Perhaps we could get a cup of tea,' said Chinese Lady.

Polly stared at her. Cup of tea? Cup of tea? Did

this Victorian-minded woman think a cup of tea would work a miracle? I'll go mad if she asks the nurse for a pot for four. God, I'm bitching now. Stay with me, Boots, stay.

The nurse took them to a waiting-room and said she would find out if cups of tea could be brought.

Chinese Lady and Mr Finch sat down. Sammy stayed on his feet, hands thrust into his trouser pockets, expression tense. Not Boots, he thought, not Boots, for Christ's sake. But people were taken, however close they were to their family. Emily had been taken, and thousands of other families' nearest and dearest.

Polly paced about with long restless strides. Chinese Lady did not attempt any comforting words. She looked on silently, her own emotions close to the surface. Mr Finch emitted a little sigh.

Someone did bring tea.

It was now mid-afternoon.

They waited, hope struggling with anxiety, Sammy not sure whether or not to phone Susie or Lizzy.

Chapter Twenty-Seven

It was Mr Saunders, an eminent brain surgeon of austere appearance, who himself finally brought news to the waiting relatives of Mr Robert Adams. For Polly, Sammy, Chinese Lady and Mr Finch the wait had long become unbearably protracted.

Mr Saunders introduced himself, then said, 'Mrs Adams?'

Polly, very pale, said throatily, 'I'm Mrs Adams.'

Mr Saunders regarded her kindly.

'I have to tell you, Mrs Adams—'

'You have to?' The words, impelled in a rush, were suggestive of the worst kind of apprehension.

'I felt I should speak to you myself. We did indeed have to deal with a case of middle meningeal haemorrhage resulting from a temporal skull fracture in front of the left ear. By the time your husband was brought to the theatre, his condition was critical.'

'Mr Saunders, for God's sake, tell me yes or no,' entreated Polly.

'Of course.' A smile broke through the surgeon's austere front. 'Your husband's condition now is

343

stable. The operation was difficult and delicate, but—'

'He's going to live?' said Sammy.

'He's very much alive now,' said Mr Saunders, 'and by this time tomorrow will have emerged from sedation and be able to say hello to his family.'

Polly, who had lived a life of many variations from the time she first came to know the horrors of the 1914–18 war of the trenches, felt swamped by bright and lovely light of a totally blissful kind.

'Mr Saunders, you dear man,' she said, 'how can I thank you?'

'You can thank your husband's excellent health as much as you can thank me,' said Mr Saunders.

'Is it possible to see him?' asked Polly, eyes overbright.

'There's not much to be seen beyond his bandages,' said Mr Saunders, 'but come with me, Mrs Adams.'

A minute later, Polly stood beside the bed of the patient. True, his head was swathed and even his eyes were covered, and he lay inert and unconscious. But what did that matter when set against his recovery and the miracle of his deliverance from death?

She touched the hand that lay outside the blankets. Her lips moved silently.

'Dear old sport, thank you for staying with me. Love you for it.'

Patsy and Daniel, knowing nothing of what had happened to Boots, were in Ruskin Park, sauntering in the way of lovers, hand in hand and wanting very little at this stage of their lives except each other.

'Daniel, was it really bad for you in Haifa?'

'Not as pleasant as it is here.'

'Did you have nightmares about what they might do to you?'

'I had worrying moments about missing our wedding.'

'You're still happy about that?'

'Eh? Happy about missing it? What a question, considering I shan't miss it.'

'Daniel, you know very well I didn't mean that.'

'Well, what I do know, Patsy, is that you usually make sense, which is a sign you're not just a pretty face.'

'Oh, thanks, and how would you like a poke in the eye?'

'Anything coming from you, Patsy, will receive a note of kind thanks, even if it hurts a bit.'

'Daniel, how did you and so many of your relatives come to be so droll?'

'Is droll good or bad?' asked Daniel.

'Oh, I guess I'll be able to live with it. By the way, I meant to ask, why did you ask your Uncle Boots to be your best man instead of one of your cousins, or one of your Army buddies?'

'Well, cousins Tim and Bobby both chose him, so it's now a family custom,' said Daniel. 'Like the custom of Mr Greenberg driving family brides to the church in his pony and cart.'

'Some custom,' said Patsy, laughing, 'but I guess I'd better conform. I meant to ask, is his cart like a surrey with a fringe on top?'

'No fringe, just the sky,' said Daniel, 'so wear an umbrella in case it rains.'

'Pa can wear the umbrella,' said Patsy, 'but if it does rain, I'll be disgusted. Daniel, is your Aunt Polly really an English aristocrat?'

'Her dad, Sir Henry Simms, is, and so's her step-mother, Lady Simms,' said Daniel, 'but Aunt Polly hasn't worn her tiara for a hundred years.'

'A hundred years?' said Patsy.

'Say thirty, then,' said Daniel. 'She was an ambulance driver during the First World War, and that made her one of the people. Grandpa Finch told me so.'

'I'm going to have some interesting English relatives,' said Patsy. 'And I like Uncle Boots as your best man, Daniel.'

'Well, he is a bit special,' said Daniel.

That evening, however, along with almost every-one else in the family, Daniel came to know that Boots had had a dangerously close encounter with the Grim Reaper. The fact that he would be unable to attend the wedding mattered little by comparison with his escape. Phones delivered details. Lizzy's reactions were mixed. On receiving the news from Sammy, she expressed thankful-ness, but then asked complainingly why she hadn't been told of the accident at the time Boots was rushed to hospital.

'Sorry about that, Lizzy,' said Sammy, 'but Polly couldn't have coped with everyone in the family turning up.'

'I'm not everyone,' said Lizzy, 'I happen to have been Boots's sister all my life, and considering how dangerously ill he was, I ought to have been at the hospital.'

'I'd have phoned you if he'd got worse,' said Sammy.

'You should've let me know, in any case,' said Lizzy. 'I'm sure I can't think that Polly had the right to keep me away. Emily wouldn't have been like that.'

'It was all a bit unnerving,' said Sammy. 'I was dizzy with shock and alarm meself, and Polly was worse. Still, all over now, Lizzy, Boots is on the mend and you and Ned can uncork the bottle.'

'Well, all right, I know Ned would want to drink good health to Boots,' said Lizzy. And since Bobby and Helene were with her and Ned, all four of them celebrated Boots's recovery with a bottle of Ned's best red wine. Lizzy got quite tiddly after a second bottle had been opened.

A little drop of what one fancied by way of celebration meant that bottles were uncorked in more than one household. Chinese Lady, in fact, not only had a large sherry, she followed that with a large port.

Rosie, who had arrived from Dorset with Matthew and their children, went with Tim, Eloise and Polly to the hospital. There, for a while, the son, the daughters and the wife of the heavily sedated patient were allowed to dwell with glad relief on his peaceful repose and his condition of stability.

Daniel thought about who to ask to take Boots's

347

place as best man. Tim, as Boots's son, would have been a natural substitute, but he'd be keeping close to his blind wife, Felicity. So Daniel phoned Bobby, and they had a chat about Boots, about what an office door had done to him, and the welcome outcome of a successful operation. Then Daniel spoke of needing a new best man. Would Bobby take it on? Bobby said what an honour it was to be asked to stand in for a bloke like Uncle Boots, even if at such short notice he couldn't guarantee a knockout speech. Daniel said he wasn't asking for anything like that. Patsy was a well-brought-up American girl, with a fair share of innocence, so he'd be obliged if Bobby kept it clean.

'Well, young feller-me-lad,' said Bobby. 'I—'

'Yes, Grandad?' said Daniel.

'I think you'd better keep an eye open for what Patsy's got behind her fair share of innocence,' said Bobby.

'You know something about American girls?' said Daniel.

'No, I only know what Uncle Boots himself said once, that all young women everywhere know a lot more than we think they do, and a lot more than blokes do.'

'That's a fact, is it?' said Daniel, treating himself to a grin.

'Yes, but there's a compensation,' said Bobby.

'Which is?'

'It's fun finding out,' said Bobby.

At their home, Emma and Jonathan also cel-ebrated, Emma opting for cider, Jonathan for beer. At nine o'clock, Jonathan answered a knock on the front door.

'Oh, hello, Jonathan,' said Mrs Duckworth, a slightly soppy smile decorating her plump face, and a carrier bag in her hand, 'I just thought I'd call and ask if you and Emma enjoyed the wedding.'

'Well, actually, no,' said Jonathan, 'seeing it's still Friday and the wedding's not until tomorrow.'

'Lor', what a silly woman I am.' Mrs Duckworth took a mental swipe at herself. 'Fancy me not knowing what day it is, and treating myself to a little drop of port on your be—' A little hiccup arrived. 'On your behalf. And I've brought the bottle too, for sharing, like,'

Jonathan guessed she needed company, and since he and Emma were in a convivial mood on account of her Uncle Boots surviving what a door could do when it cracked your head open, he decided to invite the old girl to join them.

'Come on in, Maudie, and your bottle,' he said, and Maudie brought the bottle of port into the light from the carrier bag.

'Oh, I'll be pleasured, I'm sure, to have a little drop with you and Emma,' she said.

Emma greeted her with smiling and sociable hospitality. Well, good quality cider did give her a lift, and she was on her second glass. She and Jonathan explained why they were having a little celebration in advance of the wedding. Maudie said it wasn't ever a good thing to walk into a door, but what a blessing that the operation had been done in time. Jonathan, taking the bottle of port from her, poured her a glass, a full one, although it was obvious she'd already had a couple.

'I'll see you home later, Maudie,' he said.

'How kind,' beamed Maudie, 'but I'm only next door.'

'Next door might be a couple of steps too far,' said Emma, noting that her neighbour was already a bit mellow.

Maudie giggled.

'You're settling down fine these days,' said Jonathan. 'Making a go of it, that you are.'

Maudie smiled a little vacuously and drank some port.

'Mind, I won't say that I don't still miss Charlie,' she said, 'and he'd have liked it that the war's—' She paused, blinking. 'Over,' she said. 'Well, yes, it was over, wasn't it before he had his fall down the stairs? I just hope he's happy where he is.' She rambled on about Charlie having his good points. Emma and Jonathan let her talk. Emma wondered if she really had resigned herself to being a widow, or if she needed the consolation and company of a regular bottle of port. 'Wasn't it a shame—' Another pause, followed by a hiccup. 'Wasn't it a shame about the stairs?'

'Falling down them?' said Jonathan. 'Fatal, as it happened. But cheer up, Maudie, you've got your life to live.'

'Mind you,' murmured Maudie, 'it wouldn't have happened if I hadn't pushed him.'

'Eh?' said Jonathan, startled.

'What did you say, Maudie?' asked Emma, staring.

'What?' said Maudie, and swallowed more port. It turned her eyes bemused.

'Maudie, you just said you pushed him,' breathed Emma.

'Well, there he was,' mumbled Maudie, well past a mood of discretion by reason of the bottle. 'Up there on the landing shouting about where was his clean shirt. It got me so cross I went up, took his shirt out of the drawer where I always put them, and brought it out and showed it to him. I said he ought to know where to look by now. He laughed, yes, out loud. The next minute he was falling.'

'Maudie, you were down in the hall, at the foot of the stairs,' said Jonathan. 'You saw him fall, you said so more than once. You're imagining any push.'

Maudie blinked and a little bubble trembled on her lips.

'Oh, I gave him a push all right, I was that cross him standing there laughing,' she said. 'Mind, I didn't know he was going to land on his head.'

'Oh, my God,' breathed Emma.

'Poor Charlie,' murmured Maudie. 'Still—' She bucked up. 'Still, his life insurance, that's been paid, and it's helped my sorrowing.'

Oh, Christ, thought Jonathan, no wonder the poor old biddy has always got a port bottle somewhere around. He looked at Emma. Emma, stunned, had a hand to her throat.

'Jonathan?'

'Look at that,' he said, 'she's done it again.'

Maudie, chin close to her bosom, was asleep, her breathing bubbling away.

* * *

By ten-thirty, Emma and Jonathan had taken Maudie home, put her on her bed, covered her up and returned to their house. Now they were discussing her tipsy confession.

'She won't remember,' said Jonathan eventually, 'I'm certain sure she won't.'

'But what do we do?' asked Emma.

'What would you do?' asked Jonathan.

'Let me hear what you think,' said Emma.

Jonathan rubbed his chin. Emma eyed him in the knowledge that although he was a Sussex-born country chap, brought up in a quiet village, he was no simpleton, nobody's fool.

'Well, there'll be a come-back from the insurance company if they find out Charlie was pushed,' he said. 'And the police could come knocking on her door. Best, I reckon, Emma, if we both do nothing and say nothing.'

'That's my lad,' said Emma. 'Well, the poor old dear, she did it in a temper. It wasn't deliberate.'

'No, not what they call premeditated, nothing like that,' said Jonathan.

'Jonathan, remind me, what was the inquest verdict?'

'Accidental death,' said Jonathan.

'Can we live with that?' asked Emma.

'I'm certain sure we can,' said Jonathan, 'and it's a fact that Maudie's got to live with it herself. And, after all, accidental death is about right, isn't it?'

'I'll go along with that,' said Emma, 'and in any case, I'm not going to let anything spoil how glad I feel about Uncle Boots surviving a brain haemorrhage, and cousin Daniel's wedding tomorrow. My feelings about all that aren't for spoiling, not by anything or anyone.'

Jonathan put his hand under her chin and kissed her.

'It's a time for not talking out loud, you reckon, Emma?'

'Yes, if there's a skeleton in a cupboard somewhere, let it stay there,' said Emma.

Jonathan and Emma weren't alone in having a visitor that evening. Not long after her return from the hospital, Polly heard her doorbell ring.

'Shall I go, Mama?' offered Eloise, home from Bloomsbury for the weekend and about to help Rosie prepare some sandwiches.

'I'll see to it,' said Polly, and found a staid-looking gentleman on her doorstep.

'Good evening,' he said, raising his hat. 'I must apologize for disturbing you at this hour.' It was a few minutes past nine. 'But is it possible to have a word with Mr Adams?'

Polly, still existing in warm bright light, was able to smile as she said, 'No, not at the moment. My husband won't be available for a few days. He's in hospital.'

'Oh, I'm sorry.' The gentleman looked sincerely so. 'Not for any critical reason, I trust?'

'No, not now,' said Polly. 'Can I help?'

'I know Mr Adams quite well. It won't offend you, I trust, if I refer to his first wife.' The gentleman had the precise speech of a lawyer. 'The late Emily Adams.'

'No,' said Polly, 'I shan't be offended, Mr—?'

'Oh, my name is Fletcher, and while Mr Adams and his first wife were living with his mother and stepfather in Red Post Hill, they were neighbours of myself and my wife.'

'Mr Fletcher, if this is important, please come in.'

'I think it most important, Mrs Adams.'

'Then do come in,' said Polly, and took him to the room she had insisted Boots use as a study. Boots did write the occasional letter there. More often he used it for entertaining either his stepfather, Mr Finch, or his father-in-law, Sir Henry Simms, or both. It was, in effect, a small club for men, where a nip of whisky was always available as an accompaniment to reminiscences.

Polly let Eloise, Rosie and Matthew know she had a visitor, and would rejoin them later.

'What kind of visitor?' asked Rosie.

'Oh, I can cope with any kind at this moment of my life, Rosie old love,' said Polly, and dashed back to the study like a woman reborn to the sound of trumpets. 'Now, Mr Fletcher, you've my full attention.'

'I've not had the pleasure of meeting you before,' said Mr Fletcher. 'You and Mr Adams never took up residence with his mother and stepfather.'

'We were both in khaki,' said Polly, 'and stationed in Dorset.'

'Yes, quite so,' said Mr Fletcher, shifting a little in his chair. 'Well, I really don't wish to take up too much of your time, so might I begin by asking a very relevant question?'

'Fire away,' said Polly, thoughts on Boots and whether or not he'd come to.

'Has Mr Adams received some unpleasant phone calls and an unpleasant letter?'

'Good grief,' said Polly, 'you know about those?'

'I know, unfortunately, that my wife was responsible for them,' said Mr Fletcher, and his correctness took on a look of discomfort.

'Then I'm sorry for both of you,' said Polly.

'That's very kind,' said Mr Fletcher. He explained that on arriving home early from his office today, he found his wife absent. As it turned out, she was walking the dog. Going into their living room, he noticed the bureau top was open, and a letter visible. He looked at it. It was unfinished, but what had already been penned in his wife's handwriting was hardly believable. He confronted her as soon as she returned from her outing. He endured the most tormenting moment of his life when, in final answer to his many questions, she confessed to the most shameful kind of behaviour. There was some excuse, perhaps, that she had undergone a personality change in late 1944 following the explosion of a flying bomb in Norwood. The bus in which she was travelling had its windows shattered by the blast. She and other passengers had suffered injury and shock, since when, despite medical treatment, she had not been herself. However, he could assure Mrs Adams that there would be no more phone calls or letters to Mr Adams.

'Mr Fletcher, I can't thank you enough for coming,' said Polly, 'and for telling me something that must be embarrassing and uncomfortable for you. Perhaps you'd like to know it's something my husband and I have kept to ourselves.'

'That, Mrs Adams, is a relief to me.'

'I sympathize with you and Mrs Fletcher,' said Polly, 'and I know my husband would share my feelings.' A slight smile showed. 'I can understand why your wife selected him as a recipient of her imaginings. He can be charming as a friend or neighbour.'

'Yes, quite so,' said Mr Fletcher. 'My wife never made any secret of her liking for him. Well, I'm glad to have been able to talk to you, and thank you for being so understanding.'

'I wish you well, and your wife,' said Polly, and saw him out. She did not, however, tell Eloise, Rosie and Matthew of the exact nature of the call. That, she thought, was not what Mr Fletcher would have wanted.

Following the exhilaration of Boots's recovery, she had not expected a bonus: an end to the unpleasant worry of Mad Martha.

Chapter Twenty-Eight

Saturday

In Tommy and Vi's home, the bride woke up to the sound of falling rain.

Oh, bother, she thought, the summer wasn't going to take the day off, was it? What a crazy country, always getting its four seasons mixed up.

Daniel ought never to have mentioned umbrellas.

Daniel awoke under his parents' roof with something on his mind.

What was it?

Holy Joe, it's my wedding day.

I hope Patsy remembers.

What a curse, it's raining. Unless it takes off for somewhere like Scotland, it could mean Patsy will have to ride to the church in a wet pony and cart.

I should never have mentioned umbrellas.

Polly woke up with Boots on her mind. The thought that he would miss the wedding was secondary, however, to her fervent hope that today his condition would be such as to definitely point to a complete recovery.

Well, she would visit him before making her way to the church with the twins. She was sure the family would understand if she spent the day at the hospital, but she knew Boots himself would want her to attend the wedding, particularly as the twins were excited about it.

Only a relapse would keep her at the hospital, and she refused to let that dire thought stay in her mind.

By nine o'clock, Mr Eli Greenberg was at his Camberwell yard, polishing up his cart and grooming his pony. The rain was moving north-west, and the sun was breaking through clouds that looked fretful and sulky at being commanded by the governing elements to move on. The elements, despising sulks and favouring the bride, stuck to the task of clearing the southern skies.

Out came Patsy's sun.

Later, in various households, there was a flurry of activity relating solely to the social propriety of getting to the church on time.

In Walworth, South-East London, Jim Brown and his missus, Bessie Brown, were all togged up with somewhere to go. Jim was sixty-six, with wrinkles around his eyes, which he cheerfully accepted at his time of life, and spectacles, which he didn't find quite so acceptable. Made a bloke look a bit of a wally. Still, as his eyesight wasn't as good as it had been, he put up with them.

Mrs Brown was sixty-two, plump, placid and one of the kind known as motherly bodies. A pot of tea and a nice gossip with a neighbour, or listening to 'Bandwaggon' on the wireless, constituted contentment for her. If other people wanted the moon, well, she'd say, what could they do with it if they got it?

She and Jim had been invited to the wedding because their elder daughter, Susie, was married to Sammy, and Daniel was their grandson. What a nice young man he was, thought Mrs Brown, and imagine his bride being an American girl. She and Jim had met her, and found that among her many nice ways was the fact that she didn't chew gum. During the war, all those GIs had chewed gum and left it on the floors of London cinemas. It stuck to your shoes and you took it home with you. Still, they'd brought a great breath of life to the country, and given Hitler's armies a real beating.

Standing in front of the hallstand mirror in the passage of her home in Caulfield Place, off Browning Street, Mrs Brown put on her new hat to complement her new dress and spring coat. Jim had said to doll herself up and blow the expense. Having spent most of the war as a full-time ARP warden, he was back to working for his son-in-law Sammy, a few hours a day, and presently redecorating the firm's offices and shop at Camberwell Green. Past retirement age, he was drawing his state pension and earning a useful bit from Sammy.

'There,' said his missus, her hat on, 'what d'you think, Jim?'

Jim regarded it, a post-war cloche-style hat with an upturned brim and feathers at the back.

'Well, me love, I wouldn't wear it meself,' he said.

'There'd be a riot if you did.'

'But I like it on you,' said Jim, wearing a new dark blue suit himself. It had a 'Utility' label, which meant it was the kind of suit you put up with on account of the country going through a period of austerity. Of course, if you were affluent and knew a spiv or two, you could get something better. Jim wasn't affluent, didn't know any spivs, and anyway, a suit was a suit as far as he was concerned. Also, he had a cockney's typical aversion to being dressed up like a tailor's dummy.

'Well, I'm ready now,' said Mrs Brown, 'and I just hope it don't start raining again.'

It was eleven. The service was at noon, in the church on Denmark Hill.

'Well, let's go and catch a bus, Bessie me love,' said Jim.

At this moment, Mrs Cassie Brown and her husband Freddy emerged from their house in Wansey Street. They too were togged up for the wedding, being old friends of the family. Cassie was wearing a light spring coat over a lilac dress, and a little white hat on her dark curling hair. Freddy, sporting a chalk-striped grey suit, was topped by a natty dark grey trilby. At the open door stood their fulsome and big-hearted neighbour, Mrs Hobday, and their son Lewis and daughter Maureen. Mrs Hobday had volunteered to look after the boy and girl for the day.

'Enjoy yerselves, duckies,' she called to the departing couple, 'no-one's going to mind if you come rolling 'ome a bit tiddly.'

'If Cassie gets a bit tiddly, she won't do any rolling,' said Freddy, 'I'll have to carry her.'

'You and your muscles,' said Cassie, and she and Freddy went laughing on their way, their children coming off the doorstep with Mrs Hobday to wave to them.

Chinese Lady was in favour of weddings. Still a classic case of principled Victorianism, she considered marriage signified the acceptance of what was natural and necessary. Her beliefs embraced the infallibility of the Ten Commandments, respectable behaviour, bringing children up to know what was right, wrong and proper, and people doing what God had ordered for them. She meant ordained, and that, as she'd told herself and her sons many times, meant men were born to become providing husbands and caring fathers, and women to become good wives and loving mothers, and to keep the peace in families. She dressed neatly but primly, taking no notice of any fashion length that was more than six inches above the ankle. In her time, she had had very good legs, and if they were thinner now, well, no-one noticed because no-one ever saw very much more than her ankles. She had never undressed in front of her first husband or her second. Her first husband had suggested that as they were married, she could drop a veil or two. After all, he said, Adam saw a lot of Eve. Yes, she said, and look what happened, God punished them both.

Today, her dress wasn't at all prim. It was of rich chocolate brown patterned with wandering yellow daisies. Her hat was new, and so were her light brown gloves. Her court shoes were those she wore only on special occasions. Being the woman she was, however, she wondered if she ought to have dressed a little more soberly out of respect for Boots being in hospital.

Mr Finch, quite elegant in a fine-tailored suit of light grey and a dark grey cravat, regarded her with a smile. There she was, the only woman he had cared to marry in his long career as a Secret Service agent. Born a cockney, she was the most resilient and commonsensical woman he had ever known, and unshakeably loyal to everything and everyone she held dear. She still had an upright carriage, but there was, at last, the visible touch of grey in her dark brown hair. At seventy-two, his own mane of hair was uniformly silver.

'Maisie, a picture,' he said.

'What picture?' she said.

'You, my dear.'

'Oh, go on with you, Edwin, I'm sure I must look like mutton dressed up as lamb.' The front door knocker sounded. 'There, I expect that's Ned and Lizzy. It's nice they're early.'

'Yes, there's enough time for a small sherry,' said Mr Finch.

'Oh, I don't know we ought to – well, all right,

just a small one,' said Chinese Lady. 'Edwin? Now where's he gone? Oh, to answer the door, of course. I hope I'm not getting a bit flustered, I ought to be used to family weddings by now. Still, it's the family's first American bride. American, well, I just don't know, I never thought I'd have a granddaughter-in-law from America. Lor', suppose she'd been a Red Indian? I'm sure Red Indians don't go to church, and all my family do, some time or other, even that Sammy.'

Into the parlour came Lizzy and Ned. Lizzy, close to forty-eight, showed an abundance of chestnut hair, large brown eyes and a figure that could now be termed buxom. She had tried to fight it by dieting. Dieting, however, made her feel hungry. Look, said Ned, you're a fine figure of a woman, and if you only eat apples and bananas, you'll lose most of what I'm fond of, and end up sagging. Lizzy, horrified at the thought, accepted her buxom look, put the diet chart on the fire, and bought a new and expensive corset of matchless design.

She entered the parlour exuberantly. Weddings did that to her, especially family weddings.

'Hello, Mum love. My, that dress is a treat on you, I never saw you in anything more colourful.'

'It's like I just told Edwin,' said Chinese Lady, 'I'm sure it makes me look like mutton dressed up as lamb. Me at my age with daisies on my dress. Mind, I'm not actu'lly old yet.'

'Nor do you look it,' said Ned, kissing her cheek. He was showing lines, and his greying hair

363

was thinning, but in Lizzy's eyes he was still an asset as a husband and provider. 'Auto-suggestion, that's the thing these days.'

'Is that foreign?' asked Chinese Lady suspiciously.

'No, you simply keep telling yourself you're not what you don't want to be, and it all goes away.'

'What does?' asked Chinese Lady, still suspicious.

'All that you don't want to be,' said Ned. 'Better than dieting if, for instance, you don't want to get – um – a bit overflowing.'

Lizzy rolled her eyes at him, and said, 'I'd say something to you, Ned Somers, if it wasn't a wedding day. Where's Kate, Mum?'

'Oh, she's gone to Polly's house,' said Chinese Lady, 'she's staying there now for the rest of her leave. Well, she and Rosie and Matthew will give Polly comforting company over the weekend.'

Mr Finch came in then with a tray on which stood four glasses of sherry. They drank to the wedding and to the family, chatted about the bride and groom, and spoke feelingly about Boots. Phone calls to the hospital had elicited the welcome news that his condition was excellent. Chinese Lady said what a relief that was, but a shame he was missing the wedding.

'The relief's the main thing,' said Ned.

'It is, Ned, it is,' said Mr Finch fervently. A man with no children of his own, he had always regarded Boots as the kind of son he might have had if his life had been different.

'Well, as soon as we get to the church, we can give thanks,' said Chinese Lady.

'We can and we will, Maisie,' said Mr Finch, and Ned ther drove them to the church.

'Sammy, come and look,' called Mrs Susie Adams from the marital bedroom.

From Daniel's bedroom, Mr Sammy Adams responded with a question.

'What at, Susie?'

'The bridesmaids, of course,' called Susie. 'They're ready. Come and look. You too, Daniel.'

Sammy appeared, Daniel with him, and they regarded the bridesmaids, Bess, Paula and Phoebe, all in pink crinolines, with circlets of crimson silk roses on their dressed hair. Well, well, thought Sammy, my dear old Ma's wireless set might still be aggravating her now that it's going on about austerity, but look what we've got here, a trio of treasures.

'Mother O'Grady,' he said, 'where did these fancy angels come from, Susie, and whose are they?'

'Daddy, we didn't come from anywhere, we've been here all morning, and we're yours,' said Paula, growing long-legged and skittish.

'Then I'm a lucky old dad,' said Sammy. 'I think the bride'll like the turnout, don't you, Daniel?'

Daniel was dressed in a hired morning suit, not his uniform. The war was over, and this wasn't a day when he wanted to be reminded he was still in the Army. The well-fitting suit paid its tribute to his lean body, and maturing good looks.

'Well, Dad,' he said, observing pictures of enchantment, 'I can't fault 'em. That's a full quartet of angels.'

'Crikey, can't you count, Daniel?' said Bess. 'There's only three of us.'

'I'm including your mum as well,' said Daniel.

Susie was in a delightful royal blue suit, its skirt calf-length, its jacket showing a line of shining silvery buttons, her lemon-coloured blouse finished with a decorative neck bow. The outfit had been created by Sammy's fashion designer.

'Mummy's ever so nice,' said Phoebe, the adopted daughter and visibly the prettiest. She glanced up at Susie. 'So am I,' she said, giggling.

'Not half,' said Sammy. 'Just a pity your Uncle Boots is going to miss seeing you and your sisters all looking like May queens.'

'Still, he's better, though,' said Bess.

'As good as he could be,' said Sammy, who had also phoned the hospital for news of the patient.

'What a blessing,' said Phoebe.

'Daniel, isn't it time cousin Bobby arrived to take you to the church?' asked Susie. 'You must be there before the bride.'

'He's not due for another ten minutes,' said Daniel, and went down to talk to Jimmy and to have another drop of what he fancied on his wedding day. Just a small nip of his dad's whisky. Well, his dad, his uncles and Grandpa Finch all believed Scotch was beneficial to a bloke, so it was probably very beneficial to a bridegroom. On top of that, he could drink good health to Uncle Boots. Which he did.

Fashion, the other name for Paris, had decreed
that in this post-war era nothing was smarter for
daytime social occasions than midnight blue worn
with pure white.

Well, a wedding was a social occasion of importance, and so there she was, the wife of the
erstwhile best man, inspecting herself in the long
mirror on the inside of the left door of her wardrobe. Her wide-brimmed hat, of delicate white
straw, worn with an upward tilt, was trimmed with
orange and lemon silks whose ends floated lightly
over the rear of the brim. The dress, pinched
at the waist, had a stand-up collar, a trim bodice,
long sleeves, and a straight calf-length skirt
backed by flying panels. The long-sleeved gloves
were dazzling white, the stockings light grey, the
shoes medium grey.

'Well, old sport,' said Mrs Polly Adams to her
reflection, 'I think you'll do, yes, I think so. If one
can't be young, or look young, one can at least be
fashionably smart. What, I wonder, would his
Lordship have to say?'

She had been allowed to see him at the hospital
at nine-thirty. He'd been conscious but drowsy,
and Mr Saunders had assured her his condition
did point to a full recovery. Polly, intending to
make a further visit during the evening, said she'd
look forward to having a little chat with her
husband by then. Mr Saunders said she could be
optimistic about that.

Meanwhile, the twins and Rosie's children were
dressed and ready for the church, and so was

Matthew. Rosie and Kate were applying last-minute touches to their preparations. If the absence of Boots was all too noticeable, the surgeon's assurance that there were no worries meant the wedding could still be an enjoyable occasion.

In the house of Tommy and Vi Adams on Denmark Hill in South-East London, the voice of the bride was heard from the landing.

'Pa, I'm coming down.'

'OK, Patsy, make your entrance,' called Meredith Kirk, American radio newscaster. Turned fifty now, he was still impressive in his appearance.

Down came his daughter Patsy in white silk organza, the gown made in Boston. It shimmered and softly whispered as Patsy descended the stairs, her veil up over her headdress of traditional orange blossom, her bright eyes dancing.

Pa Kirk felt a lump rise in his throat. Patsy, his one and only child, looked no less than beautiful. He had come all the way from Boston to see her married to her English guy, to give her away, bringing with him his second wife, together with the sister and brother-in-law of his late first wife, and their son and daughter, Patsy's cousins. These five people had already made their way to the church.

'Patsy, you're a triumph,' he said, and lightly kissed her cheek. 'And I want you to know I'm a hundred per cent in favour of Daniel, even if he's going to put a couple of thousand miles between you and me.'

'Pa, you'll never really lose me,' said Patsy, 'you're my lovely dad, and I'll write every week, I promise. Only there was never going to be anyone for me except Daniel.'

'Your fun guy, sure, I know,' said Pa Kirk. He picked up her bouquet from the hallstand. 'Let's go, then, shall we, honey?'

Patsy brought her veil down, took the bouquet, and they left the house. Waiting at the kerbside by his pony and cart was Mr Greenberg, tophatted and Sunday-suited. He raised the hat, a broad smile opening up his beard and touching his teeth with a benign gleam.

He bowed.

'Miss Patsy Kirk and respected father, ain't it?' he said.

'It sure is,' said the delighted Patsy. 'It's an old family custom, Pa.'

'Well, I guess every old family custom should fight for survival,' he said, and Mr Greenberg saw them aboard.

A few minutes later, the passengers on a passing bus were tickled up to their eyebrows as they caught sight of a bride riding in an open green cart drawn by a trotting pony.

Chapter Twenty-Nine

It was over, the service, and Patsy Kirk, now Mrs Daniel Adams, emerged with her bridegroom from the church to pose for photographs. Minor chaos of a happy kind took over as the official photographer fought a professional battle with all the amateurs.

Bystanders looked on as relatives and friends milled about. Mr Greenberg, his pony and cart waiting to take bride and groom to the reception, joined Rachel and Leah.

'Vell, although it's sad about Boots, it's still vun more happy day for the family, ain't it?' he said.

'Yes, one more, Eli,' smiled Rachel.

'Lovely,' said Leah, thinking of her forthcoming marriage to Edward, who would soon be on his way home from Cyprus.

Rachel thought the forecourt simply overflowing with Granny Finch's descendants and the men and women who had married into the family. Except for Edward and Boots, they were all there, including grandchildren and great-grandchildren. Some faces were not as familiar to

Rachel as others. Colonel Lucas, for instance, Eloise's husband, who had lost an arm in the war, and Horace Cooper, married to Susie's sister, Sally. Also Tommy and Vi's elder son, David, away all through the war and now on short leave from his RAF unit, his arm around his fiancée, Kate Trimble, a WAAF.

Sammy and Susie with their daughters, the bridesmaids, looked as happy as the bride and groom. And there were many friends, and couples like Cassie and Freddy Brown. Each contributed to the atmosphere of surging life and exultant celebration in this leafy area of London, the city that, battered though it was, still stood mellow with age in the sunshine, the pride of its teeming cockneys. The Adams family with its own cockney roots had a new branch. American. And soon, thought Rachel, it will have Leah as its Jewish offshoot. I should worry about that? My life, I shall be happy. She picked out Patsy's father and the little group of American relatives now within the embrace of surrounding Adamses.

The guests swarmed, and in the forecourt of the church the wedding became a riot of colour and a tumult of happy voices.

That evening, when the bride and groom were well on their way to their Lake District honeymoon, and celebrations were quietening, Polly drove to the hospital, hoping that yesterday's traumatic hours could finally be consigned to limbo by finding Boots awake, aware and capable of words. She was not going to ask for a bookful,

371

just enough to convince her that the pressure on his brain had not left him mentally impaired in any way.

A nurse, talking to the receptionist, turned as Polly walked in.

'Oh, Mrs Adams,' she said.

Polly, who had changed from her colourful wedding outfit into a dress of sober hues, said, 'Mr Saunders did agree I could see my husband this evening.'

'Oh. Oh, yes,' said the nurse.

'How is he?'

'Just a moment, Mrs Adams.' Away the nurse went, leaving Polly to put her question to the receptionist.

'Do you know if my husband's condition is still improving?'

'I've only just come on duty,' said the receptionist, 'but I'll check. It's Mr Adams?'

'Yes,' said Polly, and the receptionist consulted the information pad.

'There's no mention of a change, Mrs Adams.'

'Thank you,' said Polly.

Down the corridor, the nurse reappeared. She beckoned instead of calling, as if she did not want to disturb the evening peace of the hospital. Polly hurried to her.

'This way, Mrs Adams,' she murmured, and Polly followed her to the ward and into it. 'Don't worry if—'

But Polly was gliding in swift movement towards the bed in which Boots lay on his back, his head still swathed in bandages. His eyes, however, were uncovered. Reaching him, she placed her hand lightly on his.

'Darling?' she said. His lids flickered. 'Boots, are you awake?' There was no response. She pressed his hand. 'Boots?'

His eyes opened.

'Polly?'

'Yes, it's me, old scout.'

'What's in your bag?' he asked, voice a little lazy.

Polly shot a glance of anxiety at the nurse, who said quietly, 'I meant to tell you he isn't fully conscious of everything yet, so don't worry if he doesn't make sense.'

'Darling,' whispered Polly, bending low, 'what are you asking?'

The faint smile touched his lips.

'I'm asking what you've brought me,' he said. 'Is it grapes or a slice of the wedding cake?'

Polly's anxiety vanished beneath a quick tide of delight. She laughed softly.

'Oh, he's fully conscious,' she said to the nurse, 'and he's making sense. In his own kind of way.'

Some months later, in October, eleven of the Nazi defendants at Nuremberg were sentenced to death by hanging. These included Goering, Ribbentrop, Keitel and Streicher. Goering, however, cheated the hangman. Given a vial of cyanide, almost certainly by the Texan, Sergeant Wheelis, he used it to commit suicide. The other condemned Nazis died at the hands of the hangman.

The bodies of all eleven men were cremated. Their ashes and crushed personal effects were taken to a river and thrown into its running waters, which carried them into the Danube and ultimately into the sea, thus ensuring that not a single relic remained of Hitler's chief perpetrators of evil.

'They're done for at last, Susie,' said Sammy.

'I know, Sammy,' said Susie, 'and I know something else.'

'What's that?' asked Sammy.

'The world's a safer place now for us and our family.'

'You're right, Susie,' said Sammy. 'Mind, I'll never exactly know how we managed to stay alive.'

'I know what helped me most,' said Susie.

'And what was that?'

'Being with you, Sammy, all the way through.'

'Well, I like you for saying that,' said Sammy.

'Oh, you're welcome, lovey,' said Susie.

Ex-Sergeant Freddy Brown was gradually coming to terms with the happy fact that he was home with Cassie and the kids, and not in the jungles and malarial swamps of Burma. There were still nightmares, however, still ugly dreams of fanatical Japs and savage ambush that made him wake up sweating. But they were fewer by the month, and in any case, waking up to find himself next to Cassie meant moments of blissful relief. Cassie was a comfort and a treasure, the kids a joy. Every bloke ought to have a wife like Cassie, and happygo-lucky kids like Muffin and Lewis.

Cassie, very bucked that she and the children

had Freddy home for good, showed a sprightly front to her little world in Walworth. Meeting her good friend and neighbour, large Mrs Hobday, in Walworth Road one morning, she greeted her warmly.

'Hello, Mrs Hobday, you're out bright and early.'

'Well, hello yerself, ducky,' said Mrs Hobday, generous of bosom and disposition, 'how's that 'andsome hubby of yourn?'

'Oh, he's fine,' said Cassie, 'he's gradually getting over all he had to put up with out there in Burma.'

'Beating the little night devils, is he?' beamed Mrs Hobday, a knitted brown jumper straining to contain the upper reaches of her ample person. 'I call that 'appy news, specially as I've heard there's soldiers that just can't get over what they've been through in them Japanese prison camps, poor blokes. Me old man says all the Japanese prison guards ought to be boiled alive.'

Cassie said she was trying to help Freddy put on weight, that his years in Burma had slimmed him down chronically. A lot of good meat, like roast beef and a thick steak now and again, would build him up. But there was still all this meat rationing to put up with. Mrs Hobday said that considering other foods were also still rationed, no-one would think we'd won the war.

Cassie said that while the war had been going on, soldiers like Freddy wouldn't have lost all that weight if the Government had made sure the Army supplied them with decent food. Freddy and lots of other men, she said, soon got to know the American soldiers fed a lot better than they did.

'That was because the American Government knew it was only right to care for their soldiers,' she added.

'Here, d'you know what me old man told me?' said Mrs Hobday. 'That when the Americans were fighting in France, they 'ad ice cream for afters. Ice cream all the way from America. Would yer believe it could last that long and not turn runny?'

'No wonder men in our Army, Navy and Air Force voted for the Labour Party last year,' said Cassie, 'they'd had enough of being treated like they weren't very important. Still, now the war's well and truly over, let's forget our grumbles. How are your new neighbours getting on?'

'What, that nice Polish couple, Mr and Mrs Kloitski?' said Mrs Hobday. She pronounced it 'Kloski'. 'Well, I know they're glad they've been allowed to settle 'ere, seeing they don't want to go back to Poland, not now it's gone communal.'

'Communist?' said Cassie.

'That's it, ducky,' said Mrs Hobday. 'I wouldn't wish that on a nice couple like them, not after what they went through with other Polishers in Hitler's concentrated camps. They were rescued by the British Army, y'know, Cassie, and they talk very grateful about that.'

'Well, we'll all do our best to make them welcome,' said Cassie, 'and I hope the Labour Government helps by doing away with meat rationing.'

'That's right, Cassie me dear, and so say all of us, eh?' said Mrs Hobday, thereby echoing not only Cassie but the population generally.

The year went on.

In late October, Rosie, Matthew and their children took a trip to South London to stay with Jonathan and Emma for a weekend. Emma, by then, was expecting her first child and having to put up with Jonathan's regular assertion that it was fair amazing what a chap with a tin kneecap could accomplish with his better half.

The visit had a purpose. Jonathan had lately come to feel that his years in the Army had made him less amenable to office work, that he'd like something more challenging. His job with a firm of City accountants was, in fact, boring him. Emma, remembering the vigorous years they had both experienced in Somerset, understood perfectly. During a phone conversation with Rosie, she mentioned the matter.

'Well now, I wonder . . .' said Rosie.

'Wonder what?' asked Emma.

'Yesterday,' said Rosie, 'Matt and I were offered fifteen acres of farmland in Surrey.'

'Surrey?' said Emma. 'Surrey?'

'The offer was relayed by an ex-Army friend of Matt's,' said Rosie, 'and Matt says fifteen acres would be ideal for a chicken farm and a small number of sheep for cropping the grass. Our chicken farm here is small by comparison and we're only earning a modest turnover.' Rosie herself still had twenty-five thousand pounds invested in Sammy's property firm, and it was paying her well, but Matt insisted it should remain untouched until rainy days became very rainy. 'Emma, look, if Jonathan is keen on an open-air job, why don't the two of you think about joining Matt and me in a partnership? Matt would need a partner, as I'm so occupied with Emily and Giles. It's a daily fight to keep them civilized.'

'Rosie, a chicken farm in Surrey?' said Emma. 'Help, wouldn't the family like to have you and Matthew, and the children, that much closer?'

'That's a consideration,' said Rosie. 'There are still times when I miss you all, and Matt won't raise any objections to emigrating.'

'Emigrating?' said Emma.

'He's a born and bred Dorset man,' said Rosie.

'Oh, I see,' said Emma, and laughed. 'Rosie, I can't wait to talk to Jonathan about this.'

'Matt and I are arranging to inspect what's on offer,' said Rosie. 'We won't make a decision until we've seen the land. Matt can afford to purchase, he has just about enough capital left out of the insurance settlement on his burned-out garage.'

'Rosie, come and stay with us for the weekend,' said Emma.

'Lovely,' said Rosie, 'and I promise to do my best to make sure Emily and Giles don't break too much of your furniture.'

'Oh, what's furniture compared to having all of you for a whole weekend?' said Emma.

'All the same, put a guard on your piano,' said Rosie.

Emma spoke to Jonathan on his arrival home

from the City, and Jonathan said well, if that don't beat all by way of the six o'clock news, I be a Sussex parsnip. You are, near enough, said Emma, and I hope our infant doesn't turn out looking like one.

Jonathan said he'd phone Matthew in the evening. He did and they had a long conversation about what was on the cards.

The upshot of the weekend visit, that took in a survey of the farmland in question, near the village of Woldingham in Surrey, was an agreement by Rosie and Matthew to make the purchase, and an agreement to create a chicken farm in partnership with Emma and Jonathan. The purchase included a large cottage-style farmhouse, and the intention was to make a start some time in the New Year.

Foremost among those in favour of the venture were Chinese Lady and Boots, both of whom were delighted at the prospect of Rosie being much closer.

Susie and Sammy's daughter Bess gave up any idea of going in for chicken farming herself in concert with brother Jimmy. They were both tending the family's ten chickens installed in a wired enclosure at the end of the back garden, and the fiddly work entailed convinced Bess she'd be wise to let her future time at Bristol University point her at a different career. She'd be joining cousin Alice there some time, she hoped.

*　*　*

November was never the best of months. It was too often sulky or murky. It was murky on a day when Mrs Helene Somers, French wife of Bobby Somers, presented him with a baby girl. The weather, however, didn't lessen Bobby's delight at the gift of a little bundle of joy. He reciprocated fully the day after the birth by presenting Helene with a huge bouquet of carnations and a bedside speech, most of which was incoherent on account of the celebratory tipple he'd imbibed in company with his happy dad and his Uncle Boots.

Helene, body now pleasurably relaxed, stared up at him.

'Bobby, what are you saying?' she asked.

'I'm saying I'm so – I'm so chuffed – chuffed – I'm lost for words.'

'You're drunk.'

'Never slept a wink last night – last night – thinking of – of you and her. And where's a chair? My legs feel wonky.'

'There's a chair,' said Helene, 'and yes, you are drunk. Everyone is looking at you.'

'So they should be. I'm a – a new-born father.'

'New-born father? You're crazy!'

'You're a dream.' Bobby bent and kissed her. 'Love you. And her. I've just seen her again. Thought she'd turned into twins since yesterday. You look as if you have too. I think I'm seeing double.'

'How disgusting,' said Helene, but laughed softly. 'Bobby, you have been celebrating?'

'You bet I have, you darling,' said Bobby.

'You are pleased with me?'

'Intoxicated.' Bobby took her hand then, and pressed it. 'Have you thought of a name?'

'Yes, I would like my mother's name for her. Estelle.'

'We'll take her to see your parents after Christmas, and invite them over for Easter. How's that?'

Helene, lying back, her auburn-tinted hair looking rich against the white pillow, let a contented murmur escape.

'It was a terrible war, *chéri*,' she said, 'but see, it was the war that brought us together, and I am very happy.'

'I'm tiddly, but just as happy,' said Bobby. Life was good these days. He worked in the Foreign Office, a well-paid post secured through influential recommendation and by reason of his wartime record as a resourceful member of SOE(French). 'My parents are waiting outside, wanting to see you and our infant. Shall I bring them in?'

'Yes, of course, if you can do so without falling over,' said Helene.

Bobby laughed and went to fetch Lizzy and Ned, the delighted grandparents of Estelle.

Chinese Lady added another name to the birthday book that was many years old.

In December, Emma was also delivered of a baby girl, and Jonathan also celebrated. But not to the point of being lost for coherent words. He let Emma know she was the best wife a simply country chap could have.

'Well,' said Emma, taking him off, 'you be a

fine old performer for a simple country chap, Jonathan.'

They called their first-born Jessie.

Chinese Lady was close to losing count of her descendants as she added yet one more name to the family birthday book.

Polly, investigating the reason for the shrieks and yells coming from the living room, found Boots lying on the settee and the twins scrambling all over him. They were in harum-scarum hilarity, and Boots was begging for mercy.

'You pickles,' said Polly.

'Us?' said Gemma.

'All three of you,' said Polly.

Boots sat up and the twins tumbled off him to the floor. More yells. Polly laughed. There they were, her family, her husband, son and daughter, all representing that which was to fashion the years ahead, the years of peace and civilized endeavour for this branch of the Adams family. There was a scar at Boots's temple, but it did nothing to mar his looks, or to make him less than the man he had always been, grateful for what his years of life had given him.

'Well, Polly?' he said, smiling.

'Yes, apart from the fact that you're turning the twins into hooligans, all's well, old love,' said Polly.

THE END